CATRIONA McPHERSON w. 1965 and educated at Edinburgh University. Formerly a linguistics lecturer, now a full-time writer, she is married to a scientist and lives on a farm in a beautiful valley in Galloway. Find out more about Catriona and the series on dandygilver.co.uk.

Praise for Catriona McPherson and *After the Armistice Ball*

'In this first novel from McPherson the period setting is spot on . . . [and] in Gilver we have a winning character who will hopefully find many more crimes to solve.'

Good Book Guide

'*After the Armistice Ball* superbly evokes the feel of the 1920s . . . I look forward to [the] next adventure.'

Euro Crime

'Catriona McPherson . . . has given us a novel that even Dorothy L. Sayers would have been pleased with . . . This looks set to be a series that will really take off'

Crime Squad.com

Also by Catriona McPherson

The Burry Man's Day

AFTER THE ARMISTICE BALL

Catriona McPherson

ROBINSON
London

Constable & Robinson Ltd
3 The Lanchesters
162 Fulham Palace Road
London W6 9ER
www.constablerobinson.com

First published in the UK by Constable,
an imprint of Constable & Robinson Ltd 2005

This paperback edition published by Robinson,
an imprint of Constable & Robinson Ltd 2006

A copy of the British Library Cataloguing in
Publication Data is available from the British Library

ISBN 13: 978-1-84529-341-3 (pbk)
ISBN 10: 1-84529-341-X
ISBN 13: 978-1-84529-130-3 (hbk)
ISBN 10: 1-84529-130-1

Printed and bound in the EU

1 3 5 7 9 10 8 6 4 2

For my parents, Jim and Jean McPherson,
with all my love and thanks

Prologue

Lustre. That was what had been missing and was suddenly back. The Esslemonts' Armistice Ball was lustrous in a way feared to have disappeared for ever; and for once, as Daisy Esslemont observed, the emphasis was not on *lust*. Husbands were recently demobbed and there was none of the usual marital ennui, so in spite of the glitter a strange wholesomeness prevailed.

The ladies dazzled. Young and old, their hair shone with setting lotion or twinkled with ornaments; lips glowed red if *maquillage* had been ventured upon, cheeks glowed pink if not; frocks sparkled or gleamed with the bristle of sequins or the stately drape of satin. The ladies, though, were not uncontested. Men, usually no more than a backdrop to their wives, were resplendent that night since no man without a dress uniform in which to strut around would have dared show his face. The epaulettes and medals from the Boer campaign and the one or two surviving costumes from the Crimea lent a faint air of light opera along with their whiff of camphor and outdid, somewhat impertinently the young men felt, the lesser peacockery of more recent heroes.

So everyone glistened. And they laughed and the music was sprightly and even the smell was different. In the heat of the ballroom, the ladies' sweat and sweet talcum mixed with the spice of cigar-breath and drove away sourness, the reek of worry, which was all there had been for five chill years.

Then there were the jewels. Out from the safes, home

from the banks, tipped from their velvet bags, came the jewels. Tiaras, brooches, bracelets and bangles, clusters, half-hoops and solitaires. The rubies, the emeralds, the sapphires, the diamonds, the diamonds, the diamonds.

The Duffy diamonds, almost forgotten, newly mesmerizing, raised a round of applause as Lena Duffy shed her wrap; people jostled to the banisters to look down at them and cheer, enchanted. Then Lena's simpering and swishing about made the onlookers turn away, murmuring that she might, she really might, have let one or other of her daughters have a look in instead of hoarding it all to herself still. Silly to have two pretty girls in pearls and their ageing mama stooping under the weight of the family jewels.

Later, when a footman came round at supper to make the collection for widows and orphans, she took off her bracelets and dangled them over the hat, laughing, before snatching them away again in whitened fists and fastening them back around her arms. Silas Esslemont frowned until the younger Duffy girl, twinkling at him, brought a smile back to his face. After all, if one were honest, what was being celebrated here was things going back to how they were before when one owed no sombre piety to life and cruel little jokes gave it savour. It was half the joy of this evening, *if* one were honest, that only those whose loved ones had returned were here; that the others, of whom there were so many, could be forgotten and that just for tonight glee could bubble up and over unchecked.

Chapter One

I am not – and I say this with neither pride nor shame – a
sensitive soul. Not one of those women whose recreation
lies amongst 'things she cannot explain', sudden powerful
convictions of who knows what exactly. I should not go so
far as to say I have *no* finer feelings, but whenever I compare mine with those of my acquaintance they do seem
somewhat coarser in the main. I have never smiled that
curling smile and nodded when told of some engagement,
some divorce. Rather, any news of that kind tends to take
me by surprise and leave me, let us face it, coolish.

How am I to explain then the conviction I held from the
earliest stage of the Esslemont affair that somewhere here
was such hatred, malign and unstoppable, that it must
lead, as flood-water up and melt-water down, to violent
death? On the surface (my usual habitat) it was a matter
merely of commerce. At stake was a good business name
– a livelihood at the very most – and while the theft of
property might be distressing it does not usually, need
not, stir the dust of life to much extent. I am at a loss,
therefore, to account for my instant certainty last spring
that somewhere near at hand and sometime rather soon
blood would spurt and be staunched in murder's furtive
scuffle.

Who can say how far back it had its beginning, at what
moment the first turning was taken away from light and
cheerful ordinariness towards the festering dark where
thoughts of killing can gather? As far as *I* was concerned
it all began on a squally spring morning in my sitting

room, the little room of mine overlooking the flower garden which my mama-in-law insists on calling my boudoir, conjuring up images of Turkey rugs thrown over low settees, air thick with burning pastilles and me with satin sleeves dragging on the floor as I pace. This is a picture gapingly at odds with reality since I do not recall that I ever have paced in the whole course of my life, in my sitting room or anywhere else.

Anyway, there I sat sans satin, sans incense, dressed in wool and tweed, in a room smelling frankly of coal and nothing much draped over anything beyond a dog blanket on my pale chair since it had been wet on our walk. I was bored, and the pleasure of boredom was beginning to run out just then, in the spring of 1922. For a few years after the Armistice it had been delicious to be without occupation. The war had ended at last, and Hugh had come home as I had always known he would, since he had been tucked away miles and miles from the front, behind even the hospitals, so that my worrying had been no more than a wifely duty and a politeness, saving me from the crime of too much visible tranquillity in front of other women whose worries were real. Now none of us was worried nor were we busy and I daresay I was not the only woman in the land for whom, her husband home, her children at school, her uniform growing musty in an attic, boredom was getting to be a burden again.

Understandable then that to help a couple of hours shuffle past we clung to the routine of doing our correspondence and managed still to make a morning's work of it, but the silliness of it all made me cross; not the best mood for considering a sheaf of invitations and had I not forced myself to accept in spite of it Hugh and I might have ended as hermits.

Daisy's letter made me even crosser than usual. Before, an invitation from Daisy and Silas would always have been accepted and if Hugh grumbled (which he did) about the company, I could retort (which I did) that if he cared to

10

take over the organization of our social life I should be happy to go where he chose.

The problem with Esslemont, as far as Hugh was concerned, was Esslemont Life. Esslemont Life, begun by Silas's grandfather in the 1860s, was exactly what it sounded as if it was. Where Grandfather had got the notion no one knew, since for generations before him Esslemonts had been content to kill their stags and collect their rents like everyone else. When the old man died – I was too young to remember this but it was still murmured about – people waited for Silas's father to sell the shameful thing and retire to his grouse moor with a sheepish shrug But far from it. Esslemont Life became by degrees Esslemont Life, Fire, Theft, Flood, Retirement Pensions and heaven only knew what next. Eventually, the Esslemonts having an insurance company with offices in George Street and advertisements in the worst sort of morning paper came to be seen as a mere quirk, something to smile and wrinkle one's nose about, something which gave one the chance to feel broadminded as one forbore to mention it.

Still, when Silas took over, upon his father's death in 1910, we all once again expected he would sell. Indeed, Hugh pronounced more than once that he should *have* to sell, to raise the estate duty. Or rather that he should have to sell something, for everyone did, and that surely he would sell a grubby old office and a lot of dusty papers before he would touch an acre of land.

Nothing was ever said, but Silas dealt with the estate duties, running just then at forty per cent, without selling off a single sprig of heather and from then on our friends began to shut up rather about Esslemont Life. After the war, of course, it became nothing short of pitiful to compare the Esslemonts and ourselves. And now this: Silas was about to float. I was not entirely sure what that meant, only that somehow it was the sale we had been expecting for three generations, and yet also the most blatant swank Silas could have dreamed up to rub our noses in it.

11

Indeed, rubbing our noses in it, or rather inviting us to rub them in it ourselves, was a yearly fixture for Silas. At the first Armistice Ball, on Armistice Day itself, the hats had brimmed and spilled with banknotes. Partly champagne bravado, but partly too our belief, soon to be shown up for the foolishness it was, that very soon and for evermore we should be as before. I wonder how many of us, sober in dreary meetings with our agents, thought back to that night and wished that some of what we had stuffed into the out-held hats was safely under our mattresses still. When the invitations came for the ball in 1919, I for one never dreamed that the hats would come round again. The embarrassment, the crawling mortification and shame as we scraped together what we could, for none of us had come prepared and clearly none of us walked around with cushions of banknotes about our persons any more. 1920 was better, since at least we knew it was coming, and Hugh made sure he was well buffered by Silas's brandy before the moment came to toss in the five twenty-pound notes he had drawn from his bank for the purpose. In 1921, I thought of declining, but Hugh would not hear of it and we were not the only ones there looking hurt, proud and grimly determined all at once, watching Daisy and Silas through narrowed eyes as they floated around amongst their stricken guests without a care.

All in all, as we shut our London houses and decided against restocking our salmon rivers, we felt that Silas was letting the cruel, cold light of a most unwelcome dawn shine into the burrow where the rest of us were still huddled, and knowing that we should all soon have to waken to this dawn made neither it, nor Silas its harbinger, any less blinding.

So we had to go once a year, pride saw to that, but must we be always dashing off there in between times? Might I refuse? It was terrifically short notice, and to decline it would excite no surprise. 'Darling Daisy,' I wrote, 'how sweet of you to think of us.' I imagined her rucking open the envelope with her thumb, scanning the prose for a pip of sense and then ripping the sheet across and dropping it into the basket, as I had done an hour before and should do again tomorrow and the day after that. I dipped my pen and had just set it against the paper once more when the telephone at my elbow shrieked.

This telephone in my room was a new departure and was thought by Hugh and by Pallister our butler to be taking modern manners to the furthest point of decency. I should never admit to either of them how it made me jump each time it erupted beside me, like a sleeping baby whose nappy pin had given way and pierced it, just as inconsolable, just as demanding of being picked up and made a fuss of with one's whole attention for some length of time not of one's own choosing. I composed myself and lifted the earpiece.

'Dan? Dan, is that you?' Daisy's voice was as brisk as ever, talking over the girl at the exchange. 'Listen, I'm ringing to make certain you're going to come, darling. I should have sent you a proper letter to explain things but I did so want to speak face to face. And then I was suddenly convinced this morning that you wouldn't come and if you don't I have simply no idea what I shall do, so you must. And don't call me a goose for caring, because I did think it was all a joke at first, as one would, but it's Silas, you see. Silas has gone very peculiar and is talking about capitulation. So whatever Hugh says, you quite simply must come.'

Even from Daisy, renowned as she was for enormous plumes of enthusiasm, this feverishness needed an explanation.

'Darling, is everything all right?' I began, then I listened as a kind of chalky gulping came over the line, a sound which might have been the very end of a long bout of sobs but which, since Daisy had just spoken, must in fact be laughter.

'Oh Dandy,' she said at last. 'Haven't you heard? You're impossible! Nothing is all right or ever will be again. Dandy, the Duffys have long been booked this Friday to

13

Monday because poor darling Silas has a contingent of bankers and other unspeakables to be sucked up to. Yes, even as far as actuaries, darling – don't ask – whom I couldn't have borne to inflict on anyone else. So I asked the Duffys. And a few satellites. They're dreariness made flesh but so respectable I thought they would be perfect. And then Cara is such a dear and always cheers up Silas no end, although Clemence has undoubtedly washed ashore on a tide from the Arctic. Naturally, I assumed that they would cancel after last week – Do you really not know?'

'I really think I mustn't,' I said, since nothing had made a whisker of sense so far.

'Hence the late summons to you and Hugh. But they're *still coming*, if you can believe it. And in her letter confirming it she said she wanted to speak to me most particularly and she imagined I would know what about. As of course I do. And she further imagined that I would agree it could all be dealt with quite amicably. Which I most certainly do not. Anyway, all four of them will be here on Friday. Dandy, you've got to come.'

'Of course,' I said, 'but –'

'You were so splendid that time on Cuthbert's yacht, darling, and I just know that you will be able to get to the bottom of it and do it again.'

'The bottom of –?'

'All of it,' Daisy yelped, and I jerked the earpiece away from my head. She continued on a rising note. 'Find out what Mrs is doing, where on earth she got the idea. Or find out what really happened, speak to the servants if you must. Always assuming we have any left. McSween is threatening notice. McSween! Because he was on duty with the luggage that day. The under-gardener is beside himself. As are we all. It's unspeakable, it must be stopped, and you are the only one who can stop it. You're the only one whom no one will suspect of anything.' She was beginning to speak more slowly now. 'I shall never forget it; you sitting there on deck under that ludicrous hat

14

piping away like a choirboy and everyone else simply squirming with shame, wondering how you dared. I was the only one who knew, I think, that the innocence wasn't an act. You'll be perfect.'

I flushed. The memory of it was still painful. She asked how I had dared? I hadn't dared, of course. I was just chatting, no earthly clue what I was saying, but Cuthbert Dougall's yacht had sailed out from Anstruther harbour the very next day and never been seen again (and it was a testament to the vileness of Cuthbert that neither his mother nor his sister, our dear friend, felt anything but gratitude towards me).

'I see,' I said. 'I'll be splendid. In the way a new novel is splendid if it happens to be just the right thickness to wedge under a wobbly table. I'm very flattered, I assure you.'

'Well, so long as I've offended you anyway,' said Daisy, 'it won't hurt to tell you that I'm willing to pay.'

'Pay?' I said. 'Pay me? And in return I do what?'

'Sort it,' said Daisy. 'As that divine nanny of yours used to say. Sort it. Get to the bottom of it, then take a deep breath and tell us all. Preferably at dinner. Throw your head back and howl. I give you carte blanche, because of course it's all nonsense and we can't actually *be* in a compromising position. Ask Hugh to tell you about it, then come on Friday and sort it for me.' She rang off.

I padded lightly towards the door, not quite on tiptoe for it would be too ridiculous to go to such lengths to avoid waking a dog, but certainly taking care. Bunty believes, with the perfect confidence of all dogs, that her presence at my heels (or under them) is my heart's desire every time I move from my chair, but she annoys Hugh. I do not mean that she barks at him or takes his cuff in her teeth or anything, but her very existence annoys him and so any errand of supplication is the better for her having no part in it. I closed the door almost silently and breathed out. A little housemaid was busy with a dustpan on the breakfast room rug and she smiled at the soft click of the latch.

'I've escaped,' I said, and she giggled, before ducking her head lower still and redoubling her efforts with the brush.

My sitting room is delightful, and the breakfast room, facing east to the morning sun, has walls of yellow stripe and cheerful pictures of flowers, so it is not until one emerges from this jaunty corner of the house that one begins to feel the true spirit of Gilverton. Mahogany the colour of dried liver encrusts the passageway and hall; the cornicing so very elaborate, the picture rail so sturdy, the dado intended apparently to withstand axe blows and the skirting board so lavish, almost knee-high I should say, that there is barely room for wallpaper, and what wallpaper there is is hidden behind print after sketch after oil of the outside of the house. Views from every hill, taken every ten years since the place was built it seems, go pointlessly by as one passes, and from above them glower down the mournful heads of stags and the snarling masks of foxes. I suppose though that I should be grateful for the hall; it serves as an acclimatization to brace one against what waits as one passes the front door and enters what I think of as the Realm of Death.

In this part of the house are the business room, library, gun room and billiard room. They sit in a miasma of cigar smoke, stale gunpowder and damp leather, and are adorned by corpses – no creature being too mean to be stuffed and stuck behind glass. I always avert my eyes from the pitiful squirrels, scuttle past the horror that is the eel case, and hold my nose as I round the corner past the forty-pound salmon landed by Hugh's father and most inexpertly stuffed but still, more often than not, I turn back deciding that whatever it is can wait until luncheon.

Today I felt quite different, although I still took great care not to breathe in anywhere near 'Sir Gilver' or look too closely at the mouldy patches on his noble sides where the scales had sloughed off to lie in heaps beneath him. Daisy's call, lacking in useful detail as it undoubtedly was, seemed to have acted upon me like a patent tonic and

16

I felt, as I neared the library, as though a Japanese servant who knew his business had stepped on the knobs of my spine and reset it with extra bounce and slightly longer than before. I was going to sort it, whatever it was, and my chin rose like a ballcock.

'Dear,' I said, putting my head round the door. I swung on the heavy handle but kept my feet on the hall carpet and therefore did not, technically, enter the room uninvited. 'We had no plans for the next week or so, did we?'

Hugh looked hard at my feet then glanced at the door hinge as though fearful that my weight might bring all twelve feet of oak crashing down.

'Only I've just accepted an invitation for the Esslemonts.' Hugh started to rumble. 'For the twenty-first,' I added hurriedly. Brown trout opened on the twentieth and Silas's river was simply bursting with them, I knew. Poor Hugh, stuck between the end of the ducks and the first roe buck and with his one winter run of salmon long gone, stroked his moustache and weighed the competing temptations and irritations the visit held out to him.

'The Duffys are going, I'm afraid,' I said, hoping to slip it all past him while he wasn't really listening, 'and, worse, some business pals of Silas. Daisy seems to think she might need a shoulder or two.' I watched, while recounting this, as Hugh's initial frown unravelled and his eyebrows climbed higher and higher up his head until his crow's feet showed white against his brown cheeks.

'Duffys going to Esslemont's?' he echoed, then blew out hard as though cooling soup. 'How interesting.' He waited for my assent, and when it did not come he spoke again with some exasperation. 'You have heard, haven't you? About the jewels?'

'No,' I said, feeling a chill begin to creep around me which might, might, only have been the through-draught from the open door.

'They've gone,' said Hugh. 'All of them, the whole lot.

17

I had it from George and he had it direct from . . . I forget. But the young Duffy girl took them to be cleaned or something and – paste!' He laughed, not a kind laugh. 'George said the jeweller started to polish the things, they crumbled under his hands, and the poor chap fainted, fell off his high stool and broke his arm. Although that might just be George making a better story.'

'How extraordinary,' I said. The chill was seeping further into me. 'Why though, should Daisy and Silas . . .?'

'Well, that's the thing,' said Hugh, bridling over his news most unappealingly. 'They've all gone, you see. Head, neck, arms and ears.' (Jewellers' terminology was not Hugh's strong suit.) 'And guess when and where they were last worn together? George said Lena Duffy is going around telling anyone who'll listen that it was an "inside job" at Esslemont's. So what with this stock market thinga-majig coming off any day now –'

'But that's ludicrous,' I said. 'Or even if it was some servant of Daisy's gone to the bad, surely Silas himself can't be blamed. They must be insured, after all.'

'You don't know bankers,' said Hugh. 'They are not like us, my dear. A whiff of a scandal and they scatter like pigeons. No substance, you see. One generation from a flat above the shop most of them. No nerve. I've always wondered how Silas could bear to rub shoulders with them so. And now see where it's . . .'

I straightened and let the door swing shut. Hugh is not really a spiteful man and I did not want to witness this, most understandable, lapse. Besides, I was shivering by this time, my memory of the Armistice Anniversary Ball playing like a faulty newsreel in my head, flashy, raucous and swirling, so that I sank on to the bottom step and caught my lip, waiting for it to pass, as I had had to do in the mornings when the babies were coming, but never since. I tried to pep myself up, telling myself that fate had handed me an occupation again at long last, one with no ghastly uniform, but I could not quite, with such bright

18

speculations, shake it off. So there I sat, feeling for the first time the sickening thump of dread which would become so familiar in the days ahead of me that when what was to happen finally did, I met it not with the shock one might think, but with recognition and, almost, relief.

Chapter Two

Looking at the map, one might imagine that the Esslemonts' place is at one end of a good straight road, the other end leading right to us at Gilverton, and Hugh can never resist this notion. So while there is an excellent train from Perth to Kingussie taking the lucky passengers within five miles, there never has been and never will be the remotest chance of my finding myself on it. As I expected, I found Hugh poring over his Bartholomew's half-inch at tea-time on the day the invitation came. He started slightly as I happened upon him, but thrust out his chin and prepared to convince me. Poor thing, I can see how irritating it must be; the road on the map marches across the countryside like a prize-winning furrow, cleaving forests and moors with an almost Viking-like forthrightness, but there are a good many features in each *actual* mile which cannot be packed into those neat little half-inches. The real mystery is why Hugh should imagine, having found out the first time how great the discrepancies were, that it might be the road which would change before next time, bringing itself in line with the map. Suffice to say that once again we arrived dishevelled and wretched after slightly more than twice the length of time he had calculated, and several hours after the other guests had stepped down from the train and been whisked five little miles in the greatest of comfort in Silas's Bentley.

Croys is a great stone barracks of a place, thrillingly ancient in parts, built as two wings flanking a huge, square tower; a staircase with rooms, Daisy calls it. It is unusual for the Highlands in sitting balefully at the end of an avenue so that one approaches it much as one used to approach a displeased parent who had arranged himself at the furthest corner from the door, the smaller to shrink one during one's penitent advance. Most of my favourite houses take the other tack, hiding around corners like plump and kindly aunts so that one comes upon them suddenly, close enough to see the lamplight and flowers on the tables inside. Still, I am fond of Croys, despite the glaring improvements that Silas's business triumphs have furnished: the thick carpets laid right up to the walls, making the fine old rugs on top of them look scrawny; the bathrooms which have colonized almost all of the old dressing rooms in the guests' wing, so that one is pitched willy-nilly into intimacy not only with one's husband but with the full range of his ablutions too.

I sat forward eagerly as we swept through the gates, preparing to be diverted in spite of my exhaustion. Most places in this part of the world are at their best in the spring, before the midges awake and begin their savagery, but at Croys the soft uncurling leaf and the peeping primrose are drowned out by a display of vulgarity unequalled in Christendom. Daisy's gardener, you see, the redoubtable McSween, has made it his life's work to perpetrate upon the bank opposite the front of the house, in splendid view of all of the best rooms, a three-ring circus of rhododendrons and azaleas in every shade, but with a particular nod towards coral and magenta. They jostle like can-can dancers in the breeze off the moor and can make people laugh out loud.

'Your rhodies are a picture,' I murmured to Daisy as she came to the door to meet us. Most hospitably, I thought, since the dressing bell must have gone. Daisy rolled her eyes at me.

'I shall tell McSween to give you some cuttings, darling,' she said. 'If you're not good.'

Grant, my maid, had come sensibly on the train with Hugh's valet and most of the luggage (the dickey of the

21

two-seater being full of fishing rods) and so, refreshed first by a pleasant journey and further no doubt by a leisurely tea, she had my evening clothes ready and was on her marks. De-hatted, hastily washed and wrapped in a dressing gown, I sat in front of the glass and surrendered myself to her. She frowned lightly (my hair is a great disappointment) and got to work.

I find it best to try to detach myself while Grant is busy about my scalp with hot tongs and rose-flower water. Any shrinking away or wincing unfailingly brings the irons near enough to scald. Accidental, I am almost sure, but still to be avoided if one can manage it. So I sat there quite docile until she was done and then plied the brushes and puffs myself as usual, guided by her small shakes of the head and sighs, until having hovered with the rouge brush for longer than I could afford I delivered myself into her hands again.

'Only not too much,' I said, as I always do. Grant comes from a theatrical family and having spent the first fifteen years of her life turning her parents and elder siblings into monarchs, gypsies and the like with a smear of greasepaint and a blob of white in the inner corners, her face-painting still tends towards the dramatic. I, unfortunately for her and me both, do not have a face which easily absorbs her efforts. At rest, I must say, I have cheekbones to reckon with and a little rouge dabbed on in the fashionable place works wonders, but when I smile my cheeks make egg shapes, the pointed ends reaching almost to my hated dimples, and then the rouge is quite wrong, its position curiously unrelated to the face underneath. However if I put it, unfashionably, where my cheeks will be when I *start* to smile, then until I *do* smile, I look like a doll. Don't smile then, is Grant's solution, which is hardly helpful. She explained once what is wrong with my face in this respect and even fixed it for me with strips of highlight and shade which looked wonderful, but only at twenty paces.

Still, the moss green dress is something we agree on. Most flattering in shape, although it takes stitching on to my petticoat straps, and with a miraculous effect on my complexion, which can be shadowy around the eyes if I am not careful. And tomato red lipstick to finish. Grant had to get quite fierce with me over this shade of lipstick, but she was right. Blue-ish red makes one's teeth look yellow, she explained, whereas a yellow-ish red turns them white. For the same reason, diamonds near the face are best surrounded by pearls, very few ladies of diamond-wearing age having the teeth to stand up to them otherwise. Grant and I think it a pity that more ladies do not grin at themselves in the glass before they go downstairs with pink lips and diamond clips, but I had never once smiled at my own reflection until the first time she told me to and I do not suppose it occurs to many others.

'Uncommonly pretty frock, that,' said Hugh, entering. Grant bowed her head in discreet acknowledgement of the praise. Hugh would never dream that I had done any *more* than put on a frock in the time he had spent bathing and shaving, and I mused, not for the first time, that if men believed a frock could do what had happened to me from the neck up in the last half-hour, their world must seem a magical place indeed.

People were standing around in the gloom of the great hall waiting for their cocktails as we came down the last sweep of the stairs. Twelve or fifteen people as well as the Esslemonts: the four Duffys whom I knew, and a lot more I did not, the men splendidly anonymous in their dinner jackets but with wives who were undoubtedly the wives of bankers. Hugh blinked around for a bit then took himself off to speak to Silas and I approached Mrs Duffy like an old friend.

She was a fair woman, slight except for an almost too splendid bosom, the type of woman one assumes must have been rather fine in her youth, but now getting raddled and colourless for want of flesh. Tonight she was dressed unbecomingly in grey silk, cut very low, drawing attention to the plain gold locket around her neck.

23

'Simply wonderful, Lena,' I said, kissing her. 'Such a long time.'

'What a delightful surprise,' she cooed back.

For want of anything as definite as a topic to converse upon, I admired the girls to her and, as I had hoped, she launched into an exposition on the coming wedding of her younger daughter.

The Duffy girls, both of them, had rather more to recommend them in the way of looks than their mama, although they were each quite unlike the other: Clemence, the elder, tall, languid and fair, with a sharp chin and high, wide cheeks (which seemed, I could not help but notice, perfectly rouged no matter what her expression); her face overall, then, reminiscent in shape of an heraldic shield, making her almost Slavic-looking what with this and with that peculiar habit of giving an upward pinch to her full lower eyelids. Even in the dimness of Daisy's candelabra, she looked as though she were squinting against light coming from below, as one does wading at noon in the bright sea.

Then Cara, the younger, smaller by half a head; she had always made me think of a woodland creature, a changeling. Not a goblin exactly – she was a pretty thing, after all – but certainly nothing so pink-and-white as 'fairy' or 'pixie' suggests; a velvety little elf perhaps, for although her hair too was fair her general complexion was dark and her brown eyes had a soft twinkle which echoed the upward curl of her lips. Hers was an expression which brought an answering grin from anyone who saw it, having about it none of that insolence which in life or in oils can sometimes make a permanent smile look so very smug and annoying. There was, I thought, something almost simian about this smile. The upper lip had a downy softness to it, as did indeed the whole of her face so that her dark brows seemed merely an intensification, rather than looking like the two worms painted on to the fashionable nakedness of her sister's skin or, I feared, my own. Was she pretty? I think so, but it is hard to know where looks stopped and personality began. Cara Duffy, you see, was what disapproving matrons used to call a hoyden, which is to say she was always in the highest of spirits, burbling over with jokes and giggles and seeming, even when just sitting quietly, to be surging with fun like a child's balloon tugging harmlessly at its string. So perhaps this is where one's pleasure in her sprang from, since on paper, I must admit, a furry little creature with velvety eyes does not sound half so alluring as an alabaster vision such as Clemence. Even tonight, though, when Cara seemed unnaturally subdued, standing beside her father and not speaking, one knew where one would rather rest one's eyes. And she *was* subdued, poor thing; marriage and womanhood looming, I supposed, and hoydenish girlhood almost gone. Such a pity it has to come to that.

I brought my attention back to Lena Duffy's voice.

'. . . should have opened Dunelgar if home was too far, but her father was fully determined on St George's or St Giles', and there was nothing I could do to change his mind. Anyway, now, under the circumstances –' She broke off and stared at me, fingering her necklace chain and apparently waiting for some response. 'Under the circumstances, none of us has the heart for a lot of fuss and commotion, so she will be married at home as she should be. Not much of a silver lining though, is it?'

Lena Duffy's purr had coarsened. To be honest it always had something else in it besides the comfortable chuckle that was its main ingredient, something more rasping, as though a single crow had got into a chorus of pigeons. Now though there was a note of real spitefulness. I have already touched on the subject of my feminine intuition. At this moment it stretched just far enough to tell me I was supposed to understand something here, but it went no further.

'I don't think I've met the young man,' I said, making what I hoped was a harmlessly general remark, 'although Hugh tells me he was once in a coxless eight with a brother.'

'Elder brother,' said Mrs Duffy. 'But he died at Arras.' One thinks one is tired of the euphemisms and casual endearments, but this bald statement in place of the 'lost at Arras, poor sweet' was shocking. It was only too clear, even to me, that it was meant to convey not even the mildest of honours to a hero, nor a warning that there was a dead brother to be tiptoed around should I find myself in conversation with the young man later. It was quite simply a point of information: Mrs Duffy had done nothing so lax as let her daughter become engaged to a second son without any prospects. The brother was dead and thus the engagement was a triumph. I turned away slightly to hide the expression I could not bring under control and wished that someone might come up and save me replying.

'So a younger son for your younger daughter,' I said at last, no saviour having appeared. This was inane even for me, but I was surprised to see from the corner of my eye a sour kind of twist wrench at the woman's mouth. My mind raced. Did it sound as though I was putting a gypsy curse on her other daughter? This was surely too fanciful. Should I not have made such outright reference to his changed status? Why on earth did I not learn simply to keep my mouth shut? Or if it was too late now for such a wholesale transformation, at least drink a little more and talk a little less.

Daisy's butler was circling with two trays balanced on his fingers like a waiter in a Paris restaurant. Sherry glasses on one and cocktail glasses on the other, he swooped amongst the guests proffering a tray to each and seeming always to guess which one was wanted where. I muttered an excuse to Lena and bore down on him, not caring how unseemly I appeared so long as I escaped her. The butler, who knew me of old, held out the cocktail tray, but from sheer perversity and temper I reached for sherry. His face fell, and we parted, he a disappointed man who feels he is losing his touch, and I a disappointed woman who fears she is becoming curmudgeonly with age and has only a quarter pint (it seemed) of nasty, oily sherry for comfort.

I scanned the room for an empty perch, but apart from Lena sitting alone on a sofa large enough for two and staring at me coldly, all I could see in every direction were settled clumps of people chatting amicably and sipping huge drinks. Daisy's drinks before dinner always go on for an age.

Just then Daisy herself peeled off from the group around a stout dowager ploughing through a long story and ignoring the fidgets of her listeners the way old ladies do.

'What on earth were you saying to the hag?' Daisy whispered. I was unable to answer; I did not know. 'Talk about sucking on a lemon,' she went on. 'And have you seen what she's wearing? How could you not? She's twirling it like an old man with a new watch chain. A gold locket! I'll bet she had to borrow it from her parlour maid. How I have managed not to kick all of their bottoms, I cannot tell you. Even one of the Mrs Bankers is wondering aloud.' I said nothing (for the usual reason) and Daisy rejoined the circle of listeners just in time to join in with gales of relieved laughter as the dowager's saga wound to its close.

I drifted, trying to look self-contained, if not quite inscrutable.

'You look heavenly, Dan,' breathed Clemence Duffy as I passed her, her face more mask-like than ever and her eyes blinking sleepily as she glanced down at herself waiting, I supposed, for the return of the compliment. Despite the fact that there is nothing so very dignified about the name Dandy I dislike being called Dan by girls fifteen years my junior, and I bristled just slightly, before looking her up and down for something to praise. She was dressed in a black shift, chiffon over a plain slip, and wore a small cameo on a black velvet ribbon around her neck, which looked as all cameos always do as though it might have come from Woolworth's. Just then I noticed that her earlobes were bare of any decoration. They were pierced for earrings and the little naked clefts looked hardly decent

27

against her painted face. She arched her brows at me, staring hard at my choker.

'But you look heavenly,' she said again. 'Beautiful emeralds. Very loyal, I must say.' She turned away, and I caught sight of Mrs Duffy fingering her locket chain again. At last light began to dawn on me and I took a few steps and craned to look at Cara Duffy. Dressed in a shimmer of pale blue silk, she wore a gold cross on a fine chain around her neck, slim hoops in her ears and nothing on her wrists at all, only her engagement ring to show that she was not just wearing rather an odd frock to a tennis party. All three of them on parade, ostentatiously bare of jewels, screaming that they dare not wear anything but trinkets here. How dared they! They certainly did need a kick on their insolent bottoms, and I was ready to oblige. I caught Daisy's eye and saw that she had been watching my realization. She mimed my stupidity briefly, eyes crossed and tongue lolling out, thankfully unseen.

Mrs Duffy still sat alone on her sofa. Very well, then. I should employ the tactics for which Daisy had sought me – the Cuthbert Dougall strategy, one might call it – of discussing loud and plain what everyone else is thinking about but dare not mention. I marched back over to Lena and sat beside her.

'My dear,' I said. 'I've only just heard your dreadful news. About the diamonds, I mean. What a thing to happen.' She intensified the stare and spoke again in that horrid murmuring way of hers.

'It has been a great blow to us,' she said. 'Almost like a death. A dreadful loss for Clemence.' This was a strange thing to say. Why so much more to the elder girl? Except perhaps that Cara had her fiancé to distract her. Unless the diamonds were intended for Clemence in the long term, as the elder child. But would not 'The Duffy Diamonds' have to stay in the Duffy family, entailed on some male somewhere? Even I couldn't ask any of this.

'And have the police got anywhere yet?' was what I settled for.

'The police?' she said, with a slight shriek. Clemence raised her head on the other side of the room and gave me a very fair copy of her mother's basilisk stare, a look which belied her friendly words of minutes before. What was wrong with these people?

'Of course, it must be horrid for you to have them tramping around,' I said, smiling across at Clemence and keeping my voice low, 'but think how wonderful, if they got to the bottom of it all.'

'The police,' said Lena Duffy again, quieter but no less witheringly, 'have not been called in. And I very much hope that they never will be.' I could quite concur with this, for with the police tends to come the press and no one welcomes the indignity of having their misfortune devoured by the jealous and therefore triumphant masses. But I knew enough to know that unless the police were called to investigate there was no way the insurance company would pay up and so . . . My thoughts snagged as an idea spread through me. Could someone be so desperate to avoid publicity that she thought it worthwhile to coerce Silas and Daisy into making good her loss, instead of just going to the police and claiming the insurance? Could anyone be so selfish? The Duffy jewels were fabulously, spectacularly precious, worth more than the rest of Mr Duffy's estate put together we always believed, and there was no way on earth that Silas and Daisy, rich though they were, could afford to replace them. I could think of nothing to say, but some of my incredulity must have shown in my face and she spoke again.

'Naturally we assumed that Silas meant to do the right thing. That is why we came today. It is galling indeed, then, when I hoped that my husband and he might talk things over in peace and quiet, to find ourselves being expected to help entertain these persons. We of all people who put our faith in him, to be asked to aid Daisy in providing a pleasant visit for these financiers, to support Silas in his pursuit of even further success for the very institution which will not honour its commitments. I know

29

the world has changed, my dear, but it is a great shock and a sadness to my husband and me to find out how much.' It took me a minute or two to digest all of this and even when I had, I could not believe I understood her.

'Do you mean to say that the jewels were insured with Esslemont Life?' I asked, knowing my voice had risen to a squeak. Mrs Duffy inclined her head.

'And I was naïve enough to believe that might make a difference,' she said.

I do not know that I should ever have called her naïve, but I could sympathize. Even if no member of the Esslemont household had actually stolen the jewels, Silas could surely have smoothed things through. He must own Esslemont Life outright since the death of his father, although I had a vague notion that owning companies was not like owning farms and woods. I had heard Hugh huffing on about something called limited liability which he appeared to think of as a kind of swindle and I had inhaled a morsel of watercress sandwich once when Daisy had said that Silas's sisters were his sleeping partners, and had had to be banged on the back. So my understanding of high finance was uncertain, but I was sure that if you owned the company you could do more or less whatever you liked. The only possible reason for Silas to insist on the police – if indeed he was insisting – would be if he hoped to wriggle out of paying at all, and even if he felt no personal obligation over the theft, surely he had too much honour for that. And why had Daisy not told me this? Did she know herself? I suddenly hoped not.

'It's unbelievable,' I said at last to Mrs Duffy. 'I can't believe it of Silas. Even on his own terms, as a businessman I mean, surely he can see that this will destroy him. A theft in his house is bad enough, but this!'

'The theft in this house is not the half of it, Dandy dear,' said Lena. 'And Silas knows that. Not that the evidence isn't clear on that point. It is, as I could tell you in plain words if propriety did not demand otherwise. Very clear. But even setting that aside, there are other things I happen

to know, which I am sure Silas wishes I didn't.' Her voice
had sunk to a spiteful mutter, and I squirmed.

'There's no need to say *anything* more,' I said, praying
that she would not. I loathe confidences. 'No need for plain
words. What you've told me already would sink Silas for
ever with anyone who matters.'

She turned to me, turned fully, and it was perhaps
owing to old-fashioned corsetry but it nevertheless gave
the impression that she was sizing me up. Then she
seemed to soften.

'Who matters to you and to me, my dear,' she said, with
a significant glance at Daisy and a shake of her head, 'may
not be anyone who matters to others.'

'Well, then you shall just have to be businesslike and call
the police in,' I said. 'Even though it will be beastly. And
you can pack your things and leave here in the morning.
Tonight even. There is no earthly reason for you to feel you
should have to stay. Unspeakable cheek.'

She hesitated then, just for a moment. 'There is an
irregularity,' she said. 'With the paperwork. Nothing that
Silas could not put right had he sufficient will to do so. But
enough of an irregularity to mean that unless this can be
handled as a matter of honour between friends then it
cannot be handled at all.'

'Oh, but paperwork!' I said. 'How could that matter?'

Mrs Duffy looked discomfited and chewed her lip for
quite some time before she answered. When she did it was
with the distant chilliness of one who feels her dignity will
not withstand her words.

'It is possible that a back-dated premium payment now
could be misconstrued,' she said.

I groaned to myself. So Mr Duffy had allowed the insurance to lapse. It was hard to believe when one thought of
the staggering value of the diamonds, but then I suppose
that was rather the point. The premium must have been
vast and the Duffys were in the same boat as we all were,
with two of their houses closed despite all their ships and
their forests in Ontario. Still, as she said, between friends

it should make no difference at all, and if Silas traded on friendship to his own benefit as he most certainly did – this house party being just one example of it – then friendship, if not common decency, should see to it that he did what was *not* to his own advantage too.

'Would you like me to speak to Daisy?' I said. 'Perhaps if just one of her friends makes it clear how shockingly we think Silas is behaving? Perhaps they are sunk so deep in with bankers and accountants and goodness knows what grubby little moneybags, that they can't see what this would mean.' I was quite sincere. My view of the proceedings had shifted one hundred and eighty degrees and I was very angry. I had been taken advantage of and Daisy had barely even bothered to hide it. She had said quite openly it was my denseness and resulting artlessness that were what she needed. Lena Duffy was smiling at me and nodding. It was the calmest and least complicated expression I had ever seen on her face, and I swelled slightly with righteous pride to think that I had put it there.

'You are very good, my dear,' she said. 'But, if you do, please make it plain that we are not expecting an instant payment of the whole amount. That would be far too much of a strain, even for the Esslemonts. Something now, and then a regular sum . . . I'm sure we can come to an arrangement.'

I wavered on hearing this. A something now, and then a regular sum, because Lena had proof and could harm Silas? That arrangement could be called a very plain word indeed.

Lena was still watching me intently and I imagine that my thoughts were clearly painted on my face, for her chumminess started to chill again and she drew herself up and away from me. Before I could summon my wits to speak though, the gong sounded, at last.

'I've put you beside Cara Duffy's intended deliberately, darling,' said Daisy, as we shuffled about, pairing up to go in. I said nothing to her; now was not the time to launch into it. 'And since she's on his other side, I fear you'll be

32

looking at his back all evening, but it's not because I'm a slave to sentiment, nor because you're dear to me and so beyond protocol, it's all in aid of your investigation. It gives you old Gregory Duffy on your other side, you see. Plenty of scope for grilling and snooping there. *Bonne chance!'*

My shoulders drooped. It is perfectly all right, of course, to sit an engaged couple side by side even if it is rather sickening to watch, but it is hard on the other neighbours and I feared I could make no use at all of Daisy's gift. I knew I should not dare to grill Gregory Duffy. He is not a fearsome old gentleman, but silent, with a vague sadness about him. It could be no more than an unsatisfactory marriage, for I am sure that a man of his stamp must be unhappy with such a wife even if her faults are as vague as his virtues. However, if a lack of bliss in marriage was enough to settle such a shroud around the shoulders, the whole nation would be sunk in permanent gloom and I have always thought there must be something more to it. Perhaps the lack of an heir, but then he always seemed much fonder of his younger daughter than his elder and it would surely be the second child, the last one, whom he would loathe for her femaleness, if he harboured such unfair grudges against either. Anyway, wherever the sadness sprang from, it drew out of one a kind of respectful pity, or perhaps a wariness is a better word for it; wariness that if one were *not* respectful he would only seem the *more* pitiful and then it would be embarrassment all round.

This was my usual attitude to Gregory Duffy, then, and it was not affected by any current anger towards him regarding the diamonds. There was only pity there too, for I was sure the 'arrangement' Lena hoped for with Silas was her idea alone. I was sure too that she must have made her husband's life a perfect misery over the lapsed premiums. How dreadful it was of Silas not to do the decent thing, not to feel enough respectful pity for this man.

I felt I could not possibly broach any aspect of the

33

subject during dinner, but as Daisy had predicted, my view of Cara's young man was restricted to the broad stretch of his coat shoulders and I foresaw a very dull time for myself unless I made some effort, so I cast about for something else to say Mr Duffy, and eventually found it.

'My congratulations. For your daughter, I mean.' His eyes flicked towards his wife at the other end of the table then rested on the dark back which hid Cara from view, warming as they did so, melting I should almost have said.

'Yes,' he said, and went on softly with a steady, falling cadence, 'yes, indeed, sometimes, most unexpectedly, matters resolve.' With this he turned his attention to his plate, and I put my head down too, puzzled. I knew he was very fond of Cara, his favouritism was famed, but how he could look around him and call matters resolved just at that moment was beyond me. (The store of things beyond me was bigger every time I looked.) We drank soup in silence for a while until a combination of grumpiness at being neglected and recklessness, for which I can only blame the enormous sherry glasses, loosened my tongue.

'I was very shocked indeed, though, to hear about your diamonds.'

'Were you?' he said, quietly, his eyes swivelling again between Clemence, her mother and Cara's fiancé's back. 'Were you indeed. I can't say I was, but my wife appears to have taken it very hard.' His voice and face were calm and unreadable, just the constant swivelling eyes, reptilian between wrinkled eyelids.

'Yes. She called it "a death in the family",' I said, suddenly remembering this.

At that, he turned his benevolent gaze upon me and watched me with one eyebrow slightly raised, almost smiling. I was in far over my head again, my feet tangled in weeds and no use thrashing. No use either fighting the sensation of foreboding creeping through me again. What was it? Perhaps just the sherry wearing off. I took a gulp of water and when I looked up he had withdrawn into

34

himself in some way quite indefinable but as clear as though he had walked out of the room.

I amused myself as best I could during the rest of soup and through fish, by studying the bankers' wives, storing up details with which to regale Grant later. They all wore such similar art silk dresses that it might have been a uniform, and one had to assume these dresses were the very latest fashion since they were so ugly – with the cut and colour of old bandages – that they could not possibly have been selected on any aesthetic grounds. Grant would know. Indeed, if this was to be the next fashion, she would no doubt soon be campaigning for me to buy some old bandages of my own.

Unexpectedly, the lure of young love proved to be more resistible than either Daisy or I had imagined and at the proper moment, my neighbour turned away from Cara and smiled at me.

'Alec Osborne,' he said. 'We've not met.' His tone was like a cold splash of water on my face after all the undercurrents and intrigue and I felt my shoulders unbunch immediately. He was a young man of close to thirty, I supposed, striking to look at, of an unusual type for this part of the world, and my mind went back fleetingly to the brother at Arras, wondering if he had been the same. He had tawny hair, that is the only word for it, silly as it may seem, for it was not fair and not red. Blond I suppose would cover it, were not that word faintly disreputable and, for a male, ridiculous. His eyes were almost the same colour, and his skin was from that palette too. Golden without being sun-tanned exactly. I took a closer look. It was as though a great intermittent freckle covered him. Most unusual, and I wondered if it was just his face and hands, before I caught myself mid-wonder and blushed.

'Have you been abroad or are you always so burnished?' I asked and immediately felt my little store of social pride begin to wither at yet another ludicrous remark. Alec Osborne, however, threw back his head and laughed. An artless peal of sound, which drew startled looks from up

35

and down the table. I was aware that Mrs Duffy's attention did not quite return to her neighbour afterwards.

'And you are Mrs Gilver,' he said, instantly making me feel like his grandmother.

'Dandy,' I said, and understandably he did not at once perceive that I was offering my Christian name. 'Dandelion Gilver,' I explained and his lips twitched just once before he organized his face into an expression of interest.

'My mother and father were great devotees of William Morris,' I said. 'And in the spirit of the times, they honoured me with the name of one of our most beautiful and unfairly neglected wildflowers.'

'Very trying for you.'

'Typical, I'm afraid,' I said. 'They also did great work in the house – much ripping out of Adams plaster and substitution of greengrocery in bog oak. My brother is only now beginning to put matters right again.'

'They're no longer with us then?' he said, and as I shook my head he went on: 'Let's hope then, Dandy, that heaven is less baroque in reality than it's usually rendered in paint, or they will not find it much to their liking.'

I think it would have been at that moment, if I were the type to fall in love, that I should have fallen in love with Alec Osborne. It would have been the first and last time in my life (and of course I should not have admitted it to myself) but, despite the presence two feet away of the girl he was to marry, as he teased me so very gently and said my name, that is when it would have happened.

Chapter Three

No further progress was possible that first evening. Silas shouted down the table to Alec Osborne to clear up some argument about fishing tackle, and at that the men were lost and the ladies retreated into a huffy but dignified silence which carried us through until we could retreat bodily to the drawing room, the coffee cups and the desultory house party chat which always makes one long for bedtime.

Hugh was up and off at early light the next day, slipping out in his stockinged feet in a way I thought most considerate until I realized that he was headed for his rubber waders in the boot room. I opened my eyes once he was gone and lay with my hands laced behind my head. I was thinking over the evening before and trying to plan a useful day, when the door opened and Daisy came in still in her nightie and the bathing cap she always wears in bed in the hope that it will keep her hair set while she sleeps.

'Wretched thing,' she said, plumping down at my dressing table and peeling it off. Her hair underneath was almost grotesque in its dishevelment. 'As ever,' she said, sighing, 'hair by Picasso.' Then she rumpled it into its naturally mop-like state with both hands and got into bed beside me. I looked straight ahead of me and spoke with no emotion. And it is just as well I did, for here is what happened.

'Well, I drew out Mrs, as you witnessed,' I began. 'She is adamant that the theft took place at the ball and she fully expected, therefore, that Silas would pay out on her claim, even though as she put it there is an irregularity in the paperwork. She seems dreadfully shocked that it's not simply happening that way.'

Daisy stared at me.

'An irregularity in the paperwork?' she said. I raised my eyebrows non-committally and waited for more. 'Is that how she described it to you, Dan? An irregularity in the paperwork? She must be insane. If anyone were to find out that Silas had done such a thing he would be finished.'

I hoped that my mask continued to function but I feared my face was hardening as I heard this. Daisy's idea of 'finished' was evidently very different from mine.

'Yes, I suppose his financial chums would look down their noses rather,' I said, trying to sound as light as I could.

'Well, that too,' said Daisy. 'But from his prison cell, I rather think that would be the least of his worries.'

'Prison? Surely not?'

'Of course prison. Fraud, false accounts, embezzlement. Why do you think Gerard Bevan is on the run?'

'Who?' I asked.

'Don't you ever read the papers, Dandy? She must be mad to think that this could happen hush-hush and no questions asked. She must –' Daisy sat straight up and glared over her shoulder at the corner of the room, towards, I guessed, the part of the house where Lena's bedroom lay. 'She must have some kind of proof.'

Daisy did not seem to notice, so lost was she in the tangle of her own thoughts, that I was silent. I knew no more than that the clear view I thought I had got of the thing had clouded over once more.

'What I don't see, though,' she said, 'is why on earth they weren't insured for real. That makes no sense at all.'

'They weren't insured,' I echoed.

'Which makes no sense at all,' said Daisy again.

'They weren't insured by Silas,' I said, slowly and carefully, mostly to myself. 'But she hoped he might fake an insurance arrangement and cover their loss, risking ruin and jail, rather than let whatever it is come out.' Fortunately my thinking out loud was taken by Daisy to be a helpful summary and she simply nodded. 'I agree then,' I said. 'She must have proof.' Something was nagging at me, but I was so confused already I knew I should have to think long and hard before illumination came.

'Yes,' said Daisy. 'Nothing else would explain how she could even dream that Silas would . . .' I tried again to catch at the nagging thought, the way one does, looking mentally off to the side and pretending one isn't. It did not work.

'This is going to do for us, Dan,' said Daisy, morosely. 'Oh, I don't mean there's anything in it, of course. We shan't have to pay it. But just a hint, just a whisper. You've no idea what they're like, these bankers. Not to mention the actuaries.' She shuddered again, just as she had when she had said the word to me over the telephone. I began to wonder with dread what an actuary was, exactly.

'I think even Lena realizes that,' I said. 'And in a way that makes it worse.' Daisy frowned at me, waiting. 'She said last night, very clearly, that I should ask you for a little something and then a regular arrangement.' Daisy's mouth dropped open.

'But that's . . .' she began, and then blinked and shook her head. 'How did you do it, Dan? What on earth did you say to get her to simply pour it all out like that? You are a marvel.' I hoped Daisy would take my sudden flush and inarticulate gulping as modesty. She smacked her hands down on the bedclothes making me jump.

'Five hundred pounds,' she said, cutting into my fizz of shame. 'Five hundred pounds if you can get to the bottom of it, darling. And, um, a daily retainer. Expenses too, of course.'

'A daily retainer?' I echoed. 'Expenses? Daisy, have you done this before?'

'I went to an agency last week and sounded them out,'

Daisy said. 'But I funked it. They would have been hope-less, lumbering around in serge, you know, like having a rhinoceros come to tea and expecting no one to notice.' She looked piercingly at me. 'Can you, Dan? Can you spare the time?' I tried hard not laugh. 'And more to the point, can you bear to cosy up to Lena enough to find out what she's up to? Can you do it?'

'Leave it with me,' I said, managing not to blush who knows how at my temerity. After all, less than two minutes before I had almost let it slip that I hadn't a clue. 'I accept your terms. Now just leave it to me.'

To my great surprise, Daisy fell for it. She sighed with contentment and snuggled down under the blankets with a slow, luxuriating wriggle like a warm dog, then emerged again and, saying she was going to write me a cheque that minute, she dashed off.

My breakfast tray appeared, although it was as hard to concentrate on eggs and toast as it was to force my thoughts to the question of the theft, the fraud or any of it. All I could think of was five hundred pounds, five *hundred* pounds; the first money of my own I should have had since the last coin had been pressed into my hand by a kindly uncle, and the first money I should have *earned* in my entire life. Daisy had tossed it casually towards me as though not only was the sum negligible but also the fact of her having it, to do as she pleased with it, was nothing out of the usual way.

Giving up on breakfast at last, I began to dress. Tweed, of course, but I always make sure to have some rather pretty tweed, such is the amount of time one spends in it when one is married to a Scotsman. Today's were a heath-ery colour flecked with amethyst, which looked quite acceptable with those purple-fawn stockings in the shade I think of as 'alcoholic nose'. I have countless other tweed garments, all heathery at heart, but flecked with any num-ber of greens, blues, pinks, yellows even. On one point I am immovable, though: country life is bad enough with-out wearing brown.

By half-past ten, recovered from my excitement, heathery and flecked, I sat down beside Lena Duffy in the hall. She was installed at the comfortable end of a chaise from where she could keep an eye on Cara and Alec, who were sitting in another corner of the room. (Alec, as an engaged person, was clearly exempt from the day's sport.) Lena did not exactly welcome me, issuing no more than a curt nod, but she did not actually scowl, so I guessed that matters between us were as we had left them, frosty – no overnight thaw – but at the sorbet rather than the iceberg end of the scale. Besides, although she was reading *Vanity Fair* she very selfishly had the *Tatler*, *Bystander* and *Graphic* on her lap too, saving them for later. This left only the dreary old *Spectator* for my amusement and so I swallowed my qualms at disturbing her.

'They seem very contented,' I said, nodding towards the corner. This was harmless enough I thought, but Mrs Duffy's mouth puckered for a second and she did not answer. Either she disliked me, ladies, people in general, or I had already managed to say something displeasing. I wondered if, despite appearances, there was something unsatisfactory about Alec Osborne. If I could soften her up with enough sympathetic clucking on this point we might switch topics with the greatest of ease. 'A thoroughly satisfactory young man,' I continued. 'Well done, Cara, for bringing him to all of our notice, I say. Where was he hiding until now?'

'Dorset,' said Mrs Duffy. 'He's a distant connection of my husband's.'

So that could not be the problem. Was it the Dorset angle that was troubling her?

'And will they settle there?' I asked. 'Rather a wrench for you.'

'They will be living here,' she said. I imagined that by here, she meant Perthshire, or Scotland, at any rate not Dorset.

I gulped, and wished that Daisy would bring the Mrs Bankers into the hall and save me. Of course I knew there

41

was no hope of that; Daisy would be keeping them scrupulously out of the way to give me a clear run and the only other person who might well appear would be Clemence – it was odd for her to be parted from her mother for even ten minutes – and that would be no help.

We watched in silence. Alec and Cara were sitting together at a table bent over some illustrated brochure or other. I supposed they might be choosing honeymoon excursions but they were making rather a solemn affair out of it if so, Cara seeming just as unlike her usual buoyant self as she had the evening before. She was turning pages idly and as she did so her engagement ring winked in the sunlight pouring through the window, making a little burst of reflected light dance over the staircase opposite.

'I used to do just that with my own rings when the boys were tiny and I went to tuck them in,' I said. '"Make Tinkerbell, Mummy," they would say. Did you play those games with your two?' Silence. Realization spread through me like an inkblot. 'Oh God,' I said. 'I *am* sorry. Oh, I could just kick myself sometimes, really. Going on about jewels.'

She heaved an almighty sigh, slightly ragged at its peak, and began to speak.

'You can't possibly imagine, my dear. My diamonds – our diamonds, I should say. Poor Clemence.' There it was again. Poor Clemence – they *must* have been meant for her. 'They were quite simply the most beautiful, the most heartbreakingly beautiful . . . I can't bear to think about it.' She was almost plausible; that is to say I quite believed that she loved the diamonds this much, but still there was something unmistakably manufactured going on.

'One hears people – and not just poets – in such raptures about mountains and oceans and flowers, and I always think, "Ah, there's someone who has never seen my diamonds or they wouldn't be going on so about a daffodil or a newborn baby."'

'Well, yes,' I said. 'A newborn baby perhaps has to be one's own newborn baby before one can rapture properly.'

42

I was half-teasing, looking at Cara as I spoke, expecting some guilty blustering to break out.

'When I think that I shall never see them again, it's more than I can stand,' said Lena. She could not have been listening to me, for no woman could maunder on so about stones after a direct appeal to her to show some motherly sentiment. What is more, while this wailing over her lost diamonds was less irritating than any wailing over her soon-to-be-lost baby would have been, it was nevertheless quite bogus since the hoped-for arrangement with Silas was all to do with hard cash and not at all to do with outdoing the wonder of the Alps and Atlantic. Anyway, it was getting us nowhere. I took a deep breath and began.

'Lena –'

'I far prefer Eleanor,' she said. So much for our bosom friendship, then.

'I beg your pardon. Eleanor, I spoke to Daisy as we agreed, and I think – no, I'm sure – that I managed to give the impression simply of gossiping and of being entirely on her side.'

'Thank you, my dear,' she said. 'And are they disposed to be reasonable?'

'Not without some evidence, I fear. I really do think they don't see how it can have happened.'

'Is this Daisy we're speaking about or Silas?' I considered how to answer. I was not sure what Silas knew about what was going on here. All I had was Daisy's remark from our telephone call that he was so unnerved as to be ready to give in. But whether this was pre-flotation jitters or meant that he knew something we did not . . .?

'Both,' I said at last. 'Both are tremendously sympathetic, of course, and sorry. But both are quite adamant that nothing can have happened at the ball. You will need to produce some proof.'

'Proof?' asked Lena sharply.

'Yes, so can you – fearful cheek, I know – but can you tell me what makes you so sure?'

43

'Of course,' said Lena. 'First of all, that was the last time the jewels were all out of the bank together.' She produced this with an air of triumph, just as Hugh had, but it still bothered me.

'If that's all –' I began, but she interrupted.

'No, there's much more.' She settled almost visibly into her story. 'I was awakened in the night, by someone scuffling around in my room. I thought it was the maid lighting the fire, you know, but when I glanced at my watch I saw it was only just five o'clock and so I leapt out of bed and put the light on. The door banged shut and whoever it was was gone. Of course, my first thought was for my jewel cases, and imagine my horror when I looked at them and saw the locks all scratched and buckled as though someone had been trying to prise them open with a blade. My dear! I opened them up and everything was still there. Or so I thought, and if only I hadn't been so ready to believe it! But the paste copies were so convincing. Well, then I just went back to bed and tried to think no more about it.' She sat back and looked almost as though she were merely relieved to have got it all off her chest, except that I could tell she was watching me very intently.

'I see,' I said, buying some time while I tried to settle on the most diplomatic way I could of asking the questions I needed to ask. It was all I could do not to shout 'Nonsense!' and count the lies off on my fingers, for it was the least convincing tale I had ever heard. I began to wonder at her nerve – to think she could get money out of Silas with this rot.

'Did you not worry,' I said at last, 'that the thief might go to another room and have better luck there?'

'Oh, don't think me selfish,' said Lena. 'I knew the others would have put their jewels back in the safe after the end of the party. I didn't imagine anyone else would have anything lying around worth stealing.'

'And why did you not do the same with yours?' I asked, hoping I did not sound as peremptory as I felt.

'My maid was ill,' said Lena, 'and I did not want to entrust them to someone I didn't know.'

'But didn't you wonder there and then – when you saw the state of the locks, I mean – about pastes?' She was beginning to draw herself up again and I saw that we were heading back to sorbet and beyond. This should have to be my last question.

'Such a thing never crossed my mind,' she said, through pursed lips.

'Well, it wouldn't,' I agreed. 'I shall certainly speak to Daisy about all of this.'

'And Silas too,' she said. I was beginning to put her down as one of those ladies who, even when past the age to flirt, cannot rid themselves of the idea that the husband is the head of the household and the valve – do I mean valve? – through which all must flow. I am the other kind; I know very well that husbands have all the money and all the say, really, but somehow I never remember to behave as if it were so. (The very strange thing is that if one lives one's life with this point of view, as though husbands barely exist, they do seem to fade.)

'And Silas too,' I assured her.

'He needs to be brought to an understanding that although what is lost can never be got back again, and although it may have taken some time to come to light, life does go on and reparation must be made.' She spoke in a noble tone as though delivering hot tips from an oracle, so I gave the kind of slow nod I thought oracles' tips demanded.

There was no chance to talk to Daisy at luncheon (the usual half-hearted luncheon dished up to ladies when their husbands are enjoying lavish picnics somewhere else) but afterwards she and I loitered long enough to let the Duffys settle themselves in the hall again and the bankers' wives begin an inept game of summer ice in the pavilion while they waited for the croquet lawn to be set, then we lit our cigarettes and strolled down the drive. McSween was up a ladder about a quarter of a mile away towards the gate,

45

lopping industriously at the fresh growth in one of the trees in the avenue, a boy down below catching the clippings, and although they made a plausible object for our walk should anyone wonder why Daisy was neglecting her guests, I certainly wanted to have the conversation done with before we reached them, so in I plunged.

'Silas must be brought to an understanding – this is a direct quote, darling – that although what is lost is gone for ever, life goes on and no matter how much water has passed under the bridge – how did it go? – no matter how many tides have ebbed and waned, he must still, um, cough up in the end.'

'Hmm. Ebbing and waning are the same thing, aren't they?' Daisy said. 'So does she have any proof?' I drew a large happy sigh; I was looking forward to this bit.

'She thinks she does, but you've never heard such a taradiddle in your life, Daisy, I can assure you. Ahem! She was proceeding to take her rest on the night in question,' I spoke in my best PC Plod, 'when she was awakened by the sound of an intruder,' but at this I lost control of my cockney vowels and had to give up.

'This is serious, Dan, please!' said Daisy.

'Yes, very well,' I said. 'Only wait until you hear it. It's hard to remember it's supposed to be serious. She heard an intruder, thought it was the maid, glanced at her watch and saw that it was five o'clock.' I waited, but Daisy said nothing. 'Glanced at her watch at five o'clock in the morning in November with no lights on, darling? I think not. Anyway she got up and put on the light. She heard a thief running along the corridor, saw that her jewel cases had been tampered with, didn't tell anyone, didn't raise the alarm, didn't mention it to her husband and didn't get the jewels looked at until months had passed. Twaddle!'

'What did she mean, "tampered with"? Did she mean they were open?'

'No, I don't think so. Just scraped and bent out of shape. As though someone had been at them with a knife. It was this scraping that woke her up, she said. As to why the

46

cases were in her room instead of back in the safe? Her maid was ill, if you please, and she didn't trust anyone else. This must be some maid, if she's so much more to be trusted than any number of burly footmen. How do you always manage to get such burly footmen, Daisy, anyway?' Daisy did not answer and we walked on for a while, heads bent, until she stopped and ground the end of her cigarette under her heel.

'That's rather awkward,' she said. 'The bit about the knife, I mean. Silas and I have been over and over that night as you can imagine, trying to think of anything out of the ordinary, and there is the thing about the knife.' She lit another cigarette and talked with her head down. 'A day or so after the ball, one of the tweenies produced an oyster knife and tried to give it to a footman to give back to the butler. Of course, all of the upper servants immediately decided this poor thing had stolen it and then lost her nerve, but she maintained and continued to maintain under all the glowering of butler and cook combined – and they should have had us begging for mercy, Dan, I can tell you – she would not budge from the story that she found the knife down the back of the dressing table in a bedroom while she was dusting. Lena's bedroom, before you ask.'

'Oh Daisy, really!' I said, almost cross. 'What is wrong with everyone? We had oysters that night, didn't we? Very delicious they were too, even though treacherous Hugh dared to blame them for the state of his head the next morning – such ingratitude – so Lena could easily have put one in her bag and dropped it herself. She probably did over her locks with it too. All to add a little verisimilitude to her story.'

'Do you think?'

'Of course! What do *you* think? A thief comes to steal jewels that no one has any reason to believe won't be in the safe, comes without a knife, breaks into the butler's pantry to get one, scrapes away at the locks right by the bed of the slumbering owner instead of just stealing the cases . . . I can hardly be bothered to finish it, it's so feeble. I say,

47

I don't suppose anyone will remember whether she really did keep her jewels in her room that night? Or whether her maid really was ill?'

'I can check,' said Daisy, 'but surely she wouldn't just make all that up?'

'That is just my point,' I said. 'The whole tale is so silly and so half-hearted one can scarcely believe she thinks it will work. And actually – Hah!'

'What?' said Daisy, stamping out another cigarette and looking at me excitedly.

'Oh, the cheek of the woman. There's something else. She as much as told me last night that, even if the proof of the so-called theft wasn't all it should be, she knew something else that Silas would much rather she didn't. So you see, it's nothing to do with the silly jewels being stolen here, and she knows it and doesn't care if we guess as much. It's not reparation or compensation or anything decent at all. It's blackmail, pure and simple.'

'Well, how completely bloody horrid of her,' said Daisy, comical in her indignation. 'After all we've done for them!'

'Such as?'

'Well, all right, putting up with them mostly. But remember how we took Cara off their hands that winter to let Mrs and the Ice Princess go gallivanting? Wheeled her about for months.' What I love about Daisy is her lack of guile.

'As I remember it, darling, you spent most of that winter gallivanting yourself. Didn't you swan off to New York for weeks on end and leave poor Cara here with Nanny?'

'It was just after the war, Dan, and I hadn't seen Mummy for five years – hardly gallivanting. And I brought you back some lovely things, didn't I? Anyway, Silas was here. He taught Cara to shoot.'

'And Mrs Duffy has never forgiven you for that,' I reminded her. 'She was still scowling when Cara took a gun last Boxing Day, do you remember?'

'You don't think . . .' said Daisy. 'That couldn't be why

48

she's got a down on us, could it? Something as silly as that?'

'No, of course not,' I said. 'Even Lena wouldn't threaten you with ruin because one of her daughters has learned an unladylike sport. She isn't as mad as all that. Unless you get her on to the diamonds, that is – you want to hear her on them! Gives me the creeps. But otherwise, no. Leave the detecting to me.'

'Darling Dan,' said Daisy, giving me a squeeze. 'I must go now and deliver croquet lessons for beginners until tea.'

'I'm going to walk around down here a bit more, out of harm's way, and plan my next move,' I said. 'Also there's something tickling at me that I can't put my finger on.'

'Absolutely,' said Daisy. 'I'll say it again, Dandy. You're a marvel. You only spoke to her for half a minute and the whole thing's out in the open.' She beamed at me, while I tried to look modest, then she swept off towards the lawn leaving me to carry on down the drive towards McSween on his ladder.

'I'll lift they dog-ends for you on my road back,' he called out by way of a greeting, glaring up the drive towards where Daisy and I had stubbed out our cigarettes on his precious gravel. I murmured a stream of thanks and apologies – he really is the most fearful bully – and walked on past him.

Leaving the drive just before it crossed the bridge I followed the edge of the river towards the start of the woods. The men were fishing miles away to the other side of the park out on the open bank and I felt sure that I should find solitude enough here for whatever it was to percolate to the top of my mind and turn itself into a thought.

First, though, to sort through what had happened. Mrs Duffy had used me as a go-between, relying no doubt on my celebrated callowness – hah! If she only knew – to be sure that I should pass the message straight to Daisy, as indeed I had. She might not appreciate the full enormity of what she was asking. Brought up to be unworldly as girls were in her time, and I supposed in mine, she might not see that what she called the correction of an irregularity was in fact an act of criminal fraud. On the other hand she might know exactly what was at stake for Silas but be sure that she had the means to ruin him anyway and so he had nothing to lose.

There it was again. It was not the sick feeling I had had right at the start; that was still with me, lumpen and disquieting somewhere deep inside, although it had receded a little over the day. Action seemed to dispel it, funnily enough, which was odd if it was a premonition of doom. Unless, of course, it was a premonition of some doom that my actions might avert. That made sense but was such a terrifying thought, that I refused to entertain it. Besides – I shook myself – that was not it. There was something else, something entirely different, like a hair across one's face that one can neither locate nor ignore. It was not only Lena's veiled hints about some hold over Silas; I was sure it was something to do with the diamonds. I tried to empty my mind of all conscious thought to see if it would reveal itself. Nothing happened. Then I wondered if perhaps I should chant or try to balance on one leg, having a vague idea got from honeymooning in Morocco that there were ways to strike a channel through to one's other plane or something and let it all out like a . . . the only image that sprang to mind was a farrier draining an infection with a nail driven through the rotted hoof. This thought made me laugh out loud and I saw something ahead of me move at the sudden sound. Alec Osborne and Cara Duffy were standing close together just where the trees began.

My first thought was to be glad that I was not wobbling on one leg and chanting, my second that had it been Hugh and I when we were engaged (had we ever stood together in the long grass at the edge of a wood?) we should have sprung apart and blushed. Times were changed; for the better I supposed. I shifted from foot to foot, deliberating whether to go on or veer away discreetly, but they both turned towards me and stood waiting for me to approach, all calm welcome, and so I walked up to them beginning my apologies. If anything, though, Alec Osborne looked relieved to see me.

'Very timely, actually,' he said in protestation as I wittered and took half-steps backwards. 'There is so much to be discussed before a wedding, and so little of it that I can discuss convincingly. I shall hand you over, Cara, and melt away.' I looked studiously towards the far bank in case he wanted to kiss her, but he shoved his hands into his pockets and strode off whistling, leaving the two of us looking after him, I rather more struck than Cara by his offhandedness, as far as I could tell from her face. We turned towards the start of the river path and fell into step.

McSween takes no interest in the woodland at Croys, woods being too close to 'Nature' to yield easily to his ministrations, and the result is charming, not least at the time of year when the last of the primroses meet the first of the bluebells and the canopy above them is unfurled but still fresh and pale. Cara, picking her way along the path ahead of me in the cool green light, would have looked like some little creature from a fairy tale, but for the fact that her rather clinging afternoon frock was covered with large, angular roses in black and pink. She sighed audibly, and again I wondered at how subdued she seemed. Such a doleful little sigh; not at all the chirruping and giggling one thought of as her wont. But then I probably had fixed in my head the Cara of years ago, a schoolgirl and then a debutante, and when I cast my mind back over our more recent meetings, it was clear that she had been on her way to this sombre state for quite some time. It is often the way, I have found, that one fixes one's view of a person based on the time in their life when one met first them and then subsequent laziness prevents one from ever updating it. This is why, I suppose, old men who have known some old lady since she was a girl still cluster around and smooth their moustaches for no reason apparent to youngsters.

51

'Do men always assume if a girl wants to talk about something, it must be something silly?' Cara asked me presently.

'I'm rather afraid so,' I said. 'But just before your wedding is no time to think of it. You must waft along on a cloud of blossom until after your honeymoon, and then you can begin on truths.' She laughed at this. 'And Alec is right,' I went on. 'Your mother and your sister are the ones for flowers and dresses and whatnot.' She bent her head a little lower at this, studying the soft bark and old leaves under her feet. I felt an unexpected and quite fierce protectiveness towards her, but I also saw a handy opening.

'Let's us have a good long twitter about it,' I said. 'I expect your poor mother must be distracted by all this trouble about the jewels. But I should love to hear about your wedding. Where are you going afterwards? Where are you to settle?'

'I can't stop thinking about the jewels either,' said Cara. 'Everyone is being so peculiar. Mummy, of course, is bereft. Clemence is as Clemence-like as ever, although I shouldn't say it about my own sister, I suppose. And Daddy just doesn't say anything at all. How I wish it hadn't come out until after I was married.'

'How did it? Come out, I mean?' I knew how it had come out, of course. Hugh had told me, but I needed to start her talking.

'Haven't you heard? Gosh, I thought everyone knew absolutely everything. I can hear whispering behind my back everywhere I go. It makes it almost a relief to be here with those dreadful little women for a few days, and I expect by the time Monday comes they will be buzzing with it too.'

I said nothing. I was quivering for more, but if I prodded her too sharply she might retreat with distaste. My recent experience with Daisy had shown me, however, that if one keeps perfectly quiet (even if one is only keeping quiet because one is utterly lost and therefore incapable of sensible speech) someone else will say something. It worked again.

'I took them out of the bank to have them valued, and the poor jeweller's apprentice who was inspecting them, as a special treat and with his boss breathing down his neck, took one look through his little monocle and almost died of fright.'

'He must have, poor lamb,' I said. And then I ventured, 'Do you have to have them valued every so often then? I'm just being nosy because I have nothing so sumptuous of my own. Hugh's insurers don't force us to submit my little baubles for regular inspection.' She seemed to find nothing strange in this. Another important lesson: say nothing at all, or say much too much – it's the unadorned question that raises the hackles.

'No, it wasn't an insurance valuation, as it happens,' said Cara, with a small suggestion of laughter in her voice. 'I've no idea how often those have to be done. But I bet my eyes they just stamp the form and sign it and never look at the things. Nobody ever does. I bet more than half the "jewels" you see are fakes, no matter how closely guarded and heavily insured they are.' She was even nearer laughter now, but a weary kind of laughter which suggested to me that she was ready to tell all to anyone just for sheer relief.

'The last time they were all out together was here, you know. Since then they've been out of the bank once to have pastes made and twice to be cleaned. All at different times, too, because our usual jeweller doesn't care to have the whole lot in his safe at once. Do you see what I'm saying?'

'Yes, but there's something bothering me about that –' I began, then I really did see what she was saying.

'He cleaned them all,' said Cara, burbling with a laughter that almost did away with the weariness in her voice, 'solemnly refusing to acknowledge that they were worthless. And then he made pastes of pastes, again solemnly going along with it. Such excruciating discretion. And after

53

the whole thing came out, it was clear that he does it all the time. It's killing.'

I could see the funny side of this, of course, and we smiled ruefully for a moment before I spoke again.

'I wonder what happened to them,' I said, carefully, probing. Again Cara spoke as though letting out the words was a relief of some unbearable pressure.

'Well, it must have been someone who had time in advance to have copies made for the substitution,' she said. 'Someone who had seen them before. You see? Someone we know.' Much as I loathed to admit it, she was making perfect sense.

'And I suppose,' I said slowly, 'I suppose it's a mere fluke that you found out at all. That you decided to have them valued, and took them to a different jeweller, that a callow apprentice got his hands on them and blew the whistle.'

'Well, not quite,' said Cara.

I thought furiously, kicking into the path with the toe of my boot, but I could make no headway with this. Cara was chewing her lip and looking at me out of the corner of her eye. Suddenly she seemed to make up her mind and spoke again.

'I was having them valued to sell,' she said quietly. 'I rather think that's what brought the jeweller to his senses. And I've simply got to talk to someone about it before I burst.'

I was nodding, trying not to look too eager.

'But you must promise not to tell anyone,' Cara went on. 'Oh Lord, listen to me! I've always hated that, haven't you? *I* promise not to tell anyone, and then tell *you* not to tell anyone, and you'll extract the same promise from whoever you tell . . .' She sounded almost hysterical.

Just then we were forced to abandon the conversation to negotiate a birch sapling which had fallen most inconveniently across the path. It was slim enough for us to step over, but we had to concentrate on keeping our skirts clear of the up-thrusting branches and so I had a little time to think. My questions, none of which I could possibly have asked her out loud, were: first, why in heaven's name with marriage to Alec Osborne weeks away was she planning to sell the diamonds she was surely to wear at her wedding; second, what could she possibly need the money for; third and most important, why on earth had she told her mother about it? Had it been me, I should have bribed the jeweller with everything I owned, and then simply slipped the things back into the bank and kept my head down.

Over the tree at last, we patted ourselves down and regarded one another.

'You poor dear,' I said at last. And I meant it. Mrs Duffy was not someone I should care to cross, unconnected and unbeholden as I was. I could hardly imagine Cara revealing to her mother not only that she had been planning to offload the famous collection for cash – and how did she manage to get them out of the bank, anyway? – but that the family treasure was Woolworth's best.

Cara was shaking her head and spoke in a very calm voice.

'Please forget I said anything at all. It's just that I'm so very confused and I don't know who to turn to –' She broke off, shook her head again, then repeated even more firmly: 'Please just forget I spoke. It's probably nothing.'

We were just emerging from the wood then, and we could see across a stretch of parkland the coloured frocks of the ladies on the croquet lawn, and a short procession of dark-suited footmen carrying tea trays across to a ring of chairs where Alec Osborne and Daisy were seated, with Silas in turned-down waders looking like Dick Whittington standing between them. My heart sank. Tea outside in summer one must learn to put up with, but this early in the spring one ought really to be able to count on a crackling fire and an armchair; Daisy has gone terribly hearty and Scotch in some ways over the years. Still, I could see a footman on his way with a pile of rugs and at least the tea would be hot. Cara, beside me, laughed suddenly.

'Silly old me with my wedding nerves,' she said, unconvincingly.

'More than likely,' I said, unconvinced.

'Although to be honest I don't care how awful the wedding is, as long as it actually happens and isn't called off.' She had lost me again. Why should the wedding be called off? Were the diamonds her dowry and Alec unlikely to take her without them? But then why should she sell them? To get rid of him? If so, it had not worked, for he didn't look like jilting her. What was going on? I forced myself to pay attention to what she was saying.

'I don't say that I shall lock myself in a tower and pine to death if it all falls through, but I am very keen to be good and married, and no going back.'

I looked at the distant figure of Alec Osborne, lying back in his lawn chair, laughing at something Daisy was saying, and wondered at Cara's easy admission of her indifference. I could quite see that she would want to be off despite it, though, since things must be unbearably frosty between her and her parents. They ought to have been grateful really; she might so easily not have told them. At the very least it had been brave of her to come clean.

'You mustn't berate yourself, Cara dear,' I said, wondering if I was yet old enough to pull off this kind of wise condescension, and fearing that I was. 'You are a good girl, you know, to tell your mother. You mustn't fret about it. And whatever spot you have got yourself in, everything will be different after you are married.'

'What?' said Cara, turning towards me and blinking, clearly having drifted off and making me wonder if maybe her feelings for Alec were less impeccably modern than she had implied. 'Oh yes, I'm a good little girl,' she said. 'I always have been, you know. I do exactly as I'm told every time and it brings me nothing but joy.' I grimaced, pained to hear such world-weariness in one so young.

Mrs Duffy and Clemence came out as we arrived at the tea table and in the fuss of arranging chairs, cushions and parasols, a few whispered words were exchanged.

'What have you been asking Cara?' Lena demanded. 'Much better for you to come to me.'

I was startled. Was it quite settled in her mind then that I had undertaken to do her bidding? I supposed it was.

'Why, nothing,' I said, my startled look backing my words nicely. 'We were chatting about dresses and flowers, actually. But I do need to speak to you, certainly. Certainly I do.'

'Come when we are home again,' she hissed. 'Come for luncheon next week.'

A few more of the men began to drift back from the river as tea got under way, and there was much protestation from the ladies, who affected to be outraged by the mud and fish scales clinging to their husbands' clothes and shrieked at the trout tails peeping from basket lids. Daisy, as I might have predicted, was stony-faced; she has always loathed the sight of women flirting in public with their own husbands. Alec and Cara were no help, chatting quietly to cach other and ignoring everyone else; Mrs Duffy and Clemence were as thick as ever, sitting close together with identical expressions of pursed disapproval on their mouths, and I'm ashamed to admit I was very poor value too, for I sat utterly silent, brooding.

What was the hold Lena believed she had over the Esslemonts, for it could not be the lame tale she had concocted about the theft? Why on earth did Cara want to sell the jewels? And how could she? Were they not her father's? And were not all the signs that they were intended for her sister in the end? I was heartily sick of the things already and the trouble they caused. Was there any chance that they would simply turn up again? If not, how would one set about trying to track them down? In the favourite parlour game of my childhood – what was it called? – there was a set of enamel tiles to be passed around, what, who, why, where, when and how, and it did make things a great deal easier to –

Suddenly there it was. When. The little wisp I had been swiping at was in my grasp at last. It was simply this: if the

57

pastes were good enough to fool everyone but an expert and if what Cara had said about the jeweller's discretion were true, then how could her mother possibly know that the jewels had not *already* been stolen, by the time of the Armistice Anniversary Ball? Had Mrs Duffy had a valuation done on them just then? One that she trusted? If not, it seemed to me, the switch might have been made at any time at all. It might have been years ago. I wondered if this simple point had occurred to no one but me. What a coup if it had not.

I must pump the Duffys for more details. I might even hint at a softening of Silas's resolve to worm my way deeper into Lena's favour. So long as nobody signed anything, surely it was worth a sprat to catch a mackerel; ladies could not, I was sure, be accused of entering into gentlemen's agreements. I should have to conduct the entire thing with my fingers crossed behind my back, of course. In fact, should I perhaps check with Daisy first that she approved of my spinning a line to reel them in on? No, I would fix my bait and land this all by myself.

'Are you all right, Dandy?' asked Alec Osborne. I had been staring in his direction, not looking at him exactly, but he and Cara had fallen silent and were both watching me.

'You look as though you'd seen Banquo's ghost,' said Cara, and Alec shouted with laughter.

'That's it,' he said. 'Lady Macbeth. What dread deed are you plotting?' I gaped, which of course only made it seem worse, and Daisy had to hurry to my aid.

'Or are you trying to remember if you've left the bath taps running?' she said, raising a good laugh from the banking ladies.

'I was just concentrating hard on something,' I said, then to make sure I had thrown them off I added, 'Fishing, actually. Bait, cast, catch. There's a great deal more to it than at first it seems.'

Clever, clever Dandy. Making my little plans and dropping my little hints. At that point, you see, I still thought it was a game. And my intuitions? I had never had any before, and so had never learned to respect them as others do. I ignored the distant, sickening drumbeat and, full of pride at how I had winkled out my little pile of facts, for the first time in my life I tried to play a cunning hand. If only I hadn't, if only I had bumbled and blurted as usual, I could have prevented it all. And so although I know they are right when they tell me that evil and madness cannot be contained, I blame myself and I always will.

Chapter Four

Imagine my surprise and disappointment when I heard that the Duffys would be at their Edinburgh house until the wedding and not in London, where I had been looking forward to following them buoyed along on Daisy's expenses. I wondered again if there could be money troubles greater than the depressing pinch we were all pretending not to feel. Severe money troubles after all might go some small way towards explaining Lena's behaviour to Daisy and Silas but Mr Duffy, so far as anyone knew, was still comfortable enough. He had a great deal of his property in Canada of all places; and it was well-tended property, that I did know, because I remembered that he and his young wife had been obliged to go there and look after it for what must have been a few rather bleak years in their early marriage when forests in Canada were all the rage.

Hugh had tried to persuade his father to buy some of his own. I just remembered this, since he had not quite given up by the time of our wedding although his efforts were beginning to move from urgency towards a sulky despair as the march of the cross-Canada railway made the venture more and more alluring even as the price crept ever upwards out of his reach. In the first year of married life I had heard the words 'Grand Trunk Pacific Railroad' repeatedly until I was ready to scream and I could almost feel sorry for Lena Duffy when I thought about her ordeal and could believe that this period of exile was when she began to turn sour. Perhaps, though, one's mental image of

Canada is unfair; perhaps she did not *actually* live in a log cabin with teams of Chinamen clanging their mallets against the tracks right outside. On the other hand, sometimes clichés get to be clichés by being true, as is the case with the heather, whisky and tartan view of Scotland; these can be found, at least in Perthshire, in unfortunate abundance.

Even if Canada was civilized, however, all the evidence pointed towards a distinct lack of social whirl for Lena went a bride and returned a matron, her two girls born in quick succession out there, and one imagines (coarsely) that it was not only the desire for an heir which hastened their arrival since after the Duffys' return home no heir, nor anyone else for that matter, had ever appeared.

I now understood from Hugh that the war had 'done for' the Canadian railway and the forests along with it, in a way I did not pretend to understand, that even the Grand Trunk Pacific Railroad itself had had to call in the receivers, and that the Canadian Government was now running the show. Of course, Hugh took some bitter pleasure in that, reaching back twenty years and trying to recast his failures as foresight. Miles of Ontario pine trees were not Mr Duffy's only nor even his chief concern, and so whatever the reason for poor Cara's trousseau to be coming from worthy George Street (which had to be depressing) I could not believe it to be a matter of economy.

Still, a trip to Edinburgh although galaxies less fun was more easily managed without raising Hugh's eyebrows than a trip to London would have been and, I supposed, I could combine it with some dreary Edinburgh shopping of my own. So I caught the train from Perth on Friday morning, telling Drysdale to meet me again off the 6.15, and two hours later I was turning into Drummond Place. I supposed the Duffys kept this townhouse to be handy for the port of Leith and yet more of the pies in which Mr Duffy had a finger, and while most of our set laughed at their stodginess, I was struck that day with an unaccountable feeling of envy. I should loathe to be here when

I might be in London, of course, but so long as it was never used *that* way by an unscrupulous husband, I saw how a house in Edinburgh might make a welcome dent in the long months of country life up in Perthshire. And Drummond Place itself was rather fetching in that austere way that Edinburgh has, in parts, when the sun shines.

'The ladies are away, madam,' I was told by the equally austere butler who admitted me to the entrance hall. Now, 'away' in English, as we all know, suggests a trip far from home but for Scots, who can talk of going away to the shops or even away to their beds, it is always worth some careful checking.

'Might I wait, then? Are they gone for long?'

'The ladies are away to the cottage, madam,' he explained, speaking rather more slowly to me, as though now unsure of my brainpower. 'The master is at home however, if you care to wait.'

I began shaking my head before he was finished. I could not imagine grilling Mr Duffy for clues and to serve him up the confection of half-truths that was to be my report from Daisy was unthinkable.

'I shall write to them, then,' I said. 'About the wedding. A letter to the cottage will be fine. I only wanted to ask them about bridesmaids' – um – anyway.' I did not know the address of the cottage, of course, but thinking I could get it from somewhere, I shrank from asking this terrifying individual to produce a card for me. He was already looking at me suspiciously, although that might have been my guilty conscience, or might have been caused by my peculiarness in offering him so much information (far from normal behaviour). I could feel a blush begin to engulf me and sticking my nose in the air I turned to sweep out.

'Mrs Gilver?' came a soft voice from the stairs. Mr Duffy was there, halfway up with his finger keeping his place in a book. I cringed for an instant, then realizing that I was being ridiculous – my fear that everyone around me could divine my purpose was on a par with a child's belief that it becomes invisible by shutting its eyes – I shook off my silliness and called up to him.

'I was hoping to find your wife and girls. But I won't dream of asking you to relay a message. Unless you have a hidden interest in voile which you rarely get the chance to indulge?'

'Voile?' he echoed, frowning.

'I see not,' I said. 'It's a kind of silk.'

'Ah yes. The wedding,' he said, and again his face smoothed into a smile as it had at dinner at Croys, a droop of relief followed by a weightless rising in his shoulders, as though he had put down two heavy bags and straightened again. 'Not long now,' he said. Very curious, this beaming happiness at the thought of losing his favourite daughter. Offloading Clemence would be a relief to any parent (although Lena seemed to like her well enough) but fathers are usually more gloomy to see the backs of their darlings and I was puzzled. I looked at him for a moment then, seeing the speculation of my own regard begin to draw a matching look from him, I made my goodbyes and fled.

I was only minutes away from Abercromby Place but, unable to face the desolation of the ladies' lounge at the Caledonian Club, I resolved to slog back up the hill to the National Gallery, there to sit and think until I could get myself some luncheon and begin my afternoon's shopping.

I had been in a huff (if I am honest) over missing London this year, but I was now beginning to see that I still had to get *some* clothes for summer. I would give a wide berth to horrid Forsyth's, sitting there on the corner like a skeletal wedding cake, where I had spent far too many hours of my life kitting out boys for school, and would go instead to dear Jenner's. I could not quite agree with its besotted architects that it looked just like the Bodleian Library but it had always seemed especially welcoming to ladies, what with the Caryatides and now with the new extension too, where an even larger dress department was to be found. My step quickened, until I remembered: shopping after lunch, thinking and Improving Art first.

On the way, I set myself to come up with a list of innocent reasons why a bride, her mother and her sister might desert their obligations and remove to a country cottage three weeks before a wedding, but before I had entered anything on my list, I was distracted by the sound of someone saying my name.

Alec Osborne was standing ahead of me on the pavement, looking very different in grey town-suiting and rather wan despite the freckle. I stopped and was glad of the chance to catch my breath although I resisted the temptation to puff and put my hand to my ribs.

'I've just come from where I suspect you're going,' I said, managing to make my breath last to the end of the speech with only a little rasping.

'You've just seen Cara?' he asked.

'Well, no,' I said. 'They seem to have gone off to their cottage. Unaccountably,' I added, for no reason I could have explained. Alec Osborne nodded and screwed up his face.

'They're still there?' he said. 'I assumed they'd have come home . . . I mean since something seems to have . . . She's broken it off, you see.' I blinked once before realizing what he meant.

'Are you sure?' I said. 'I just spoke to her father and he certainly didn't seem to think so.' Alec Osborne fished a rather crumpled letter out of his breast pocket and made as though to unfold it.

'I assumed she'd written from town,' he said. 'But I suppose they would have stayed away, wouldn't they?'

I could do no more than stare at him uselessly. One would expect a jilted lover to look puzzled and upset but the way he was casting his eyes around and shifting from foot to foot spoke of something else besides.

'Are you busy, just at this minute?' he said. I shook my head. 'I wonder then if you would be so kind –' He broke off. The expression on my face must have revealed the lurch of dismay I felt at the prospect of holding his hand and there-there-ing maternally while he wept for his lost love. 'It's not what you think,' he said. 'At least, I think you think something, and I do too.'

I gaped. What did he know?

'I saw you talking to Lena and to Cara,' he said. 'Don't you feel . . .? I hardly know what to call it, but don't you have a feeling . . .?'

'Yes,' I said. 'Yes, I do.'

We walked to the gallery without speaking again, and only when we got there did it strike me how completely distracted he must be to trot along wordlessly beside me when only I knew where we were going. When we were climbing the steps, however, he raised his head, took in where we were, and nodded his approval.

Inside, it was more work than I had anticipated to find a suitable stopping place. The landscapes upon which we might have rested our eyes for refreshment without stimulation all had scribbling schoolchildren clustered before them, and the blood and swagger of the Biblical tableaux or the cavortings of various Venuses and Cupids (in those simpering pastel orgies fit only for cutting up and covering screens) were not at all appropriate. After all, however distracted Alec Osborne might be by suspicions akin to my own, he had still just been sacked with less than a month to go by a very pretty girl of whom I had no reason to believe he was not fond.

We trudged past a po-faced Madonna with one of those peculiar lanky babies on her lap then sank at last on to a rather collapsed circular velvet ottoman in front of a blameless view of Venice by Guardi. I waited for him to speak.

'This came this morning,' he said after a short silence, shoving the letter into my hands. I felt an equal pull towards devouring every word of it for clues and dropping it back into his lap in horror at the thought of reading it in front of him.

'I know,' he said. 'But describing it to you instead would

only add furtiveness to the brew and how would that help?' I could not suppress a quick smile. He was right. Sometimes a little coarseness is all that makes a thing endurable. Nothing, for instance, could be more excruciating than a bashful midwife. I resisted sharing this thought and began to read.

'Dear Alec,' it began and I was enough of a Victorian to be mildly surprised not to see 'Dearest'. 'I cannot marry you. I am very sorry for the hurt and trouble I know this will cause, but it is much better than what would come to pass if I were to keep quiet and go along with it. I cannot explain my reasons, except to say that I am convinced I could never make you happy, and that knowing that, I should be miserable myself.' It finished with 'Yours sincerely,' which I quite saw was the only possible option, and was signed with a large, sweeping C.

'Fanny Price,' I said.

'What?' said Alec.

'She's quoting Jane Austen.'

'I doubt it,' said Alec. '"Soppy old rot", she calls it.'

'And it came completely out of the blue?' I said after sitting a moment looking the letter over again. 'Have you no idea what lies behind it?'

'Only this,' said Alec. 'Which came earlier.' He fished in his inside pocket again and drew out an envelope on which I could see more of the same large, looped writing in the same purplish blue ink. He took a single sheet of paper out of the envelope and handed it to me.

'Dear Alec, Mummy, Clemence and I have come away to the beach cottage for a few days but I should like it so much if you were to come and visit us here. There is something momentous I need to tell you. Please, when you arrive if you could pretend to Mummy that you came in search of me off your own bat that would help enormously. I think she's being perfectly ridiculous but I don't want to make her any crosser than she already is. Sorry to be so mysterious, Alec dear, but I do think it would be best told not written. I trust completely in your affection for me and hope that I am right to do so. All my best love, Cara.'

'And have you no idea what she was referring to?' I said. 'It's all very vague.'

Alec took the letters back from me and studied them both, frowning.

'She had something to tell me, which her mother believed would make me want to call off the wedding,' he said. 'Between the first letter and the second she clearly had a change of heart. I can only assume that her mother managed to talk her round.'

'But why would Mrs Duffy go from trying to persuade Cara to keep the thing secret, to trying to make her break it off?' I said. 'I mean, surely the only reason for keeping quiet was to make sure that the wedding went ahead.' Alec was nodding.

'If we knew what it was,' I said, glancing at him and catching him glancing at me.

Neither spoke for a while, each waiting for the other to take the first step. Alec Osborne gave in first, but he inched forward only very slightly.

'What were you talking about while you walked by the river?' he said.

'The wedding a little,' I said. Another glance and a deep breath and I gave in. 'But the jewel theft, mostly.' Alec relaxed with a puff of breath.

'Exactly,' he said. 'And did Cara seem to you to think the two were related?'

I nodded.

'I agree,' said Alec. 'She hinted the same to me but as to exactly what's up . . . . Let's try to work it out, Dandy. If you don't mind, that is. I mean, it's my problem really, mine and Cara's, but if you don't mind.' I was shaking my head vigorously and he looked pleased, but neither of us had a clue where to start. I decided to try one of my two previously successful tactics: the one where I start to talk and listen for what comes out.

'Perhaps,' I said, 'Cara was mixed up in the theft.' I bit

my lip and waited for him to leap to his feet and shout slander, but he only nodded, so I carried on. 'That might easily be what she trusts will make no difference to your feelings, and what Mrs Duffy assumes will send you fleeing.'

'Possibly,' he said. 'But what would suddenly make Cara go from being sure I wouldn't mind, to being so sure that I should mind that she doesn't even give me a chance, but breaks it off herself? And if Cara was tied up in the theft, why on earth would she have willingly taken the fakes to the jewellers?'

I was suddenly aware of a well-upholstered woman in an elaborate hat, and her droopy daughter, both leaning precariously towards us from the far edge of the ottoman, clearly agog.

'Let's walk around a little,' I said in a loud voice and I was vindicated by seeing the stout woman sit up sharply and fix her gaze at a painting opposite.

'Any number of reasons,' I went on in a suitably hushed voice as we moved at the required reverent pace past some portraits of scowling Puritans. 'Perhaps she wanted to find out the value of the pastes. Perhaps she needed money and that would be enough. Perhaps not all the jewels were meant to be replaced in the first place, but her accomplice "double-crossed" her.' Alec's mouth twitched. 'I have two little boys,' I said, with an attempt at dignity. 'And their taste in reading matter is not what it might be.'

'I'm sorry,' he said. 'Just that I can't quite take it seriously – Cara with an accomplice!'

We passed one of those nasty Flemish paintings of greasy goblets and overgrown vegetables – barely still although only too life-like.

'But the undeniable truth is that she did try to sell them,' I said, 'and it's not really such a step from that to stealing them, is it? They do actually belong to her father, after all. Anyway, the real mystery as far as I'm concerned is why on earth she came clean about it. Surely she could have hushed the little jeweller man?'

Alec had stopped and was staring at me, reminding me unpleasantly of Daisy. I decided to keep talking.

'Unless – and don't laugh at this – unless she just wanted the whole thing out in the open to be off her conscience before the wedding. Perhaps she couldn't face going through the sacrament of marriage with such a stain on her – You are laughing.'

'Yes,' he said with a lift of one eyebrow that threatened to tug an answering laugh from me, even though it also made me want to box his ears. 'The sacrament of marriage, quite. But never mind that. Did you say that Cara tried to *sell* the jewels?'

'Didn't you know?' In my surprise, I spoke much, much too loudly for the gallery and we were both startled to hear my words echo around the high room. 'Really, didn't you?' I whispered. 'That's why she had them at the jeweller's. To sell them.'

'I can't believe it,' said Alec. 'Cara would never take it into her head to do such a thing.'

'It's true,' I began. 'She told me so herself.' But even as I said this, I felt the facts begin to shift and resettle. Cara had said to me that she was a good girl who did what she was told and I had not known what, if anything, she meant by it and so I had dismissed it. I should add this, in thick black letters, to my growing list of Very Important Facts: people always mean something whenever they speak; if they appear not to, the fault is my own.

'That is,' I went on, 'it's true that she did it, but it might not have been her own idea. In fact, she gave me the clear impression that she was doing someone else's bidding.'

We lapsed again each into our own silent thoughts. Why would anyone want Cara to sell the jewels? And why would she allow herself to be forced into it if she had been mixed up in the theft? And most of all, who might it be? The obvious person to sell a thing is the thing's owner, but why would her father sell his diamonds?

'Utterly enthralled!' The voice cut into my thoughts no less because of its acoustics – it was a just suppressed shriek – than because of its undoubted and unwelcome familiarity. 'Two circuits of the room, with not a glance at the pictures, really!'

Renée Gordon-Strathmurdle, the last person on earth I should wish to see at such an awkward moment as this, was bearing down on us flapping her gloves and pursing her lips coquettishly.

'Dandelion, my darling,' she cooed as she bent her head – she is immensely tall – to kiss me. 'And sweet Alexander, plucked from darkest Dorset to join the happy hielanders.' Renée always talks like that, a mixture of hell and damnation preacher and circus barker. Loud with it.

'Your dear sweet mother was worried, Alexander darling, that Perthshire for all its air and fish might prove too, too plain pudding for you. I'm simply thrilled to be the one who can write and tell her how marvellously you're settling in.'

'And what brings you here, Renée?' I asked, when she drew breath.

'Oh yes, indeed,' she roared. 'You do both look rather startled to see me. But don't worry. Allow me to have dragged myself into the twentieth century, please. Although, Alexander darling, with your wedding in three weeks' time you have opened my eyes, I must say.' Alec had turned the most peculiar colour; the few spaces there were between his tawny freckles had gone a pure, clear pink and the freckles themselves were liverish.

'I was dropping off our Gainsborough for the summer,' she went on, her voice rising to a bellow as she said the name. I quite believed this; Renée would always want any largesse she dispensed to meet with full and immediate gratitude and if it meant her driving from Perth to Edinburgh and back like a grocer on his round then that was what she would do.

'And how is poor sweet Cara?' she chortled.

'Very well indeed,' said Alec, rallying at last. 'I'm tootling off to see her later today, as a matter of fact. Although, Dandy, if you did decide to go,' he gave me a significant look, 'I could hold off till tomorrow and run you down there.'

Such openness was the perfect tactic to throw Renée off her stride, of course, but to my shame, between catching up with the idea that I should visit the Duffys, digesting the notion of driving 'down there' (wherever that might be) with Alec, and wondering how to serve this up to Hugh, I funked my cue and instead of answering in the same cool manner, I gulped. This sent Renée into peals of such loud laughter that the little curator rose from his chair by the door and got near enough coming to tick her off as to adjust his tie and polish his boots on the back of his trouser legs before sitting down again.

I had regained my composure by the time the train drew back into Perth station that evening, but I was exhausted. It had taken me until after luncheon to shake off Renée, although Alec had pressed his card into my palm and fled, as men can, within minutes of her landing on us.

Pallister met me in the hall.

'Telegram came for you, madam,' he murmured with some disdain. Receiving a telegram unless it was to announce a birth or a death was always taken by Pallister to be yet more proof of extravagance and general giddiness.

It was from Mrs Duffy, Reiver's Rest, Kirkandrews, Galloway – the beach cottage, I assumed – and after apologizing for misleading me as to her whereabouts, it invited me to join them there for a day or two if I was free. I enjoyed a short period of wonderment that this invitation should fall into my lap, until I remembered that, of course, she must be as keen to see me as I was to see her. I had to remind myself that she was plotting Daisy and Silas's ruination to prevent myself from feeling a twinge of guilt at leading her on.

So how was I to get there? Blushing furiously again, I drew Alec's card from my bag, resisted the urge to look over my shoulder, and gave the number of his hotel to the operator in a loud, careless voice.

I telephoned to Daisy next and she gave me leave to incur what expense I might in the trip only begging me to ring her with news as soon as I could. Hugh, as I should have expected, barely registered the announcement that I was going away. He was closeted with his steward planning improvements to field drainage in some far-flung and, I must suppose, soggy corner of the estate and so, with the prospect of extra men and a great deal of muddle in view, he could be counted upon not to miss me.

Thus bidden on my way by both my master and my mistress, then, I summoned Grant to begin packing.

Alec had warned me that it would take a full day to reach the Solway coast, so I had Drysdale take me on the first leg after a very early breakfast and deposit me on to the Forth ferry like a parcel for Alec to meet at the other side. I quite saw that I should have to think about a little motor car of my own if this investigation were to run into weeks and months, something more reliable than the battered Austin in which I rumbled up and down to the village. I wondered whether Daisy's fee would stretch to one of the new Wolseleys. That was something to be looked into, but for today I was very content to tuck myself into the passenger seat of Alec's hired Bentley and be whisked away.

For much of the morning we drove in silence, a silence which deepened as we entered the pass at Dalveen heralding the beginning of Galloway, not for nothing known as the Highlands in miniature. The road plunges down between the glowering lumpen mountains, clinging to the side of the north slopes so that any little car daring to pitch itself in at the top positively hurtles to the bottom, like a child on a helter-skelter, making carefree drivers want to say 'Wheee!' and timid passengers clutch the door handle and shut their eyes.

Alec and I emerged from the bottom of the pass without

incident, however, and pulled up at the inn at Thornhill for luncheon. Since the food at this inn was barely middling I am quite sure that the bustle in the dining room owed itself chiefly to customers coming from the north and celebrating after being so recently convinced that their days of eating and drinking were over; it was certainly busy enough to prevent us from much useful discussion while we ate.

At last though, as we pushed cheese around our plates and waited without much enthusiasm for coffee, the party at the next table rose to leave and I could abandon polite chat and ask the question which had been consuming me since the day before.

'Who could it have been telling Cara to sell them?'

'The obvious answer is that it was the owners, her parents,' said Alec. 'One or both.'

'But why would one or both of the Duffys want to sell their jewels?' I asked.

Alec shrugged.

'Is there money trouble?' I persisted. 'Would you know if there were?'

'Probably not,' said Alec. 'My prospective father-in-law is not open in his discussions with me; rather secretive and peculiar about Cara's settlement in particular. But I think things are all right. I mean the Canada property isn't what it was and he's thinking of getting out of shipping, but I shouldn't have thought selling the family treasures was on the cards just yet. What I'd like to know is why Cara went along with it if she knew they were fakes.'

'Might it be a double bluff? Cara pretending to *sell* them to make it look as though she had nothing to do with *stealing* them?'

'It's a bit involved,' said Alec. 'And who was she bluffing? Who knew she stole them?' I took a sip of coffee and then, realizing it was not hot enough to require sipping, a gulp.

'Her mother, I suppose,' I said. 'After all, how could Mrs Duffy have enough evidence about the theft to use as a lever on Silas without her knowing of Cara's involvement too?'

Alec clattered his coffee cup into its saucer, both of them thankfully too sturdy to be affected by such treatment, and stared at me.

'A lever?' he said. 'What on earth do you mean?'

I stared back. Was it possible? Could it be possible that yesterday in the gallery, I had somehow managed not even to mention Mrs Duffy's campaign? I hurriedly told him all that I knew of it.

He listened intently, but a moment after I had finished he sat back with arms folded and shook his head at me the way one would to a particularly stupid puppy.

'And you just neglected to mention this before now?' he said. I felt that any of the possible responses was beneath me. 'But how on earth did you find it all out?' There was no particular emphasis on the word 'you' but I felt his unspoken judgement all the same. I wanted very much to tell him that it was my job to find it out and only wished I had a letter of engagement from Daisy that I could show him, but I forced myself to stay quiet. He was after all to be Cara's husband – neither one of us really believed the engagement would not be remade – and knowing that I was purposely investigating his soon to be mother-in-law might cool the air between us.

'Well, you said yourself you thought I knew something,' I said, huffily. 'This is what I knew. And you can see at once how it complicates matters, can't you?' I decided to focus my attention firmly back on the facts. 'What Mrs Duffy is doing – for I'm sure it's her doing it – does not make sense from start to finish. If she were ninety instead of fifty, one would think she was gaga. And Cara's behaviour makes even less.'

'But that's a very good sign,' said Alec. 'There are so many inconsistencies already that there's no way it can stay secret. I'll bet as soon as we speak to Cara and her mother the whole thing will just dissolve.'

'I have little hope of getting anything from Lena,

74

although she may well let something slip that she doesn't know is useful, as she has already,' I said. 'But Cara, yes. Cara is altogether different. Why, she said more to me at Croys than a child would, and she will surely yield to you under the slightest pressure.' I did not trouble to keep the arch note out of my voice and was gratified to see him look discomfited.

'Yes,' he said, standing and coming to draw out my chair, talking in a mock grandiose style to meet my archness head-on. 'By nightfall tonight, it will be laid plain before us.' He went back to his normal voice. 'We just need to speak to Cara.'

We were quiet again during the long afternoon's drive through the forest and down, down towards the sea. I was engaged partly on digesting the weight of my luncheon, partly on planning approaches to Lena and Cara, but also on trying to sort what I knew in patterns, hoping to be the first one to pounce on the answer which had to, simply *had* to, be there.

By the time we were on the coast road, coming round the bay to Kirkandrews in the failing afternoon light, I was even looking forward to it. A few days spent in this soft, fresh breeze making all well for Alec and Cara, for Daisy and Silas, and even somehow I hoped for Mrs Duffy, was a pleasant prospect. My debut as an investigator was almost too easy to be called employment. A gentle word with Cara was all it was going to take, I was sure, to earn my fee.

Alec swung us off the road at the Kirkandrews finger-post and I sat up in my seat, eager as one always is for one's first glimpse of the sea. Someone was having a bonfire at the beach and the scent of wood smoke mingled with the salt tang which had just become discernible in the air. It was charming at first – I leaned my head out of the side window to sniff at the memories of Boxing Day pic-nics it carried – but it threatened to overpower us as we advanced. The smell of it rolled up in plumes, driven no doubt by the on-shore breeze, and soon we had to fasten the car windows against it. There was no visible smoke, just the engulfing smell of it, the stench of it now we were on the track which led right to the sand line. I began to think it could not be a bonfire after all, but something much bigger, out now although perhaps still smouldering. I looked towards Alec and saw that he was grim-faced and pale as he drove the car on, ignoring the bumps and hollows under the wheels and the reach of the gorse on either side of the narrow lane scratching at the paintwork. The growing acrid stink, the protesting rumble of the tyres and the ceaseless grinding of the engine all of a sudden seemed like an outside echo, horribly amplified, of the dread that had been threatening to consume me all week. Alec increased the speed again as we passed the sign for Reiver's Rest and we jounced over the close-cropped turf faster and faster until the car rounded the last of the gorse into the open and skidded to a slithering halt.

In front of us, was a large plot of clipped grass ringed around with flower beds and edged with a white stick fence. A shell path started from a gate on the side nearest us and led halfway across the garden before it vanished abruptly, obscenely, to be replaced by a ring of scorched earth on which sat the blackened, reeking heap that was all there was left of the Duffys' cottage. Such a tiny heap, almost all ash, with only a few withered sticks and splinters, unbelievable that it had ever been a building.

I stepped out of the car on shaky legs and had to hold my scarf across my mouth to save from retching at the stink of it. They must have doused the flames in sea-water – of course they had, the sea was a minute's run from where we stood – and the smell of the wreckage still sizzling and settling now and then was unbearable. Even some of the men who sat slouched beside buckets in the long grass at the edge of the dunes still wore cloths covering their noses and mouths.

A constable in uniform and gumboots was picking his way towards us around the edge of the debris, poking at the settling ash with a charred stick, clearly waiting for someone of greater seniority to arrive. Every so often he looked at a small crowd of sightseers, gathered at a respectful distance, as though daring any of them to advance. When we approached him, he touched his helmet rim and threw the stick down.

'Where are the ladies?' Alec asked in a steady voice, showing the strain only in the lack of any words of greeting.

'Away to the hotel at Gatehouse,' said the man. I reached out and squeezed Alec's arm. 'The two of them,' he added. 'The mother and one o' the lasses.' He turned towards the remains of the fire and spoke softly. 'The other lass was in there, God love her.'

Alec and I did not speak or even look at each other as we walked back to the car. There was nothing to say. It would have been ludicrous to voice the certainty that it was Clemence at Gatehouse with her mother, shameful to both of us to allude to the conviction – so strong we would have staked our lives on it – that now we should never be able to speak to Cara.

Chapter Five

Young men had died in their thousands, and I had known dozens and scores of them, sons of friends or lads from the village. I had mourned their deaths individually and collectively in the church Sunday after Sunday, year after year, and had stood in front of memorials – had even unveiled one – singing patriotic hymns and boiling with misery and rage. None of these deaths, however, not even young Sandy Masterton, to whom I had once fed broth when his mother was sick with a fever, stabbed at me like the death of Cara Duffy.

I take no pride in that. I loathe the grading of tragedy and the jostling for pre-eminence amongst the bereaved, that most disgusting example of the disgusting habit of claiming a starring role in any incident that touches one. I do not, therefore, mean to suggest either that my recent conversation with the girl made me peculiarly pained by her death or that one young girl, fair of face and gentle of birth, was materially different from thousands of coarser and plainer young men.

I wonder though. Might it be true that we are not really creatures of any imagination after all and that something, anything, happening under our noses necessarily affects us more deeply than something, anything, we merely hear about? I had hitherto suspected a grosser motive behind our menfolk's reluctance to talk about the war; a selfishness, or worse a self-important chivalry, and had wondered if that was why they all seemed to disapprove so viscerally of the poets' trying to make the rest of us understand. Now, I began to see that perhaps there was a gulf that just could not be crossed between those who had been there and seen with their own eyes and those who had waited at home. Why else would this death, sudden and shocking as it was, seem so much worse than what lay behind the names on the cenotaph?

These were the thoughts which occupied me as we drove up to the town of Gatehouse and unremarkably, typically I should almost say, they turned out to be quite wrong.

I expected to find Lena and Clemence installed in a bar parlour, smoky and dishevelled, perhaps even wrapped in blankets, with attendant police and servants talking in hushed voices. I hoped a comfortable landlady was bringing them soup and hot bottles for their feet and I steeled myself to be the one who must bring other kinds of comfort. It was with some initial relief then that Alec and I found the two of them, in the bar parlour at the Murray Arms to be sure, but looking quite fresh and somewhat indecently composed.

'Lena,' said Alec. Mrs Duffy turned with a start and looked at him, frozen, for what seemed like an age, then without moving her eyes she noticed me standing just behind and to one side of him and she held out her hand.

'Dandy, my dear, I had completely forgotten you were coming. Have you been down to the cottage?'

'Oh no,' I whispered to myself. They did not *know*. I did not understand how this could be, but somehow, unbelievably, they had not heard, and telling them was to fall to me. I felt Alec begin to tremble beside me, although we were not touching. Perhaps I only saw his coat sleeve moving, or perhaps I felt the floor underneath my feet reverberate with his tremor. I had to speak.

'Something has happened, Lena,' I began, and then, my attention caught by a sound in the corner, I turned and saw a police sergeant, squashed discreetly and surely uncomfortably into a small chair, with his cap on one knee and his notebook open on the other. He had half-risen at my words and was regarding me with wide-open eyes. But if the police were here then . . .?

'What?' said Lena Duffy, her voice stretched dry. 'What do you mean?' I was utterly lost now. Did she know after all? She must.

'Cara,' I said.

'What?' said Lena Duffy again. I felt Alec reach out and take hold of my elbow, his fingers still trembling and cold through my sleeve. Lena had risen now but Clemence was shrinking back in her chair, her blank face as unreadable as ever.

'You know, don't you, do you?' I said. 'About the fire.' Alec squeezed my arm again and a glance at the police sergeant gave me my answer. He was staring at me, with his mouth open.

'What about it?' said Lena. 'What has happened? What are you talking about? Have they found . . .' Her voice faded to a croak and she was silent.

Just then the comfortable landlady of my imagination – long apron, white cap and all – came to the doorway opposite and stood looking at all of us for a moment, before her eyes filled with tears and she retreated, mopping her face with a glass cloth. I felt dizzy, terrified that I should begin to laugh, and I wanted to turn and run, but I forced myself to walk towards Lena and take her hands.

'We've just come from there,' I said. 'No one has found anything. It's burnt to the ground.' Odd the things one does without thinking. She, whom I should have been comforting, chafed my cold hands in her warm ones as though she were my mother and I a child, such a comfortable, familiar gesture and so wrong just then. I pulled against it and she let go of me. Then returning to her seat, she surveyed the tea-things on the table with another very familiar gesture, a deep breath in and the competent, calculating glance with which a matron decides whether what is left can be stretched or if more must be ordered.

I am sure the offer of 'Tea?' got almost to her lips before she caught it and, at the gape I could not hide, bowed her head. I heard Alec turn and run out of the room behind me, knocking against the door jamb on his way. His footsteps pounded away down the flagged passageway to the front door and then could be heard disappearing along the pavement outside.

'I should go and see,' I said, gesturing vaguely behind me.

'Would you, my dear?' said Lena. 'Poor Alec. If you would.' I looked at her for a moment longer, then at the quiet policeman, then fearing again that I was about to laugh or scream or shake someone, I too turned and stumbled out.

He had gone quite a way, but was walking back towards me by the time I saw him. He waved, sat down on the broad low wall of a bridge and lit a cigarette, waiting for me to approach.

'I'm so sorry,' I began. Then I rubbed my face hard with my two hands, hoping to scrub away the tears before they fell. 'I'm hopeless at this.'

'At what?' said Alec, sounding interested and even faintly amused. Far from trembling now, he too seemed horribly unperturbed.

'At whatever you choose to name,' I said. 'I can't imagine what possessed me, but I got the idea that she didn't know anything had happened. I only hope she's too upset to take it in. Clemence too.'

'Dandy,' said Alec, gently. 'What are you talking about?'

'I don't even know,' I wailed. 'I've never . . . I felt so peculiar, that must be shock, is it? I mean, I was rattled already and then the whole atmosphere was so very odd. It's not like in books and plays – tears for sadness and smiles for joy, is it? And it feels so different, when it's someone one has only just spoken to and when there's no battle, no dispatches. Are *you* all right?' I asked, finally, feeling ashamed that what I was really asking was if he

81

could drive me right back home again to Bunty and Hugh and away from all of this.

'Dandy,' said Alec again. 'Listen to me very carefully and please believe what I say. I don't know what is going on in that room.' He waved his cigarette towards the hotel. 'But it is not, believe me, it is not a doting mother and a loving sister suffering from shock. Something is very wrong here and you know it.'

I nodded slowly at first and then faster as my thoughts seemed to catch up with the rest of me.

'I feel . . .' I began, and gave up. 'I've been thinking about Sandy Masterton from one of our farms, who died in the retreat from . . . Well, anyway, I knew him much better than Cara and I couldn't see why this should be so much worse. But I suppose that's it, isn't it? There's something wrong here.'

'That's not quite it,' said Alec. 'What you are feeling is exactly what I am feeling. I, unlike you, have felt it before.' I looked at him, shaking my head slightly to show him that I did not know what he meant. And then all of a sudden I did, and my head began to nod instead.

'It's because we should have known, isn't it?' I said. 'We should have guessed and we should have stopped it.'

'And now it's too late,' said Alec, 'and there is nothing worse than that.' My moment of inspiration had passed and pedestrian logic seemed to reassert itself in me.

'There's no need for you to feel that way,' I said.

'Cara was my fiancée,' said Alec, simply. 'It's seldom spoken of, although everyone knows about it. It's what makes it bearable when one's parents die, you know. And I'm sure it's what makes it bearable for women to be widows. Have you never wondered why women make such comfortable widows and men such hopeless widowers?' He had been gazing at the glowing end of his cigarette as he spoke, but now he raised his head and looked at me. 'At the front, you know, if a letter came and it was a chap's older brother? Well, that was bad, but we

82

knew it was bearable. When a chap's younger brother went, it was horror.'

'Is that why the officers so much more often . . .' I was going to say 'went to pieces' but stopped myself in time. This was the first time I had ever spoken to any man about the nuts and bolts of it all. Alec nodded. Then he brought himself back to the present. He took a last deep puff on his cigarette and threw it down into the river.

'A mother and an elder sister who have just survived the fire that killed the baby?' His voice grew hard. 'They would be beside themselves. They would be clawing through the embers with their bare hands, or they would be asleep, unconscious. I've seen it countless times. The body just switches off like an electric lamp going out. Sometimes for days. What they would not be doing is sitting in a parlour miles away in fresh clothes, drinking tea, and attuned to the possibility of news.'

'Couldn't it *be* a kind of shock?' I said, desperate to avoid what he seemed to be suggesting. 'Couldn't that be a kind of retreat in itself? Like sleeping? I mean, if there were anything going on, wouldn't they try to act more as they should?' I warmed to this idea. 'Wouldn't they put on a show of grief if they were hiding something?' At that, though, I remembered Lena Duffy's survey of the table and the offer of tea that she suppressed before she could utter it, the flare of panic in her eyes as she almost let it slip. 'Or even if it did seem like only a show,' I said, 'couldn't it be that their real grief strikes even them as so far from the way it is written in books that they feel they must try to . . .' Alec was shaking his head, but before I could begin a fresh assault, he waved me into silence with a discreet gesture. The police sergeant was approaching.

'Feeling more like it now, sir?' he asked, then turned to me. 'Can I just ask you what your plans are, madam? You were coming to stay, were you not? Will you put up at the Murray Arms, then?'

I stammered for a bit before I spoke. Of course there

would be some official business to be gone through, I supposed, but I was no more than one of the many onlookers.

'I'm sure Lena and Clemence would be grateful for it,'
said Alec softly. I was shocked. Of course it would suit our
purposes to have me installed but it was a bit much, on no
more evidence than our shared feeling that something was
wrong.

'The inquiry'll be at Kirkcudbright, doubtless,' the police
sergeant went on. 'In a few days' time, a week at the most.
If you could see your way clear to stay till then.'

'Aren't there friends they could go to?' I said. 'Surely
they won't stay in the hotel.'

The sergeant slid his cap back on his head and stood
looking up and down the street, rubbing thoughtfully at
the red mark from his hatband.

'Well, Cardonness Castle is all shut up, madam, seeing
Sir William's away to London as usual in the springtime,
and Lady Ardwell is practically bedridden since last winter, poor old lady. There's always Commander Cochrane at
Ruscoe, I suppose, but I don't know if they've ever met.'

'No, quite, of course,' I said, before he ran through the
whole county. Perhaps, after all, the anonymity of a country pub would be preferable to an invalid lady or Sir
William's dustsheets. I should stay. After all, Lena had an
investigation and inquiry to get through and apparently no
one around to help her do it.

'And yourself, sir?' said the sergeant, turning back to
Alec.

'Has anyone sent word to Edinburgh yet?' Alec said.
'Someone will have to tell her father.'

My bags were duly carried from the motor car into the
inn and up to a small back bedroom. I assumed Lena and
Clemence were already in the best rooms, but I was glad
of the plain whitewashed walls and the brass bed with its
cheerful quilt; my sense of guilt would not have withstood
any luxury.

Before facing the Duffys again, I went to the post office
to send a telegram to Hugh. I might have telephoned of

course, but not wanting to enter into negotiations, certainly not wanting to bring on a command to come home, I thought a telegram would be more fitting.

The girl behind the desk was weeping.

'Poor, poor soul,' she said, shaking her head and letting large tears fall on to the blotter. I bit my lip and nodded. Then she sniffed and composed herself a little, looking expectantly at me through the grille with her pen at the ready.

'I have no idea what to say,' I said. I had never read one of these telegrams, thank heavens, and had no idea how they were usually couched.

'Who is it for, madam?' asked the girl, professionalism beginning to reassert.

'Oh, no one,' I said. 'I mean, my husband. But no one close. To them, I mean. I just need to say that I'm staying to be with Mrs Duffy and why.'

She had got my measure.

'"Dreadful fire at Reiver's Rest,"' she intoned with relish. '"Poor" – it's Cara, isn't it, madam? – "Poor Cara tragically lost. Staying in Gatehouse to comfort poor mother."' And so on. It became clear that the telegram was not her natural genre, but I managed in the end to remove most of the adverbs and settle on 'perished' as an acceptable midway point between her eulogies and my apparently shocking bluntness.

'Fire at Duffys' cott. Cara perished. Self unharmed. At Murray Arms Inn, Gatehouse with Mrs D. until further notice.' She read back to me. 'Love?' she asked, pen quivering.

'Love,' I agreed, for a quiet life.

There was no sign of the Duffys in the parlour when I returned. The tea-things were gone and the table covered in what must be its usual garb of a dusty chenille cloth and a bowl of wax fruit. I crept along to the bar but, my nerve failing me at the door, decided to search out someone in the kitchen quarters.

'There now,' said the landlady, suddenly coming round

a corner and almost bumping into me. 'I wondered where you had got yourself to, madam. The doctor wants to see you.' She surveyed me briefly and then pronounced her verdict. 'You're done in. What say you come and sit in my kitchen and wait for him there? That parlour's a gloomy spot at the best of times.' She steered me along the passageway and into the kitchen where the fresh smell of linen sheets drying off on a rack before the fire fought with the aroma of tonight's stew beginning to bubble, the whole making a welcome oasis of comfort. She tucked me into a Windsor chair and set about tea.

'I'm that glad you're back,' she said. 'They just went to pieces. After you and the young man left. Jim Cairns left them for two minutes to come and speak to me and when he went back they had gone straight to pieces. Couldn't say which was worse. The poor mother roaring and crying and the young one shaking all over like nothing on earth. And so he goes for you, Jim Cairns, and I sends the lad for the doctor to see can he give them something and gets them off upstairs to lie down and as soon as these sheets are aired they'll be in their beds where they should be and maybe get some rest, eh?'

She sounded as relieved as I felt that the ladies had finally begun to behave as they ought, and she looked hopefully at me to see if I was about to break down too.

'I don't really know them all that well,' I said, in my defence. 'I just happened to be coming down on a visit.'

'And a very good thing, madam,' she said, putting a thick cup of dark tea down before me on the table. 'Now, I'll just need to get on if that's all right.' She sat down opposite me with a bowl of carrots and spread a newspaper for the scrapings. Soon a light spray of carrot juice reached me as she set about them and since my tweeds were flecked with orange and it was rather refreshing, I let it.

After a while we heard the stairs over our heads creak with a heavy step descending and presently a large man, in the rather collapsed tweeds so universally associated

86

with the country doctor that one suspects there must be an outfitter somewhere supplying them, let himself into the kitchen.

'Mrs Gilver?' he asked, putting out his hand and taking mine. 'Dr Milne.' He sat heavily and shook his head a few times before speaking again. 'I've settled them and left them something. A hot bath and a good night's rest, Mrs McCall. You'll can do more for the poor ladies than I can tonight.' Mrs McCall abandoned her carrots without another word and, wiping her hands on her apron, she gathered up the sheets and left.

'And you'll stay, won't you?' he asked, once she had gone.

'Of course,' I said. 'But you know, I'm not a *close* friend. I wonder if perhaps we should send for someone else.'

'Mrs Duffy asked for you,' he said. 'More than once, she asked if Mrs Gilver was still here.' This was curious.

'What is going to happen?' I asked. 'And what did happen? Does anyone know?'

'Well, there will be an inquiry,' said Dr Milne. 'But we'll never know exactly. These wooden houses, you know. I never could understand why houses by the sea are so often made of wood. They dry out like kindling in the sea breeze.'

'Is Mrs Duffy able to tell you anything?' I said. 'Or Clemence?'

'Not a thing. They weren't there. They had gone for a walk on the shore and the young lady stayed at home. Writing letters, they said. By the time they came back round the headland, the place was alight and the men were already there with their buckets. Futile. Futile. These wooden houses.'

'Awful,' I said. 'One can't imagine. And now an inquiry.'

'Oh, I wouldn't worry about that,' said the doctor. 'Our Fiscal is a good man. A very gentle way with him. There's a hard road ahead of the whole family, to be sure, but there

87

will be no unpleasantness at the inquiry to make it worse.'

'It was a curious thing,' I ventured, 'but when Mr Osborne and I arrived, they were so very calm I thought for a minute they didn't know. And I'm afraid I must have confused them.'

'Aye, I heard,' he said. 'Jim Cairns told me. I shouldn't worry, though, madam. Shock is a funny one. Why, I saw things in the war you wouldn't believe.'

'Yes, I'm sure,' I said, and sipped my tea in silence, uncertain whether the thought which had just struck me was my imagination or not. Did he too think that something was not right? There was a watchful and repressive air about him. Was he warning me that 'the Fiscal' would never dream of rocking a boatful of such distinguished ladies? That I should be careful not to either? Or was he right about shock, and Alec quite wrong? I was suddenly convinced that this was the case, and I flushed with shame at the thought of our muckraking. Wicked, repulsive. Poor Mrs Duffy and poor Clemence too; bewildered, so hurt and shocked that they had retreated into a kind of a stupor and all we could do in the meantime was point our fingers and suspect them of something we did not even have the courage to put a name to. Everyone in this village was weeping in sorrow along with them except for their so-called friends. At least Alec had an excuse: he was in shock too, however much he protested. But me? My behaviour? My suspicions? It was too disgusting, and I would have no further part in any of it. The silly misunderstanding about the diamonds – I had forgotten about the diamonds, to be honest – could all be resolved by Daisy without my help.

Chapter Six

The days which followed, while we waited for the inquiry, passed not quickly exactly – there was no rush or bustle about them, nothing at all to do in fact – but rather they passed elsewhere, as though I were asleep and only dreaming the meals and baths and walks and the endless overheard conversations of the townspeople about the shocking thing which had happened in their midst.

'Obliterated,' I heard an apronned housewife say to her neighbour as they met at the kerb, pouring out used buckets of floor-water.

'Pulverized,' was one word that rose out of the chorus of voices of the schoolchildren dawdling home across the bridge.

'All away to ash,' the waitress was saying to a customer as I opened the tea-shop door and entered.

Mr Duffy arrived from Edinburgh but, although he spent considerable time closeted with Alec, he took his meals upstairs in Lena's rooms with her and Clemence and so I hardly saw him.

I was still too shame-faced to want to spend much time with Alec, who in any case was lodging at the Angel around the corner, the Duffys and I having almost exhausted the accommodations of the Murray Arms.

Clemence kept to her room apart from venturing down to the parlour to read once or twice, sitting with *Emma* held up right in front of her face. Perfectly reserved, she managed to rebuff any comfort offered, not only my rather awkward advances, but also the doughty cluckings of the

89

landlady, Mrs McCall, who was far too good a woman to let it show, but who I am sure was puzzled by Clemence almost to the point of irritation. Poor Clemence, to be so very unbeguiling to all, and for no reason that one could ever put one's finger on.

Mrs Duffy, so Mrs McCall told me, did not rise from her bed again and Dr Milne became worried about her, we thought, descending the stairs shaking his head and puffing upwards into his moustache. Strangely, despite my hardly setting eyes on either of the ladies, Dr Milne insisted I stay, continuing to report that Mrs Duffy wanted me there, and this puzzled me. I am not used to thinking of myself as such a tower of strength and comfort that my very presence in the same building can be such a help.

One immediately noticeable effect of Cara's death that should be reported is that it quashed the nasty feeling of dread I had been suffering. Wretched as I was – and I did suffer to think of her smiling mouth and soft eyes never to be seen again – I was nevertheless at peace. Besides, as the sergeant had predicted, matters moved on apace; not even the fact of the body's total destruction stood in the way of officialdom and the inquiry was fixed for Friday.

When that day came, Dr Milne sought me out in the parlour after his morning call on Mrs Duffy. I rang for an extra coffee cup and he sat opposite, sipping meditatively and watching me.

'She wants to talk to you,' he said at last. 'And I must say that's a relief, for I was beginning to worry that she might withdraw altogether, and then there's no saying how long it would take.'

'Certainly,' I said, quailing inside but not showing it. 'I shall go to her directly.' As much as I dreaded an interview with Lena, it at least made me feel a bit less foolish and useless.

'But you must prepare yourself for rather a shock,' Dr Milne said. 'She is very distressed, and ill with it. As soon as this is over, I'm ordering her away for a good long rest. I should have said the seaside, normally, but as it is . . .

90

the Lakes, I think. And if we're very, very lucky we might avoid a complete breakdown and keep her out of hospital.'

I was startled, not only at the news of what a state Lena was in, but at the calm way the doctor spoke of it, as though breakdowns and hospitals were the daily currency of life. What of Clemence? And Mr Duffy?

'Her father is deeply saddened, to be sure,' said the doctor. 'But he's a strong man and then of course, he didn't have the distress of . . .' He broke off and seemed to glare at me, summing me up. 'I'll tell you,' he said. 'I promised I wouldn't but I will, and in turn you must promise me not to tell anyone else.'

That again! Passing on a secret he had promised to keep and absolving himself by passing on the request to keep it too. Cara had said how she abhorred the habit, and it struck me that here was a sign of her goodness quite at odds with the ideas we had about her conduct. I tried to signal my unwillingness to Dr Milne, while at the same time trying not to make my disapproval obvious. No one likes a prig.

'Mrs Duffy was already in a very distressed state, even before this tragedy,' he said, ignoring or failing to notice my attempts to stop him. 'A rather unpleasant thing happened recently and I was surprised, to own the truth, at how well she took it. Now, of course, I can see that she was holding fast under great strain, and had no reserves to call on to help her through all of this when it came.'

'I see,' I said. 'Well, I shall bear that in mind, Dr Milne. I don't need to know any more.' But he shifted around on his seat, bursting with it, and I saw there was no escape.

'A matter of only a week or two ago, Mrs Gilver,' he said at last, 'only days before the fire, a servant of Mrs Duffy's died, and in the most upsetting circumstances. She kept it from the girls, as any mother would. Said the creature had gone off home without warning, but it must have been preying on her, and it certainly weakened her nerves.'

I felt immediately chastened. This was something we,

91

Alec and I, knew nothing about and something we could not even have guessed at. How dare we, in all our ignorance, find Lena's behaviour wanting and pronounce upon it? I caught myself plunging into these ruminations and felt if anything even more chastened. Why must my first thought always be what light some new piece of information threw on my own actions? Listen to what the man was saying, I told myself. Poor Lena.

'What happened?' I asked.

Dr Milne gathered up a sigh as from the pit of his being. 'An all too common affair, my dear. The girl had got herself into trouble and tried to get herself out of it again. Mrs Duffy found her and sent for me, but by the time I got there it was far too late.'

'Good Lord,' I said. 'Good God in heaven. So, is this the second inquiry that poor Lena has had to go through? It's very odd, you know, because no one in the town has said anything and one would have thought, human nature being what it is . . .'

I fell silent, perplexed by the way Dr Milne was fidgeting and by the flood of colour turning his always ruddy face an even deeper shade.

'No, no,' he said. 'There was no need for that, thankfully. We, that is I, I managed to avoid any question of that. She wasn't a local girl, you know. Came down with the ladies from Edinburgh.' He busied himself draining the last of his coffee even though it must surely have got quite cold. 'Anyway, it was all – as I'm sure you can imagine, Mrs Gilver – it was all most upsetting for her. The more so for not being able to speak of it, being alone with the girls. I fear the delayed reaction to that has coincided with the shock and distress of the fire, not to mention the grief, and really laid her low. So,' he started to gather himself ready to leave, 'just be warned. She is not herself and must not be worried or bothered in any way.' With all this talk he apparently managed to regain some of his composure and bowing curtly – and rather awkwardly I thought, a bow hardly being his usual method of leave-taking – he departed.

For a while, I was unable to move. Or no, that is far too melodramatic, but I was disinclined to stir myself. I felt a sturdy reluctance to finish my little cake, dab my lips and stand up, as though that would constitute an acceptance of the ways of the world and my place in it. I was, quite simply, furious. No inquiry, no investigation, no questions asked, for this poor creature. Then less than a fortnight later, the full might of the Law grinding into high gear for Cara. And to top it all, the placid assumption that I should share the common view and hold my tongue. I would, of course, but I was glad the good doctor was rattled. No wonder he had felt the need to unburden himself. The poor creature – what an end! And yet, what had been her alternatives? I remembered a nursery nurse of my own, fatter and fatter and then suddenly gone and not to be spoken of in front of the grown-ups ever again. Helpless, I took the last bite of my little cake, dabbed my lips and stood up.

Despite knowing that Lena's indisposition was emotional rather than physical, I feared the smell of a sickroom, and I had to pause outside her door to ensure no sign of my distaste for the visit showed on my face. Thankfully, though, the room had no hint of the invalid about it. The shades were drawn up to let in the light and the bottom sashes were open a few inches letting the soft morning air flutter Mrs McCall's muslin curtains in the most cheerful way. Mrs Duffy was propped up cosily in bed, her breakfast tray pushed away, looking more like herself than I could have hoped for, only rather pale and without her accustomed dignity, owing chiefly to her hair lying over her shoulder in a thin plait. I went to sit on a little armchair, but she stretched out her hand to beckon me towards her and so, having removed the tray, I sat on the edge of her bed and let her take her hands in mine.

Close to, she looked rather less composed. Her mouth quivered as she tried to speak and her eyes, which she kept lowered, were pink-rimmed and puffy. I could hear Mr Duffy moving around in the adjoining room and I spoke very softly, asking her how I might help.

'Alec,' she said. For a fleeting moment I panicked, but thankfully before I could tell her gently that I was not Alec, she went on: 'Dandy, please speak to Alec for me, for Cara's father and me. I know she sent a silly letter and I know the dear boy will want to tell them all about it, with no thought for himself, but would you please tell him from both of us, that we will quite understand if he says nothing.'

It had not occurred to me that the inquiry would delve so far into such personal aspects of Cara's life, but I agreed instantly that it would be intolerable. Alec should not expose himself to the ridicule and pity of the townspeople in the role of a jilted lover.

'I'll tell him,' I said. 'I'm sure it will be a great relief not to have to read out the letters.' At that moment, I felt Mrs Duffy's fingers contract in a spasm just as the door to Mr Duffy's room opened and he walked in. Seeing me, he stopped short, and swept from his head the tall silk hat which completed the suit of old-fashioned mourning clothes he wore. Mrs Duffy's hand grew slick with sweat and I thought in passing how right of Dr Milne to fear for her health. She might look calm and be eating her meals but the woman was a bag of nerves.

'Mrs Gilver,' said Mr Duffy, grave and polite, as I jumped up from his wife's bedside with a few words of incoherent greeting and apology.

'I'm so pleased to have something I can do to help,' I said at last. Mr Duffy frowned slightly at me and glanced towards his wife, and I thought once again how self-centred I seemed to be. He was about to go to the inquiry into the death of his child and Alec's letters were only a tiny part of his worries. Why could I not take care of this one little matter for them without pushing myself forward and demanding thanks? 'Please put it out of your minds,' I said, seemingly unable to stop talking. I drew a deep breath. 'Mr Duffy, may I say once again how very, very sorry I am. And I hope this morning won't be too dreadful.' Mr Duffy gave a vague smile and took the hand I was proffering.

'I'll leave you now,' I said, turning back to Lena. 'But if you or Clemence should want me this morning while your husband is away, I'll be here. Just send Mrs McCall to fetch me.'

'Clemence is summoned to the inquiry,' said Lena, her voice quivering. 'I can scarcely believe it, but it's true. A court! I have tried my whole life to protect her from ugliness and now she must go to a court!' She turned to her husband and spoke piteously. 'Are you quite, quite sure that you could not have got her out of it somehow?'

Mr Duffy's face was unreadable as he regarded her, then he turned to me and thanked me for my visit. I took the hint.

I had been keeping my distance from Alec, as I say, but coming downstairs I caught sight of his blurred profile through the fancy glass of the public bar and, thinking I might as well get it over with, I pushed open the door. This was less startling behaviour than it may sound for apart from Alec the bar was completely empty. It had been so for a day or two now; I assumed that the newsworthiness of the incident at the cottage was outweighed by the sheer quelling doom of the Duffys' presence. It was much to the credit of Mrs McCall, however, that she seemed unconcerned by the quietness of her usually thriving bar trade, but turned her hand with great readiness away from pints of beer and hearty sandwiches and on to bowls of thin soup.

The public bar was rather a disappointment if the truth be told. No spittoons, I noticed, no questionable prints and no stronger a whiff of beer than there is in my own servants' hall at Christmastime. I joined Alec at the bar, resting my elbows on its glossy surface and hooking my foot over the brass rail momentarily until, at the upward lift of his eyebrow, I removed it.

'Are you going?' he asked, looking at my grey day dress and hatless head. He was dressed in only slightly less extravagant mourning clothes than Mr Duffy, his own silk hat sitting incongruously on the bar beside his glass of beer.

'Oh no, I don't think so,' I said. 'No, I don't think so at all.' I almost said that I doubted Hugh would approve, but felt a reluctance to show any such wifeliness to Alec. 'So I shall want to hear all about it.'

'I should be very surprised if there were much to tell,' said Alec. 'I foresee accidental death, much commiseration, a word for the volunteers with the buckets and a sermon on fire safety.' He lifted his almost empty glass, and drained it. 'Is it my imagination, Dandy, or have you been avoiding me? Have you had a change of heart?'

'No,' I protested. 'Witness me seeking you out now. I have a message from Mr and Mrs Duffy.'

'Exactly,' said Alec. 'You have a message for me, otherwise I shouldn't have seen hide nor hair of you. Quite.'

I ignored this and pressed on.

'They wanted you to know that they do not expect you to tell the Fiscal about Cara's letters. And I must say, Alec, I agree with them. Apart from anything else, there will be press reporters there.'

'Quite,' said Alec again.

'And it would serve no purpose,' I said. 'Besides, I'm sure you would come to regret it in the end. One often does, after all, come to regret the confidences one bestows in moments of heightened emotion.'

'It would serve no purpose?' said Alec. 'You don't see a difference between a happily engaged young girl dying in a fire or an extremely *un*happy young girl with a secret breaking off her engagement and dying in a fire, evidently unable to smell smoke, raise the alarm, or leave the cottage by any one of the many doors or windows?'

'You make it sound so sordid,' I said. 'Think what the pressmen would do with that.'

'You're right,' said Alec. 'One tale is much more sordid

than the other. And you say her parents would prefer the less sordid version to be entered into the public record?'

He sounded as angry as I had been an hour before comparing Cara and the unfortunate maid, and I squirmed as much as Dr Milne had. Suddenly I felt no better than Dr Milne. After all both girls, if one got right down to it, were being more or less tidied away, the main thing seeming to be to avoid a scandal. What hypocrites we were, all of us. How eager I had been to believe that Alec and I had made something out of nothing. And, if I were honest, it was not because the matter had actually resolved itself into plain view, but just because it was unthinkable that I should make a fuss, and make a spectacle of myself and my friends.

Alec reached into the pocket of his coat, drew out two envelopes, extracted the letter from each and spread them on the bar. I read them again over his shoulder.

Dear Alec,

Mummy, Clemence and I have come away to the beach cottage for a few days but I should like it so much if you were to come and visit us here. There is something momentous I need to tell you. Please, when you arrive if you could pretend to Mummy that you came in search of me off your own bat that would help enormously. I think she's being perfectly ridiculous but I don't want to make her any crosser than she already is. Sorry to be so mysterious, Alec dear, but I do think it would be best told not written. I trust completely in your affection for me and hope that I am right to do so. All my best love, Cara.

Dear Alec,

I cannot marry you. I am very sorry for the hurt and trouble I know this will cause, but it is much better this than what would come to pass if I were to keep quiet and go along with it. I cannot explain my reasons, except to say that I am convinced I could never make you

97

happy, and that knowing that, I should be miserable myself. Yours sincerely, C.

I had forgotten, I think, what the letters contained. Or rather, having read them that day in Edinburgh sitting in the gallery, when all that faced us was a puzzle with a happy ending around the corner, they had seemed very different from what lay before me now. Unthinkable, *unthinkable*, not to admit that something quite horrid had happened in the day that separated them. I wondered which one Mrs Duffy considered to be the silly one – 'a silly letter', she had said. Presumably the one which broke off the engagement, although it was the other, the first, which touched unflatteringly on Mrs Duffy herself, and I have found one is more likely to brush off as silly something which shows oneself in a bad light, than something which is hurtful to others.

Life makes sense. One thing is connected to another. And no matter how fastidious we are in turning away from ugliness, or how brazenly we stare down the world to hide our ugliness from others, things are as they are. That maid, poor creature, caught the eye of some man somewhere and so set herself on the path towards her death, each thing connected to the next, no matter how confidently the man responsible might have reassured her at the beginning nor how discreetly Dr Milne handled it all at the end. It was no different with Cara, no matter how we all shrank from it. The theft, Cara's secret, the broken engagement and her death, coming all on top of one another like that, must be connected. They each had to be a thread in a pattern I could not see, a story whose organizing element was hidden from me. It was a much more complicated story than the tale of the maid, of course, or at least more unusual and therefore much harder to make out from the glimpses of it we had caught so far, but it had to be there. Things are connected. Life makes sense.

'I think you should read them out,' I said at last.

'I wasn't having a change of heart, you know. Just a failure of nerve. But I'm over it.'

Alec, to my great surprise, shook his head.

'No, Dandy. You underestimate the power of respectability, I think. If I read these letters out today, then later, once we – you and I – have found out what we need to know, we will come up against a brick wall. I can see us trying to make a policeman listen to us. "But these letters were heard at the inquiry," he will say, "and it was agreed then that they were not of any significance." No, much better to keep them up our sleeves until they can do us some good. Accident, commiseration, commendation and safety warning is the order of the day today.' He took out a black-edged handkerchief and pressed it to his lips, possibly fighting a display of emotion, but more likely wiping away traces of beer, then he set his hat dead straight on his head and gave me a grim smile.

'Can you wait five minutes for me to change?' I asked. Bother respectability, bother Hugh and bother the reporters. For Cara's sake, and somehow, obscurely, for the sake of the servant girl whose name I did not even know, I was going to the court.

Chapter Seven

Like the days before, the inquiry seemed to slip past
almost at one remove, as though the witnesses were speaking in a code that only the Procurator Fiscal himself could
understand, frustrating the crowd's desire for details, a
desire so keen as to be almost tangible in the stuffy atmosphere, like citric acid spilled somewhere. If ever a witness
seemed to be edging towards sensation – as when one of
the volunteers described the heat and high leap of the
flames – the Fiscal would first stifle the witness into
silence, then quell the rustle of pleasure in the room with
a look so pained, so superior, that I wanted to shrink down
into my seat, slither to the floor and crawl away.

I had expected the Fiscal to be a desiccated, Dickensian
character, blinking behind half-spectacles and using Latin
where English might do. Had this imagined figure
appeared, the chasm between his chill disapproval and the
vulgar delight of the crowd might have been put down to
his age and unworldliness and I might have been able to
feel affronted by him and a little justified in being there. As
it was, though, he was a young man of hardly forty with
gleaming chestnut hair swept back from a handsome brow
and with powerful shoulders which, even though draped
in sober blue suiting, looked incongruous above a sheaf of
documents. I imagined him summing up and directing the
jury, then pulling on a helmet and goggles and, with a
sweep of a white silk scarf, stepping back into his Avro and
roaring off.

I brought myself back with a jump. Clemence had taken

the stand while my mind was wandering and the room had stilled into perfect silence, broken only by a few soft cluckings from some of the more maternal townswomen. The younger females in the audience simply craned and stretched in an effort to see her shoes.

Could she describe what happened on the morning of the fire, in her own words and taking her time? He could hardly have been gentler, but still Clemence's eyes pinched up in that wary way of hers and her head went back so that she seemed to be looking down her nose. I heard a tut behind me and from somewhere else in the room a scornful noise like a little pff! of gas escaping from a beer bottle, and I knew that poor Clemence was not going down well. But just then, although she could not possibly have heard them, she moved her head slowly, putting her chin down and looking up, her eyes scared and huge. That's more like it, I thought and there was a confirming murmur of satisfied pity from the tutters and pff-ers around me. Clemence started to speak in a small voice.

Mummy and she had set out for a walk along the cliffs as they did most mornings, leaving Cara alone in the cottage.

Why?

Cara had some letters to write. She did sometimes go walking with them – she took quite as much pleasure as her mother and sister in life at the cottage – just that this morning she had letters to write and elected to stay at home. The fire in the little sitting room was burning and, Clemence expected, the kitchen range must have been lit, but the fires in the bedrooms were not, it being warm spring weather. Cara might have fed the sitting-room fire, although it was well built up when Clemence and her mother left. There were no other fires in the cottage, no wireless or other contraption that might have overheated, and no cellars or windowless rooms which might have necessitated Cara's lighting a candle. Cara did not smoke, none of the ladies did, and so there were no hot ashtrays for her to overturn. No, she did not use a seal on her envelopes, and so would have had no call to strike a match to melt the wax.

Was Miss Cara in the habit of keeping all her letters?

Clemence hesitated, and then answered that she did not know what proportion of letters Cara kept or discarded. She expected she would keep letters from her family and other loved ones, but might throw away unimportant notes. What exactly did he want to know?

The Fiscal merely wondered whether, as part of dealing with her correspondence that morning, Miss Cara might have had letters she wanted to destroy, in fact, to burn? Clemence hesitated again and moved her head as though to look at Alec. Her eyes stayed on the Fiscal's face however and at length she answered him in a slightly firmer although no louder voice.

No, Cara did not as a matter of course burn letters, although it was certainly possible that if there was a letter she did not want specially to keep and there was a fire lit in the room, she might throw it on as the easiest way of discarding it. But she tended usually to write letters up in her own room where she had a little table in the window looking out over the sea.

Not in the sitting room where the fire was burning in the grate?

Another long pause, and then – No. At this point, Clemence caught her father's eye, where he sat black and stiff in the front row of seats, and began to weep into her handkerchief, at which she was released from the stand and joined him, putting her head down against the shoulder of his coat although he kept both hands clamped on his knees and did not move to comfort her.

'We shall never know for sure,' said the Fiscal, summing up, 'the chain of events by which the fire started and took hold before Miss Duffy was able to escape. We can, however, take some comfort in the knowledge that it was so unlikely as to be impossible that she suffered in the slightest way.' This he directed towards Mr Duffy and Clemence in the front row, still sitting there, one rigid, one huddled

102

and seeming not to hear him. 'The unfortunate young lady would certainly have been rendered painlessly unconscious through inhaling smoke long before . . . any other part of the tragedy occurred. Indeed, the very fact that she did not escape leads one to suspect that she had fallen asleep when the blaze started and would have known nothing at all.' He continued in this vein for quite some time, carefully quashing all possible sources of prurience, before pronouncing, as we had expected, upon the courage of the volunteers and the pressing need for constant vigilance in the home. The jury retired and very shortly returned.

'Let it be recorded, then,' said the Fiscal, 'that Miss Cara Duffy met her death by accident. No further investigation is required and I hereby release the remains and grant leave for the funeral to take place.' He was slightly, just slightly, knocked off his sonorous course by a recollection, visible to the crowd, that the remains were so utterly destroyed that the timing and nature of the funeral were rather by the by as far as evidence was concerned. These grisly thoughts struck all in the room at the same time causing a collective shudder and the Fiscal's euphemizing, sanitizing efforts were thus completely undermined. We filed out with quite the most unpleasant possible images fixed in our heads.

Had I not known how weakened Mrs Duffy had been a few hours previously, I should have thought she had spent the morning packing, so promptly after our return from Kirkcudbright were she, Clemence and Mr Duffy installed in their motor car and leaving Gatehouse. I barely spoke to either of the ladies, actually not at all to Clemence and only enough to a rather calmer Lena to find out that they were taking Dr Milne's advice and going away to the house of a friend of theirs at Grasmere, and from there on to Switzerland until they could face coming home. Switzerland I could see and the sooner the better, but Grasmere – if that was the spot where the Wordsworths led their peculiar lives – I had always thought of as dank and joyless, all puddles and forest and likely therefore to have what we used to call 'bad air'. One does not hear so much about 'bad air' as one used although whether because modern science has given it a grander name or has proved its non-existence I could not say for sure.

Alec and I met up in the parlour at tea-time. The public bar had clearly sprung back into full life concurrently with the Duffys' driving away for we could hear the men's voices from where we sat. I was glad of it. Mrs McCall would be busy at the other end of the inn and we were that much more likely to have peace for our talk.

'What did you make of Clemence?' asked Alec, as an opening. I had been thinking about Clemence's evidence most of the day and welcomed this indication that my thoughts had been usefully directed.

'Very interesting,' I said, washing down a mouthful of rather overly soda-ish scone with a draught of tea. 'My overall impression was the slanderous one that she was well drilled and therefore not able to think on her feet nimbly enough to take advantage of an unexpected opportunity.'

'Exactly,' said Alec. 'It was all she could do not to smack the table and say "Damn!"'

'And do you think that it's an actual possibility?'

'That Cara was burning my letters and set the house alight? No, I do not. Ludicrous.' I waited for him to justify this, hoping there was something more behind the dismissal than his natural wish to avoid even this much responsibility for her death. 'Try to imagine the scene,' he went on. 'Cara sits by the hearth stuffing papers into the grate, and not armloads at that. I'm no great writer of love letters, I can assure you. One falls out, or wafts out or however it may have happened, and the rug starts to burn. The fire spreads despite Cara's efforts to beat it, forcing her further and further back until she reaches . . . ?'

'The door,' I said. 'Yes, I see. Or even if she left the room and then came back to find the fire already going, it wouldn't be between her and her escape, would it? Unless she tried to get beyond it, to save something. She didn't have a dog down here with her, did she? I should quite likely have plunged into a fire for Bunty.' Alec shook his head.

'She might have tried to beat the fire down and then, when she couldn't, panicked and fled and tripped and hit her head on something,' I suggested.

'Of course,' said Alec. 'At any moment of any day a person might suddenly become unconscious by simply tripping and hitting his head, but it tends not to happen. Have you ever fallen down and knocked yourself unconscious? Do you know anyone else who has?'

'I've fallen,' I said. 'Mostly on the curling pond. And my younger son once got hit on the head by a low branch running along a riverbank, but you're quite right. People don't generally react to tripping by falling headlong like felled trees, do they?'

'Unless they are very drunk. So let's discount the letters in the grate, shall we?'

'One other possibility occurs to me,' I said, reluctantly. 'Would it have been at all in character for Cara to have lit the corner of a sheet of paper and held it aloft, watching it burn, before dropping it into an ashtray with a contemptuous curl of her lip and a toss of her head?' Alec was speechless. 'I saw Clara Bow do it,' I said, 'and I remember thinking what a pity I should probably never get the chance to repeat it. Rather an extreme reaction to an inflated greengrocer's bill, you know.'

'I shouldn't have thought that was Cara's style at all,' said Alec drily, and remembering how she had laughed that day at Croys about 'pining' for Alex, I agreed. This recollection led me back with a jolt to what I had been all but forgetting. What we were talking about here, the two of us, cosily over our tea, was the death six days ago of the girl Alec had been to marry. I took the opportunity of his being busy buttering a teacake to have a good long look at him. In his expression and demeanour he seemed, and had seemed since this morning, quite different from the creature I had found shaking and pale on the bridge the day it happened. Also, he was displaying only suspicion about what *had* really happened and outrage that it might go undetected; there seemed to be no personal sadness, much less raw new grief. And he had changed his clothes already, out of mourning and into a Norfolk jacket – still with a black tie which looked very peculiar – as though Cara was not worth the discomfort of an afternoon in black cloth as well as a morning. I could think of no way to broach any of this with him, however, indeed no real excuse for doing so beyond curiosity, so I decided to stick to the subject in hand.

'Very well, then,' I said. 'The Fiscal was thorough in dreaming up possible sources of flame, but did he miss anything out?' We thought in silence for a while.

'For instance,' I said. 'Did Cara really not smoke?'

'Of course she did,' said Alec. 'But not in her mother's house and certainly not in the morning. Is there any beauty routine that requires a naked flame?'

'Such as what?' I asked, amused and not hiding it to get my own back for Clara Bow.

'Well, I don't know,' said Alec, shifting. 'Curling irons or what have you.'

I thought back to Cara's perfect shingle and stifled a laugh.

'I suppose,' I said, 'she might have needed burnt cork – if she were blacking up for a minstrel show. I wonder that the Fiscal didn't think to check –'

'Oh shut up,' said Alec. 'Let's leave this. We both know that Cara did not die as a result of accident and we're wasting time.'

'What do we think did happen?' I said. I knew what I thought, but at that early point in our investigation it still seemed too fantastical to say it plainly aloud.

'I think Cara killed herself,' said Alec, 'and so do you. And so does her mother, and possibly her sister too. I think it's something to do with the theft, and I think the same thing – whatever it is – is why they suddenly rushed off

down here and why Cara became convinced, or was persuaded, that she should break off the engagement.'

'Yes,' I said slowly. I was wishing against wish that
I could deny this, but it was no use. He was right.

'But,' I went on, 'should we do anything about these
convictions of ours? Shouldn't we just let matters lie?'

'Another failure of nerve?' Alec asked, looking at me
very hard.

'No. Just that even if we do find out what happened and
even if her mother knew enough to stop it from happening
– and I'm sure she did – so even if we feel Lena deserves
it to be out in the open, what about her father? Do we
really want to put her father through the ordeal of a
verdict of suicide?' Alec looked uncomfortable at this.

'And *how* do we find out what happened?' I went on.
'And actually, *why*?'

'What do you mean "why"?' said Alec.

'I mean who are we to?' I said. 'Who am I to? On what
authority? I'm only supposed to be sorting out the diamond theft.'

'You're *what*?' said Alec, and I remembered, too late as
usual, that I had not told him this. There seemed little
reason to pussy-foot around it now, however, so I briefly
filled him in.

'Well, there you are then,' was all he said, when I had
finished. 'That's your authority. I think it's all connected, as
a matter of fact – it must be – but if you're squeamish, then
concentrate on Silas and Daisy by all means. You can leave
Mrs Duffy to me.' He spoke grimly, and at my questioning
look, he said: 'It sticks in my throat, that's all. She thinks
she's handling it so beautifully, and there's something
repugnant about that. Her daughter's death should be all
she cares about. Any potential scandal should hardly regis-
ter. So, I mean to find out what happened and face her
with it. Then even if no one knows the truth except her and
me, at least she won't be able to pride herself on having
handled it all.'

Again, I was struck with a familiar thought. Disgusting

107

as it was to think of Mrs Duffy's scheming (and I was sure Alec was right about it) weren't we just as bad? How, rather than thinking only of Cara and his own loss, could he be busily planning revenge? At least, *his* schemes were for Cara, though, in Cara's name. When one got right down to it, it was only Lena and I who were vile; she containing a scandal and I preventing another.

'But I ask again,' I said, pushing all of that aside, 'what are we to *do*? I can hardly chase off to Grasmere, much less Switzerland if it comes to that.'

'No, the last thing we want is to ask any more questions of the Duffys,' said Alec. 'Not just because we don't know what to ask and if we did they wouldn't tell us, but we don't want them to know that we're interested. Do you see?' I didn't. 'Because when the time comes that we do want to ask something of them, we must not be suspected. What we need to do now, is stay here and try to find out something, anything, that will tell us about Cara's state of mind that last week.'

'But how?' I said. I suppose I had thought vaguely that I should go home and think things over, perhaps talk to some of Cara's friends and . . . I *hadn't* thought; that was the trouble. I certainly hadn't thought of snooping around for clues.

'Well, there must be countless people who spoke to her,' said Alec. 'Servants, for instance.'

'No,' I said. 'They didn't have a servant with them.' I saw no need to discomfit both of us with details of the poor little maid.

'Well, a village woman then,' said Alec. 'To cook and clean. And the postmistress would know what letters Cara sent and if she made any telephone calls. You must take care of the women. I'll speak to tradesmen – the milkman and suchlike – about any comings and goings. It's sure to lead somewhere. Small town gossip, you know.'

'Yes, and then the fire will have made everyone think back carefully for any titbit that puts them close to the action. People do that, I've found.'

'Quite,' said Alec. 'We won't have to dig. It will be impossible to help finding out whatever there is to know.'

'There's still the problem of Hugh,' I said, reluctantly. 'What on earth shall I say to him about why I'm still here?' I was not entirely sure why I did not just tell Hugh about Daisy employing me as her sleuth. Perhaps because although he might have roared with laughter, patted me on the head and given me his good wishes, he might just as easily have put his foot down.

'You must lie,' said Alec. 'Either by commission or omission, depends how Jesuitical you feel about it. But lying is the only option, I'm afraid.' He spoke with great jollity, but did not quite meet my eye. 'Either make something up – tell him you're interested in a little house, or a boat or an orphanage which need a patroness – or send a telegram. A nice ambiguous telegram.'

And so, blushing and feeling that my life, having jogged soberly along during all the years one is supposed to run wild, was certainly making up for lost time now, I sent another telegram to Hugh. 'Inquiry found accident. Duffys shattered. Am staying to help. At least one week. Dandy.' I tried to see the startled look of the girl at the telegraph counter as a good thing; I hoped it would put her and me on the cosiest terms when I came to question her about Cara. Of course, the story of how I stayed at Gatehouse with Alec Osborne would be all that our mutual friends could talk of for weeks once the first one found out, but knowing our mutual friends I could be sure that Hugh would never hear of it, and what is more, knowing Hugh, that he would never speak of it to me if he did.

I went early to my room that night, feeling rather like a pea in a drum downstairs now that everyone else had gone, and sat propped up in Mrs McCall's brass bed in the lamplight as the sun faded outside, plotting away like mad. My first task should be to track down the individual (or individuals) who had gone in to do the rough work at the cottage, and I had my excuse for snooping after them all ready. I was rather proud of it and was trying to ignore a small misgiving I had that it would land me in a great deal of trouble if it didn't come off. Then – I removed one of the three fat pillows and snuggled down – just when the girl at the telegraph desk should have had time to regale all of her friends with my wickedness and be agog for more, I would seek her out again. I should not need any further story to cover my designs, she being as keen to speak to me as I to her. I turned out the lamp, closed my eyes and fell asleep to the comforting drone of the men's voices in the bar.

Chapter Eight

'Well, Miss Madam,' said Agnes Marshall, 'you had better come in.' I had tracked her down disappointingly easily, simply by asking Mrs McCall after breakfast, getting Alec to drop me in the village of Borgue, and setting out to walk to her cottage 'right facing you at the Kirkandrews road end' where I was assured I would find her at home, Saturday being baking day.

I followed her and was shown into a small parlour, aggressively clean and obviously seldom used. She shut the door firmly on the warmth and delicious smells emanating from her kitchen and sat down opposite me on the edge of a hard chair, carefully folding her apron around her floury hands to save a speck falling on to her well-brushed horsehair and gleaming linoleum.

'Can I get you some tea, Miss Madam?' she asked. Her mode of address, which I had taken at first to be a slip of the tongue arising from fluster, was evidently as habitual as it was original. 'I cannot offer you coffee,' she said, 'for I wouldn't have the stuff in the house.' This fierceness put me off accepting anything.

'I am a friend of Mr and Mrs Duffy,' I began, 'and I believe that you were Cook at the cottage up until –' Mrs Marshall was shaking her head.

'Not "Cook"!' she said and I wondered what bitter insult I had dealt her (I never can keep up with the tortured questions of rank below stairs). 'I just went in first thing, got the range het up again, not that it was ever cold, did the dishes from the night before and got one or two things

111

sorted for the day. Peeled the tatties and dressed a bit of meat for them and that. And then I was off and away mid-morning again. A gey queer set-up if you ask me. But them that pays the piper calls the tune. It fidgeted me I can tell you, sitting here at home all night, knowing they dishes were in the sink growing ears. Still.'

'And I believe that Mrs Duffy didn't get a chance to speak to you before they left,' I said, crossing my fingers in my lap.

'No indeed,' said Mrs Marshall. 'I doubt I was the last thing on the poor woman's mind.'

I relaxed.

'Well, I daresay, but she did think of you, and asked me to be sure to give you this.' I unclasped my bag and handed her the envelope. I hoped she would show the proper Scottish reserve around money and not open it until I was gone – I had no idea if the sum I had enclosed was outrageously small, outrageously large or just right. She laid it aside without so much as squeezing it for a clue.

'Well then,' she said. 'There was no need for that, tell her when you see her, Miss Madam. No need at all. I'm affronted.' I took this as it was meant, as a thank you, and went on.

'I wonder if you could tell me where I might find the other maids?' I said.

'Others?' she said. 'That's what I'm telling you. There weren't any others. Just me in the morning to get redd up and they did the rest of it their own selves.'

'How odd,' I said. 'Were they waiting for more staff to be sent from town? After the poor girl – After the maid –'

'Very private ladies,' said Mrs Marshall, and I wondered if I imagined the note of reproof. 'Having a bit of fun to theirselves playing at houses, or so I thought at first.' Either Dr Milne had done even better than I imagined at hushing up the maid's trouble or Mrs Marshall was one of the least gossip-prone women I had ever met. And just my luck to have come up against what must be one of the few individuals for miles around who would not jump at the chance of being centre-stage.

'So you thought at first,' I echoed. 'But then?'

'Well, I daresay you'll know anyway, Miss Madam, being a friend of theirs, if there's anything to know. But I did begin to wonder if maybe they had their reasons. I wondered if maybe there was illness, for they kept the place gey hot for the spring. Or some other trouble. Not with the mother – the mistress, I should say. But those lassies.'

I waited, trying not to seem too eager, and avoided her eyes by looking with absolutely feigned admiration at the pot dogs on her fireplace.

'I got to thinking they had had a fall out, for they weren't close like you'd think sisters would be. It was near like their mother was trying her best to get them to make it up, but as far as I could see they'd have nothing to do with each other. Aye well, I suppose there's no saying that two peas in the pod have to be pals as well as neighbours, eh?' I recognized another of Mrs Marshall's own expressions, and nodded my agreement. This was a new angle, I thought. Trouble between Clemence and Cara. What might it be? Mrs Marshall seemed to answer me.

'But there, it can't have been easy for the girl to see her wee sister getting wed before her. I wondered myself why the man would have gone for the one and not the other.'

'Did Clemence – the elder girl, that is – seem unhappy to you then, Mrs Marshall?' I asked. This was obviously much too frank, and she reacted as though stung.

'I'm sure it's no more my business than it is –' 'Yours', she had been about to say, I am sure, before politeness stopped her. I decided, since I had probably ruined my chances anyway, that nothing more could be lost by pressing on.

'I had rather thought it was Cara who was feeling glum. Not going out for a walk on that last morning for instance, poor girl. Still, as you say, if they had quarrelled, I daresay neither one was thrilled to be thrown together in a tiny cottage in the middle of nowhere.' I realized halfway through this that I was currently sitting in possibly an even smaller dwelling in the same remote spot, and too late I bit my lip. Mrs Marshall bridled but said nothing. I am sorry to say that what came out of my mouth next was not even reckless inquisitiveness so much as babbling, pure and simple.

'I wonder what they had argued about, don't you? I mean, they're normally as close as close can be. Devoted sisters, wouldn't you agree?'

'I couldn't say, Miss Madam,' said Mrs Marshall, predictably. But as it happened she was not merely being snooty, for she followed this with: 'I had never met the family before.'

'Oh really?' I said, sensing safer ground. 'You are new in the area, then?'

'I am not, then,' she said stoutly. 'My grandfather was born in this house. It's them that's new. I took the job on to help them out this once, but a month ago, I wouldn't have known them to pass in the street.' My eyes strayed to the envelope on the table, thinking that under these circumstances I had been rather too generous with Daisy's money. Mrs Marshall, most unfortunately, caught my look and all hope of amity between us was lost. I quitted her parlour and, imagining her removing my taint from her sofa with a stiff brush, I stamped back towards Borgue in a temper, cursing myself for my foolishness.

'Stupid woman, stupid woman, stupid woman,' I chanted, in time with my steps. I should be reliving that visit, that wasted chance, in my sleep.

'That makes two of us then,' said a voice, sounding only feet away from me. I jumped and wheeled around looking for the source. An ancient, crooked but sturdy old woman slowly unbent herself from where she had been stooping behind the wall which edged the lane to my left. She put her hands into the small of her back and stretched herself with a groan, before coming back to rest, not upright but gently curved forward like a feather. 'Aye, the Dear knows why I'm crippling myself with this caper,' she said, pointing to the ground at her feet with a knobbled and earthy finger. I peered over the wall at a vegetable patch, laid out between brick paths, in which stretched long rows of tiny green plants, looking like stitches in a brown blanket. 'I've near kilt myself planting out they cabbages and now I'll be out here every night with my candle trying to keep the snails off them, and then when I've been out in the snow to cut one and washed it and cooked it and laid it down, they'll all turn their noses up anyway.' She spoke with great weariness but her eyes were twinkly and she looked back at her poker-straight rows with pride. 'And what have you done?' she said. 'Here, I hope you've not stepped in muck in they boots.' She bent again and delving her hand into a bucket she began to sprinkle something around the neck of a tiny cabbage plant.

'Oh goodness me, no,' I said, thinking that I had no idea and deciding not to check, 'I've upset and offended one of your neighbours, I'm afraid.'

The old woman's head bobbed up instantly at this and I saw the twinkle in her eye intensify as though someone had turned the gas up to full. She stood straight again and wiped her hands, beaming.

'Well now, Mrs Gilver madam, how did you manage to do that?'

She knew my name; this was more like it.

'I say, I don't suppose you'd like a hand with that?' I said, stepping along to the gate and coming into the garden. 'I could do with something to work off my bad temper and you look as though you need a rest.'

She held the bucket out towards me wordlessly, and eased herself back against the wall with her feet splayed. Crushed eggshells was what the bucket contained, and I took off my glove before grabbing a handful and crouching down amongst the cabbage seedlings to set about my inexplicable task.

'I was charged with giving a little something to Mrs

115

Marshall to say thanks for her trouble. From the Duffys, you know. And it seemed to me the most natural thing in the world to have a little chat about this and that, but the lady seems to think I was prying and – oh bother!' A clump of eggshell, still with some of its contents clinging about it, dropped on to a seedling and bent it down. I flicked it away.

'Och, you shouldn't worry yourself about her, madam. She's far too big for her boots. It's no as if she was slaving for them. In and out in the morning as fast as you could blink she was, but even that was too much trouble.'

'Well, it beats me why she should take the job if she had no taste for it,' I said, glad to have someone with whom I could share my many thoughts on Mrs Marshall. The old woman rocked with laughter.

'Aye well, her man, Sandy, he was in about the wee hoose painting and papering for them and when madam said did he know of any "domestic help" he just said his Aggie would do it and glad, never thinking a woman would grudge to work with the two good hands God gave her.'

'Ah,' I said. 'I imagine that would cause a little coolness.'

'Well, Sandy was none too cool, I can tell you. Fit to be tied more like it. He's near had enough of her airs and graces, for it's not what he's been used to.' I wondered how she knew all this. Did the hot-tempered Sandy and the frosty Agnes have screaming matches in the garden? Did the sound carry this far?

'No,' she said again, 'Sandy has never been used with seeing a woman too proud to turn her hand. Why, his mother still grows all her own vegetables, madam, and she's over eighty, God love her old bones.' She brought this out with great enjoyment and watched me closely to see if I was catching up with her.

'I see,' I said, with an inward whoop of delight that my gamble had paid off so lavishly and I was not grovelling around in the dirt for nothing. There is no greater source of scurrilous gossip than a mother-in-law with a grudge in her heart and if 'Sandy' had worked for the Duffys he might have well have told his mother something I would like to know. 'Well, Mrs Marshall,' I said, playing her at her own game, 'if she felt that way, I suppose my dropping in with a tip was just about the last straw.'

'I wish I'd been there to see it,' she said. 'Oh, but madam, to think here we are laughing and there that poor lassie is. Ashes to ashes and dust to dust is what we're promised, but please God there's not many of us bound for that kind of end.'

'Did you know her?'

'Naw, not me. I didn't know the family at all. They don't belong here. They just bought that wee hoose to play in, I think. No that any folk round here would want they wooden hooses. Built as hidey-holes for Edinburgh and Glasgow folk and that's all they've ever been. Mind you, they had theirs lovely. Sandy showed me what they were putting up and it must have been a palace. Shame to think all that new paint and paper and all they curtains gone just like that.'

I privately agreed with her, but thankfully said nothing because she clapped a hand to her mouth in horror.

'Devil take my tongue,' she said. 'Listen to me going on about paint and paper when they've lost their bonny lassie. Oh dear God, it's true what they say. It's as well we don't know what's coming, or we'd none of us get out of our beds in the morning.'

'Were you at the inquiry?' I asked, knowing the answer, but making the most of Mrs Marshall, to whom I felt sure one could say anything.

'I was not,' she pronounced. 'Although I heard you were, madam, and if you don't mind an old woman speaking her mind, you should have known better. My own man, God rest his soul, was taken home ten years since and I would no more have gone to his funeral than I don't know what. A graveside's no place for a woman, and as for a courtroom! Aye, I know there's plenty of those clackety pieces from Gatehouse went and now we'll not say a word to them for all they'll say is that Mrs Gilver was there so there can't be harm in it. I don't know!'

'But you'll have heard all about it,' I said, rightly surmising that none of what had preceded required a response. 'Does your Sandy have any idea what caused it? He must know the place well.'

She shook her head.

'He's near gone daft with thinking about it, madam. Here, just mind out and not put too much down at once! That bucket's to do the whole row and you'd not want to be scratching it back up again if you're short at the end. It gets terrible under your nails.'

I was warming to Mrs Marshall as much and as quickly as I had cooled to her daughter-in-law.

'He cannot think how it happened,' she went on. 'Mind you, once it was going he's not surprised it went like it did. They kept the place that hot! Sandy was fair sweating when he was working there, if you'll pardon me. And he tellt them and tellt them they could not have it so warm with new paper or it would be hanging off again. But softborn, soft-bide, eh?' She gazed innocently at me, crouched in the earth, scrabbling in the bucket of eggshells, and I smiled in spite of myself.

'Mind you, it's all just habit, this lighting fires in God's good spring, for I know they found it close. I walked past this one day and every door and window in the place was wide open. New curtains all blowing out and getting clarty, so I think madam was just digging in her heels and refusing to do what she was told solely because she was told it. A stubborn old woman is a terrible thing, is that not right?' She chuckled and smoothed her apron.

When I had worked my way up the row to the top of the vegetable patch and almost to the cottage door, Mrs Marshall stumped inside and came back with a glass of water for me and one for herself, and we sat companionably on the bench against the house wall looking down the row of cabbages with, I daresay, equal pride. Mrs Marshall sighed heavily.

'Poor soul,' she said. 'Her mother will be lost without her, and maybe that sister of hers will be sorry now she wasn't more like what a sister should be. I cannot stop thinking about it. Daft like, for I didn't know the lassie. I'm not even sure now which one of they girls it was that died. The younger one, they said. But there wasn't a spit between them. So was it the bonny, cheery one or the other one with the – I shouldna say this, but – with the face that would turn the milk?'

'I'm afraid,' I said, having no trouble applying these descriptions to Clemence and Cara, 'that it was the pretty little thing who died, and her elegant sister who is still with us.'

'Aye well,' said Mrs Marshall, 'God gathers his own.' She seemed to recollect herself and shrug off some unwelcome thought. 'It's not like I ever heard any harm of Teenie-bash.' I took this to be a reference to Clemence. 'It just beats me how two lassies fae the same mould can be so different in theirselves. Mind you, two girls together can just as easy be at daggers drawn every day of their lives as they can be chums.' She gave a shout of laughter. 'I had nine, madam, and there's ways that's easier – although the work would kill a mule – for they all jist have to shake down and get on with it.' I nodded solemnly and I did agree with her, as a matter of fact. I had often thought that had my boys been girls I should have been quite happy to add to their number until they were well diluted by siblings. Of course, had my boys been girls, I should have been obliged to keep on in pursuit of an heir for Hugh, even as far as matching Mrs Marshall's nine, and I quite saw that if it might kill a mule it should certainly have done for me.

'I was sure there was three,' Mrs Marshall was saying when I turned my attention back to her. 'But Aggie said definitely jist the two lassies. And that's right enough, is it, madam? So I turned to Aggie and I said, "Well, who was the wee bit thing I saw riding a bicycle up fae the wooden hooses on the Tuesday night?" As if the devil was after her,

119

mind. "I'm sure I don't know," says Aggie. "Your eyes are not what they were." Cheeky besom. "Och well," says I, "it was probably one of the other maids." That shut her up. The *other* maids. She didn't like that, I can tell you.' Mrs Marshall wheezed with laughter again, and did not seem to notice me staring, open-mouthed. This must indeed have been 'one of the other maids'. The poor creature, having begged or borrowed a bicycle from who knows where, racing up to Gatehouse to . . .? To send a desperate letter to one of her friends? Or to try to procure a way out of her troubles? But in Gatehouse? Was that possible? Or perhaps the furious pedalling itself was the idea.

'Madam?' said Mrs Marshall bringing me back from my wool-gathering. I drained my glass of water and stood up, forced to screw my hands into my back just as the old lady herself had done. She beamed at me, hugely entertained by having got a soft-born besom to do an a honest job of work. I held out my hand to her.

'Thank you for a most pleasant morning, Mrs Marshall.'

'Well, you know where I am, madam. Don't go past the door.'

Returning to Gatehouse on the midday bus, I was met at the door of the inn by Mrs McCall, who happened to be passing along the corridor and who clutched my arms in her big hands and asked me in a shocked voice what in the Lord's name had happened? What has she heard, I thought? And was about to ask her the same thing, when I caught sight of myself in the fish-eye glass above the fireplace. This glass never throws back a flattering rendition of one's face, tending to give more bulbous prominence to the nose than is usual and making one look, overall, as though one's features have been painted on to a child's balloon blown up a bit too far. Now, though, I looked really quite savage. My hat was askew, my hair was sticking straight out to the sides (I assumed from having been squashed into my collar as I crouched) and there was a smear of dirt across one cheek. Looking down I saw that the hem of my coat was earthy and my stockings, frankly, a disgrace. Fearing that if I told her I had been planting cabbages I might lose any little scraps of dignity I had left, however, I made no explanation but ordered a bath and luncheon in my room and swept upstairs.

In the afternoon, refreshed, although still rather in need of a manicure, I sailed forth to deal with the girl in the post office. I had had a tremendous idea in my bath and was eager to set it in motion.

The post office was quiet, as I had expected, the people of Gatehouse being the sort to deal with all High Street business such as letters and parcels nice and early in the morning and not dash in and out in the careless way that city dwellers do. I have never quite been able to understand the exact nature of the moral rectitude that springs from doing things in the morning rather than the afternoon, but since it served my current purpose I had no quarrel with it. The postmistress herself, Miss Millar, was just visible up a ladder in the back-shop with a list in her hand and a pencil behind her ear. I leaned companionably against the counter at the telegraph desk and smiled at the girl.

'I wonder, my dear, if you will be able to help me with a little matter,' I began. The young person glanced very briefly to the side as though to check that her boss was well out of the way and then leaned towards me eagerly.

'I find that I need to send a telegram to a friend of mine. She is also a friend of poor Mr and Mrs Duffy,' I added hastily, seeing her face fall, disappointed at this prosaic beginning. 'But the difficulty is this. I know that poor Mr and Mrs Duffy have gone off for a few days before they go home to begin to make the funeral arrangements. So I cannot be sure whether they have told this particular friend yet, about the terrible thing that happened. Do you see my problem?' The girl shook her head slowly, and I saw that

121

I should have to be rather more frank than felt comfortable. 'You see, my dear, if I send a telegram to my dear friend and make no mention of it, she will, if she has heard the news, think me terribly callous. If, however, she has not heard and I *do* mention it, then not only will I give her the most frightful shock, but I might offend the Duffys. After all, it is their decision how and when people are to be told.'

'But – pardon me, madam – but won't your friend have read all about it in the papers?' said the girl.

'The papers? The newspapers? Oh, yes,' I gabbled. 'Well, no, because this friend is very, very sensitive, and in poor health and doesn't read the newspapers for that reason.'

'Well, madam,' she continued, 'can you telephone to this friend and ask a member of the household whether she has been told?' I could feel a prickle of perspiration begin at the back of my neck. Confound the girl.

'I had thought,' I went on, 'that if you showed me your list of telegrams sent – you do keep a note of them, don't you? – I could look and see if there had been anything sent to my friend.' This was my wonderful plan. My vision had been of the girl, docile and eager to help, sliding a list of names across the counter to me, and of my thus finding out all manner of things.

'But her father might have sent word from Edinburgh, before he came here, madam,' the girl persisted. 'Or he might have telephoned. I don't mind of him coming in here, but he might have rung her up from the hotel. Or they might have sent letters. We don't even see the letters, madam. The postman picks them up and they're sorted and off to Kirkcudbright.' I nodded, more and more vigorously as she ran through all of these things I had never thought of. 'What's your friend's name, madam?' she said suddenly. 'And I'll check.'

I gaped at her and blushed. 'Gordon-Strathmurdle,' I blurted, the least authentic-sounding name of anyone I know in the world.

'Oh no, madam,' said the girl. 'I would have remembered a name like that.' I blushed even deeper. 'And besides,' she said, generous now that we both knew which of us had the upper hand, 'there were no telegrams sent from the Reiver's Rest all week except that one to you yourself.' I smiled my thanks and fled next door to let an ice-cream sundae in Frulliano's cool my cheeks from the inside out.

Alec had had a rather less eventful day than mine, closer to what we had both foreseen in the way of gently coaxing information from simple bucolics who did not even know it was happening. No dressings down from shop girls for him; no mud nor eggshells. There had been time before our rendezvous, however, to compose a report which skated over these less triumphant episodes. I had even made notes for myself and although I had lost my nerve at the last moment and hidden them amongst my nighties, still I was eager to pass on what I had learned.

'I'll begin, shall I?' I said. 'I have found out first, that Cara sent no telegrams, nor did Clemence, and Mrs Duffy sent only the one to me that we knew about anyway. Also, that the Duffys were troubled about something and very keen to be alone, to the extent that they did not want their housekeeper to linger in the cottage a moment longer than she had to each day. Lastly, that Clemence and Cara were at odds with one another over something, so perhaps their mother did not want the housekeeper to hear them quarrelling – she's quite terrifying, by the way.'

'The telegrams are good work, Dandy,' said Alec, 'but forgive me for being frank, won't you? The rest of what you have just told me are not "findings out" but your interpretations of findings out. I want to hear the facts, not the theories, then we can add them to my facts and build our theories together.' This last sounded so very enticing that it took away some of the sting. I dashed upstairs, got my notes from my underclothes drawer and started again.

Alec listened in silence, making a great deal of work out of clearing and refilling his pipe, while I relayed Aggie

Marshall, old Mrs Marshall and young Miss Telegram in turn, missing out the worst of my blunders, and scrupulously avoiding any reference to cabbages.

He puffed steadily for a long moment after I had finished, and I lit a cigarette of my own, rather wishing I could share his pipe, which smelled mellow and cool against my more acrid smoke (best gaspers from the grocer cum tobacconist up the street). Gentlemen's brilliantine too always smells so much more dignified than the poisonous cocktail we pour over ourselves in pursuit of a lasting curl. Why did men always keep the best of everything for themselves?

'So two different people commented on how hot the house was,' said Alec. 'Three including Sandy Marshall. I caught up with him myself and that was one of his main themes.'

'And his mother makes two, and who is the third?' I asked.

'His wife,' Alec said. 'She told you the range was never cold when she went in in the morning. Yes. That may very well be significant when we put it alongside something else I found out today.' I noted that Alec did not feel he was compelled to report verbatim what his informants had divulged, not too scared to mess things up with interpretation before I could mull them over. 'Mr McNally, the coalman, had something very interesting to say. I included him in my round-up of possible visitors for the sake of completeness and I'm very glad I did so. Not least because pickings were otherwise rather slim – don't you think it just a bit suspicious that they seem to have kept themselves quite so utterly to themselves, Dandy? A couple of ladies glimpsed on a distant cliff-top is about it.'

'Yes, but you were about to tell me something about the coalman?'

'Quite. Mr McNally delivered five hundredweight of best house coal, as well as two sacks of sticks, the week before the Duffys arrived. It was ordered by letter from Edinburgh. Now, the coal store at Reiver's Rest – somewhere between a large bunker and a shed proper – sits separate from the house itself, quite some way away, owing I suppose to the local wariness about wooden houses –'

'Or possibly the complete lack of concern on the part of the builder for the little maid who had to trot back and forth with the buckets,' I put in.

'That too,' said Alec. 'Well, after much hemming and hawing, Mr McNally admitted to me that he went back to the cottage yesterday, to "check on" the coal. For which I think we can understand "take back and resell", but why not? Coal would be the last thing on anyone's mind, and as McNally pointed out to me, a heap of it just sitting there is a temptation to any troop of wee rascals who might happen past with a box of matches and a heidfu' o' naethin'.' Here Alec dropped into a dreadful approximation of a Scots tongue, painful to the ear.

'Now, the coal shed was kept locked,' he went on, 'but Mr McNally has a key and when he opened up yesterday, what do you think he found?' For a horrid moment my mind ran skittering over some of the things I imagined might be found in a locked coal shed, rats being the very least. Then Alec went on.

'He found nothing. Nothing. The coal was finished. In one week, enough coal had been used to have kept a family of ten warm all winter.'

'I've just remembered,' I said. 'Mrs Marshall – nice Mrs Marshall – told me that one day when she went by she saw that all the doors and windows were thrown open. She remembered particularly, because the new curtains were blowing out against the outside walls getting dirty, and she was puzzled because she knew the fires were hotter than Sandy thought was advisable with new paper.'

'And yet didn't Clemence say at the inquiry that the bedroom fires weren't even lit?' said Alec. 'I wonder why no one corrected her? No matter. You know what this means, don't you, Dandy?' I thought I did but it seemed not only far-fetched, but beset with problems. 'All the fires

125

lit, the range stoked and the windows flung open. That little house, that little wooden house, was being dried out like kindling. It was *supposed* to catch fire and it was supposed to burn to the ground when it did.'

'Yes,' I said, 'but there's a problem, Alec, don't you see? Cara couldn't possibly have arranged that and carried it out, could she?'

'No indeed. Indeed she couldn't.' Alec's voice was grim. 'Our suicide theory begins to crumble. And anyway, didn't you say that both the Mrs Marshalls remarked how happy Cara was?'

'"A cheery wee thing",' I agreed. 'Yet that second letter she sent you seemed anything but cheerful.'

I took a last puff at my cigarette and threw it into the fire. Alec was busy fiddling with his pipe. (Perhaps he was welcome to it; who could be bothered, after all?)

'The second letter aside,' I said, 'if Cara didn't kill herself, what did happen? Was it an accident after all?' Alec resettled his pipe, raised his eyebrows and said nothing. I began to shake my head, horrified. 'No, Alec, no, you can't mean that. That Mrs Duffy or she and Clemence together . . . and then calmly went for a walk and left her there. And how on earth could Cara be made to stay in the house and let it happen?' I asked.

'We said ourselves that she must have hit her head and been unconscious,' said Alec. 'And we agreed that people don't just hit their heads.'

'But it's impossible,' I said. 'Her mother? Her sister? It's utterly preposterous. And why?'

'It would explain their oddness, their watchfulness,' said Alec. 'Their peculiar reaction to seeing me. Mrs Duffy's attempts to quash all hint of trouble at the inquiry.' I was beginning to feel sick. To think of them (or just her?) banking up fires and stoking the range, the windows open and everyone still sweltering. Wait! No, it couldn't be. Relief rolled over me like a wave of warm water.

'It can't have happened that way,' I said. 'Don't you see? Because how could they have explained it to Cara? She

126

wouldn't have sat quietly while they made a tinderbox of the cottage around her, would she?' Alec's shoulders dropped and he smiled.

'No, no, of course not.' He gave a sigh that was almost a laugh. 'I'm sure we're right about what all the coal was used for, but it must have happened with the knowledge and acquiescence of everyone in the house. It must have.'

'And since we can't countenance the idea that Cara was a willing accomplice in her own death,' I said, 'where does that leave us?'

'You're wrong,' said Alec, sitting suddenly upright from where he had slumped down in his chair with relief. 'That's exactly what must have happened. Cara, Clemence and their mother were all in it together. It was a deliberate scheme, what the Americans call a frame-up. And what it means – of course! – is that Cara is still alive.'

'What?' I said, but the sense of it hit me almost at once. 'Oh, yes, I see! Oh thank God! She's not dead. She's disappeared somewhere and that's why the house had to burn right to the ground – to make it plausible that nothing remained of her.' I beamed.

'And it all went according to plan,' he said. 'Including you turning up as a convenient witness, except that I was not supposed to turn up with you and that rattled them.'

'And do you think that was the secret she wanted to tell you? And do you think that she and her mother couldn't agree on whether you might be told? And she couldn't bear you to think she was dead while you were still engaged and that's why she wrote to break it off?' Alec nodded faster and faster as I rattled through all this, and as his smile deepened I thought to myself that yes, it must have hurt him at some spot between his heart and his pride to have got that letter, despite how cool he had seemed, and that he was glad to have an explanation of the jilting that was nothing to do with his attractions as a husband, even if we now had more questions, and more puzzling ones, than ever.

'So . . . why?' I asked. 'And how did she get away? And where is she? And how are we even going to *start* to find her?'

Chapter Nine

We could be sure of one thing: there was nothing more to be learned in Galloway. Clearly the Duffys had chosen the spot because they could go about their business unobserved there. So I telephoned to Gilverton, telling Hugh with a nice truthfulness that the Duffys had gone off to the mountains and that I should like Drysdale to fetch me from Edinburgh the following afternoon. I was glad; despite a growing fondness for the peace of my little room with its striped flannel sheets and its view of the barrels in the yard, my lack of success with the locals (around whom Alec seemed able to run the expected rings) was a constant thorn, and I was missing Bunty, growing tired of the clothes I had brought and, after this morning, I needed Grant to attend to my coat and gloves as a matter of urgency.

We spent the journey up to town dividing the tasks ahead. I was to tackle the jeweller who identified the pastes, since both Alec and I felt a lady could best achieve the right combination of tenacious interest and muddle-headedness to find out all there was to know while not putting the man on his guard. Besides, the jewels were my proper concern, being Daisy's only one. I thought it rather unlikely that Cara would have said anything useful to a jeweller, but thoroughness is to be recommended in most arenas and, also, there was not much else for me to do.

Alec had rather wider scope. Under cover of unbearable grief, he was to make visits to Cara's closest friends and beg them to talk about her. We both thought it certain that they would speak of the last time they had met, or the last letter they had had, and that something about the pickle she was in might be revealed. I secretly hoped, as I daresay did he, that he should actually discover much more than this; that is, that he should discover Cara herself holed up with a chum somewhere. We did not, however, give voice to this hope.

So, after a blissful night back in my own bed and having submitted myself to one of Grant's most punitive toilettes – it always incensed her to have me go off on my own – I found myself in Edinburgh again, descending Frederick Street, approaching the jeweller's with the reluctance of a dog being led to its bath water. Stopping at the corner of the street and pretending to look with interest at a suite of hideous mahogany bedroom furniture in the window of a shop, I ran through my plan once again. I hoped this plan was a wily testament to my growing skills as a detective, but I feared it was another rag-bag of unnecessary lies and pointless indiscretions. Briefly, it was this: I had decided to tell the jeweller that I suspected suicide and was convinced that Cara's attempt to sell the jewels was connected. I should ask him not to tell the Duffys about my interest, and I felt sure that out of common decency, even if not out of any sense of obligation, he would agree. I should begin calmly but was ready to dissolve into tears if the occasion arose and a corner of my handkerchief was soaked in Thawpit to help with the dissolving.

An hour later I was striding out along the pavement again, with my head high and a bounce in my step like the first day of spring and I had swung around the corner past the mahogany furniture and begun the uphill climb before I began to falter. It was true that I had performed brilliantly. The jeweller was flattered by my confidences and only too eager to discuss every detail of his meeting with Miss Duffy. He hoped to be struck dead if he breathed a word of such a distressing thought to her family or anyone else and (my final triumph) he made a cup of tea and put my feet up on a stool when I broke down and 'despite

130

dabbing my eyes' succumbed to a fit of weeping. However, the thought struck me only now that my visit had in fact been a complete failure. Put simply, I had not found anything out. Miss Duffy had said nothing at all about her reasons for selling up, and remarkably little about the jeweller's discovery of the fakes. She had seemed neither very surprised nor suspiciously unsurprised but only rather distant, as though unconcerned in the transaction. This, he had assured me, was not uncommon. Ladies selling their jewels often masked the unpleasant feelings it aroused with haughty remoteness. She had not even reacted when told that, had the jewels been genuine, she would have needed to produce proof of ownership before a sale could go through, but the jeweller considered that this might be put down to, as he called it, breeding.

I was forced to stop at the kerb on George Street while a number of taxis passed and, glancing along, I saw a willowy figure dressed in black emerge from a shop on the other side, followed by another, bulkier, outline in deeper and yet more garish mourning. The second was undoubtedly an upper servant of some description but the first, now walking in my direction, was Clemence Duffy. I scuttled across between taxis and, composing my face into friendly sympathy, approached them.

'Darling,' I exclaimed, attempting to press Clemence to me, maternally. 'What happened to the Lake District? Is your mother better? Not worse, I hope. Not too ill to travel?' Clemence, after recovering from her initial surprise at seeing me and, I expect, at being clasped so inexpertly to my bosom, looked rather pleased, or as pleased as her unanimated face ever did.

'Mummy and Daddy are still at Grasmere but I came home to pack for Lucerne.'

'You're alone?'

'No,' she said, waving vaguely behind her. 'Nanny's here.' I nodded towards the elderly servant who hovered nearby clutching a bulky parcel done up in brown paper. 'I'm to go through Cara's things before Mummy comes

131

home, and then there are such a lot of letters to be answered.' I was still puzzled. It was authentic enough that Mrs Duffy might not be up to this, but it looked very odd to leave Clemence to deal with what would have been such upsetting tasks. Even while this fresh evidence that Cara was not really dead cheered me, I suffered exasperation that their act was so unconvincing.

'Besides,' Clemence continued, 'there was something else I particularly wanted to attend to.' She patted the parcel in Nanny's arms and then, struck by a thought, she turned back to me with her sleepy, beatific smile. 'Would you care to join me for luncheon, Dandy? And see it first? It will have to be at home, I'm afraid, because of the mourning, but you're very welcome.'

We lunched off boiled chicken and asparagus jelly against a background of studied gloom in the dining room at Drummond Place, the shades being half-pulled, the room unadorned by any flowers, and the maid who served us red-eyed and sniffing. The servants at any rate were responding suitably to what they believed about Cara's death, however bogus the family might appear to my over-informed eye. Afterwards, we carried coffee upstairs to a sitting room which, being at the back of the house, was allowed its full measure of sunlight. It was hardly more comfortable for that, however, being antiseptically modern. The white floor shone like glass, making one fearful to walk upon it too heavily, and it was hard to believe that one might sit on one piece of the gleaming white furniture and put down a coffee cup on another, so like sculpture and so unlike chairs and tables did they seem.

Clemence caught me gaping and said: 'Mummy just had it done. Isn't it delightful?'

I thought it looked silly against the Georgian windows and under the Georgian cornice, but could hardly say so. Luckily, Clemence turned from me and pounced on the brown paper parcel laid on a white cube of a table before the Georgian fireplace and began to pull off the wrapping.

It was a large black leather book, wider than it was long, its covers held shut by a ribbon. Untying this and flicking aside a sheet of tissue paper, she pushed it towards me and I saw it was a photograph album. The first photograph was of Cara. I caught my lip in my teeth to stifle a gasp; it was so beautiful, so light and soft-looking, quite unlike the usual snaps in which moon-faced freaks barely recognizable as one's relations sit propped up like corpses. In this photograph, Cara, close up, only her head and shoulders showing, was standing in a room posed very casually with one elbow leaning on a chimneypiece, and although she was evidently facing the window (for I could see it reflected in the glass above the fireplace behind her) something to do with the light bouncing from behind as well as in front gave her an intensified version of that back-to-the-window glow every woman tries to arrange whenever she can. It was not just the light, though. Cara's expression, too, was like a distillation of all that was so charming about her. She had her face half-turned away as though shy and was smiling the curling smile I remembered, but with such a serenity that, forgetting for a moment that she was still alive, I felt a lump form in my throat.

'Look,' said Clemence, turning the stiff page, 'they're not all of her.' She showed me pictures of Mrs Duffy and of Clemence herself in the same room, sitting in plump armchairs or standing against the windows, sprigged cotton curtains billowing around them.

'These are heavenly, Clemence,' I said, turning to the next, which had Mrs Duffy and Clemence sitting at a garden table with teacups. With a jolt, I recognized the shingle path and the white fence in the background and realized that this was the beach cottage. Quite a substantial structure, I saw, almost to the point that calling it a cottage was an affectation, and I thought again about the way it had been reduced to such a small pile of ash. My detective instinct prompted a question.

'Did someone from the photographer's shop come down for a visit, then?' I thought that such an individual would surely have something to tell me, and felt a surge of excitement to think of him five minutes' walk away in George Street. Alec would be astounded.

'No,' said Clemence. 'These are mine. I mean, I took them.'

'Well, they're splendid,' I said. 'People usually look like propped-up . . . dolls, don't they? But these are lovely.' Clemence's face does not pucker into easy frowns any more than it breaks into grins, but something did happen in her expression then.

'I hope Mummy doesn't mind,' she said. 'Only I went to such trouble.'

'Of course she won't mind, Clemence dear. She will be delighted. What luck that you should have taken them. And what extraordinary luck that they should not have been lost in the fire too.'

We were both silent for a moment considering this. Then Clemence blinked and her next words came in the quiet, careful voice she had used in the court.

'I carry all my plates together in a special case – the fresh ones and the ones I've used – so naturally I had them with me on our walk.'

'Naturally,' I agreed.

Her face smoothed again. 'I took the plates into Rollins' when I got home,' she said. 'And I didn't ask them to hurry or anything, so imagine how touching when they telephoned this morning to say they had made them up already. They must have done it because of Cara, don't you think? They must have heard.'

'People are sometimes too extraordinarily kind,' I said.

'Yes,' said Clemence. 'Only it's not – I just hope Mummy isn't angry.'

I could see how one might as easily think it ghoulish as touching, but I gave what I hoped was a reassuring smile, and went back to the topic of the photographs.

'How did you take the ones with you in them?' I asked, examining the picture of the garden more closely. Photographic tricks held no interest for me, but I thought a good

134

run on her hobby horse would put Clemence back at her ease. However, when she spoke she sounded strained, starting the speech with a strangulated little laugh.

'Oh, Cara took that one. She wasn't very good at it. Look, you can see this is not as clear as some of the others.' I could indeed. This was much closer to Hugh's efforts with his Box Brownie, nothing like as beautiful as the picture of Cara in the house. Clemence cleared her throat. 'She got very cross with me,' she said, 'when I tried to explain what she was doing wrong. I suppose I must have been lecturing. One does, doesn't one, when it's one's passion. And then she flounced off. Look.'

The next picture was of the same scene with Cara disappearing into the french windows and Mrs Duffy caught between her camera smile and the expression of annoyance which was just about to replace it.

'I didn't really mean for this one to be in the album,' she said, 'since we were quarrelling.'

'Oh, but such a little quarrel,' I said, meaning it, thinking that this could not possibly be the quarrel of which Agnes Marshall had spoken. Indeed, it was hard to reconcile these touching pictures with the kind of quarrel Mrs Marshall had felt was going on. Perhaps she was a scandal-monger after all in her own small way.

'Yes,' said Clemence, still rather brittle. 'And we made it up beautifully anyway. A man came past walking his dog – hideous little thing – and I asked him if he would take a snap of all three of us together, but he was hopeless! I tried everything except writing it all down for him. After he had wasted three plates we gave up, and by that time Cara had such giggles that she had forgiven me.' She stopped tittering and sighed. 'Of course if I had known that it was our very last chance, I should have persevered with the silly man.' With that, she turned another smile on me, stretched lips and watchful eyes above. Before I was forced to think up something to say, however, we heard the muffled peal of the front doorbell which was clearly bound up in rags for mourning, and Clemence leapt to her feet.

'Telegrams,' she said. 'Such heaps of telegrams and letters every day. I had better deal with them, if you'll excuse me, Dandy. The parlour maid was in floods yesterday and forgot to tip the boy.'

'Can't your butler –?' I began, thinking that the paragon of propriety who had admitted me on my first visit would not stand for the young mistress out on the step tipping the telegram boy.

'He's not fit to be seen, I'm afraid,' said Clemence. 'Drunk. He adored Cara.' Her voice was cold, although whether from jealousy or from disapproval of the butler's collapse I could not say.

'We all did,' I said, and then grimaced at my own sugariness. 'She was –'

'You hardly knew her,' said Clemence, startling me with her vehemence, but as I peered into her face to see what she could possibly mean by such a thing, the shutters came down, the bell clanked again, and she left.

This was getting stranger and stranger by the minute. I did not recognize, and nor would anyone who had known Mama and the girls for more than a week, the joyous rustic trinity in these photographs. But there it all was, incontrovertible, interleaved with tissue and bound in leather for all to see. Unless, I thought. Unless . . . Of course! This was part of the cover-up. For after all, was this record of a perfectly ordinary week in the country not somewhat too complete to be believed? Was it not, in fact, a deliberate attempt to construct a fairy tale, told in pretty pictures, of a happy family and especially a happy Cara? And when one thought about it, really, the angelic beam of Cara in that close-up was rather an over-egged pudding. Even some of Clemence's oddness began to make sense. The album had clearly been planned to dispel any suspicions of suicide. These suspicions had not arisen in the end (except in Alec and me) but Clemence was too proud of her own cleverness to resist showing off to someone. Hence my very warm welcome and invitation for luncheon at a time when one might more naturally have expected her to be shunning all company.

They had all the practical details very much off pat, I thought. But they just did not quite get the emotions right. Either too little, as when Alec and I first came upon them in the parlour at the Murray Arms, or too much as when Mrs Duffy suddenly took to her bed or languished in Grasmere sending her now only daughter home alone. And Clemence today was making the same hash of it: more interested in how her plates had turned out than in the face of her dead sister, and then brusque to the point of rudeness trying to amend things.

I perused the photographs again, this time somewhere between cynicism and a grudging admiration for how it had all been managed. Clemence really was an excellent photographer, and quite an actress besides. The little sisterly quarrel was a nice touch, as was the bumbling man with the dog. I wondered if he was real. Might it be worth going back down to Galloway, or sending Alec, to seek him out? Probably not, since whatever he had to tell us would not answer any of the big questions such as where Cara might have gone. Or where the diamonds had gone for that matter.

Thinking of the diamonds suddenly made me remember Silas and Daisy with a guilty start – I was disgusted with the way I kept forgetting about Silas and Daisy – but with them now in mind, I began to feel less generously disposed to these photographs. And their artistic merit did not actually bear repeated examination, I found, excepting perhaps the one of Cara posed inside the cottage. And something about that was beginning to bother me.

I turned back to the start to look through the whole collection again with an objective eye. There was another of Cara which I now saw for the first time. Another in the same pale dress, but this time leaning, laughing, over a wooden fretwork banister in a painted staircase, her hem drooped to her feet by her stoop, her hair ruffled out of smoothness and glowing as the sun shone through it from

137

the elegant sash window on the landing behind her. In this picture she looked, quite simply, like an angel. A bobbed and shingled angel in a crêpe-de-Chine frock and comfortable shoes, to be sure, but again my conviction of her safety wavered.

I was still gazing at the angel-on-the stairs picture, when Clemence came back into the room and I saw a flare of something on her face as she caught sight of me bent studiously over the album. Aha! I thought. You didn't mean to leave me alone with this for quite that long, did you?

'This one is simply divine,' I said, and showed her. I expected some kind of reaction, naturally, but not what came. She winced and then to get control of herself she made a sudden gesture which drew the corners of her mouth down and made the tendons of her neck leap out briefly. I tried to behave as though I had not seen this curiously unsettling little show but at the same time I tried to fix everything about it in my mind to pore over later.

'You know, Clemence dear,' I said, 'you are very talented. I should love to see what you would be capable of in a studio if these snaps are anything to go by. Have you ever thought of it?' Having thus praised her, I thought, into malleability, I went on: 'And how about making another copy of this album for Alec Osborne? He would be utterly – well, I daresay enchanted is not quite the right word, is it? But I think it's an idea you should consider.' What I wanted, of course, was a copy I could study at leisure and I thought I could chance laying it on a bit thick; the worst that could come would be that she would think me a dreadful Victorian and this she probably did already. 'After all they *were* engaged, and it would be a great shame if she just slipped out of his life completely. Even if it is too painful for him to look through just now, it would be something for him to treasure in years to come.'

Clemence stared at me, chewing her lip, and I thought I could imagine at least some of the conflict that fluttered inside her. She could not think of a single good reason why she should not make an album for Alec, but she could not agree to something so far outside her mother's plan without at least asking Mrs Duffy first. And although she was sure that Mama's answer would be the firmest possible 'no', Clemence's own pride in her pictures made her want to say 'yes'. Despairing of her ever answering, I took pity and said goodbye.

Alec was staying at the George. We had planned to meet there for luncheon if our allotted jobs were finished on time and for tea if not, but since I left Clemence at a quarter past two I could not be quite sure which it was to be. Luncheon at the George does not have quite the ring of sobriety and respectability that 'tea at the George' evokes. Tea at the George goes along in the imagination with pantomimes, stiff taffeta petticoats and the smell of mothballs from Nanny's best winter coat and so I was torn between a desire to share my morning's gleanings as soon as I could and a desire to be too late, so that it was tea blameless tea that we shared. I supposed, irrationally, that our lunching together would bring Renée Gordon-Strathmurdle to town, to the George, and to the adjoining table as though on a pulley. And what if it did? Luncheon was hardly breakfast in bed. The only explanation for these twinges of conscience was that spying and snooping on those who thought me their friend – and doing it for a fee! – was interfering with my judgement regarding all kinds of innocence and guilt.

Confirming, as always, that the world operates quite independent of my desires, the waiter assured me that 'my party' was still there and led me to a quiet table at the back of the dining room where Alec sat, not quite concealed behind a parlour palm, but with that general idea.

'I've lunched already,' I said as I sat, waving away a menu. Then I turned to Alec. 'And I'll bet you can't guess where?'

'Two mugs of soup in the back shop of the jeweller's?'

139

said Alec, playing along. He could see that I was bubbling over with something.

'Tell me yours first,' I said firmly, determined that my meeting with Clemence should be the finale.

Alec had made no progress at all.

'I dined at Posso last night,' he began. 'Dalrymple's place, you know, down in the Borders, but Chrissie Dalrymple had nothing to offer. She hasn't seen or spoken to Cara since Christmastime. A little coolness, I imagine, arising from not being asked to be a bridesmaid.'

'Well, what does she expect?' I said. Chrissie Dalrymple towered over Cara and was stones heavier, with a round pink face and bright yellow hair that stood out all around like a thatched roof. I should not have wanted her in my wedding photographs either.

'Yes,' said Alec, clearly not following. 'They were school friends, though, and as thick as thieves, united in their dislike of Clemence, Cara always said. Clemence was just a year above and fearfully haughty as a result, I gather. Anyway, I had thought if Cara had anything she didn't want to get around her current set, but which was pressing too heavily on her to be kept quite secret, an old school friend would be just the thing. As it was, I achieved nothing except indigestion from too much high game and sympathy.'

I could well imagine. Chrissie Dalrymple would have been cock-a-hoop to have Alec, newly eligible, descend.

'She told me not to feel that I had to answer her letter of condolence when it arrived, if I preferred instead to come back to Posso and chat again in person.' Alec spoke with the bleak panic of a man accidentally drifting closer than he cares to towards a girl of greater determination and less politeness than himself. I tried to hide my smile as I answered.

'That's a thought, though, isn't it?' I said. 'Letters of condolence? I mean, one always is quite desperate for something different to say, isn't one? And the last con-

140

versation one had with the – in this case temporarily – departed would be a natural source of material.'

Alec summoned a waiter and asked if any letters had arrived for him during the morning.

'Of course, my mother might not be sending them on at all,' he said. 'I might have them to look forward to whenever I go back to Dorset. Anyway, while we're waiting – this morning I had coffee with three very good friends of Cara's whom I have met upwards of half a dozen times but whom I still think of interchangeably as Boo, Koo and Shoo. Do you know who I mean?'

'Booty, Koo and Sha-Sha,' I said, laughing again. 'Yes, I know them very well, but how spine-chilling for you, darling.' Alec nodded fervently.

'I *had* thought that grief might have tempered them somewhat, and they are very shaken, but all it meant was that they were even more inclined to throw their arms around me and each other and had lost all sense of conversational restraint. If I hadn't known she was going riding afterwards, I should have said the tall, dark one was drunk.' The waiter, approaching with a large stack of letters, caught this most unfortunate snippet, and put them down on the tablecloth with rather a smack.

'Good old Mother,' said Alec. 'I paid extremely close attention to their outpourings, Boo-boo and Co-co I mean, and was on the lookout for any sign that one might have something to say to me she might not want the others to hear, but I'm fairly certain there's nothing. I went as near as I dared to asking. So, neither Cara's oldest chum nor any of the current gang seem to suspect a thing.'

He picked up the pile of letters and began to leaf through them absently, then suddenly stopped and sat very upright staring at one of the envelopes. He let the others fall to the table and held this one up in front of his face.

'It's from Cara,' he said and turned it towards me. There was his name and address written in the same, rather faint, rather loopy hand, familiar now from the two letters we had both pored over at the gallery and again in Gatehouse. Without another word, Alec slit open the seal with a table knife and began to read out loud.

'"Dear Alec, I hardly know how to begin to say how sorry I am."' He gave a high-pitched exhalation of breath that was almost laughter. 'Dated the day before yesterday,' he said, and I felt my eyes fill with tears.

'"I hardly know how to begin to say how sorry I am,"' he read again. '"I am almost too shocked and bewildered to know how to write this letter and I hope you will forgive me if I am clumsy as a result. Your suffering is without a doubt fathoms deeper than mine, but believe me when I say that I loved Cara . . . enough . . . to understand –"' He broke off and stared at the letter, frowning. '"I loved Cara enough to understand what you must be feeling in these first days of your loss and grief."' He turned the letter over and looked at the back of the last sheet. '"With my deepest sympathy, Christine Dalrymple."'

I hied the waiter and demanded that some brandy be brought. Alec's face was the colour of gutter snow under his freckles, and his hand scrabbled around his lapel for several seconds before he managed to extract Cara's two letters from his pocket and shove them towards me.

It was remarkable, so much so that I considered for a moment whether Chrissie's letter of condolence might be from Cara after all and be in some kind of code. A further moment's examination, however, showed me that only the handwriting was identical, the brains behind the two had little in common. Were Chrissie Dalrymple ever in a position to break off an engagement the recipient would be lucky to get away with fewer than ten pages.

The brandy, to which the waiter had added a measure of port off his own bat, quickly brought Alec back to a more usual colour. He shook his head over the letters again and again, and I had cause once more to wonder about his feelings for Cara and also whether he believed in his heart that she was safe, for all the conviction that logic had put in his head.

142

'But it's not really so peculiar,' I said. 'Girls' schools are notorious for jamming one and all into the same mould. Well, no more than boys' schools I daresay. In fact, you know, my own boys are much more like each other after three terms at school together than when they were just two brothers. Last hols Hugh had occasion to slipper them both for –' I broke off, confused. 'Sorry,' I said. 'This can hardly be of any interest.'

'Tell me,' said Alec. 'Tales from the nursery are just what I need for a minute while I try to stop shaking.' I went on reluctantly, tales from the nursery not being what I liked to think of as my forte.

'Donald had gone off shooting rabbits after being expressly forbidden to do so, since there was a real shoot that day with several inexperienced guns and we didn't want the boys getting peppered. Well, they were suspiciously quiet all morning but when Hugh bellowed up the nursery stairs demanding to know if they were there, they answered one after the other that yes they were but they were in a ticklish spot with a recalcitrant engine and couldn't come down. Imagine our surprise, then, an hour later when Donald arrived in a neighbour's motor car wrapped in a blanket, having fallen in the burn trying to get home without being seen. Little Teddy had answered for both, you see. "What is it, Daddy, we're dashed busy." And then "Yes, Dad, we're almost there with this blasted engine. Must we come down?"

'This wouldn't have been possible before they went off to school. One spoke like Hugh and one spoke like his hero Angus, the cook's son. Now they both just sound like schoolboys, like every schoolboy, as though they were turned out of a press in the dormitory at the beginning of their first term to be fostered on us.'

Alec looked quite calm again now, even managed a laugh, and I thought it was safe to turn the talk to my eventful morning. The failure of the visit to the jeweller was dealt with first and then I settled with some relish to what came after. I told him, without editorializing in the least, about Clemence being at home with Nanny to 'take care of things', and my puzzlement got its corroboration from his.

'However,' I said, 'all that is nothing.' I hunched forward over the table on my elbows and told him all about the photograph album, my idea about its original purpose, my disquiet about its contents and Clemence's start of alarm at finding me poring over it.

'You're quite right,' said Alec. 'There is a strong smell of fish here.'

'And,' I said, becoming more sure with the warmth of his agreement, 'I can't help but wonder about such a painstaking record of what is ostensibly a very ordinary week in the country *en famille*. And then the chumminess in the pictures – it's absolutely at odds with what we've heard about the frosty atmosphere.'

'But what exactly have we heard about the atmosphere?' said Alec. 'Remind me what you were told.'

I cast my mind back over the Mrs Marshalls' accounts and came to a rueful conclusion that I had made a great deal out of very little, merely that Cara and Clemence seemed not to want to be companions to one another and that Clemence was grumpy. Even added to the strange decision to all but dispense with a housekeeper, it did not amount to much. I fell silent, disappointed.

'But tell me some more about these feelings you had about the photographs,' said Alec. 'What did you think was wrong with them?'

'That's just it,' I said. 'I don't know. Only that there was something off. Not just the fact of their existence; we agree on that. But something about the photographs themselves just wasn't right.'

'Say again what they were,' said Alec. 'As much as you can remember.' To my surprise he got out a pencil and a pad of paper and poised himself to make notes.

'Well, there were the two portraits of Cara in the crêpe-de-Chine fr –' I broke off. 'The two portraits taken inside the cottage, I mean. And some of Clemence and of Lena in the same room, although these were not portraits exactly, more like snaps. So it's almost as though they knew that the pictures of Cara were the ones that mattered and that's not right, is it? Then there were some taken in the garden which were very pretty. Everyone under a tree in blossom with the french windows open to the house. Really very happy pictures, except that Cara got cross with Clemence for telling her what to do and flounced off, spoiling one. The only other I remember is of Lena and Cara on a cliff-top with their dresses blowing about in the wind. Clemence must have scrambled down and taken it from the beach, unless Lena and Cara climbed the cliff to have it taken. Oh, Alec, I don't know. I need to have another look at them.'

'Hmm. Hard to see how you could do that without making Clemence's whiskers twitch,' said Alec.

'Which is exactly why I want you to pester her for a set of your own. Or at the very least you should take a good look at them to see if you can spot whatever it is that's bothering me. As a man, you might alight on different aspects of . . .' I fell silent, chasing a wisp of thought.

'What?' said Alec, but I shushed him.

'Men and women, what was I thinking? Men and women . . . Oh!' I sat up and slapped my hands down on the table. 'I think I know what it is. Read me back exactly what you wrote down, Alec darling.' He did so and before he was finished I interrupted him.

'Yes, I'm sure I'm right. It's the crêpe-de-Chine dress. They are supposed to be a record of a week in the country. A whole week. But don't you see? Cara's wearing the same crêpe-de-Chine afternoon frock in every one of them. And that's not all.' I stopped and stared down at the tablecloth trying to summon the pictures back before my eyes.

'The picture on the cliff-top,' I said. 'The picture on the cliff-top has the sun behind them, that is, on the east, making it morning.' The white cloth was dancing before my eyes, little purple and yellow spots blooming in it as

I tried to concentrate. I shut my eyelids tight and thought furiously, trying to call to mind every detail.

'Were you ever at the cottage?' I asked. 'I should love to know where the landing window sat in relation to the compass, because in the photograph with Cara looking over the banisters the sun is simply pouring in.'

Alec shook his head.

'They'd only just got the place. This was their first visit to it.'

'Well, Scottish architecture,' I said. 'Not exactly varied. I bet the staircase went up from the front and turned making the landing to the back and thus the landing window face east. Morning again, you see. And therefore extremely odd for Cara to be wearing a crêpe-de-Chine dress. That's it. The pictures were all taken in one frantic session. Now, why should that be?'

Alec whistled softly and clapped his hands.

'Well done,' he said. 'I should never have thought of that. But I wonder why *they* didn't? Three ladies. Why didn't they think to change their clothes?'

'Perhaps they didn't have time,' I said, trying to remember if in fact all three ladies had been in the same clothes in all pictures. I only seemed to remember Cara, gleaming in her pale frock, and could not bring the others to mind.

'Presumably,' I went on, 'they were trying to make a record of Cara's presence throughout the week when in fact she was leaving in time to get far away before the fire, her "death", and any investigation. What odds that if we managed to find the man with the dog who botched the picture of them all together, he'd tell us not only that it was morning but that it was the start of the week.'

'I'll bet that's it,' said Alec. 'I'll bet if you went back now, Dandy, and asked your Mrs Marshalls just when they saw Cara, they would tell you they saw a great deal of her at the very start of the visit and then not again. Shades of your little boys, don't you think?'

'But how can she have gone?' I said, coming back down

to earth with a thump. 'Never mind why or where. How can she have got away without anyone seeing her? She had no car and there is no train station within miles and rather few buses, never mind that Cara travelling alone on the Gatehouse bus would have been pretty conspicuous to all the interested locals.'

'Well, consider this,' said Alec. 'We've been thinking that they went to Kirkandrews because it was a quiet spot to stage a fire, but what, when you get right down to it, is its main feature?' I looked at him blankly, and he continued: 'The sea, Dandy, it's on the coast. And how better to get far away with the greatest possible discretion than in a boat?'

'It's all a bit Bonnie Prince Charlie,' I said. 'But I suppose you may be right. Although, if someone was coming to get Cara in a boat, then they might just as easily have come in a car. We hadn't thought of her being fetched before. I wish I did have a good excuse to go back to Gatehouse and quiz the Mrs Marshalls.' I was speaking idly.

'And find the man with the dog and try to find out if someone saw a boat,' said Alec, who clearly was not.

'I think the local fishermen might be more in your line,' I said, but Alec shook his head.

'We can't possibly both go again. You need a plausible motive for your return and I should only undermine it. Besides, I intend to cultivate Clemence and get a hold of those photographs by hook or by crook. I might just let slip to Kiki and Kuku that the album exists and let Clemence try to resist their attempts to winkle a copy out of her.'

I was rather hurt that Alec felt he needed to see them for himself, as though my conclusions could not be trusted, and my face must have shown some emotion, which he correctly interpreted.

'I'm sure you're right,' he said. 'Don't, please, be in any doubt about that, Dandy. But the time may be coming close when we find ourselves trying to convince someone that more official investigation is needed, and at that point we shall need some proof.'

147

'So I'm off to Gatehouse again,' I said. 'What on earth am I going to tell Hugh this time?'

Alec had already stopped listening, I think, although he answered, after a fashion: 'Say you've gone to see a man about a dog.'

Chapter Ten

After a long, fruitless attempt to think up something better, I did, in fact, in the end, tell Hugh that I had gone to see a man about a dog.

Clemence had described the one being walked by the man who tried to help them with their pictures as 'a hideous little thing' and for some reason I got it into my head that this meant a Jack Russell terrier. Assuming her to be as snobbish about dogs as most people are, I felt sure that any of the hideous breeds which happened to have some social cachet – bulldogs, King Charles spaniels, all the bulging of eye and bald of bottom – she would perceive with scrupulous correctness as adorable, but that a sweet little Jack Russell terrier would be an affront.

So I told Hugh in an innocent voice at breakfast, that whilst in Galloway I had met a man whose terrier bitch had recently been brought to bed and that I had resolved on going back to procure one of the puppies. Hugh looked rather pulled about by this. He has always despised what he calls my silliness about Bunty, not seeing why she should not sleep and be fed with his dogs, and the news was most welcome that I was considering another to dilute my adoration, and a terrier at that. On the other hand, there was the possibility that two dogs on cushions in my sitting room being fed chicken from two little china dishes might only be twice as annoying. I have to say I do not agree with Hugh's assessment of my sentimentality over Bunty. She is simply my companion, as the hairy pack which follows him around is his, and since I spend my

149

days inside in the comfort of my sitting room it is only common sense that she should be clean and sweet-breathed, while his dogs can with just as much common sense be reeking of carrion and caked in mud as he and they tramp around the woods and farms. Besides, Bunty is a Dalmatian and it is quite simply a waste of God's considerable efforts to let a Dalmatian get dirty.

'I thought you would approve,' I said. 'The breed as a whole and these puppies' parents in particular are excellent molers.' Hugh's ears perked up at this. He is inordinately fond of his gardens, to the point of being quite peculiar at times, and we were suffering just then from a savage attack of moles, causing him acute pain each morning as he surveyed the desecration of yet more of the sward. Add to this the lamentable fact that a good mole-catcher is one thing the neighbourhood of Gilverton lacked (what mole-catchers there were being variously incompetent, lazy and, in one case, drunk by noon) and it is easy to see why a Jack Russell terrier from a talented moling lineage might be a very welcome addition to the household.

For one dreadful moment I thought I had gone too far and he was going to suggest he come with me but, thinking quickly, I put a stop to it.

'I shall go in the motor car and take Grant with me this time,' I said. 'And Bunty, of course. There's no use in bringing home a puppy she hasn't met and might not take to.' He disappeared behind his newspaper with a deep frown and one of those little harumphs he has begun to emit since he turned forty. Hugh is bored and pained by Grant's and my conversations and would have been irritated beyond anything by the sight of my letting Bunty choose a puppy. I myself was quite looking forward to this bit, until I remembered that it was part of my cover story and was not actually going to happen.

Mrs McCall was delighted to see me again, all the more so since this time I was travelling as she obviously thought I should, with my maid and my chauffeur, and she took to

150

Bunty immediately although not to the extent of letting her sleep in my bedroom; she treated this suggestion of mine as a joke.

Early the following morning I got Drysdale to drop me off at a convenient spot north of the patch of coast in question and arranged to be met again on the road to Borgue in two hours' time. The morning was fresh and bright, a stiff sea breeze making me glad I had put a great deal of cream on my face but bringing no low cloud to threaten my walk. I had a snapshot of Cara, taken from Alec's wallet, to jog memories and Bunty was straining to be off, plunging around with excitement and wagging her whole body from the shoulders backwards in delight.

'That's a grand-looking beastie,' said a voice behind me, and I turned to see a young man in corduroys and a rather shabby mackintosh smiling at Bunty as he came towards us. 'As they say in these parts,' he went on. 'What a beauty.' He was not, after all, I saw as he drew nearer, a young man in the usual sense of the phrase, being rather creased about the eyes as well as the mackintosh, but 'young man' was his type in that he looked unburdened the way young men do, and utterly unmarried.

I looked about him for a dog of his own, thinking what luck it would be if this were the bumbling photographer already. There was no sign of one, but I tried my theory anyway.

'Yes, she's a dear,' I said, falling into step with him as it seemed our paths both lay towards the beach. 'Do you have a dog of your own? Only I'm on the hunt for someone around here – not sure who exactly – who has some Jack Russell puppies going begging.' I stopped short, too late. I should never find an unknown man with a dog of some inelegant kind by making it a bitch, having it pregnant and dreaming up a breed for it all out of my own fluff-filled head. 'Or so I heard. But I daresay the puppies are spoken for, if they even exist. Village gossip being what it is there's a fair chance that some blameless little dog just happened to have a large meal of rabbit one day. Do you?

151

Have a dog, I mean?' I tried a light laugh, as though unaware of or at least unconcerned by the inanities I was spouting.

'Cats,' said the young man. 'Cats for me every time, I'm afraid. Although this handsome creature gets close.' With that he tipped his hat and disappeared into an opening in the hawthorn hedge which marked the start of a path.

'Faint praise for you, Bunty,' I muttered.

The walk along the cliff-tops was splendid although I made no further progress with the mystery man or his hideous little dog. None of the lounging youths or bustling old women I met was able to think of any such pair who walked along the coast, although I established that Sandy Marshall had a collie and that another branch of the seemingly endless Marshall family had a fearful mongrel; 'mongrel' excited me for a moment, since I could guess what Clemence would make of one, but it was clear from its description that it was far too big for the role. 'Feet the size of your face, madam,' said my informant, an image which made me hope I never encountered the thing. Eventually, I was persuaded by an aged worthy that I was wasting my time: 'It could easily have been a tripper, a tourist, a visitor or even a hiker, madam, come to that.' I agreed ruefully that it could be any one of these, whatever the differences were.

When the cliffs dipped into grassy hummocks, I scrambled down on to the beach, not wanting to walk through Kirkandrews and have to pass the burnt patch where the cottage used to be if I could help it. Presently, I identified the spot at which Clemence must have taken the photograph of Cara and Lena on the cliff-top; I remembered the jagged look of the rock, and that tortured little hawthorn clinging to the lower slopes had shown up clearly on the snap. One very interesting thing I noticed was that there was no easy path from the cliff just there, and so to set this picture up Clemence must have brought her camera and other accoutrements along the beach from the dip where I had joined it. Had she been photographing rock pools and happened to see her mother and sister above her, it might have made some sense, but trying to pass the scenario off as a plausible posed shot was ludicrous. I stood frowning up at the cliff, puzzled. Even once one knew what one knew, that is that the Duffys were constructing a record, it was still odd for part of that record to be this particular picture. What was gained by Clemence's hauling her things along the shore and by Lena and Cara's long wait at the top in that wind which whipped their clothes into a blur and must have chilled them? My imagined pretext, that Clemence was otherwise engaged and the others were caught impromptu, would only have gained merit if some of Clemence's rock pool studies or whatever were in the album to support it. I wondered what she had done with them, then I shook my head to clear it – there *were* no rock pool studies. I was finding it increasingly difficult to keep a clear boundary between what I actually knew and what I surmised. Worse, conclusions based on my surmising threatened constantly to mix themselves in with known details and when that happened I should be lost.

On I trudged, leaving Bunty racketing about, snuffling in piles of damp seaweed and getting more and more excited by the unfamiliar slip and spray of sand under her paws. Each time I got further from her than she liked she gave a chorus of offended barks and raced to catch me up, overshooting and skidding to a halt in yet more of the enchanting sand and bladderwrack whereupon the whole performance started again. She was therefore quite exhausted by the time we had completed our loop, and she trotted quietly up the lane beside me, seeming – sand and scent apart – in a fit state to go visiting.

Still, I quailed at the thought of young Mrs Marshall's reception – how I pitied Sandy, whom I had imbued with all of his mother's good qualities – so I went straight to the old lady herself. From sitting slumped at the bench by her door after my labours I knew that she had a good view of the sea and I surmised that a cottager only has a bench by her door if it is her habit to sit there, so I felt some hope that she might be able to help me out in the matter of the boat, if indeed this romantic departure of Cara's turned out to be true.

Old Mrs Marshall was 'tickled' to see me, as she put it, and took very readily to the unusually sedate Bunty, but she had no information to offer about any hideous little dog. What's more she looked at me with piercing incredulity when I trotted out this excuse for my presence, and so for a while I sat quietly, looking out to sea – for we were indeed installed on the bench by her door – breathing in the scent of the new mint growing around our feet and enjoying the weak sunshine. I wished for a fishing boat or something to bob into view and help my next round of questions into being, but since nothing came I had to do what I could.

'This is a very quiet spot,' I said.

'Aye, it is that,' said Mrs Marshall. 'A tiny wee cottage in the middle of nowhere.' I recognized the words I had used to Agnes and gave a snort of self-deprecating laughter, only blushing a little.

'Yes, but I meant the sea, really. One expects there to be little boats and ferries and things and yet look at it – nothing. Is it always like that?'

'The boats are out there right enough, off at six this morning and back at six tonight, if they're spared.'

'And are there ever pleasure boats?' I asked. 'Sailing boats? Is there anywhere for them to land hereabouts?'

'Come the summer,' said Mrs Marshall.

I paused again, planning my next enquiry, when she took me by surprise, saying: 'Why don't you just out and ask, madam, whatever it is?' I looked at her from the corner of my eye and saw that although the twinkle was as ready as ever her face was serious, so I took a deep breath and decided to trust her and my instincts about her. I ignored the nagging voice in my head totting up the growing column of people I had either told outright about

154

my theories or told such nonsense that they must suspect something worse.

'I believe,' I said, 'and I am not alone, either – I firmly believe that the fire at the cottage was deliberate, but –' I held up my hand as she started to babble – 'but that no one died in it. We, Miss Duffy's fiancé and myself, both strongly suspect that Cara left the cottage long before the fire, and this is where I hope you can help me.'

'Who would do sich a thing?' said Mrs Marshall. 'There's never been anything like that here in all my days. I mind of a boy in Kirkcudbright years back but he went into a home.' I saw that I should have to explain some more, but I did not even get to finish the first sentence before Mrs Marshall's remonstrances broke out again.

'Nonsense, nonsense, nonsense,' she said, shaking her apron smooth and glaring at me as though I was one of her own many children with a hole in its stocking for her to darn. 'What for why would a woman do sich a thing? After getting the whole place newly painted and papered not a month before. It makes no sense.'

This, it was true, did make no sense that Alec and I had yet established. Why had Mrs Duffy had the cottage decorated when she meant to burn it down?

'Unless it was to guard against these very suspicions,' I said. 'Because she thought that people would say exactly what you have.'

'Och, that's too clever for me,' said Mrs Marshall, getting to her feet and stamping away inside as the kettle started to whistle. I followed after her and leaned against the doorway. She poured a little water into a fat brown teapot, swirled it around and then sloshed it out into the stone sink with a contemptuous gesture that could hardly have been more so had she actually spat. And I agreed. It was too clever a double bluff, but then so was the photograph album, and that was true.

'Did the cottage need the redecoration?' I said, thinking that perhaps if they had stayed a week in real squalor it

155

would look as though they knew in advance that a fire was about to remove the need to do something about it.

'Not a bit of it,' said Mrs Marshall. 'But there! That's "ladies" for you.' I cringed, sure that I came within the sweep of this judgement.

'Mrs Marshall,' I said, summoning courage, 'why not just humour me? What harm will it do at least to discuss it? And imagine if I were right, and poor Cara is not dead after all, only hiding somewhere in some kind of trouble and we find her.' Thus, unscrupulously, I overcame her better judgement and wiping her eyes and sighing, she submitted to my questions at last.

'Think very, very carefully,' I began. 'You know which Miss Duffy is which, don't you? Now, when was the last time you saw Cara?'

'The day before the fire,' said Mrs Marshall. 'Her and her mother were out for a walk after their dinner and I heard them laughing away about something and looked up and there they were.' This was not at all what I wanted to hear and it perplexed me.

'You're sure?' I asked. 'You're absolutely sure that all three ladies were at the cottage right up until the day before the fire?' This would undo my idea about why the photographs had to be taken in just one session.

'No doubt about it,' said Mrs Marshall. 'I even thought there was four of them to start with, till you tellt me that was a maid. Some maid, I thought, you don't see a lass in service dressed like that round here, but she'd be Edinburgh, eh? However, that's by the by. There was definitely three right up until the end. I couldn't get peace for them marching up and down my lane and talk talk talking at the tops of their voices. The mother and the cheery one, then the mother and the miserable one and I thought to myself more than once if those two lassies were mine I'd take the back of my hand to both. The Dear knows why they could not all go out for their walk together and save their mother's feet. That poor woman must have been worn out by the end of the day.'

156

'What do you mean?'

'Or if the lasses were at daggers drawn why could one of them not go out by her own self? Chaperones! I thought we'd got past all that nonsense by now.'

I stared at her, my cup of tea halfway between its saucer and my lips. First one and then the other? I banged down my cup and fished in my pocket for Alec's snapshot of Cara.

'Tell me who this is, Mrs Marshall,' I demanded. She took the snap and holding it at arm's length for her long sight she scrutinized it for an agonizing time before pronouncing.

'That's thon wee maid I saw, and dear God in heaven, this get-up's even worse than the other one. Where do they get the money to dress like that? I'm wondering if I'm not too old to go into service in Edinburgh myself.'

'This,' I said, coming to stand behind her and look over her shoulder at the smiling face under its velvet hat and over its squashy fox fur, 'this is Cara Duffy. Now, tell me again exactly when you saw her.'

It took a good half-hour and another pot of tea for Mrs Marshall to get off her chest everything that she knew and everything she felt, and to decide whether it was wickedness or merely cheek. The bare bones of it were that she had seen Cara pedalling furiously in the direction of Borgue on Tuesday evening and had not seen her return. No unknown boat and no car at all had been seen or heard. Neither Mrs Marshall nor, we were sure, her daughter-in-law had seen 'the girls' together at any time. I cursed my own stupidity as I remembered young Mrs Marshall's calling them two peas in a pod and old Mrs Marshall herself not being able to tell which was which. Clemence and Cara Duffy were the least like one another of any pair of sisters one could hope to see, and only a dolt like me would not have heard alarm bells long before now.

'Aye well,' she concluded at last. 'It's a wicked thing to do and I'm glad I'll never likely see them again for I could not promise to bite my tongue and let them think they'd

157

fooled me. But praise God that lassie didn't go up in flames after all, madam, and I hope you get to the bottom of it so's I can tell everyone, for I'm sure I'm not the only one that cannot sleep for thinking about it.'

'Oh, I'll get to the bottom, Mrs Marshall,' I said. 'Don't worry about that. They've made far too many stupid mistakes for me not to. I can hardly believe they let Cara cycle away in full view of whoever happened to look and see her. Such a silly risk to take.'

This thought was still troubling me as I made my way back down the lane at last. Time was getting on, but Drysdale would come and look for me if I missed our rendezvous, I was sure, and I wanted to go and stare. Now I knew for a fact that a fraud had been perpetrated, I felt no concern at all at being seen standing there like a ghoul. I passed Sandy Marshall's cottage and carried on to the road end and the start of the dunes, then turned left along the path to the Duffys' cottage gate and stopped. The blackened depression in the earth and sudden cutting off of the bright shingle path seemed even more grotesque than they had before. It ought not to have been so, now that I knew no one had died there, but perhaps it was because I had now seen the place for myself. I had seen the photograph of the tea-table under the tree, the blossom-heavy branches in the foreground half-hiding the cottage behind. Now the tree – cherry, I rather thought – had its blooms and soft green leaf buds shrivelled and browned on one side by the heat of the flames. I felt my mouth twist in distaste and I turned away. Then I turned slowly back, looking at the tree and trying to summon the image of the cottage behind it, with its funny little peaked windows and something else I knew had been there but could not bring to mind. The branches of blossom, the upper part of the house showing through it here and there, and what? I stood opening and shutting my eyes, trying to dredge up the picture as though from my boots, until Bunty, sensing my tension perhaps, or maybe just bored, began to whine.

When I emerged on to the lane again, I noticed a second path leading off directly opposite, suggesting another house. Immediately, I remembered Mrs Marshall's scorn about 'they wooden hooses'. There must be another; the Duffys' was one of a pair. I walked along the narrow path and sure enough around a bend and past a clump of gorse lay another white gate and another shingle path. Even though I had hoped for it, it stopped me short to see a cottage identical to the one I had glimpsed in the photograph album, as though the patch of black earth was a lie. I crept forward and stood at the fence.

It was a pretty house of the kind one must call a cottage despite its size, although a very different sort of cottage from the Marshalls' homesteads. It had a wide porch, bounded by decorative wood banisters, and the peaked dormer windows I remembered to its upstairs. Most sweetly of all it had a single chimney right in the middle of its roof which made it look like a toffee apple standing on its head with its handle sticking out at the top. I felt a stirring of misgiving again, one that I could not quite place, but before I could give it my attention I was startled by the sound of a door creaking open, and the untidy young man with the cats appeared on the porch.

'Hello again,' he said, amicably enough. Certainly as amicably as I deserved, leaning on his gate and staring at his house.

'I was just admiring your adorable chimney,' I said, adding nothing to the store of dignity which my earlier ramblings on dogs had left me. However, the young man merely laughed and looked upwards.

'I think it looks like a sink plunger,' he said. 'Rather inconvenient to tell the truth, but even in a wooden house the chimney must be brick and it's easier to make one stack in the middle and have all the fires opening off it. And fires and wooden houses are rather a hot topic at the moment, aren't they? If you'll pardon my pun.' I flushed, realizing that he thought I was sightseeing, come like some villager to gawp at the nearest thing to the place it all happened.

'Inconvenient?' I said, making conversation to show him I was unaffected by his insinuation and plumping for the only bit of his speech which seemed to offer scope for further chat.

'The central chimney. Having to have all the rooms open off one another without a hallway and having all the fireplaces across the corners.' He stretched luxuriously, a stretch with just a suggestion of a scratch at the end of it. 'Not bad for me since I live on my own and can draw up my chair and hog it, but I'd hate to be jostling with a wife and a gaggle of frost-bitten children.'

Feeling very much that I represented the world's producers of unwanted brats, I withdrew from this unpleasant individual and took myself off to meet my motor car.

Frustration was evidently the order of the day, however, since Drysdale and I now chugged back to Gatehouse at an infuriating five miles an hour behind a coal cart whose driver seemed not at all concerned with our plight. And when we turned into the wide main street of the town and Drysdale pulled out to work off the tension by roaring the last five hundred yards with his foot to the floorboards, I frustrated him yet further, for having spied 'E. McNally' painted on the side of the cart as we flashed past it, I instructed him to stop while I got out and had a word. I had to ask about Mrs Duffy's coal order, I thought; that final check would establish beyond the doubt we were already beyond that she had set the fire and burned the cottage down.

'Mr McNally,' I called, hurrying forward to catch him before he hefted a sack on to his shoulder. He turned, showing me that spectacularly dirty face that a coalman always has, and for which I have often felt envy, thinking how very satisfying it must be to bathe when one starts out so filthy, and how unlike my own bathing which is almost completely for the sake of form except when I've been hunting. Mr McNally blinked his blue, dolly's eyes in his black face and flashed a friendly smile with his dazzling coalman's teeth.

'I'm Mrs Gilver,' I began. 'A friend of Mrs Duffy, and I was asked by her to take care of settling up with the housekeeper and anything else that was left unfinished in all the confusion.' I waited, hoping that this would be blunt enough. It was not. 'I just wondered, just now when I saw your cart, whether there was anything outstanding that I could take care of.' Still nothing. 'Did Mrs Duffy have a regular delivery and pay up at the end of the season or are you all fair and square? Please don't hesitate at all if you're waiting to be paid – I'm more than happy.' Mr McNally was shaking his head.

'No, ma'am,' he said. 'Mrs Duffy said she'd drop me a note when she was getting low and she paid me when I delivered.'

'But of course you would know not to deliver it now,' I said, making doubly, trebly sure. E. McNally looked at me as though I were an imbecile.

'There wasna any order outstanding, ma'am,' he said. 'But I'll venture if there was I'd have known to ignore it.' I nodded, gave him a little something anyway for his trouble and got back into the car. So, Mrs Duffy was to have dropped a line when the coal got low, and there was the coal hole at Reiver's Rest scraped clean for all to see with no order outstanding. I wondered if this detail had escaped her planning or if she had decided not to advertise in advance the fact that she had used all that fuel in case the news of the fire should jog an uneasy thought and start the coalman's tongue wagging.

Drysdale turned the car again and I knew he took the chance while checking over his shoulder to fire a look at me, searching for some clue as to why I should leap from the car and accost a coalman in the street. His look was matched by that on the face of Mr McNally as he watched me pull away.

Thus after a single day, with my work in Galloway complete, and one or two more of the world's populace now believing me to be an idiot, I headed for home again. I was ready to tell Hugh that the puppies were all ear-marked for friends of the family and that I had changed my mind anyway after both Bunty and I had been snapped at by the mother with her teeth like little icicles and been told by her doting owner that this was something for which the breed was known.

We arrived back at Gilverton just as lamps were being lit, and while Grant took herself off in high dudgeon to unpack the case of clothes for a week's visit she had packed only two days before, I sought out Hugh to tell the tale of woe. I could hear voices from his library and smelled pipe smoke alongside the usual reek of Hugh's cigar so arranging a smile of wifely and hostessly serenity upon my face I threw open the door and strode in. (When visitors are there I do not knock and keep my feet on the hall carpet.)

'Dandy my dear,' said Hugh. (When visitors are there he reacts with delight to any glimpse of me.) 'Just in time. What will you have to drink?'

'Welcome home, Dandy,' said Alec Osborne. 'This is an unexpected bonus, I must say. I feared I might miss you.'

But for some reason the sight of the two of them on either side of the fire like that, a heap of dozing dogs between their feet, presented a domestic and social challenge to which I felt unequal after the long drive and the excitements of the day before. I excused myself hastily, promising that a half-hour's rest should render me fit for the dinner table.

Up in my room, Grant was slamming around with her mouth still set in a grim line but with a tell-tale loosening of her shoulders which told me that she was happiest really to be home again with her own irons and well-drilled laundry maids waiting below. I sat at my dressing table and began to remove hatpins until I caught her eye in the glass. She looked significantly at me and then at my bed where, miracle upon miracle, there against the pillows sat a familiar black leather album tied with a ribbon. I threw off my coat, kicked off my shoes and climbed up on to the counterpane, drawing the album towards me like a lover, sure that inside it cast-iron, rock-solid, gilt-edged answers were soon to be found.

Chapter Eleven

I saw it immediately this time, of course. Added to the fact of Mrs Duffy's redecoration, it was so obvious that I felt some shame for not seeing it before. Because really, how could these dowdy stripes and sprigged muslins have been freely chosen by the same woman who had turned her drawing room at Drummond Place into an ice-cube?

I resolved to subject the idea to my harshest criticism while dressing, and see if it was still standing up by the time I was done. I was late already, but since Grant was in far too foul a temper to be let loose on my hair, I saved myself a good twenty minutes by pulling on a silk turban instead. Thank heavens for turbans in the evening. I hoped they would stay in fashion for ever, or at least until I was old enough to go on wearing them whether they were in or out. I pulled a couple of curls out at the front and tried to make them rest against my forehead, but this was wasting time. I still could not see any flaw in my discovery and could wait no longer to tell it to Alec, nor to quiz him on how he had wrested the album away from Clemence.

When I joined him and Hugh, moreover, I could see from his dancing eyes that he was bursting to tell me. Hugh, though, was well away on the relative merits of dry-stone walls and hedges and I had to wait until we were sitting down to dinner before I got in.

'Tell me, Alec,' I said, 'to what do we owe this pleasure?' For I could not imagine on what pretext he had insinuated himself into my household at less than a day's notice. Hugh is not antisocial but he needs to be led up quite gently to the idea of a single visitor; they require so much more attention than does a crowd of twenty.

'Came to see a horse,' he said.

'Uncommonly decent of you to take the time too,' said Hugh. I, with a wife's keenly attuned sensitivity, understood this to mean that Hugh had mentioned something in passing at Croys and meant nothing by it, so was now more than a little surprised to have it followed through. However, from his tone I also divined that he found Alec Osborne agreeable company and did not therefore mind too much.

'I find myself with time to fill,' said Alec. 'I was expecting this week to be the run-up to a wedding, you know.' Hugh gulped and turned to me beseechingly.

'Have you seen any of the family since we left Gatehouse?' I asked, knowing he had and wanting to know more.

'Yes, indeed,' said Alec. 'Lena is still away of course, but I spent the day with Clemence yesterday. She's bearing up terribly well, and I took three good friends of Cara to visit which I'm sure helped. She seemed very much soothed by them.'

That explained it, I thought. Clemence could not withstand the combined efforts of Koo, Booty and Sha-sha (who could?), hence the presence on my bedside table of the leather volume. I could bet, though, that Clemence would be anything but soothed to reflect on having let it out of her clutches, and if she knew it was here with me she would be having absolute kittens.

'Dreadful, dreadful thing,' said Hugh, and we fell silent. Just as well, perhaps, since we were having mutton and if one does not shut up and eat it while it is hot, especially in a chilly place like our dining room, it can congeal quite horribly before one is halfway done.

I fetched the album down to the drawing room when I left the dinner table, and was sitting staring at the picture of Cara on the landing when the door opened. Hugh and I rarely sat together after dinner and I had expected Alec and him to return to the library. Indeed I was beginning to despair of getting a chance to talk to Alec at all, knowing that he should be out at the stables the next day, but here was a piece of good luck: Alec entered the drawing room alone.

'Hugh asks you to excuse him, but he has work that must be done tonight. Something about a contractor? And asks me to excuse him, and asks me to ask you to excuse him to me, and generally wants us to spend the evening apologizing to each other on his behalf. Are there contractors?'

'There are certainly drains,' I said. 'I rather thought it was clearing, which would suggest plumbers, but it may have been building, so contractors might be indicated.'

'Or perhaps he just can't face it,' said Alec. 'I've noticed people simply not knowing what to say to me.'

I poured him some coffee and decided to indulge in a little straight talking.

'People *don't* know, Alec dear. That is, they don't know – and I didn't myself if it comes to that – how you are taking the whole thing. You don't seem perturbed. And it's not –' I said, holding up my hand to stop him interrupting, 'it's not because you know she's not dead, before you say that. Because it was exactly the same when you thought she was. Bluntly, no one wants to extend the hand of sympathy for a sorrow you don't appear to be suffering.'

Alec came and sat on the other end of the sofa; I think so that he might speak without having to look at me.

'It wasn't a great romance, if you must know.' He spoke with a quiet, hard deliberation as though pushing the words out of himself as one forces notes from a brass horn. 'But I liked her. Well, you know Cara, Dandy – she's impossible not to like. And she seemed to like me, although I admit she seems to like everyone, so I can't feel too flattered.'

'Yes,' I said. 'She's that rare thing: an absolute darling who doesn't make one sick. Less so recently, perhaps. More troubled. But generally, one would rather wonder

166

why she wasn't engaged long ago than marvel at her being so now.'

'Quite,' said Alec. 'So I daresay I should think myself lucky she didn't want a great romance any more than I did. We should have been happy, though, I'm sure. For one thing we had known each other all our lives, or known of each other at least, and that's a start.'

'Yes, you're a distant relation, aren't you?' I said, only now remembering that someone had told me this. 'And so were you always meant for Cara? From the cradle? Very touching.'

'What a Victorian you are,' said Alec, laughing. 'From the cradle, indeed! Cara was just a cousin in Canada as far as I was concerned.'

But there was a shifty defiance about the way he spoke despite the laughter, and I knew he was rattled, embarrassed by more than just my teasing, and I remembered something he had mentioned lightly just in passing.

'The mystery you hinted at, to do with Cara's settlement? Have you any idea what it was?'

I was lucky again; Alec laughed so hard and so long this time that I could not help but join in.

'You should have seven daughters, Dandy, instead of your sons. Talk about Lády Bracknell! But to answer the question . . . I always imagined that Gregory was to settle everything he could on Clemence and felt he couldn't tell me this outright.'

'Why on earth would you think that?' I said. 'Cara is by far his favourite, so much so that I feel sorry for Clemence sometimes.'

Alec turned to face me, to enjoy the look he was about to put on my face.

'I rather thought he would settle what he could on Clemence because Dunelgar, Culreoch and the London house are coming to me. I'm Gregory's heir.'

I choked on my coffee.

'How too Mr Collins for words,' I said at last, and

luckily Alec gave another bark of laughter instead of slamming out of the room as I should have deserved.

'What an idea! What things you do say, Dandy! No, I didn't quite resolve to "make my choice from among his daughters" – although you've no idea what the girls in Dorset would have thought of moving to the Highlands; they shrank away at parties when they found out. Broke into a run, some of them. Anyway, as it turned out, my elder brother . . . And so I might have stayed in Dorset after all.' He laughed again, but this time absolutely mirthlessly, and went on in a loud, blustering voice with a small tremble at the back of it that made me want to take him on to my lap like one of my sons. 'Since I was getting Gregory's pile, I convinced my father to settle on my younger brother after Edward was killed. Now what do you bet Gregory changes his mind and I end my days in a home for old soldiers?'

'But could he change his mind?' I said. 'Isn't it an entail?'

'Liferent,' said Alec. 'I don't think you get entails up here, do you?' I shrugged. 'Meaning he can't sell them but must pass them on along the male line. So, more or less an entail really, except that it needn't be me.'

'But you're an Osborne,' I said. 'Not a Duffy. How can you be male line? I've never understood how Mr Collins can be Mr Bennet's male heir, come to that.'

'My grandfather, Gregory's father's brother, married a Miss Osborne,' said Alec. 'She was an only child and so, much to the delight of her family although to the disgust of his own . . .'

'He changed his name?' I was laughing again.

'It's not so unusual really,' said Alec. 'Much commoner than you'd think.' He was looking away from me again and seemed defiant.

'No!' I said. 'Darling, tell me you weren't going to!'

Alec had the grace to look sheepish.

'As I say, when there's land or loot hanging on it, it's not as unusual as you'd think. And in my case I'd be changing back anyway, to what I should have been if my grandfather hadn't been swayed by the Osbornes.'

'I suppose so,' I said. I thought about all of this for a moment, wondering if it had any bearing on the case. 'It's all very dynastic,' I concluded.

'To tell the truth,' said Alec, 'I hardly thought about it until after the war. When I went off to the front, Lena and Gregory might easily have had a son of their own and I might easily have not come back.'

'Yes,' I said, sobered. 'In 1914, Lena can barely have been forty and the girls were still children. I suppose because they had the two of them so quickly and so close together and then no more, one doesn't think of it. But look at Queen Victoria.'

'Exactly,' said Alec. 'So it was only when I came to visit a year or two ago that I really began to believe in it.'

'And you met Cara again, and your eyes locked over the estate accounts and –'

'Oh, shut up!'

'What if Cara never comes back?' I said. 'And the only way to keep the estate together – your bit and Clemence's bit – is for you to –'

'Will you shut up!' said Alec louder, but still laughing. 'I am not quite such a Mr Collins as to run through the family, even if there is no Mary waiting at the bottom of the barrel.'

'What about the diamonds?' I said. 'Are they part of the "boys only" bit? I must say it's very unfair if they are.'

'Don't know,' said Alec, shortly.

He didn't know? This was strange. Diamonds as precious as the rest of the estate put together and he didn't know whether they were to be his? Or his wife's, if she ever came back. It spoke volumes to his credit to be so unconcerned about their fate, I thought. But did he know they weren't insured? Had I told him that? Or was he perhaps this careless only because he assumed that a huge insurance cheque would be his instead?

Finding the diamonds seemed to be the best idea all

169

round, and the best way to go about it seemed just as clear: find Cara. I turned with relief to something I knew, spreading the album open on the sofa between us. Alec looked as pleased as I was at the change of topic.

'Two pieces of earth-shattering news, darling,' I said. 'These pictures, this one and this one,' I flipped back and forth between the two images of Cara's smiling face, 'were not taken at the cottage at all.'

Alec looked at each them for a long time, then at the others, and began nodding slowly. I was disappointed; I had hoped for a chance to explain. Gratifyingly though, when he spoke at last, he said: 'I think you're right. There's something funny about them, but I can't put my finger on it.'

'Look,' I said, eagerly, bending over the album with my head beside his. 'Here she's resting her arm on a mantelpiece, and it's directly opposite a window, which means it's in the middle of a flat wall. Now the fireplaces in the cottage were all set across the corners of the room. Look at the picture of the garden, see? Just one chimney with eight pots right in the middle of the roof. Sitting room, dining room, morning room, kitchen range and four bedrooms; I could practically draw you a floor plan. And just to make sure, if you look closely at this one of Lena in what is supposed to be the same sitting room, same wallpaper, same curtains, you can just see that this corner of the wall doesn't turn at a right-angle and look! What's that?' Alec bent even closer over the picture and scrutinized the object in the corner.

'Dark wood and brass hoops,' he said. 'It's a coal bucket.'

'A coal bucket, yes. By the fire in the corner. That dark block that stops halfway up the wall is the fireplace. And there's no way it could be the same fireplace as in the picture of Cara, is there?' Alec shook his head.

'Now the one on the staircase. This one isn't at the beach cottage either. You see how the window behind her is set into the wall like an ordinary window? Well, the upstairs windows at the cottage were all dormers, you know, set into the roof. And once again if we look at the picture in the garden you can see the side of the upstairs windows sticking out. If there was a landing window flat on a wall on the front of the house we should be able to see the taller part sticking up from this angle and we can't. These two pictures were not taken at the cottage.' I waited for the praise that was to come. Alec flipped back and forward a couple more times and then nodded firmly, with his lips pushed out in a pout of either satisfaction or grudging admiration, I was not sure which. I should tell him, I knew, about the other cottage and not let him think I had got all this from looking with a better eye at what he himself had also seen. Perhaps I would some day, but for the moment I was content to be thought of as a detective genius.

'Now,' I went on. 'The question is why? Why did Lena go to all the trouble of redecorating the cottage to make it look as though these pictures were taken there? Why not simply take pictures of Cara at the cottage?'

'Are you really asking?' said Alec. 'Or do you already know?' He said it in a good-natured enough way, but I thought I should be careful not to be so triumphant as to be sickening.

'There are two possible reasons,' I said. 'Either because Cara was never there, or because the pictures had to be taken after she left, or without her knowledge.'

'That's three,' said Alec, but I ignored him. 'And we know that she was there because of the other pictures.' He flipped through the album until he came to the snap of Mrs Duffy in the garden with Cara disappearing into the house behind her.

'That,' I said and paused dramatically with my finger on the crêpe-de-Chine back, 'is not Cara. It's Clemence in Cara's dress.'

'Did you find the person who took the picture?' said Alec.

'You are looking at her,' I said. 'She's there.' Alec stared first at me and then at Clemence/Cara's back in the photo-

171

graph, and I took my finger and put it down on the paper, just where Lena's hand disappeared behind a fold of her dress, then I traced the path of the cable down the back of the chair leg and under the picnic rug into the foreground, stopping where just the tiniest little piece of it was visible at the edge of the frame.

'Very clever,' said Alec. 'It did seem odd that Cara should flounce off the way Clemence described. Not typical Cara at all.'

'And if she were flouncing,' I said, 'she'd be blurred.' We both looked in silence at the sharp outline of the figure in the dark doorway.

'But what about all the others?' said Alec. I waited in smug silence for him to discover what I had discovered as soon as this idea began to take hold.

'There's only one more,' he said, presently. 'On the cliff.'

'And that could be anyone,' I said, peering at the figure in the billowing dress standing beside Lena in the distance, with her hands jammed into her pockets while Lena waved. 'Although in fact I think it's no one. I think it's a dressmaker's dummy and that's why it was taken from so far away and why they had to pose in long grass. You know, I had thought that it was a silly mistake to take all of the pictures with "Cara" in the same dress, but actually it was only the dress that made us believe it was Cara in the first place, and it almost worked.'

'So she wasn't there?' said Alec, closing the album. 'She was never there at all. She just wrote the letters at home before they left and Mrs Duffy or Clemence posted them from the cottage, timing them perfectly so that I should arrive just too late.'

'Now for my second staggering piece of news,' I said. 'She was there. At least for one night. Mrs Marshall saw her on Tuesday.' I described to him the old woman's glimpse of the 'third' girl and the elaborate attempts to establish the existence of two identical sisters during the

172

rest of the week. Alec shook his head as I spoke and looked increasingly troubled.

'I should have got to the truth much quicker,' I said. 'Only when Mrs Marshall mentioned this girl on a bicycle pedalling hell for leather I naturally thought it was the poor little maid.'

Alec's mouth had dropped open and far too late I realized what I had said.

'A poor little maid? Why is this the first I've heard about a poor little maid? And why poor?' I shrugged, hoping to avoid the unpleasantness of explaining. Alec spread his hands wide and practically shouted at me.

'You must find her, Dandy, and see what she has to say. You must talk to her as soon as you can. I don't know what's got into you!'

'I . . . Well, I can't talk to her, if you must know,' I said, and took a deep breath. 'She died.'

'When? How? What are you talking about?'

'Suicide, I suppose you would call it,' I said. 'Dr Milne told me. Rather against his will since he had hushed it up for them and was embarrassed. And I didn't tell you because Dr Milne asked me to keep it to myself.' Alec was still looking at me as though I were a halfwit, and I suppose with good reason. I was still bowdlerizing. No wonder men end up unable to deal with the grislier aspects of life, when they go through their lives being invited by nannies, wives and daughters to look the other way while hurried drapes are thrown over anything ugly.

'Suicide,' said Alec and whistled. 'That must have given them pause. I wonder they had the nerve to go ahead with the fire. And I wonder why she did it.' I looked back at him blankly.

'But about your Mrs Marshall seeing Cara,' he said presently and I was glad that the little maid was dropped. 'Why would they let her bicycle away in the daylight after all the other precautions? The redecoration, the photographs, the letters. These things are all so very careful and elaborate, and Cara rolling along the country lanes would ruin it.'

'Well then, perhaps she wasn't "leaving". Perhaps she had just slipped out on some errand or other.'

Alec thumped his hand down on the black leather of the album, making me start and rattle my cup which was, thankfully, empty by now.

'Of course,' he said. 'We know she slipped out on an errand. She went to post a letter, didn't she?'

Once again the letters were taken from his inside pocket and spread out side by side.

'"If you could pretend to Mummy",' he read, '"that you came in search of me off your own bat . . . I think she's being perfectly ridiculous, but I don't want to make her any crosser." She sneaked out to post this to me, Dandy. I'm sure of it.'

'As we thought. You were never meant to be there,' I said. 'I was supposed to turn up on my own and be taken in.'

'Oh, my dear,' said Alec. 'I'm afraid so. I'm rather afraid Lena was grooming you for the role of the stooge from the time she got her claws into you at Croys. Yes, I'm sure of this now. The second letter was the only one I was ever supposed to see.'

'Yes!' I said, suddenly remembering. 'Lena referred to "a silly letter" when I saw her in her bedroom on the day of the inquiry. And I remember now, when I mentioned about you showing the Fiscal the letters – plural – she flinched.' I knew this was right, unflattering as it might be to have been cast as Lena's puppet.

'I still don't see what the point was, though,' I said. 'All that furious bicycling to deliver such a casual letter. If she wanted to see you badly enough to send it she would have told you to hurry, not said you might like to come when you had a free minute. Why did she not ask you to come straight away?'

'Oh, Dandy,' said Alec, suddenly reaching out and taking hold of my hand. 'Don't you see? Can't you?' I didn't and couldn't, but I knew some part of our story would soon have to give way under the weight of all the things that no longer made any sense.

'I don't think she knew she had to tell me to hurry,' said Alec. 'I don't think she *knew*. Back to your reasons for faking the pictures – she *was* there and if they were all done on the same day, they could easily have been done at the start of the week while she was *still* there. So it must be the third reason. They had to be done without her knowledge. She didn't know what was going on.'

'But the second letter?' I said, but even while I was speaking I began to wonder. 'She did write it, didn't she?' Alec shook his head.

'No. Clemence wrote the second letter.'

'But it's so perfectly identical,' I said.

'As was Chrissie Dalrymple's letter of condolence,' said Alec. 'They all were at school together. Why did we not think of it that day at the George when Chrissie's letter came? And I should have known from that "C". Cara always signed herself "Cara" even on a note, but I suppose . . .'

'Clemence knew that her handwriting would convince but she wasn't so sure about attempting a signature?'

'Precisely,' said Alec. 'Now where does that leave us? What exactly are we saying?'

'We seem to be saying,' I said, 'that Cara was not in on the plot. That's good, in one way, isn't it? From your point of view, I mean. Doesn't it make you feel a little better to know that your wife-to-be was innocent – at least to begin with? I do hope she was filled in at some point, though. I mean, I hope Lena and Clemence and whoever came to take Cara away told her what it was all about and got her consent, because otherwise . . . Well, it sounds too silly for words, but otherwise it's kidnap.'

'I have the most dreadful feeling,' said Alec, 'that I'd be quite happy to settle for kidnap, Dandy, right at this moment.'

I got up to throw logs on to the fire and was astonished

to find, glancing at the clock, that it was after eleven. Hugh, it seemed, would not be joining us at all. I sat down again, rather heavily, and scrubbed the heels of my hands into my eye sockets, doing who knew what to my make-up, but the lights were low.

'So, what if the plan was to kill her?' said Alec. 'Let's just allow ourselves to think it for a while, think it through.' For I was shaking my head already. 'Just go along with it, Dandy, please. Kill her at the beginning of the week, dry out the cottage, fake the pictures, fake her presence and make sure the fire was so severe that no one could tell she was dead before it began. That would explain why she didn't take part in the fakery.'

'But why?' I breathed, trying and failing to stop myself from believing such a repulsive idea. 'Never mind how – and Alec, my dear, the how is a huge obstacle. I don't mean how was it managed? I mean how *could* she? It's unspeakable.'

'Unspeakable things happen, Dandy. Every day they do. And as for why: to stop Cara from telling me she had stolen the diamonds. To stop me from telling the police. To save the family name –'

'To cover up a theft!' I said. 'For pride? Alec, please listen to me. A mother, any mother, and God knows I'm far from being the Madonna in modern form, but any mother would rather have her two daughters at her side in the workhouse than that one should die so she could hold her head up.'

'Your opinion does you credit,' he said. 'Do you have a better theory?'

'How about this?' I said. 'Cara stole the jewels. Mrs Duffy and Clemence planned the fire to cover her disappearance and were to collect the insurance money for the diamonds. Cara, though, was not convinced until the very last minute that she *had* to disappear, hence her letter to you saying that she thought she might be able to talk you round.'

176

'And did Cara have to get away because she stole the jewels or did she steal the jewels to fund an escape? In which case what did she have to get away from?'

'Well, I suppose the obvious thing is you,' I said. 'Her engagement.'

There was a very long silence at this, and one for which I could hardly blame him.

'Why not just break it off?' he said at last.

'Because you are her father's heir. We keep forgetting about Cara's father in all of this, because we're so sure her mother and sister worked the whole thing themselves. Perhaps she dared not tell her father she wouldn't marry you.'

'Nonsense,' said Alec. 'Cara could wind Gregory around her finger and frequently did. And why wasn't she in on the faked photographs? Can you explain that?'

No,' I said. 'I can't. I'm too tired. In fact, we're both exhausted; we're probably just seeing shadows.'

Alec shook his head.

'This isn't going to go away,' he said. 'But you're right – we are tired. Let's sleep on it.'

Leaving him to finish his pipe I retired. I had indeed rendered myself comical with eye-rubbing and I was glad Grant wasn't there to pour silent scorn upon me. (Our arrangement was that on ordinary evenings if I stayed up after eleven I shifted for myself.) I left my frock inside out on a chair in a small act of defiance, and got into bed to lie on my back while my cold cream soaked in, glad to have a little thinking time without Alec there to sway me.

He was leading me off the track, I was sure, because he would not pay attention to the diamonds, discomfited perhaps about being Mr Duffy's heir and fearing that any concern on his part towards the question of the diamonds might be mistaken as self-interest. I felt it increasingly, though, that he was letting his squeamishness overcome his judgement. They had to be important. I had to be able to come up with a solution to the mystery which took the diamonds into account. I resolved not to sleep until I had done so.

Cara, dressed in a frock of pale, striped wallpaper, was up to her elbows in a washtub, suds spilling over the top and down the sides washing the gold colour off the brass bandings. I stepped closer to see what she was washing. Under the water, clear now, the bubbles magically gone, she was rubbing handfuls of diamonds together as small children do with shells on the beach.

'You see,' she said, turning towards me and smiling, with the sun glinting through the stray golden hairs which had risen from the sleek cap of her bob in the steam, 'gone. Quite gone.' I looked back into the tub and saw that indeed the diamonds were melting in the water, disappearing. And as I watched Cara's hands, too, were beginning to wear away, until they were down to fingerless stumps like the hands of a burned child I had seen once and never forgotten.

I sat up in bed, glad of the moonlight, glad not to be in the dark where that image might linger, but still I jumped and clutched the covers under my chin as my bedroom door opened a crack. There was a soft knock before it opened further.

'Dandy?' Alec whispered, coming right inside and waiting a bit for his eyes to adjust before he moved again. Still groggy and rattled as one is after waking from a dream, I was unable to speak and only blinked and gulped as Alec came to sit on the edge of my bed. He started with a reassurance.

'I'm sorry to disturb you,' he said. 'And don't be alarmed: it's not a social call.'

'What's up?' I asked, recovering my sangfroid. 'Can't it wait till morning?'

'No.' He stopped and ran his hands over his face, and I could hear the rasp of the stubble which somehow made him sound even more tired than his weary voice.

'Do you have a glass of water there?' he asked. I passed it to him and waited for him to speak again.

'I think I've had the whole thing wrong,' he said.

I sank back on to my pillows with relief, but worse was to come than I had even imagined up to now.

'This evening,' he went on, 'I was arguing that Lena and Clemence killed her, kept the body somewhere, faked their record of a happy holiday with the photographs, and then set the fire to explain her death. But . . . Well, they're hardly seasoned arsonists, are they? If there had been a sudden downpour, or if the men managed to put it out and there was a body left to be examined, it would have been obvious that the fire was a cover-up job, and that would mean the noose, for one or both of them.

'However, if they tried to burn an empty house and put it about that Cara was in there, all they would have to say – if the house *didn't* burn, you understand – all they would have to say was that she couldn't have been there after all. They could even say that she must have started the fire and run away.' He reached out both his hands towards me and I put mine into them.

'Tell me about this maid,' he said. 'This poor girl who was supposed to have committed suicide most conveniently for everyone and who seems to have departed her life leaving not a ripple.'

'What about her?' I asked, whispering again and fighting against the idea forming in my mind.

'Two things,' said Alec. 'Had Dr Milne ever seen her before? And more to the point, did Dr Milne ever meet Cara?'

Chapter Twelve

'You look knocked up,' said Hugh, as I went in to breakfast the next morning. He has a particular way of saying this, not quite accusing, not triumphant exactly (and I should be thankful he says anything, I suppose) but there is a silent coda to the remark that always puts me on the defensive.

'I didn't sleep very well,' I said, not looking at Alec but seeing him anyway shifting uneasily in his seat.

'Well, all this chasing about,' said Hugh. 'You should go out for a good long walk with the dog you already have.' He broke off and began again in much the same vein but in rather gentler tones, as befitting the presence of a guest. 'Yes, a good walk in the fresh spring air, my dear, and you'll be right as rain by luncheon.'

'That would be lovely,' I said. 'Are you offering an arm? Or are you busy?'

This suggestion produced the desired result: Hugh huffed, puffed, turned to Alec and said: 'Would you think me a boor if I showed you the mare after luncheon, Osborne? And asked you to wheel Dandy round the park this morning?'

'I should be delighted,' said Alec, and his politeness seemed to sting Hugh into further explanation.

'Only I must just get my contractors off on the right foot,' he said. 'Wonderful chaps once they're set on their way, you know, but they do need a firm early hand or God knows what might come of it all.'

With everyone thus satisfied, Hugh dropped back

behind his newspaper as Pallister came in. Mrs Tilling, our cook, sends up two eggs freshly poached every morning just as I arrive in the breakfast room. I do not know how she gauges the moment of my arrival, for I am often unwitnessed and I trigger no obvious trip-wire en route from my bedroom to the ground floor, but every morning Pallister appears with a chafing dish just as I'm sitting. His disapproval at my being coddled and his being put to such trouble when there are perfectly good eggs under a hot cover on the sideboard is mammoth (as is Hugh's irritation at the performance, but Hugh always makes sure he is behind his newspaper and no doubt tells himself it is not happening). I cannot remember why and when this ritual began, which probably means it was while I was pregnant and inattentive on account of the all-enveloping haze of nausea, but I look forward to it. I smiled at Alec as I scooped the eggs on to my plate, feeling what a good light it cast me in that my cook loved me even if my husband would rather play in the drains than wheel me about, as he so charmingly put it.

An hour later, we let ourselves into the walled garden. My recent toils in Mrs Marshall's cabbage patch led me to look at the ground around me with greater interest than I could remember having felt before but April, while so pretty in woods and parkland, is unrewarding otherwise and the borders on either side of the gravel path were in a most undignified state. Great hoops of wire were waiting above the budding plants, great swathes of net suspended between sturdy poles, and bare canes everywhere, so that one felt one had come crashing into an actress's dressing room and caught her in only her corsets.

'Now Alec,' I began, firmly. 'You had me at a disadvantage last night – I was half asleep, but now I am going to convince you you're wrong. I left out a few of the more unpleasant details about this servant girl, you see.' Alec waited silently for me to continue, and I tucked my arm into his before I did, a very mild embrace and one sanctioned by my husband, besides.

181

'I'm glad I'm not looking at you while I say this!' I exclaimed and then I cleared my throat and plunged in.

'I see,' said Alec, when I had finished. 'Yes, I see. But consider this, Dandy. You already know that Dr Milne has been grossly less than thorough in his dealings with this unfortunate creature. Why, there should have been policemen and a proper investigation. So how far do you think he would go? As far as accepting Mrs Duffy's account of what had happened and dispensing with any examination at all? Might he have done no more than enter a servant's bedroom, glance at the unknown girl lying there under a sheet and sign a certificate?'

I leapt on this suggestion. Even if it meant that the girl was Cara, I should almost prefer the idea of *her* drifting off on laudanum than *anyone*, alone and wretched, bleeding to death at her own hand.

'You need to speak to Dr Milne,' said Alec. 'Find out, as I say, whether he knew Cara. If not, find out if he had ever seen the maid before. If not again, then find out just exactly how closely he examined her body.'

'Me?' I said, aghast. 'It can't possibly be me, Alec. I couldn't.'

'Well, *I* can't,' said Alec as though this should have been obvious and reminding me just a little for the first time in our short acquaintance of Hugh in particular and men in general.

'I don't see why not,' I said. 'Man to man. And if you're about to say it's a woman's concern, may I just remind you that the poor girl – if such she was – didn't get herself into that state on her own and I doubt that the other party has perished in an attic for shame.' We walked along in silence for a bit after that. Furious huffy silence on my part and, I hoped, newly conscious and heartily ashamed silence on Alec's. In we went at one end of the peach houses, trudge trudge trudge along the slatted walkway over the pipes, green with moss and treacherously slippy, then out again.

'And anyway,' I said at last, 'I can't go gallivanting off

to Gatehouse again. You heard Hugh at breakfast. What would I tell him this time?'

'You might say Mrs McCall's famous mouser of a cat is just about to have kittens,' Alec said, resisting my attempts to elbow him off the path into a soggy patch of that decayed matter that gardeners are so fond of heaping up everywhere. 'Yes, all right, all right. Does Dr Milne shoot? Might you invite him here? He needn't bring his wife, you know.'

'Impossible. There's nothing *to* shoot. Not a stag to be had these days. I could always write to him.'

'Impossible yourself,' said Alec. 'A letter couldn't be casual enough not to raise suspicions. Besides, we'll be skirting very close to slander if we need to ask about the death certificate, you know. The last thing we need is to write it down and turn it into libel.'

This sobered me again. One of the most striking aspects of being caught up in all of this, I was beginning to find, was the sudden giddy lurches between blood-curdling horrors and a feeling that we were at some kind of parlour game. Perhaps one caused the other: the reality too awful to bear so that one constantly retreated into one's intellect and let it become a mere puzzle.

In the end, I came around to the idea that Dr Milne must come and stay. Living where he did, he had to be a fisherman, I decided, and so I would get Hugh to include him in a fishing party. I could then feign some indisposition and do a little fishing of my own. How though to get Hugh to use up some of his precious fish on a country doctor he had never met? Even coarse fish; salmon would have been unthinkable. I myself quailed at the thought of entertaining a Mrs Milne if she existed, but ducking out of my part of the fixture turned out to be my masterstroke. Hugh was so delighted to have me suggest, for the first time ever in our married life, that a party of fishermen might come to stay without their wives and to suggest further that I should be quite happy to dine off a tray in my room to avoid the imbalance of a dinner table with just one lady to go around, that he swallowed the slightly odd inclusion of a mysterious Dr Milne from Gatehouse with scarcely a murmur. I felt a little pity, truth to tell, that he could not see through me more easily than that. He actually thought I was being generous offering to forgo a dining room full of men talking of nothing but fish and probably still smelling of it a little.

Alec was to be of the party, for Dr Milne was being presented as a particular friend of his. So when he left Gilverton on the evening of our walk, bearing the album to return to Clemence, it was with his quick return guaranteed.

In the dull meantime, all I could think of to do was write a long-overdue letter of progress to Daisy. Swearing her to strict secrecy, Silas apart, I told her what we had discovered about Clemence's impersonation of Cara, the deception of the photographs, the deliberate setting of the fire and the pains taken to make sure it burned like the bottom pit of Hades. I glossed over the fact that it seemed Cara had not been in on the plan, feeling (or perhaps more honestly *hoping*) that this apparent anomaly would soon be explained. I outlined my belief that Cara had stolen the diamonds and absconded with them, and that her mother knew. I admitted that I had not yet discovered whether Mr Duffy's allowing the insurance to lapse constituted an unforeseen hitch or whether setting up Daisy and Silas to make good the loss was part of the original plan, designed to keep the police away. I also admitted with admirable frankness (I thought) that I did not know why Cara, or Cara and her mother, or Cara and her mother and Clemence together, had planned the disappearance in the first place. The letter finished with my assurances that I was just about to double-check for my own satisfaction the last plausible scenario in which Cara had actually died at the cottage.

I had no pang submitting my account of lodgings and travel to Daisy's scrutiny along with my report but my nerve deserted me a bit, I must own, when by return of post there came back a cheque lavish beyond my initial comprehension, representing not only my expenses and retainer but half my fee and a sizeable bonus. My hands were damp with guilt as I read the accompanying note.

Darling Dan,

Wonder of wonders! I hope you don't think my astonishment is any slur on your abilities, darling, only when we heard about poor, darling Cara we naturally thought that there was an end to your investigations and our hopes of an answer. Do you think me a hag from hell if I admit it crossed my mind that her death, poor darling, might also bring an end to Lena's machinations? I never should have dreamed in a hundred million years that it was simply the plot thickening. How dared you, Dan? What resolve you must have needed to stick to your guns and keep Sherlocking away regardless! But what vindication! One can scarcely believe one is in the presence of such scheming – I'm talking about Lena now, darling, not you, although . . . !! – and really I think it almost amounts to wickedness, when it gets to putting the death notice in (although I suppose they could hardly not) and sending out invitations for a memorial service – have you got yours yet, darling? – in fact the memorial service makes my absolute blood boil, doesn't it yours? Because they might perfectly easily have said they were much too upset and since there's nothing to bury anyway . . . I don't know how I shall get through it without being sick, darling, but do let's sit together,
    Yours very impressed indeed and agog for more,
    D xxx

I *had* been invited to the memorial service and had been facing it with as little relish as Daisy. Now, as well as the general disinclination, I had the worry that Daisy would blurt out, as established fact, in front of Alec, some part of what I had told her in my letter and she had swallowed whole. (It was chastening to realize just how strongly I had

185

played the suit of Cara's still being alive.) Well, I certainly would not meet trouble halfway, by showing him what she had written. Apart from anything else one should shield Daisy's stylistics from the gaze of strangers; I like her letters myself but I wonder if she ever reads them through.

Presiding over my most enormous silver teapot on the day the fishing party assembled, I hoped to fix such an image of my fragrant presence in the minds of Hugh's cronies that they would overlook hardly seeing me again for the rest of their stay. Dr Milne appeared with Alec and seemed quite equal to his company, droning away about rods and flies and the poundage of his last triumph, neither listening to the droning on either side of him nor caring that his fellows droners were not listening to him. I foresaw success and a few days of peace for me, and that evening I put on my smoking suit and listened to dance music on the wireless, as happy a pike widow as ever there was. Grant checked on me just once to see that I was lounging as decadently as the smoking suit demanded and she seemed quite pleased. She was waiting for the day I dared to wear this costume at a party, and waiting very patiently – that is, she always packed it for me when I went away but hardly ever suggested it out loud.

Dr Milne was allowed a clear day's fishing the next day, my plan being to spring an ankle on him the day after, but in the end a better excuse presented itself. I had slipped off on the second evening to *The Perils of Pauline* at the cinema in Perth and, while there, the thought struck me that I might come down with a flea. It should be noted that between my artsy crafty childhood and my adulthood in a houseful of dogs, I have been dealing with fleas quite expertly from a young age, but Dr Milne was not to know that and I thought something slightly disreputable and undignified might bring us closer together than an ankle, no matter how I shoved it in his face and howled.

186

Accordingly I sent for him straight after breakfast and was huddled in a chair in my sitting room looking sheepish when he was admitted.

'Have you had coffee, Dr Milne?' I asked, pouring a cup out before he had time to answer. 'You'll think this is a fearful cheek, I'm sure, but I wondered if I could have a professional word?' He looked crestfallen and answered:

'Yes, of course my dear Mrs Gilver, I never come away without my bag, but you should have said when you wrote.'

'Oh no,' I protested. 'This has just come up. Sheer opportunism since you're here anyway.' So he *had* been a little suspicious about the summons, then. I should have to tread lightly. 'The thing is,' I said, and I found that I was blushing, which added a great deal in the way of authenticity, 'the thing is, I think I've got a flea.' I clapped my hand over my mouth as though trying to disguise either shock or nervous giggles and waited for him to respond with the expected professional gravity. To his credit, however, he threw back his large head and roared with laughter, at which I started to giggle for real and the ice was well and truly broken.

'I can't help you with that, I'm afraid,' he said. 'Except to pass on a good tip for killing the little devils. I'm always getting them, visiting in the village. There's one family in particular . . .' He shuddered. 'Stand in an empty bath, take off all of your clothes slowly, item by item, and drop them into a basin of water set beside you. If the flea is in the clothes it will swim to the top. If not then it must be on you or on the bath, where you can see it. You find it, pinch it between your fingers – tight, mind – and put it in the water to drown. Don't take the clothes out of the basin until you've seen it belly up. And some calamine lotion for the bites,' he finished, reaching into his bag. I was scratching for real by now, always having been very suggestible on the topic of fleas and ticks.

'Thank you so much,' I said and settled back to chat. 'Well then, happier circumstances than last time.' I was

187

glad to see that he seemed ready to sit and talk, fleas or no.

'I see there's to be a service in Edinburgh,' he said.

'Are you going?' I asked. 'I know the Duffys had not had the cottage long, poor things, but did you get a chance to get to know Cara at all?' My stomach gave a little lurch as he shook his head.

'I never met the poor lass,' he said. 'I knew her father to pass the time of day. Met him when he came down to look at the cottage. It must have seemed such a charming idea. A little wooden cottage by the sea for the ladies.'

'Dreadful, dreadful,' I said vaguely, trying to think as fast as I could what to say next. 'I should think the last thing they'll want to do is rebuild on the site, don't you? So, I suppose from the point of view of the village it would be best if they just sold the land to someone else.' Dr Milne looked puzzled at the turn the conversation was taking, and I hurried on. 'I mean how awful for the local people simply to have that great big blackened hole sitting there to remind them.' Dr Milne nodded and took up the theme.

'Aye, right enough,' he said. 'I know old Mrs Marshall up the lane is in a terrible state about it all.' My stomach revolved once more. Surely my ally had not spoken of things she should not. His next words calmed me.

'She can't stand to go down to the shore for kindling I heard, and that was her daily jaunt before now. She's a wonderful old woman, one of the old kind.' I remembered in good time that I could not be expected to know who this Mrs Marshall was, in fact had better *not* know in case he wondered how, but I saw an avenue.

'Is that the Mrs Marshall who went in to clean for the Duffys?'

'Her mother-in-law,' said Dr Milne.

'I see,' I said. 'I do like the way these country places have their settled families, don't you? Hugh's tenants on the home farm have been here longer than the Gilvers. I say, Dr Milne, I've just had the most – well, I hope the

188

most fanciful idea. They never did get an explanation of how the fire started, did they?' It was hard work to remember just how little I was supposed to know and how little concerned I should reasonably appear to be. 'A thought just occurred to me. The poor little servant girl. You know, the one who died? She wasn't local, was she? It couldn't have been her family taking some kind of revenge, or . . .' Dr Milne looked flabbergasted.

'Where do you get an idea like that?' he said.

'The cinema, I suppose,' I said, sheepish again. 'Along with the flea.' I hoped he would say more without having to be prompted again, as I wanted to save all the patience he had left for the outrageous suggestion I might have to make next.

'No, that wee lass had come down with them from Edinburgh,' he said. 'I had never set eyes on her before in my life.' I took this steadily, betraying no emotion. 'It would be as like a Gatehouse girl to get herself into that kind of trouble right enough, but not to take such a way out of it. Most often what happens is someone leans hard on the boy and there's a wedding and an "early blessing". No, that wouldn't be the way of it at all.' He mused now, as though talking to himself. 'It was a shame, right enough. A bonny wee thing, damned shame.'

'Dreadful,' I said again in a murmur which I hoped would not interrupt the flow.

'And it hit Mrs Duffy hard,' he went on. 'I thought at the time it had hit her harder than she was happy to show. No weeping and wailing, mind, but she was a terrible colour and I was worried. I thought to myself, that for all she was stiff – if you'll pardon me saying so – she had a heart in her. Yes, a wee kitchen maid she had probably not seen above a dozen times and you would think it was her own –' He broke off, confused at where his meandering had taken him, and fell to nodding sorrowfully. I lapsed into a silence preparatory to my next move. After a couple of agonizing minutes had ticked by on the clock, I began to speak with a little laugh.

189

'If we'd had this conversation yesterday,' I said, 'I should have been able to account for the dream I had last night. The worst nightmare I've ever had since I was a child. In fact –' I gave him a twisted smile, and my look of trepidation was quite genuine – I did not know if what I was about to say was a masterstroke of subtly entwined truth and fancy or my biggest blunder yet. 'In fact, I wonder if I wanted to tell you about it – "subconsciously" as they say. Do they still say that? – and that's why I didn't even think of dealing with the flea by myself.'

Dr Milne looked gently encouraging, but said nothing.

'I dreamt about Cara,' I said. 'Or rather about that poor little servant girl, but in the dream they were one and the same person. Cara was lying in bed and her mother was there and so were you and there was blood simply everywhere.' I dared not look at Dr Milne to see how any of this was going, but ploughed on, finding my stride. 'I had to wade through it up the stairs to the attic, and by this time it was the attic here at Gilverton – you know the way one can never dream very convincingly about the unknown and so one substitutes something more familiar? – and the blood was hot as though it were flames and where it spattered on the walls in the little bedroom it was singeing and blackening the paper, and when it hit the people's faces – and it did, you know, it went simply everywhere – they screamed as though they were being burned. It was quite, quite dreadful, because you see I knew, in the dream, that we were all going to die there, that none of us was able to escape and there was a voice coming from somewhere reading a dispatch like in the war, telling how we had all perished in a fire and Cara started to scream, "No, no, no. Not a fire! It was the blood. It was the blood!"'

I stopped at last and squinted at Dr Milne from under my brows. He looked as thunderstruck as one might expect after what had turned out to be rather a Gothic narrative, but he did not look at all anxious or afraid.

'Most unpleasant, Mrs Gilver,' he said. 'Thoroughly

190

nasty. What were you reading before you put out your lamp?'

'Oh yes, I daresay you're right,' I said. 'At least, it was all rather torrid at the cinema. Or could it have been that dashed flea? You know, in my sleep I could feel it feasting on my blood and making me burn with itches? Or perhaps not.' I really should try to rein in these excesses; he was gaping at me now.

'But the worst thing is, Dr Milne,' I said after a pause, 'that I can't seem to shake it off even in the cold light of day. I just can't get rid of the silly idea that Cara was the maid and the maid was Cara. And so just now when you said that you had never met either of the two girls before, I suddenly thought perhaps I was right. Perhaps my dream was a premonition! Not that I believe in all that, and it would be a post-monition anyway, wouldn't it? Or a message from the spirit world or something.'

Now he looked anxious, and I hurried to put things right.

'I don't really mean that. Of course I don't believe in such things, but it would be a real kindness on your part if you could reassure me that no such thing is possible. I mean, the servant was a servant, wasn't she? And she really did – I mean, she really had – I mean, did you actually see . . .?'

Professional calm reasserted itself in Dr Milne's flushed face, now that he presumably had me placed one short step from the gates of the madhouse. He reached out and patted my arm.

'Come now, Mrs Gilver,' he said, placidly. 'You are far too mature and sensible to give way to these flights of fancy. It was a nightmare. A very shocking nightmare, but no more than that. The film, the flea, as you say, and I expect the very fact of me being here and you seeing me again, all these things together *and nothing more* are to blame for your restless night. But if you are sure it won't simply upset you further, I can put your mind at ease.'

I nodded bravely and he went on, sitting back in his chair and looking at the carpet as he spoke.

'The poor little girl whose body I examined was most certainly a servant, Mrs Gilver. Her hair, her hands . . . Go and hold your own pretty hand next to one of the kitchen maids' downstairs and you will soon see how impossible it would be to make a mistake like that. This child's hands were quite raw, you know, bits of pot scourer under her nails. And I'm afraid there was no mistaking what she had done to herself. It was the typical silly nonsense that only a very ignorant girl would believe in. And only such a creature wouldn't see that she was just as likely to die from it as to miscarry. Does that put your mind at rest?'

It did and I smiled at him with unfeigned relief, prompting him to begin to work off some of the considerable annoyance that he was much too polite to let out in any other way. After all, I had made a pretty monstrous suggestion about his professional integrity.

'We doctors don't just glance at a corpse and sign our names, you know. I only wish we did. I made a very thorough examination of the poor creature and there was no doubt at all that this was a female of the servant classes, whose body bore the unmistakable marks of pregnancy. And I assure you, Mrs Gilver, it's as easy for a medical man to tell such things as whether or not a female has borne a child as it would be for you to tell a man from a woman. I can't put it any plainer than that.'

I was beginning to have had enough and, before the good doctor could go into any more revolting detail, I rose and held out my hand to him.

'Thank you,' I said. 'And please, if I could presume on your kindness even further, please don't tell my husband about this. He thinks I'm silly enough as it is. Now, a-hunting I shall go,' I finished, picking up the bottle of calamine lotion and brandishing it before me. I was half-way to my bathroom before I remembered that the flea was not real.

Sickened and fearing nightmares for real unless I turned

my attention to gayer things, I busied myself in the nursery wing for the rest of the day, where I rather thought I should do a little redecorating before the boys came for the summer. I should shed a tear at the passing of the blue curtains with ducks on them, but they would be most gratified to find manly stripes instead, and so I threw myself into it and grew quite cheerful. Successful as this was for the hours of daylight, however, it was destined not to last.

At a little after nine that evening when my supper had been cleared and I was tucked up on a sofa with Mr Pickwick to jolly me along until bedtime, Alec appeared with a soft knock and slithered almost furtively into my room.

'Hugh's taking a contingent to look out of a telescope and I've peeled off,' he said.

'Quite right, too,' I said, putting my feet to the floor and closing my book. 'The tower room will be freezing.'

'Aren't you feeling well?' Alec asked. 'Are you just off to bed? I don't want to disturb you.'

'It's a smoking suit,' I said, trying for haughtiness. 'Right. Report from Dr Milne. Has he said anything, by the way, to the rest of you, about my mental state? He thinks I'm slightly mad after this morning.' I told Alec with as few grisly embellishments as I thought I could get away with, just what Dr Milne had told me: that he had never met either this child or Cara but that given the thoroughness of his examination there was no doubt about the creature's class nor her condition.

'That's that then,' said Alec, when I was finished. 'I still can't believe it though. A theft, a suicide or whatever you want to call it, and a fire all happening to the same family in such quick succession and none of them connected to any of the others?'

'Well, in my version,' I said, 'the theft and the fire are connected, and it's just the poor maid that's the unforeseen catastrophe. And I still think there's something fishy about that. Why on earth would they take a kitchen maid away with them in the first place? I mean to say, the rough work of the kitchen is the one thing they could be sure to have done daily by some local woman. A lady's maid, I should have thought.'

'Who said she *was* a kitchen maid?' asked Alec.

'Good point,' I said. 'It was Dr Milne, and I don't suppose he really knew, just placed the poor creature as low as he could on the scale to match his distaste for what she had done. You should have heard him this morning, Alec. Nothing but disdain for the type of "creature" who would do such a thing. I wish we knew her name. It's hateful to keep calling her a creature. It makes me no better than he is.'

'But she really is a distraction, Dandy dear,' said Alec. 'Your concern for the poor cr– for the girl does you credit, but it's Cara we need to think about.'

I sighed and said nothing. It still bothered me greatly that Cara, Cara, Cara mattered so much and the other little girl not at all. I was sure that Dr Milne's revulsion was not only for her desperate action – an unusual one to be sure – but for the all too common action which led to it. I was sure as well that if poor dear darling Cara had found herself in a similar spot . . .

Alec started to speak but I held up my hand to silence him while I followed this sudden thought through to its conclusion. Cara had something momentous to tell Alec and was sure that Alec would not mind. She might have dealt with it, had she been able to raise the money, but since the jewels were fakes she was stuck with it. Her mother did not want Alec to be told, even to the point of getting Clemence to break things off on Cara's behalf. How stupid we had been. It was obvious now.

'Alec,' I said, with great reluctance. 'Did you and Cara . . . Did you and Cara go to bed?' This was no time for skirting around the thing, I was sure.

'No,' said Alec. 'Why do you ask?' He had clearly decided to be as businesslike as me about this unexpected turn.

'Well,' I said, 'you are not at all going to like where this is leading, but I suddenly saw right now that the poor unfortunate creature could be Cara after all, and could have died in just the way we know the poor thing did. In short, I think Cara was pregnant. Listen to me, listen to me, hear me out,' I protested, as he began to interrupt. 'Had the child been yours –'

'It couldn't have been.'

'No, I believe you,' I said. 'Because if it had been, or even if it might have been, then why would Mrs Duffy be so terrified of Cara telling you? Do you remember the letter? The first letter I mean? "Mummy is cross" and "I think she's being ridiculous" and "I trust in your love". Do you see? Cara knew that they were going to force her to break it off with you and disappear and that's why she decided to try to get rid of it.'

Alec held his head in his hands, either to block out the horrible idea or simply because he was trying to mesh this new theory with all the facts and near-facts we already had spinning around us.

'What about the diamonds?' he said, and I knew he was trying to think it out.

'Well, perhaps Cara meant to sell the diamonds to raise money for a doctor.'

'Don't be ridiculous,' said Alec. 'Surely it would take a piddling fraction of what she could raise.'

'But she can't have been thinking very clearly. I know she was almost beside herself the day we spoke at Croys. And don't you remember me telling you – she was talking about the fakes and she said she thought perhaps now the wedding wouldn't go ahead? We were puzzled at the time, do you remember, trying to see a connection. So then she decided to throw herself upon your mercy, but her mother and Clemence were terrified that you would chuck her and ruin her reputation and so she was whisked off to the cottage, and her disappearance was to be masked by the fire, and Clemence wrote to you breaking it off and so

195

poor, poor Cara tried to . . . Oh God, Alec this must be right, mustn't it? It all fits.'

'Do you have any brandy in here, Dan?' said Alec. It was the first time he had called me that, although I felt a heel for noticing when I should only have been thinking about how upset he was. I poured him a glass of cognac and one for myself then stood by his chair with my hand on his bowed head as he drank it.

'What about the diamonds, really, though?' Alec persisted. 'Where does the theft fit into this?' After scarcely being willing to mention the diamonds before, he would not leave them alone now.

'It doesn't. If Cara stole them, she would hardly have tried to sell them too. But she *did* try to sell them and I think she became desperate when she failed.'

'Why not sell something else?' said Alec. 'Or why not ask someone for money? There must have been heaps of people who would have given Cara anything she asked for without a murmur. She was adored. *Is* adored. Was.' I could tell by the slump of his shoulders that I had convinced him, and now I was almost sorry I had. I sat back down at my end of the sofa and sipped my drink in silence.

'What would you have done?' I said presently. 'If Cara had told you.'

Alec looked up at me with a bleak expression on his face which made me want to take the words and stuff them back into my mouth.

'With hindsight?' he said. 'To prevent such an end for her? If she had told me she was . . . with child, I should have married her, adopted her triplets and let their father sleep in my dressing room, of course. Without hindsight, I really can't say.'

It was just at that moment that Hugh walked into my room and found us there (no knocking and keeping his feet on the carpet for him) but he clearly had no difficulty in assigning a meaning to Alec's drained and desperate

face and my look of embarrassed glumness, and he withdrew tactfully, going to tell the others that young Osborne,
for all that his upper lip was as stiff as anyone could ask,
was really quite undone about the whole thing in a quiet
way.

Chapter Thirteen

Could it possibly have happened like that? I could believe it of Lena that she would stage her daughter's death as a respectable way out of the wedding and at least if that were true one did not have to believe the even more monstrous idea that she had actually killed her child to save her own reputation. Whether she meant Cara to re-appear at some time in the future with a fantastical tale of kidnap or amnesia I did not know, nor had I any clue why Cara had changed her mind about leaving and tried with such terrible determination to put things right. Wait, though. Something was wrong with that. Cara did not know about the plan, we had decided that she could not. So kidnap was not after all so far from the truth.

Of one thing I was sure: this was cooked up by the women alone. I remembered the way Cara's father had looked at her down the dinner table at Croys, and not one man in a million would look that way at a girl three weeks from marrying his heir and carrying another man's child. A mother, though, was a different quantity altogether. A mother – a woman herself for one thing, who knew the way the world could turn on a girl – might quite easily do what Lena had done to get her daughter out of shame's way.

The question remained whether we should tell Mr Duffy now, shrivel his rosy memories in the harsh light of ugly facts, and shine the same light on his wife and elder child so that he would be left with nothing. It had been such a shabby little scheme, all the desperation one associates with people straining to keep a skin of respectability where none is deserved, and it had gone so horribly and obscenely wrong. I could not see any good coming of making him face it.

Besides, the only good I should be concerned with was Silas and Daisy's. And I knew that the only way to keep Lena from putting the squeeze on Silas was for me to squeeze her, first and harder. I was not proud of this as a plan. It was not lost on me that when there is no decent way to express an action, then the action itself is probably shameful. Still, it was the best I could come up with. Lena thought she knew something dreadful about the Esslemonts? Well, now I knew something dreadful about the Duffys, and although I had not a clue what Lena's knowledge actually was, I was sure it could not be worse than mine. I had trumped her.

I needed some more proof, of course – Mr McNally's empty coal hole, Mr Marshall's paint and paper, and old Mrs Marshall's girl on a bicycle amounted to almost nothing – and I had an idea of how I might get it, but as I regarded myself sternly in the glass on the morning of Cara's memorial service, as Grant lowered the huge black hat on to my head, I wondered if I dared. Had I lost all my humanity in the short duration of my detective career? It seemed no time since I thought I was going to find out what had happened to the diamonds and simply show Lena that the Armistice Anniversary Ball was neither here nor there. Such an innocent task! And now a few weeks later I had come to contemplate something scarcely less shabby than what had been planned at Reiver's Rest. Grant sniffed expressively and my attention returned to the present.

'More rouge, madam,' she said.

I shook my head.

'And a little something around the eyes,' she added.

'Grant, it's nine o'clock in the morning. I am not going to have a little anything around my eyes, nor more rouge.'

'You can't carry off all this black, madam,' said Grant. 'Not any more.'

'I never could,' I said. 'And I'm not trying to carry it off. It's a memorial service, practically a funeral. Anyway, I don't foresee being able to get through the day without tears and then I should look like a panda. A panda with white streaks through its rouge.'

That swung it.

'I wish you would learn to cry out of the corners of your eyes, madam, I do,' said Grant and swept out. I was left feeling a lot less charitable after this prickly exchange and besides, Grant's easy scorn of me and all my works made me want to prove to myself that I had talents, even if neat weeping was not one of them. I decided to swallow my scruples and use the day well.

'Man that is born of woman is of few days and full of trouble,' intoned the minister and from my position half-way back in the church I could see a collective droop of shoulders in the pews in front of me. I have always thought that the jolly, celebratory funerals one comes across in Scotland (whose Church is fearfully Low) are more depressing than doleful High Anglicanism, but today of all days I should have welcomed a fat little man beaming as he spread the good news from behind the coffin, instead of this shockingly empty altar and the cadaverous individual before it telling us adenoidally that each of us was doomed. Beside me, Daisy inspected her nails surreptitiously, and on my other side I could feel Hugh remove himself mentally to the riverbank, or it might have been the stable yard. Curious, that sense one gets of the moods of one's husband through the long years of habitual proximity, like the way one knows exactly the moment when he has fallen asleep and so will not be going back to his dressing room and leaving one in peace to read. I wondered idly if the flow of intuition went all one way or if Hugh could tell that I was busily thinking instead of praying like a good girl.

Still the minister droned. He was on to an appreciation

200

of Cara's life now, and far from giving voice to the howl of anger which would be any right-thinking person's view when a young girl of twenty-two dies weeks before her wedding, he was tucking a blanket of euphemism over the whole sorry mess. I thought of what Hugh had told me about the native villagers in East Africa, how they sit on the ground screeching and wailing, none of this cloying acceptance. Or now I came to think of it, perhaps it was only the women who wailed. Hugh had not said what the menfolk got up to; presumably they blustered on just like this. Men. One good thing about speaking to Dr Milne had been that he told me what he knew in the straightest possible terms. 'Clear signs of pregnancy', he had said, and 'miscarriage', not like Alec gulping and stammering and only managing to say 'with child'. Such a silly expression. Like the minister's 'born of woman'. Although to be fair Dr Milne had said it too, had he not? That a medical man could tell with one eye shut when a woman was with child.

I sat bolt upright in my pew and my prayer book fell to the floor, landing on the edge of its spine with a sharp crack. I am sure too that I said something, although I do not know what, because Daisy came out of her daydream with a jolt to stare at me and Hugh stiffened with instant embarrassment. Even the woman in front, although she would not crane round to look, was transfixed – I could tell by the sudden quivering attentiveness of the feathers on her hat.

Had I merely been drifting off to sleep? One often thinks one has had tremendous ideas then, ideas which turn out to be not only worthless, but barely expressible in anything but gibberish. But this time I was almost sure. I put my head back down again, concentrating on the wood grain to help me block out the voice of the minister, and started to think. Now, of course, I fell asleep for real and the next thing I knew was that Hugh had gripped my arm rather firmly and hauled me to my feet for the beginning of the final hymn.

Since I could do no more until the reception I turned my thoughts at last to the plain fact of Cara's death and my real sorrow for it, ignoring the equal measure of indignation – moral indignation – at the lie and at the arrogance of those in this very church who were busily at work under their show of grief covering that lie up.

Old Mrs Marshall would have been relieved, I thought an hour later, that even without a coffin and the subsequent need for the ladies to retire delicately while the gentlemen went to the graveyard, the sexes were to be segregated. We were bundled into cars and carriages to be trundled back to the house, but the men seemed determined to walk. This meant that drinks and luncheon had to be stalled until they caught us up and, meanwhile, the ladies made do with coffee, sitting desolately around the huge double drawing room in our dowdy clothes and looking, I thought, like dead ducks on a mud bank. Mrs Duffy and Clemence were nowhere to be seen, moreover, leaving us quite without occupation. I saw Renée Gordon-Strathmurdle slop a great dollop of something into her coffee cup from a hip flask and wished I had not placed myself so carefully far away from her.

Sha-sha McIntosh was slumped opposite me, without the other members of the trinity for once and looking, in her enforced mourning, like a child who has been sent to sit in the corner for naughtiness. I caught her eye and smiled.

'You saw Clemence's charming pictures, I believe,' was as good an opening as any. Sha-sha nodded and brightened. How very young she seemed to be cheered instantly by a kind word.

'Poor darling,' I went on. 'You were to be bridesmaid?'

'All three of us,' said Sha-sha. 'And now we simply can't think what to do with the frocks. It seems wrong to throw them into the dustbin, but what are we to do with three frocks all the same? It's too silly for words.' A couple of elderly ladies, aunts perhaps, looked over their spectacles at her with reptilian severity, but I understood.

202

'Cara would not have minded at all your thinking about them,' I said, with a glare at the huffy aunts. 'One can't – if one's being sincere – always make sure one has only suitable thoughts.' I wondered suddenly if Sha-sha or the others were entertaining any thoughts even less suitable, thoughts along the same lines as those of Alec and me. I decided to dip the very tip of one toe into the water and try to find out.

'Do you know what I couldn't help thinking, Sha-sha darling? I tell you only to make you feel better in comparison and you must promise not to give me away.' She mimed pressing her lips tight closed and I went on in a conspiratorial whisper. 'When I looked at those lovely pictures of Cara, instead of thinking how lucky it was and how clever Clemence was, all I could think was what a nasty frock Cara was wearing and what a shame she wore it in all of them!'

Sha-sha was silent for a moment before she answered, and I thought perhaps I had overestimated her triviality, or rather underestimated my own, for I was sure that such thoughts might have been quite in character for me. However, she answered presently, and her answer was both a relief – she was not shocked – and a disappointment.

'I can't think where she got the thing,' she said. 'Or why. It certainly wasn't part of her trousseau because we've all been instrumental in that and we shouldn't have let in such an abomination.'

'It was pretty frightful,' I said. 'Perhaps it was an old thing she kept for the country.'

'Perhaps,' said Sha-sha. 'She did have a crêpe-de-Chine just like that, you know, countless ages ago. It was pale green and fearfully baggy, but we didn't seem to notice then how ugly she looked.' She gave a little laugh. 'Perhaps in a few years we shall look back at ourselves now and think: Ugh! what frights we were.'

I tend to think this at the end of each day as I take off the clothes I put on that morning, and I felt more sure than I could politely say that Sha-sha would certainly look back with a shudder upon her current hat, sitting on her pretty head like a monstrous toadstool. One thing was clear: she had no troubling suspicions about the pictures. At that moment, the men began to arrive and the Duffys' butler came to summon us down to luncheon.

While the stair and hall were thronging with ladies coming down and gentlemen removing coats I slipped unobtrusively away to my work. It would be an exaggeration to say my heart was thumping as I closed the baize door behind me and crept down the stairs – stairs which resounded rather startlingly to my tread no matter how stealthily I moved – but I did feel my pulse thrum a little. I hoped, though, that if my face was red or, worse, my neck blotchy it would be taken as a sign of high emotion and not nerves.

Once arrived at the end of the basement passageway, I set off along it lurching blindly with a handkerchief pressed to my mouth. I even sniffed, but it echoed too much in the empty passage for me to do it twice.

The upper servants were sure to be in the dining room or at their own luncheon, I told myself, and I was much more likely to meet with some mouse-like creature of the kitchens who would be so unnerved by my sudden appearance that she would not have time to question my story until I was gone. Then, even if she reported my strange behaviour to the housekeeper, cook or terrifying butler, they would most likely squash it for fear of showing her any credence and would certainly not carry a tale from the likes of her all the way to ears of the family.

I was half right. It was a kitchen maid – or might have been a scullery maid, for I am insufficiently familiar with the distinctions to tell – who rounded a corner and came upon me blundering towards her, but far from being the timorous child of my imaginings, she was a lusty individual of squat girth, turned-up nose, wide smile, and an air of bustling self-sufficiency: in short Mrs Tiggywinkle in human form, with an Irish accent and no sign of being unequal to meeting me.

'Lord, madam,' she said, hitching a tin pail comfortably on to one ample hip and staring. 'What have you gone and landed up down here for?'

I fluttered my handkerchief and mumbled vaguely, hoping to convey enough distress to explain how lost I was. Mrs Tiggywinkle put down her pail of kitchen scraps and, wiping her hands first, took me in a competent grip and began to propel me back the way I had come. I had expected a seat and a glass of water at least, giving me time to work up my little speech, and so, seeing my opportunity passing much more quickly than I anticipated, I thought I had better quit mumbling and dabbing and get on with it.

'I do apologize,' I said. 'Quite the last thing you need on a day like this, silly women drifting into your kitchen when you're busy with all these guests.' She looked at me as though I had gone mad but could hardly say anything. 'Are you still short-handed?' I blurted out. She stared at me even more intently then, thinking, I suppose, that I must be a member of the family she had failed at first to recognize for why else would I ask such a thing?

'Or have I got it wrong?' I said. 'I thought that one of your –' I could hardly say 'colleagues' – 'that one of the maids left. I mean, died. And I was thinking how awful for you if she was a particular chum.'

'Miss Cara died, madam,' said the girl in a patient and rather tender voice, clearly having decided that I was some lunatic cousin let out for the day to come to the service.

'I'm terribly sorry,' I said. 'I had heard in the village – in Gatehouse, you know – that one of the Edinburgh families in the cottages had brought their maid from town and that she had died. I don't know what made me think it was the Duffys.' We had reached the bottom of the stairs by which I had descended, and just then the door at the top opened and we both heard the voice of the butler coldly telling someone we could not see to stop sniffing and behave herself.

205

'Jesus!' said Mrs Tiggywinkle, clearly as intimidated by the man as I was.

'Don't let him find me!' I hissed and this spurred her to action. She opened a door and shoved me inside before coming in herself and leaning against it to listen. We heard a veritable army of footsteps descend the stairs over our heads as the butler and footmen trooped down from the dining room, then we could hear the butler's voice demanding to know why a bucket of peelings was sitting in the passageway and where Mary had got to this time.

Mary, as I took her to be, leaned back against the door and let out her breath in a low whistle. We were in a little store room, utterly empty and seemingly without purpose, but I knew from my own housekeeper at Gilverton that the ability to keep a few rooms completely bare was a matter of pride, being a sign of a well-run household where detritus was not allowed to gather. An empty attic is, I believe, the pinnacle of housekeeperly excellence.

'What must you think of me?' I said, deciding to abandon my show of feminine confusion and throw myself on her as an ally now that the ice was broken. 'But that man always looks at me as though I were something the cat brought in and I just simply can't face him today.'

'Nice to have the choice, madam,' said Mary, feelingly, and my frankness had clearly made her feel quite on a level since she took a tin out of her apron pocket and, having wrested it open with difficulty, lit a cigarette.

'Still,' I said, refusing her offer of another, 'I'm glad it's not one of your friends who died after all. I can't think where I got the idea.'

'No more can I,' said Mary. 'They never take any of us down to these "cottages".' She made the word ooze with scorn. 'And we're all fine here. Peggy, Rose, Nan, Jean, Dilly, Margaret and me. What did she die of?'

I was caught off-guard by this, but righted myself quick enough, I think.

'Went swimming in the sea and drowned herself on her

206

afternoon off,' I said. Mary and I both tutted and shook our heads.

'Accident, was it?' she said, with a last deep suck on her cigarette. I nodded. 'Accident,' she said again. 'Probably in trouble and trying to put it right, don't you think, madam?' We shared a look, then she pinched out her cigarette carefully between callused finger and thumb before putting it back in the tin and into her apron pocket again.

'Well, then.' This with an air of finality.

'Indeed,' I agreed, handing over the half-crown I had ready in my glove for the purpose. Mary checked up and down the passage before slipping out and making her way back to her abandoned pail and the ticking-off to come. I slipped out after her and climbed the stairs again, knowing that at least a frosty look if not a whispered interrogation from Hugh should meet my belated entrance, but knowing too that just as Mary had her half-crown in her pocket I should have Alec's glance of expectation, an expectation I would certainly satisfy as soon as we had a chance to talk.

Luncheon was purgatory. Had the minister of the morning been there, he would have been convinced of the existence of that Popish venue well before the pudding and been lost to Presbyterianism for ever. The food was cold and depressing owing, I expect, to the upper servants having been at the service and to a feeling that nothing today should be too enjoyable. This was not the worst of it, however. Alec, if you can believe it, had been sat next to Clemence, a placing so monstrously, squirmingly, wrong that no one else at the table could drag their eyes or their minds from it. On Alec's other side Lena sat, stony-faced, although whether this was a performance of grief or because she had underestimated how shocking her seating plan was and was toughing it out I could not tell. Mr Duffy looked stricken. Grey and shaking, he sat without eating a morsel and stopped his neighbours on either side from doing so either, it seeming bestial for them to stuff away

207

while he just sat there. This reluctance to eat spread out around the table, and the servants kept coming back into the room and then stopping, shuffling in the doorway, not knowing what to do and unable to catch the eye of either of the Duffys to help. The sight of the butler half-reaching for a plate and then stopping himself and smoothing his hair instead, that classic gesture of awkwardness, made me want to weep.

And then just when one thought it could get no worse, Clemence laughed. Not a huge laugh, but a giggle which just happened to fall into a momentary pool of perfect silence. Mr Duffy's head jerked up and he sent a look of pure hatred down the table, the kind of look which in my boys' weekly papers is depicted as a thick black dotted line. Clemence did not notice and Mrs Duffy stared back at him coldly until his eyelids drooped and he bowed his head again.

Two things were clear: everyone would be desperate to leave as soon as they could after rising, and since we could not all leave at once, one's best hope was to get right in at the off. But, since Hugh was far too stiff to make the first move *and* was impervious enough to 'atmosphere' to bear it, I foresaw a long wait amongst dwindling numbers before I could escape. A plan occurred, however, and I put it into motion at the earliest opportunity.

'Alec Osborne has just told me,' I whispered to Hugh, 'that he fears he'll keel over if he doesn't get some fresh air. And he wonders if you and I would go with him.' Hugh, bless him, actually took steps backwards, physically recoiled, and I could not resist going on, although I knew it was cruel, 'Shall I come with you, or will you and he go alone?'

Poor Hugh may still have been babbling: 'You, Dandy, you go, you two go without me,' when, having collected Alec with a whispered 'Come on!', I descended the front steps and set off.

We walked through the streets in the growing damp of a chilly afternoon – there is nowhere in the world like

208

Edinburgh for making the same cheerless ordeal out of any time of the day or season of the year, even early May. Our obvious mourning clothes matched all too well the deliberation of our pace and the down-turned gravity of both face and voice as I told Alec all that I had learned. Mary's evidence could not be talked away, and he did not try.

'Yes, all right,' he said at last. 'It was Cara. Splendid work, Dandy.' This had a bitterness I had not heard in him before, but which was only too easily understood. I could imagine what he felt to find out that his pretty angel of a fiancée had killed herself trying to get rid of a baby that was not his. Whether there was still only sorrow at her death or a sneaking relief beginning to grow that he had avoided marriage to such a girl, his heart must be heavy with some mixture of grief and guilt.

I felt it most grievously myself that we *still* did not know what had happened to the jewels and so despite all my muck-raking Daisy and Silas were exactly where they had started. And there they would stay, I was sure, since the only way out of it depended on me. Oh yes, I had been all set, that morning, to blackmail – let us call it what it was – to blackmail Lena into silence. Now, though, I felt that had I the nerve to go through with it, I should never be able to look myself in the glass again. And anyway I had not the nerve, I knew.

We were there. Alec looked up as I laid my hand on the gates of the Municipal Cemetery and pushed them open, then bowed his head again while we traversed a network of paths to the back corner where some newly filled plots sat in a row. There were five recent enough. Five, packed so close that there was barely a strip of flat ground between them and they looked more like the furrows of a ploughed field than graves. Three of them had flowers upon them, some florists' wreaths as well as little hand-picked posies.

'So it must be one of these two,' I said, looking first at one and then at the other of the two graves which lay quite unmarked. 'Oh, Cara.' I felt a huge bulge of tears revolve somewhere inside me, but bit down hard on my lip to hold them.

'You're sure,' said Alec. It may have been a question.

'When I was speaking to Mrs Tig – to Mary just now,' I said, 'she pinched out her cigarette in her fingertips and didn't feel a thing. And I thought, those are kitchen maid's hands, you know, tough as boots. Not scrubbed raw, as Dr Milne said. With bits of metal pot-scourer under her nails. Kitchen maids don't have nails to get things stuck under.' Somehow that seemed the worst thing of all, imagining Lena taking her still-warm hands and setting about them with a scourer to add a convincing little touch to the tale.

'How do you know this is the place?' said Alec.

'Dr Milne told me it was in town,' I said. 'Then I just telephoned around, pretended I was organizing a little marker of some kind. It's the sort of thing a kind employer might do – Hugh has done in the past – although not Lena admittedly. I had to gamble that in fact no marker was already arranged.'

'And was one?' said Alec, his voice beginning to sound gruff.

'No,' I said. 'Apparently not.'

210

Chapter Fourteen

There then began a curious stretch of calm that was yet as tiring as any time I have ever endured. The case was closed, I believed, but one might almost have said that other parties disagreed. Had I believed in fate, I might have blamed myself for tempting it with that first nightmare served up to Dr Milne. Had I believed in ghosts, of course, I should have blamed Cara herself for her determined, beseeching presence. Perhaps though it was only the weather, a spell of heavy warmth both day and night; liquid weather, although no rain actually fell. It was as if a flood was held in the sky by a single trembling membrane, pressing dull headaches down upon all beneath it, seeping just enough vapour for one's clothes to be always limp and one's hair lank and oppressive against one's neck.

In the heat each night as I slept, short and furious dreams of Cara raged through me and then wrenched me up and out, leaving me flailing under a soaked sheet listening to the blood thunder in my ears. Night after night I willed my leaden arms and legs back to life, rose, splashed my face and changed my nightie, then lay back down in the cooling damp of my bed, hoping to slip into a gentler sleep without her finding me.

At last the month dragged to a close and I began to look forward to the return of the children for the summer – 'look forward', that is, in the sense of knowing that it was sure to happen and had to be prepared for. By and by, it came to me that if I made my final report to Daisy, if my part in the affair could be tied in pink tape and filed, then

211

the dreams might stop. There was a twinge of shame each time I considered how I was shirking my duty to tell Daisy that I had failed. And failed I had, for all thoughts of applying pressure to Lena had wilted and died in me in the Municipal Cemetery weeks before. Admittedly, if Daisy had contacted me in a sudden panic, if Lena had renewed her vague threats, I might have found courage enough in my outrage to do something. But Lena was either biding her good time or had abandoned the plan after Cara's death or perhaps was to return to extortion only after a proper period of mourning, if such a ludicrous clash of sensibilities were possible.

So one morning, dry-eyed and sick from weariness, and with Cara's stark face still behind my eyelids whenever I shut them, I sat down at my desk intending to report my failure and return my fee. As it turned out, however, I wrote something quite different, looking detachedly but with interest at what poured from my pen, and grateful once again not to believe in the spirits by which I might otherwise have felt invaded.

My letter was short on detail, extremely long on mystery. In effect, I told Daisy nothing, or nothing much: only that I firmly believed Lena would not be in touch again – I was less sure than this in reality, of course, but I hoped to excuse the terseness of my note with a suggestion that things were dealt with – but, I went on, if there *were* a renewal of Lena's hints, a fresh round of her not-quite-stated demands, Daisy was to say the following: 'I know you took no servant to the cottage.' I assured her that if she said just that, 'I know you took no servant to the cottage,' Lena would immediately and for ever desist.

Calling Bunty, I set off to the post box at the farm road-end where I dropped in the envelope, with high hopes that I should now have seen the last of the nightmares. Or perhaps my imminent plunge into family life for the summer would effect the necessary jolt. That very night, of course, I dreamed of Cara again, horribly, sickeningly, until I rose and went to the pitcher, peeling off my nightie as

I walked. So one last tremor then, caused by writing the letter, but the boys would be here in the morning, in less than five hours I saw from squinting at my mantel clock in the grey light, and my life would resume its course.

For one day it looked as though that might be true. The boys, collected from the station by Hugh, clattered into the house with the greatest possible confusion that two boys, two trunks, five excited dogs and as many excited servants might be imagined to produce, so it was just as well that their mother merely waved and smiled from the perimeter, adding nothing to the mayhem. They cantered upstairs to hug Nanny and inspect the nursery for the slightest changes, startlingly tall as they passed me, and before I had had a chance to organize their newly angular faces in my mind and remove the image of the round cheeks and sweet curls which I always substitute for reality, they were back, charging out of the house still in their grey shorts and black shoes to go and see the ponies, with Hugh marching after them, bellowing that they must not upset the poor beasts and must change into boots that instant.

'Tomato sandwiches, Mrs Tilling,' I said. She would have made tomato sandwiches without being told, of course; it was not so much an instruction as a blessing in code.

'They have been ripening on my kitchen windowsill since Sunday, madam,' said Mrs Tilling. 'And will I make cheese scones? And which do you think between a chocolate cake and a walnut cake? Or perhaps . . .?'

'Both,' I said, as we knew I would.

'This tea is quite good,' said Donald with his head tipped back and his lips tucked in to stop cake crumbs spraying as he spoke. Teddy, a year younger and thus less able to control himself, exploded into giggles although, to be fair, he did catch most of the scattering mouthful in his napkin and Bunty soon snuffled up the rest. 'Quite good' was clearly to be the phrase of the summer. They always brought one home with them; a word or two whose repetition was the last thing in wit, which Hugh would become

213

unbearably irritated by and begin to hand out punishments for before the week was out. Last year every picnic, walk and party we arranged had been agreed to by the boys 'if I'm spared' and although it made me smile to hear them repeat this dainty phrase, it drove Hugh wild with rage and produced more than one slippering.

Teddy took another huge mouthful of cake and a slurp of tea and leaned against me comfortably.

'It's quite good to be home, Mother,' he said.

'It's quite good to have you home, Teddy Bear. And you, dear,' to Donald, who closed his eyes at me slowly like a cat.

Almost enough becoming domesticity to choke on, then, but it did not work. I awoke drenched and shaking that night as usual, half-forgetting the details of the nightmare and glad of it. I crept through the silent house to the nursery wing without knowing why. I make little pretence of rampant maternal passion and have always found chocolate box displays sickening both in myself and on the few occasions when I witnessed them in my own mother. Besides, mine are boys which means that already, at ten and eleven, they are lost to me. Still there I was, standing at the end of Donald's bed, shivering slightly, listening to his breathing and that of Teddy in the bed behind me, no idea what had drawn me there. They kept pace with one another, breathing in and out in perfect time, and I wondered if it was because they were brothers or if it came from sleeping in the same room and if so whether at school a dormitory full of little boys breathed in and out in time all night. These musings, aimless as they were, drifting around and through me like smoke, nevertheless seemed to give me whatever I had come for because the dream slipped off me at last and the sick rumbling it had left behind quieted, the thoughts dissolving before I had even thought them.

All three of us were breathing in time now, and I could have stood there for ever, I think, although the hard floor began to make my bare feet ache. I thought of curling into an armchair but, imagining their scorn in the morning to find their mother mooning over them like a lovesick cow, I gathered myself and returned to my room.

Alec stood at the front of the church in his wedding clothes, Hugh as his best man and six bridesmaids in pale green crêpe-de-Chine. The cadaverous minister from the memorial service was on his hands and knees shouting down into the floor of the altar, shouting to Cara to come out, telling her everyone was waiting. Her father sat in mourning in the front row with his hands clenched on his knees and we, the rest of the congregation, pretended not to hear the scuffle and gasp of a struggle going on under our feet. 'Help me,' screamed Cara's voice. 'Somebody help me.'

I too tried to call out but could only make a dream's smothered straining mumble. When I woke I knew I had made the sound aloud and was thankful that I had got myself out before I really found my voice.

Once more, through the house, even colder now at the dead still of four o'clock when the embers are grey and even the night creatures outside have fed and killed their night's measure and turned for home.

The boys, tired out and having slept hard since ten, were drifting up to meet the morning and they stirred as I crept back into their room. This time I knew why I was there. I had not, as feared before, come up here to channel motherly feelings like some opportunistic medium whose seance looked like going flat; much less had I turned to the easy sentiment of 'my dear boys come home to me' simply to drive away the horrors. I had come to force myself into honesty and make myself face what had to be faced. I had failed Daisy and I had failed Cara. I had failed because, however short of the ideal I might fall when it came to cooing and sighing and gazing fondly, deep down I could not help thinking like a mother. Thus, hidebound, hogtied, I had allowed myself to ignore a sign so glaring that my own brain presented it to me night after night and looked as though it would continue to do so for my whole life unless I gave in. Well, I was ready to give in now.

Lena had planned her daughter's death. Lena had prepared the fire that was to have caused her daughter's death. And now Lena's daughter was dead. The missing step, where I had tried to cram Cara's inexplicable change of mind and then her killing herself, that space could only sensibly be filled one way. I could hardly bear to think it, I was such a coward, but I knew it was true: Lena had killed her child and I, least motherly woman one could imagine, could not stand listening to the breathing of my own children and ignore it.

'Cara,' I whispered, then went on even more quietly as Donald flinched and resettled, 'I promise you. I promise.' I did not need to speak the promise, not to someone who was in my head and orchestrating my dreams, but it was no less sincere for that.

There was no instant clarity, however, just because I had let go of my resistance. As to what exactly Lena had *done* to kill her child I did not know and could not bear to speculate. And as for why, I had no idea where to start. There was so much of it all and it made no sense, as though more than one story in loose leaf had got shuffled in together and I was reading now a page from this, now a page from that, never knowing where the join should be. I needed help.

Brightly, at breakfast the next morning – the children breakfast with us in the holidays, at least to start with until all parties tire of it – I announced to the boys, and hence indirectly to Hugh as well, that we were to have a visitor.

'His name is Alec Osborne and he's a friend of Daddy's and mine, but younger. He has had a rotten time lately and he needs a quiet break in the country with his friends.'

Donald groaned and said with what I hope was affected weariness, for it would not be pleasant to think that one's eleven-year-old boy was really that jaded: 'Not another shell shock case, surely, Mother. That was years ago.'

Hugh's eyes bulged but he said nothing.

'No, dear,' I replied calmly, understanding what Hugh refused to understand, that there was no way we could hope to explain to the boys anything about the true nature of the war. They had lived through it but they had been so well protected that they still viewed it as a game; one which had unfairly finished before they were old enough to play and which had left behind it only its most dreary components – the wounded, the money worries and indeed the shell shock cases. What Hugh and I did share, I am sure, was a fervent wish masquerading as a conviction that at least we should never see its like again and they had missed it for once and all.

'He was to be married,' I went on. 'But there was a dreadful fire and the girl died in it.' Donald's and Teddy's eyes grew round with delight. 'So you see he is very sad and needs to be jollied up with games and expeditions.' I hoped by this to fix their interest on the possibility of a more exciting companion than either Hugh or me. I failed, of course.

'A fire! Gosh, Mummy, did he try to save her and get beaten back by the flames?'

'And have to listen to her gurgling screams while she –'

'No!' I said, almost shouting. 'Where do you get this? Gurgling screams indeed. You are forbidden to mention it to him, do you hear?' This seemed to diminish Alec's value rather severely and both boys pulled wry faces and went back to gobbling.

Still, Hugh had been informed of the visit and had not made a murmur, so now my only task was to summon Alec, but I was not quite sure exactly where he was. He had gone to the Duffys' after their return from the Alps, had been staying with them at the time of the memorial service, but he was not there now, none of them feeling equal to the situation. Had their estate been open he might have skulked there inconspicuously for weeks until the relationship faded, but I quite saw how neither he nor the family could bear his presence in the narrow confines of the Edinburgh house, with wedding presents still arriving and having to be sent back, and visits of condolence being paid. Perhaps he had returned to Dorset.

My telephone was ringing as Bunty and I came back into the house after our morning walk and although I broke into a lope to reach it I was still only halfway across the breakfast room when Pallister disappeared through my door with a withering look at me over his shoulder. He was holding out the earpiece towards me when I caught up with him and spoke in a chilly voice even by his standards.

'A young gentleman, madam.' This of course was exactly what Pallister feared a private telephone was for and it was hard to say whether distaste or pity was the chief ingredient in his expression as he withdrew. Little I cared.

'Dandy?' said Alec's voice, and despite everything my heart lifted a bit.

'Alec, I need to speak to you most seriously,' I began, shrugging off my coat and pointing Bunty fiercely towards her rug.

'Yes, but since I telephoned to you, dear,' said Alec in his most amused drawl, 'I'm afraid you shall have to wait.' I heard the click of him resettling his pipe and waited for him to go on. This appearance of such extreme relaxation had to be a deliberate act, for if it were not why had he rung me?

'I have had the most peculiar interview with old Cousin Gregory,' Alec said. 'Last evening in his library. I was invited, not for dinner but to come and see him at ten o'clock and was bundled in and upstairs like a chorus girl being brought to a stag party. Then we had a long talk about Cara.' Alec must have heard me catch my breath and correctly interpreting my interest he dispelled it immediately. 'Nothing to the point of our investigation, Dandy, just generally, you know. I think the poor old boy can't be

218

getting much of a chance to talk about her. Lena's act of "grief to the point of distraction" is still going strong. And as you know he has no time for Clemence, so I daresay he's just had to bottle it. He looks ten years older.'

'And?' I said, beginning to feel disappointed. 'Would you like me to visit and "draw him out"?'

'Stop interrupting,' said Alec. 'I'm getting to something important. Two things, actually, and I hardly know which is more startling. First thing: Gregory wanted to assure me that I was to remain his heir. That in itself I'm sure you will agree is nothing, but he was vociferous on the topic of my marrying Clemence.'

'What?' I said, before I could help myself. 'Alec, are you . . .?' I had been going to say 'mad', but bit my lip just in time. Clemence? Clemence *knew*. She at least knew something. I was sure she did. 'Are you to be a Mr Collins after all then?' I finished lamely.

'Concentrate, Dandy, please,' he said, and his tone told me that at least I had managed to conceal the extent of my fright. 'Cousin Gregory, talking around and around, and never quite saying it exactly or even hinting at why, has let me know that if I marry Clemence I am to be disinherited and the estate will pass to another branch of the family entirely. Now what do you make of that?'

'He knows something,' I said. 'He must know that Clemence was bound up with Cara's death. But why on earth . . .? Have we got it wrong, then? Is it all Clemence and nothing to do with Lena after all? Because why should Mr Duffy be so down on Clemence alone?'

'That brings me to the second item,' said Alec. 'He's not concentrating on Clemence. Far from it. He told me that he is going to divorce his wife.'

I was speechless, my mind racing but failing to find a thought to grasp and hold.

'He is divorcing Lena,' Alec went on, 'settling the Canadian property on Clemence, who we can only assume is to be packed off there, and handing the estates over to me.'

It is to my shame that what should have been the least

219

important of these points, that Alec might be coming to live on the Duffys' Perthshire estate after all, lodged in my mind as firmly as all the others.

'How can he divorce her?' I said. 'You mean he is to let her divorce him?' Even that was a ludicrous notion. Mr Duffy, stiff, proper and sixty-five, allowing himself to be photographed at an hotel with a girl hired for the purpose. But Alec was adamant.

'He can't just cast her off with no grounds,' I said.

'He has grounds,' said Alec. '"I will have no trouble producing grounds" were his exact words, and you've no idea how grim he looked when he said it.'

I could only whistle.

'How soon can you get here?' I said, sensing that we could spend the remainder of the morning on the telephone before we had done turning this over between us. 'I've already warned Hugh that you're on your way. I'm afraid he thinks you're coming for solace and there's worse – my boys are home and there will be a fair bit of letting them win at tennis and mending kites to be got through.'

'You've already said I'm on my way?'

'Yes, darling. Because Cousin Gregory who knows something is not alone. We know something too. Or I do anyway and I can't go on pretending I don't. Look, I don't want to talk about it on the telephone, but unless I face it and do something about it, I am never going to sleep a peaceful night through again. Only –' a sudden thought had struck me – 'Mr Duffy didn't say anything about wanting you to let sleeping dogs lie, did he? I mean, it's not a condition of the inheritance that you don't make any trouble? Because if it is . . .'

'You think I might let Lena off with murder to get my hands on it?' said Alec. His voice was cold and it was that I first responded to, flushing at his offence, at my insult. Then I realized what he had said, and the silence between us lengthened.

'So,' I said, at last.

'Just so,' said Alec.

Having arranged for his arrival two days later, we rang off. I walked around the room for a while picking up and setting down ornaments and disarranging the flowers. Clemence, Mr Duffy, Lena, Alec, the fire, the abortion, the photographs, and countless other flitting ghosts of ideas too vague even to be named whisked around my head, only obliquely visible, disappearing if I looked straight on. I despaired of ever being able to organize it all and view the whole thing at once. If I could only lay out each fact in order in front of me. For things *are* connected and life *does* make sense – I had decided that as early as the Croys visit and it had served me well until now. But this was like trying to play soldiers with kittens, goldfish even, seven disappearing for every two I managed to set in place and hold there.

Despairing of a head-start then, although it galled me to admit that I must wait for Alec, I thought I could at least make some practical preparations. Slipping into Hugh's business room I helped myself to a quantity of the large sheets of paper he uses to sketch out his interminable improvements. From the day nursery I took an India rubber and some pencils, and I looked forward to standing in front of my fire sharpening them with a pocket knife; this is one of my few manual skills, learned in childhood from a rather dashing drawing master and something which I felt would give me a welcome air of competence in front of Alec. Passing out of the nursery again, I stopped at the bookcase and, feeling rather silly, extracted the illustrated volume of Sherlock Holmes stories.

For the rest of that day I sat curled in my chair devouring it, hoping for guidance, but as tea approached I concluded that the working methods of a genius are of no use to lesser beings. Besides, real life is rather less neat than Mr Conan Doyle would have us imagine, or perhaps I should say rather more neat, people (as a rule) not dropping the ends of unusual cigars and abandoning scraps of their garments on convenient thorns as they pass. Really, when one thinks about it, story-book villains must be hardly decent and must suffer terribly from draughts, considering how much of their clothing they leave behind them. I closed the volume and hid it in my desk.

222

Chapter Fifteen

Alec was a terrific hit with the boys. In fact, his commandeering of their admiration prodded Hugh into enormous efforts of his own, even to the extent of getting Drysdale to fix up an old two-wheeled carriage and teaching the boys to drive along in it behind a quiet pony; I quite saw that they would be returning to school in September utterly spoiled.

Each day, after tea, which I and Alec and hence unbelievably Hugh – Hugh! – took with the children, it was understood that Alec and I should be left alone until it was time to change.

I cannot say what Alec was feeling, but on the first afternoon I felt as bashful as a child at a recital when it came to sitting opposite him and telling. Apart from anything else, there was so little of substance to tell. I cleared my throat.

'I think Lena killed Cara,' I said. 'I'm convinced of it, although I cannot explain why. Why I'm convinced, I mean. Or why she did it for that matter. Or how. Or how on earth Dr Milne managed to make the mistake he did.'

'I agree,' said Alec. 'We need to work out what happened and then we need to find some evidence. And then, whether we like it or not, we must go to the police.'

I leapt on this.

'Couldn't we go now?' I asked. 'I should love so much simply to hand it all over.' Alec was already shaking his head.

'What on earth would you say happened? How would you even begin? What proof do we have?'

'There's Mary's evidence,' I said. 'There never was a servant at the cottage.'

'That shows that Cara died, Dandy, not that Lena killed her.'

'And there's the diamonds,' I said.

'What about them?'

'I have no idea.' He was right: we needed proof. And unless we worked out what had happened we shouldn't even know what to look for proof *of*. I saw that.

'All right, then,' said Alec.

'Quite,' I replied.

By the end of a few days, we had reams of notes and permanent headaches and with each discussion it seemed we were losing sight of anything sensible, miring ourselves in endless speculation which produced nothing except fatigue.

A typical conversation might begin with me saying: 'There's just too much of everything.'

'Run through it again,' Alec would say, sitting back in his chair with his eyes shut. He said this on average every half-hour until I began to feel like a secretary.

'And none of it makes sense,' I would conclude at last. 'No one is behaving in a way that makes any sense at all. Take Mr Duffy. If he knows Lena killed her daughter, why is he content with divorce? Or rather if he is angry and disgusted enough to divorce her, why is he not angry and disgusted enough to go to the police? And how did he find out? And if he thinks Clemence knows, why is he giving her the Canadian property? But if he doesn't think Clemence knows why is he sending her off to Canada? And why also is he concerned to make sure that you don't marry her?'

'Or Lena,' Alec might say, running his hands through his hair for the hundredth time. 'Why did she make such elaborate plans to burn the house down if she had no intention of using the fire to destroy the body? Why did she take such a risk in asking Dr Milne to hush up the maid? Why did she think she could blackmail Silas and why does she now appear to have given up? What does she know about the disappearance of the diamonds?'

'Come to that, where are the diamonds, and who stole them and why and who knew about it?'

Then a silence.

'*Might* Cara have stolen them to raise money for an abortion?' This tended to recur.

'That would be far too much money. And anyway, in November? Impossible.'

'When do you suppose it did happen?' This from Alec, very gruff.

'Not before November, darling. She'd have been immense by the time of the Croys visit.'

'When then?' he said, staring hard at his feet.

I tried to remember Cara in her slim tube of a dress walking beside the river. Silk jersey it had been, the most clinging and least forgiving of any stuff dresses could be made of. I had not worn it for years.

'Oh, well after the New Year, anyway,' I said. Within a few months of the coming wedding then. But since we were talking about it, and he was squirming with embarrassment anyway, I finally resolved to ask something I'd been ducking.

'Forgive me, Alec, but was there no sign, no sign at all, that something like that was up?'

'What do you mean? What kind of sign?'

'Well, wasn't she – I mean, didn't she – Because I've been thinking, if it had been me, in Cara's predicament, I know I would have.' I hoped he would work out what I meant. No such luck. He blinked at me and waited.

'Remember when I asked you a very impertinent question to which the answer was no? Well, might I ask why not? I mean, whose decision was it?' I was being terrifically modern, and I wondered if Alec knew, or if he believed that in my youth, so recent and yet so distant, I had turned this question over calmly as though deciding between a walk or a drive on a Sunday morning.

'I don't know that it ever came up,' said Alec. 'Why?'

'And she didn't try to bring it up? Sometime after the New Year. I mean, as soon as she found out that she was definitely going to have a baby, so long as the father wasn't a Chinaman or anything . . . and then I daresay you'd have been none the wiser.'

'I daresay not,' said Alec, drily.

'And nobody else would have cared,' I said. 'Look at Daisy, for heaven's sake. Rupert weighed almost nine pounds, hardly six months after her wedding and no one even remembers it now. Although her mother was incandescent with fury at the time.'

'And Silas has never guessed?' said Alec.

'I didn't mean that!' I said. 'Rupert is Silas in miniature. Goodness, no. Much more likely that there are many more Silases in miniature popping out where they shouldn't be. Thankfully Daisy is too scatty to notice or care.'

'I had heard as much,' said Alec, and the little awkwardness had passed.

'It's a good question, though,' he said. 'Cara doesn't seem to have entertained any of the obvious solutions, does she? Such as postponing the wedding, or even seducing me, if she got really desperate, as you suggest.'

'But we *do* think she wanted to get an abortion and that's why she tried to sell the diamonds,' I said, refusing to react to such outrageous compliment-fishing.

'Even though one would think it's a bit of a sledgehammer to crack a walnut in terms of price *and* even though she would only think of it if she hadn't in fact stolen them.' This was another point which occurred and reoccurred.

'But if it wasn't Cara who stole them . . .' would be next.

'And we're back to where we began,' someone would

226

conclude. Then we would both groan and start somewhere else.

'Let's try the fire.'

'All right. Lena planned the fire, but was it to destroy Cara's body? Or merely to hide her disappearance?'

'Oh no. Lena planned to kill her,' Alec would say stoutly. He was sure of this. 'For some reason.'

'That we don't know,' I would remind him.

'And she *did* kill her,' he went on. 'But we don't really know how, do we? Except that it could be mistaken for . . . something else.' He gulped.

'Let's not think about that, darling. It's too horrid. Lena planned to kill her and Lena killed her.'

'For some reason,' he would say.

'That we don't know,' I would remind him.

'What *do* we know?' he would ask with the regularity of a metronome. And then I would recount what we knew and we would talk for another hour and the next day at the same time Alec would ask again what we knew and I would answer him again in so nearly the same words that if the intervening day with its meals and tennis and walks had been missed out no one would have been able to tell.

The day that we finally got somewhere, the day at least that the cracks began to show, the day before the *really* momentous days began, looked like all the rest to start with.

'What *do* we know, then?' Alec said, already querulous.

'Lena changed her mind about how to cover up the crime.'

'For some reason.'

I screamed. 'Alec, please stop saying "for some reason".'

'Steady on,' said Alec.

'It's not just irritating,' I insisted. 'I think it's actually stopping us from getting anywhere. We keep assuming that there's a reason for everything and it's just that we don't know what it is. But if we didn't do that, if we very

227

strictly held to the rule that if a thing appears to have no explanation then it can't have happened –'

'The exact opposite of Sherlock Holmes, then?' said Alec, and I could not stop myself from shooting a guilty look at my desk.

'What do you mean?'

'You're saying we should eliminate the implausible on the grounds that its implausibility makes it impossible too?'

'I think we could try it out,' I said, hoping that I did not sound too defensive. I had obviously given up on Conan Doyle before the useful bits. 'We haven't been getting anywhere anyway.'

'All right,' said Alec, sitting up, and speaking with great deliberation. 'Why did Lena change her mind about using the fire to destroy Cara's body? She had made very elaborate plans and something must have made her abandon them.'

We sat in perfect silence listening to the clock ticking until I felt a blush begin.

'What I wouldn't give for a madman,' I said. 'A mad murderous tramp with an axe.'

'If Conan Doyle had dragged on madmen when he got stuck he would never have found a publisher,' said Alec. 'It has to hang together.'

'Does it?' I said. 'I believe that things have to make sense, but must they hang –?' I stopped.

'Well, a mad axe-man who just happened to have killed Cara when she was about to be killed by someone else anyway is a little too –'

I shushed him furiously and thought hard, biting my lip, until my cigarette burned down to the end and, suddenly scorching my fingertips, brought me back with a start.

'I nearly had something there,' I said. 'I think so anyway. Not a mad murderous tramp, but . . . . Listen to this, Alec. We need to explain why Lena changed her mind and did something as risky and ad hoc – the maid and Dr Milne – instead of something she'd planned – the fire. We've been thinking that she must have lost her nerve, that she must have begun to doubt the body would be destroyed. Must have started worrying that there would be enough left to tell that Cara didn't die in the fire. But don't you see? We are missing something very obvious. The only reason to kill Cara the way she did, so that it looked the way it looked . . . I'm sorry, Alec, I know, but we must, darling.'

Every time I got close to talking about the precise moment and manner of Cara's death, the same thing happened. That curious tawny freckle that covered his face like a crochet-work shawl meant that he could not turn white exactly, but his lips seemed to disappear and the shadows under his eyes became suddenly prominent as the colour drained from around them. I tried to harden my heart to this, at least not to look at it while I spoke.

'Listen. We keep shying away from it, but we must force ourselves. It's too awful to think about, so we're trying to make sense of it all some way that means we don't have to. And that's never going to work. My nanny used to tell me that "Monsters faced are mice." So let's face it. The only reason I can think of to kill Cara in that particular way is this: if the body did not burn and was discovered, the story of the abortion was to be a second line of defence. Cara was supposed to have tried to abort a child and, when she failed, was supposed to have set the fire and killed herself. Do you see? You must see.'

Alec was blinking repeatedly as though to steady himself while a new idea took hold.

'And in that case,' I went on, 'it makes no sense whatsoever, whatsoever, whatso*ever*, that Lena would dream up the kitchen maid idea, does it? Not only is she taking a huge risk with Dr Milne, who she cannot possibly have known in advance would be so disgustingly co-operative, but more importantly, she is actually removing a central piece of her original plan. The way it actually happened, if the cottage had not burned completely, it would have come out that there was no one there at all. And then all

229

the talk would be, where was Cara? And the newspapers would be full of the story that a young woman had disappeared and Dr Milne might get to wondering and . . .'

'You're right,' said Alec. 'What did we say? What was our rule?'

'If something appears to have happened for no good reason at all, then it can't really have happened,' I said. My blood was thumping now. We were getting somewhere at last.

'So,' said Alec slowly, 'what is it that we're saying didn't happen? She did plan to kill her, and she did kill her, and she did kill her in that way . . .'

'But she didn't – couldn't possibly have *planned* to kill her that way.'

'Of course not,' said Alec, and now it all came tumbling out. 'It would have been crazy. She must have meant to kill Cara by suffocation or something, so that if her body survived the fire it would look as though she died from asphyxiation – because she *would* have died from asphyxiation.'

'But something happened. Something unexpected. And in a rage, all her plans forgotten, Lena set upon her.'

'And then she panicked and in her panic decided to gamble on the fable of the kitchen maid.'

We waited, each of us expecting the other to find a flaw, to frown and say that of course it could not possibly have happened like that and we should have to start again.

'So,' I said at last, when no one had spoken after all, 'we were right about the madman. In a way. Except that it was a mad *woman*. She must be, mustn't she? I mean we thought she must be evil, to plan her own daughter's death, but to snap like that and do what she did, it must be madness. And we don't have to explain it now. If it's madness. We can stop.'

Alec gave me the kind of smile one would use to a child, then he came to sit beside me and put his hand, in a very curious gesture, on the top of my head, not ruffling my hair exactly but as though he were about to, or as though he were blessing me.

'Good people always say that,' he said. 'About madness. And about evil, actually, if there's a difference. They can't explain it on any terms they understand and so they say what you just said. That it cannot *be* explained and we should not even try.' I turned my head a little to look at him and his hand slipped slightly down my hair, making him feel how awkward the gesture was, I think. At any rate he took his hand away before he went on talking.

'But madness and evil are no different from anything else, Dandy. An evil act is done *for* something. Always. We have not got to the bottom just by saying it's mad. We don't stop now. We've hardly started.'

'Do you really think there's no difference?' I said. 'Evil and madness.'

Alec shrugged. 'I think it's in the eye of the beholder,' he said. 'The strong call it evil and condemn it, the weak call it madness and pity it.' This silenced us both and we sat side by side but not touching; wearied, I think – at least I was – and wishing we could be talking of books, sitting here, or just gossiping, or even that Alec could be pouring out his manly grief about his poor dead love and I could be patting his hand and looking at him with my head on one side like a robin.

We both jumped and clutched at each other as a volley of knocks hit the window-pane so hard that the glass grated against the putty. Outside Donald and Teddy's faces could be seen, chins on the sill, red with excitement. I leapt to my feet and unfastened the window, too rattled even to scold them.

'You don't half look glum,' said Donald.

'What were you talking about, Mummy?' said Teddy. 'You're supposed to be cheering Mr Osborne up, you know, and he looks like a dying duck now.'

'Don't be rude,' I said, flustered. 'We were talking about the nature of evil and the meaning of madness and other

231

things that rude little boys know nothing about. Now run along and leave us alone.'

'You should come on a picnic, Mr Osborne,' said Donald. 'We've got that pony licked into shape now, that's what we came to tell you, Mother. So we can all go on a picnic and the pony can lug the hamper.'

'Tomorrow,' said Teddy. 'That'll cheer you right up.' He leaned to the side to see past me to where Alec was sitting. 'Better than old meaning of madness anyway. Or I know what. I'll tell you a joke.'

'No,' I said as firmly as I could, Teddy's jokes being unfit for the ears of anyone but Nanny. 'Mr Osborne is not interested in silly little boys' jokes.'

'I'll tell you the meaning of madness,' said Donald. 'Cousin Melville.' Teddy lost his grip on the window sill at that and dropped off in fits of giggles. I fastened the window again and returned to my seat.

'I rather wanted to hear about Cousin Melville,' said Alec.

'You shouldn't encourage them,' I said. 'And Hugh's cousin Melville is "not to be spoken of". But I think you're wrong about evil and madness being the same thing, you know.' Alec, far from being annoyed to have me disagree with him, gestured for me to go on. 'I think she must be mad to think of killing her own child. But to do it, to go through with it, that's evil.'

'The desire is madness, the decision to give in to the desire is evil?'

'Yes, or even if a mad rage took her through doing it, to try to get away with it is evil.'

'And this is all your own?' said Alec. 'You have never studied the great philosophers?' I felt he was laughing at me now, and I racked my brain to remember if I had in fact read something like that.

'I don't think so,' I said. 'Have I pinched it from somewhere?'

'Don't,' said Alec, glaring at me. 'Don't pretend to be silly. Silly little boys don't deserve our scorn, but if there's

232

one thing worse than a silly woman, it's a woman who pretends to be silly when she has a choice.'

Rather typical, I thought, for the most flattering thing that has ever been said to one to be couched in terms that call one a goose and a liar and an uncaring mother to boot.

'To return to Lena,' I said, and something about the way I said it caused Alec to get up and go back to his chair.

'If what we've deduced is right enough,' I continued, 'and if you're right about evil being purposeful then we are even less far on than we were before.' Alec looked at me quizzically and then nodded.

'Lena planned to kill Cara in cold blood,' he said, 'but killed her in anger before the plan could be seen through. We now need an explanation for not one murder, but two.'

'But you know, I've been thinking thoughts like that off and on for ages and ignoring them,' I said. 'I kept thinking how it spilled out one side when you were looking at the other, you know? Just too much of everything, and we've been searching for an answer that explains it all. But really it's as though she's two completely separate people. Planning everything so carefully, then flying into such a blind, ugly rage. Then once again dealing so horridly meticulously with the mess that rage produced. And for what reason? Because what you said about Cara is just as true of Lena. If she is so concerned about respectability why not do any of the much milder things that might have been done? Postponing the wedding or arranging an abortion.'

'As you said yourself, Dandy, even if Lena is two separate people, one is mad and one is bad. Neither of them would want to smooth things through for Cara instead of punishing her.'

The dressing bell rang then, and I was glad to hear it. I was completely fagged with it all and thought if I tried to compose one more coherent remark, Alec would change his mind and think me the silliest woman who ever lived. Besides, I was still hugging his compliment to me, saving it until later when I could get it out and admire it properly.

'Goodness, madam,' said Grant, as I opened my bedroom door. 'Have you been frowning like that all afternoon? Look at the crease you've put in your brow. I shall have to press a hot cloth on that, ten minutes at least. Now, lie down while I fetch it and try not to scowl, do.'

Chapter Sixteen

It was with mixed feelings that I found myself, along with Alec, engaged for a picnic the following afternoon.

'I don't clearly remember having accepted this invitation,' I grumbled as Teddy and Donald dragged me downstairs the next morning to instruct Mrs Tilling.

'That's the nature of your madness, Mummy,' said Teddy, barely getting it out between gusts of laughter. I foresaw that the nature of madness was to take over as the motto of the holiday and I cursed myself for blurting it out to them.

'Very well then,' I said. 'But you must not disturb me all morning until it's time to leave. I have a great deal to do.'

'A great deal of *what* to do?' said Donald with a depth of scorn which tugged at me. I had told myself at the time that I hated the way they clung around me when they were tiny with their little sticky hands clutching my skirts and their little sticky faces always turned up for a kiss. Now, perversely, I should not mind at all to hear voices piping how clever I was to find rabbit when he was lost at bedtime or how pretty I looked when I was dressed for a party.

I asked for a pot of coffee to be brought to my sitting room and sat sipping it, meditatively staring at the objects on my writing desk: the blank sheet of paper, the photographs of the boys as fat babies. Also there on my desk top was a puzzle, brought back as a souvenir from my elder sister's tour of India with her bore of a husband. It was a little polished nest of interlocking structures, indivisible so that it must have been carved out of a single piece of wood, and it rattled with a pleasing, smooth sound if one shook it, but it could not come apart. So not a puzzle at all really, just an intricate curio.

That was what this case should look like, perfectly interlocking and complete, but it was more like the monkeys from the night nursery, little wooden monkeys each with one arm stretched up and its tail reaching down so that it could be suspended from the one above, arm to tail, arm to tail, in a brittle, precarious string. That was this case to a tee. Each fact could be carefully suspended from the preceding one in a longer and longer chain, but if one tried to make a loop – I remembered Donald spending hours on this – guiding the last tail gently around to the first paw, no matter how careful one was, the thing fell to bits in one's hands.

Two murders need two motives, I wrote, then I put my elbows on the desk and lowered my head, but stopped in time. It was not even ten o'clock in the morning, and I could not possibly put my head in my hands already. Sherlock, I am sure, never put his head in his hands before luncheon. That should be my rule from now on. No head-holding before luncheon, no putting of one's head on the table and rolling it from side to side before tea, and no audible groaning before dinner.

Two secrets, I wrote. Diamond theft, baby coming. I could not begin to see how either of these could lead to either of the murders, much less work out which went with which. Could a theft cause the planned death of one's child? Could anything about a theft send one mad? Not in any way that I could imagine. But it was even more ludicrous to think that a baby coming too soon and from the wrong quarter could make a woman plot to kill her child. It was shameful, scandalous, it's true, but it happened all the time and the most rigid families got over it in the end. But then Lena was such a curious mixture of respectability and complete carelessness. Clemence so protected, so coddled – I remembered Lena telling me with

236

satisfaction how she tried to shield darling Clemence from the ugly truths of life. Cara on the other hand, since she had managed to get pregnant, must have been on a fairly free rein. And that was how it had been for years. Clemence at her mother's heels and Cara racketing about with Sha-sha McIntosh and the others. Staying all on her own with Daisy and Silas years ago, walking in the woods with Alec, if it came to that. Questions of respectability seemed to influence Lena in random and mystifying ways. But could any mother, however odd she was, really care whether a child who is known to have killed herself is also known to have had a little accident as well? Daisy's mother had been wild when Rupert had made his early entry in the too, too solid nine pounds of his flesh, but she adored him now.

Of course! The revelation fizzed in my head. Of course! I had said it myself, hadn't I? It's the sort of thing that one gets over, but it rocks one on one's heels at the time. Lena had not known about Cara's baby.

I had been right all along. There *were* two stories, each quite separate from the other. The planned murder, so meticulously prepared, the cottage decorated, the engagement broken and the coal laid in, was all to do with the jewels and nothing to do with the baby at all. It had to be so. Lena already knew about the jewels; the timing was right. A known fact causing a planned killing and then a nasty surprise wiping out all the plans and ending in something savage. That had to be how it was. If I forced myself to accept the one brutal fact that threatened to choke me, that Lena really had done what she had done, it fitted.

From here, finally, I could bridge the gap. From this spot on my cliff edge I could point across to where Lena had gone and at least see what had plucked her away there. I still did not know exactly why she had planned the fire but that night at the cottage, with the plan set in motion, she must have been wound as tight as a steel spring, perhaps half-crazy already with the thought that she couldn't, but she must, but she couldn't, but she must. Then Cara went out on her bicycle to the post box and, if Lena discovered that she had gone, she must have assumed she'd gone for good, escaped. Lena must have been flung to the farthest edge of sanity at that, or drowned by a surge of hopeless relief, perhaps, that she needn't go through with it after all. Then cruelly, unbelievably, she was snapped right back to the middle of it again when Cara returned. Into all of that, Cara dropped her bombshell and the shock must have cracked across Lena like lightning. She attacked, and attacked as though to blot out the very source of all the disgust and shame.

But where was Clemence in any of this? Had she tried to intervene between her little sister and her mother gone suddenly, terrifyingly, mad? I had never seen so much as a word pass between the sisters in any of our meetings through the years, and Clemence was Lena's through and through. Poor Clemence. (Why did we always say that?) What had been her part in that ugly night? She had been there, and yet it was impossible to make oneself remember her somehow. Lena and Cara with their secrets were curved around each other, interlocking, and Clemence did not fit. I shuddered. Not 'poor' Clemence at all. It was chilling to think that there was someone else there, besides Cara and Lena, not stepping in, not stopping it from happening, just watching it with her blank eyes and then taking her plates to the photographer's shop to see how well they had come out. Perhaps whatever was wrong with the inside of Lena's head had passed itself on.

I felt besmirched by these thoughts, but not for the first time I put my uneasiness down to quite the wrong cause. I thought it was the horrid idea of what had been done to Cara that was unsettling me. I actually thought that I had pushed myself to my limits and beyond in making myself repeat the idea and see the image over and over again. In fact, of course, I had turned away in squeamishness every time, taking mincing little peeks at it and then bolting, and because of this I had not seen something glaringly obvious.

238

Had I forced myself truly to retell the tale of what had happened in the cottage that night and tried to watch it happening before me like a news reel, I could not have helped but see the gaping hole in the story. Ironic that I should then have been able to turn away from it once and for all. Nanny Palmer was right: monsters faced *are* mice, but because I had not faced this one it loomed over me like a behemoth still.

It was with some effort that I arranged a suitable face to wear above my linen frock for the picnic, an effort which I surmised from Donald's greeting was not wholly successful.

'You look dreadful, Mother,' he said, reminding me very much that he was his father's son.

'You don't half need this picnic,' said Teddy. 'But it's a shame you're so big or you could come in the trap with us instead of the boring old motor. Now I wonder . . .' He looked at the picnic things and unflatteringly at my figure, gauging their relative weights, I supposed, but Alec nipped this firmly in the bud.

'No, we're not getting it all out again when we've just spent such ages stuffing it in,' he said. 'You get in and drive the pony with Donald, and Mummy and I will crawl along behind and tell you what we think of your prowess.' This proved the magic touch, although I pitied the poor pony, envisaging much more liberal application of the whip if the boys were playing to the gallery. Still it gave Alec and me talking time as we puttered along in their dust.

'You do look ropy, actually, Dan,' said Alec as we set off.

'It's just . . .' I began, but could not go on. 'I really am all right. In fact, it's being all right that's so shocking.'

'I know,' said Alec. 'I remember this from the war. One gets used to more and more and more until one is quite happy to countenance things which would have been the

239

stuff of nightmares in normal life. I remember –' He broke off.

'Please tell me, 'I said. 'I shan't mind, because I know exactly what you mean. Every so often I hear myself saying "But since Lena killed her child that must mean . . ." and I think I shall faint or burst out laughing because it seems so impossible.'

'Faint, if you've got a choice,' said Alec. 'When one starts to laugh one's really in trouble. What I was going to . . . I once had this pie. It was in the trench, you know, and instead of the usual dried beef and mouldy biscuits, somehow from somewhere we had got these pies. Anyway, I found myself thinking that yes, I knew I had to do something about old Pinner, Sergeant Pinner, I knew he could not stay there for ever, but I was bloody well going to have my pie first and then a fag and *then* I should take him away, and it wasn't as if he could see me anyway because his head was blown off all over the shop and that made it better. I started to laugh then and couldn't stop, kept going until the whites of my eyes were red all over with burst blood vessels and then Pinner and I had to be carted off together. Look, one of them is still a bit pink.' He turned towards me and opened his eyes very wide close to mine. I could not see anything in the dim interior of the motor car, but I nodded anyway.

'So,' said Alec, horridly brisk all of a sudden, 'let's at least see if you've been wading through the same horrors as me this morning, shall we? I concluded that . . . that . . . the nature of the attack points towards its being Lena's sudden discovery that Cara was with child which brought it on.'

'Yes,' I said thankfully. 'That on top of all the strain of what she was about to do. And, as well, there's the fact that she is, must be, an extremely unstable woman. In our midst all the time, looking perfectly normal.'

And yet. Lena's madness seemed to come and go so conveniently. Mad evil thoughts, and cool sane plans. Mad, ugly rages, and calm, brave solutions. I had heard of people who had hordes of unwanted guests inside their heads, independent agents each ploughing a different furrow, and I wondered again for a moment if Lena's madness could be of this type. But no. Even when she acted like two separate people, one cleared up after the other. They were in it together.

The boys had veered off the lane and were trotting the pony over the rough ground towards our favourite picnic spot, Donald driving the trap and Teddy, totally unnecessarily, standing up waving his arms to show us where they were going. We turned and began to bump over the grass behind them.

'What about the diamonds?' said Alec 'Have you got anywhere with that?'

'No,' I said. 'At best a lot of incompatible wisps.'

'Me too, 'said Alec. 'Such as what makes Lena so sure that the Esslemonts' ball is anything to do with it? After all, Cara told you that the jewels were in and out the bank more than once since then. To be cleaned and valued and have pastes made.'

'Everything except to be worn,' I agreed. 'If I had anything as beautiful as those I should wear them all the time. Every day. I should be wearing them now.' I was forcibly trying to lighten the mood as we drew to a halt and got ready to jump down and rejoin the children.

Mrs Tilling might not have been up all night in preparation of the feast but that was clearly the effect she wanted to achieve. As well as tomato sandwiches there were chicken legs and a glorious raised game pie which Alec and the boys fell upon but which I, still trying to dispel the story of Sergeant Pinner, could not touch. A splendid luncheon, then, which would have been quite delicious freshly served in the dining room or even on the terrace, instead of damp and dishevelled on the ground a mile from home. The hardboiled eggs, as ever, were taken by Teddy and shied into the river.

'Where they belong!' he cried after them. 'Mummy, why

241

can't you tell her? It's a fearful waste of eggs apart from anything else.'

'Write me the script, Teddy darling, and I shall deliver it with feeling,' I said. 'And if you come up with a winner we can adjust it slightly and I'll use it to stamp out my birthday cologne from Granny.'

After lunch, a row broke out.

'Oh, come on, Mother,' said Donald, 'What's the point of coming if you're not going to join in?'

'I am not playing hide and seek,' I insisted. 'There's nowhere to hide.'

'There's heaps of places to hide,' said Teddy with his arms spread to the heavens and a look of incredulity on his face. 'Look around. The riverbank, dozens of good trees, long grass . . .'

'You're wearing a pillow case anyway,' said Donald, looking disparagingly at my rather crumpled linen, 'so it can go in the tub for a boiling. Come on!'

'We'll let Mr Osborne decide,' I said, and turned pleadingly to Alec.

'I say let's,' said Alec, leaping to his feet and brushing away pie crumbs. 'You boys can hunt for Mummy and me first.'

The boys draped themselves over the bonnet of the motor car and started counting. Around the next bend in the river, I knew, was an ancient and rather sickly beech tree with a hollow in its trunk and I thought Alec and I might fit there, snugly but not beyond the boundary of propriety, so I dragged him off in that direction. When we got there, however, I saw that this hollow – so commodious in my recollection – was actually only the size of an average bathtub, and while it might have done very well for one of the boys and myself, it was out of the question for Alec and me. He looked at it with one raised eyebrow and then scanned the upper branches.

'You get in there, Dan,' he said, chivalrously kicking out some old leaves, 'and I'll shin up a bit and keep a lookout.'

242

'It won't be long, I hope. This is bound to be the first place they look.'

Resigning myself to the ruin of my frock and to Grant's censure on my return I backed myself in and snuggled down, while Alec, with a great deal of grunting and rustling of leaves, climbed into the crown above me.

'Can you hear me?' he said, presently. I assured him I could. 'I have a clear view,' he said. 'We can talk now, but if I see them coming I'll shush you.'

I marvelled at his unspoken assumption. We were to speak of the murder of his fiancée, but only until it threatened to interfere with our winning at hide and seek.

We had hardly begun, though, when I heard a series of whoops and ululations from quite close by and my heart sank. Unsatisfied, as ever, with just hide and seek, they had added a Red Indian element, and, in my experience, being stalked by braves took a good bit longer than by little Scottish boys, what with endless suspensions of the action to discuss anthropological details, as well as the obvious retarding effect of them dropping to their tummies whenever they drew near their prey.

I heard heavy breathing and slow careful footsteps and I peeped out to see Teddy, bent over at the waist and carrying the knife we had used for the pie, pick his way on tiptoe along the bare earth below the beech tree, looking for tracks. He did not even glance up as he passed.

Alec waited an age before he spoke again.

'All clear,' he whispered, then in a normal voice, he carried on. 'That day at Croys, Dan. Cara said to you she was a good girl who always did as she was told.'

'Yes. I've told you several times she did.'

'No, but listen. What were you talking about when she said it? Can you remember?'

'Something to do with the diamonds,' I said. 'Something to do with her telling her mother. I blush to admit it, but I was more taken up with that fact. I mean, would you? Lena?'

'I should rather have died,' said Alec. 'But what I'm

really getting at is – Sssh!' I shushed immediately, thinking he must have had some sudden spark of an idea and needed to catch it before it evaporated, but the steady tramp of approaching feet told me, after a minute, that he had merely heard the boys coming back. I could not help a sigh of exasperation from escaping me. It was too ridiculous for words. I sighed again, rather more loudly, and then wanting only to get out of this tree and go home, I cleared my throat.

The boys, who had to have heard me, went quiet. Their footsteps stilled and then they began to move again more stealthily, barely making a sound. I held my breath, ready for their leaping attack, but gradually, unbelievably, the quiet footsteps receded. They were walking away. The little devils were deliberately walking away and refusing to find us. This was a ploy of some tradition; hide and seek when they were tiny consisted of my moving myself to more and more obvious locations in the house and their refusing to 'find' me even when, giggling helplessly, they looked straight into my eyes. I had learned, as a result, never to allow the game to begin just before bedtime and I remember saying to them in my sternest voice that I should agree to play hide and seek but refused to play 'hide and hide' or 'seek to be sought' any more. Really though, they should have been past such tricks by now.

And then suddenly something was clear, as though a bar of carbolic had been dropped into a bath full of bubbles, popping them all at once and revealing my own body lying large as life in the plain water. I struggled out of the hollow and looked up at Alec perched in the branches above me. My face must have shown it because he jumped down and took my hands, all thoughts of hiding forgotten.

'What?' he demanded.

'What about this?' I said. 'It's so obvious, you're going to kick yourself. Since November, the Duffy diamonds have been taken out of the bank to be cleaned, to be valued, and to have pastes made, but they have not been worn. Now

244

answer me this: who takes jewels out of the bank and has them cleaned if they are not going to wear them? Who has their jewels valued for no reason? What kind of person would have pastes made if they were not going to wear the pastes?'

'The same kind of person,' Alec said slowly, 'who has a photograph album of her two daughters enjoying a week in the country when one of them is already dead. Is that what you mean? Lena was constructing a record?'

'No,' I said. 'Not at all. She wasn't hiding. She was seeking to be found. She was trying to make the theft come to light. Trying to get someone to admit that the diamonds were fakes.' I laughed, shaking my head. 'Don't you see? She was desperately trying to get some jeweller or banker to blow the whistle. She must have been beginning to despair of its ever happening. Certainly the further it got from the Esslemonts' ball the more difficult it was going to become to convince anyone that *that* was where the theft occurred.'

'So who stole them?' said Alec.

'She did,' I said. 'Lena did, of course. That's why she could be so sure of when they were stolen. She stole them herself. And she probably set up the theft with as much care as she set up the fire – only to find that the theft would not come to light and all her lovely evidence at Croys was wasted. She stole them herself, Alec, and what is more, she meant to steal them twice. Once in reality and once by claiming the insurance money. Or as it turned out by extorting the insurance money from Silas.'

'But why would she?' said Alec.

'Perhaps because Gregory meant to give them to Cara. And because Lena loves them. Perhaps she still has them somewhere and always meant to keep them for herself. For herself and Clemence, I mean. I'm prepared to believe that she loves Clemence as well as the diamonds but we know that she hated Cara.'

'Do we?' said Alec. He sounded bewildered, as though struggling to keep up with me.

'She killed her, Alec darling,' I said. 'She killed her twice. In cold blood and in anger. Her own child. Of course she hated her.'

'What about Cara trying to sell them?' said Alec. 'If you're right about this. Does it help that fit in?'

Another of the bubbles popped and I looked at him through the clear water, cold and certain.

'Cara tried to sell them, my dear Alec, because she was a good girl who did as she was told.'

'Who was telling?'

'Lena, of course.'

'And Cara obeyed? Why?'

'I don't know. I don't understand the hold Lena had over her, any more than I understand the hold Lena has, or thinks she has over Silas and Daisy. Horrible woman, with all her little secrets.'

'And why was Cara to be killed?' said Alec.

'Because she could not be trusted to keep it all to herself once she was an independent married woman. She was used to bring the theft to light and then, since she was expendable, she was expended.'

'Evil woman,' said Alec. 'For jewels? For money?'

'But, you know, in her favour I don't think the sacrifice of Cara was part of the plan from the start. If one of those horribly discreet jewellers had done what they were supposed to do –'

'Mummy,' said Teddy's voice, high with indignation and wonder. 'Why aren't you hiding? And what on earth are you talking about?' I started and gobbled uselessly like some nervous item of poultry, but Donald and Teddy were clearly wearing out too and made little protest as we packed up the picnic things and bundled everything back into the cart for a hasty return. They were not too tired, however, to persist in trying to find out what we had been discussing. They kept on and on until Alec relented and told them it was a story we had not finished reading and were trying to guess the end of, and then went into enormous detail about such quelling matters as which of the

246

two heroes the heroine really loved and what kind of stocks and bonds the old banker had embezzled, until Donald begged him to shut up.

'And *why* weren't you hiding?' said Teddy.

'Why weren't you seeking?' I countered.

'We were using Indian tracking methods, Mother,' said Donald.

'Well then, I don't think much of them,' I said.

Both boys began to talk at once, Teddy's voice, being the more piercing, winning through.

'– just where you're wrong. Because they are actually very skilful – better than blacksmiths and everything that we've got here – and not at all savage at all.'

'Even scalping,' Donald put in.

'Scalping isn't savage?' I could hardly help laughing. Donald looked witheringly at me.

'Yes, but it's not just lunging at someone and ripping his hair off, Mother, there's a lot to it and . . . Mother? Are you all right?'

'Are you going to faint, Mummy?'

'Are you going to be sick? Did you eat berries?'

'Because you're always telling us not to, and really after that huge lunch –'

'Dandy?'

I could not answer.

'Right, you two,' said Alec, bundling them into the trap. 'You set off now and we'll give you three minutes and race you home.'

I sat numbly in the motor car while he started it, not quite believing where my thoughts were leading me.

'What is it?' he said, once we were under way, rolling along in the wake of the pony.

'Simply this,' I said. 'When a person flies into a murderous rage and attacks someone, what one ends up with is a battered bloody corpse, not a girl lying in a bed who looks as though she has had an abortion. And if we hadn't been so cowardly about making ourselves face it I should have seen that straight away.'

'What made you think of it all of a sudden just now?' said Alec.

'Scalping,' I said. 'It's brutal and nasty but not, as my charming children pointed out, just lunging at someone and ripping his hair off. And the same goes for what happened to Cara. There's no way one thing could be mistaken for the other.'

'But Dr Milne –'

'Yes, but that's what I've been thinking through. Dr Milne said precisely nothing. Simply that she had tried to miscarry in a very silly way that only an ignorant girl would think of. He supplied no details. *I* filled it all in, and in the most grisly way possible.'

'And you told me no details and I did the same,' said Alec. 'You're right. But Dr Milne did seem sure, Dandy.'

'He also seemed sure that the girl was a servant, and we know she wasn't. Besides, something about what he said has been bothering me all along in a way I can't get a hold of. I almost got it at the memorial service, or I thought I did, but then I fell asleep. So maybe I was dreaming.'

'Don't drift, Dandy,' said Alec. 'Concentrate. What *can* have happened? You're right, of course. Any . . . direct method would have nothing in common with a sudden angry outburst, but what else is there?'

'Hot baths? No. Gin? Clearly not.'

'What about jumping?'

'That's an old wives' tale,' I said. 'Complete nonsense – But oh! That's exactly what Dr Milne said, isn't it? That only a silly ignorant girl would believe it would work and that anyone with any sense would see that she'd be as likely to die as to miscarry.'

'And jumping, jumping off something and landing badly, would look almost identical to being shoved and landing badly.'

'And a shove is exactly the kind of thing one would do if one flew into a rage, isn't it? I'm sure this is right, Alec. It must be.'

We rattled up the drive to the house. The boys, unable to

stop the pony, who had got the bit well and truly between its teeth, swept away around the side to the stables. I gestured for Alec to pull up on the gravel then hurried inside and straight to my sitting room to the telephone.

'Who are you calling?' he said, arriving just as I lifted the earpiece.

'Hello?' I said. 'Yes, it's a Dr Milne in Gatehouse of Fleet, please. Kirkcudbright 59.' I put my hand over the mouthpiece. 'Before I lose my nerve,' I whispered to Alec.

'Well, be careful,' he whispered back and sank into a chair to listen.

Chapter Seventeen

It took the usual aeons for the call to be put through, clickings and whirrings and sudden hollow silences. While I was waiting, Alec whispered at me again.

'What are you going to say?'

'No idea. But don't worry – it's a favoured ploy of mine.'

The telephone was ringing at last.

'Yes, hello, what is it?' said a clipped voice at the other end. If this was Mrs Milne, then I pitied the doctor.

'Might I speak to Dr Milne?' I said. 'Or leave a message?'

'Can you not come to the surgery?' said the voice, surely a housekeeper.

'Oh, no,' I trilled. 'This is not a professional call. I'm a friend. Mrs Gilver. But I'll happily ring back if Dr Milne is busy.'

'Oh, Mrs Gilver,' said the voice with deep interest. I supposed I was famous in Gatehouse by now. The doctor was in for Mrs Gilver, no doubt about it, and the housekeeper, for such she must be (a wife would hardly be so accommodating in handing over even her husband's ear to such a female), bustled off to fetch him.

'My dear Dr Milne,' I began, greetings over, 'if you send me a bill this time it will be no more than I deserve, but please let me trespass for a moment. I'd like you to back me up in my efforts to get my boys to maturity in one piece. You didn't meet my little boys, did you? Well, they are monkeys. I use the term advisedly. They've been learning mountaineering at school this year and I cannot keep them off the roofs. The stable roofs have always been a draw, but now they're up on the house roofs day in and day out and will not listen to me telling them they could kill themselves. Now, here's how you can help me. I told them a heavily edited version of what happened to that poor little kitchen maid of the Duffys'.'

'You did what?' He almost shouted, and Alec too was looking at me as though I was gaga.

'What I mean is I told them that a girl I knew jumped from the tiniest height and ended up dead. She did jump, didn't she? I'm almost sure you said she jumped, or that's what I had understood you to mean.'

'Oh yes,' said Dr Milne. 'She jumped.' I wiggled my eyebrows at Alec.

'And I've been telling them that jumping is safer than falling because you've planned for it and that this poor girl jumped off something miles lower than our roofs here – you remember the house, don't you? Terrible Gothic additions, turrets everywhere – so then they said, What did she jump off, Mother? And I had to admit that I didn't know. And now they think it was a cliff-top or something and they won't heed my warnings the least bit. And to cut a long story short, we've got ourselves into a betting situation over it. There are scones at stake. Shocking when one thinks of the poor creature, I know, but there it is. Now, what did she jump off? Do you know?'

Alec's face was caught midway between stunned admiration and disbelief, but I held out the earpiece towards him to let him hear Dr Milne laughing cosily at the other end and he mimed a salute to me. I smirked back, and put the earpiece to my ear again.

'She jumped from the landing, my dear Mrs Gilver. Down the stairwell. Hit her head as she fell and snapped her neck when she landed.' We both sighed.

'Well, since there couldn't have been more than a dozen steps in a cottage staircase, I should think that might sober my little demons no end. Thank you, Dr Milne.'

'You're very welcome, Mrs Gilver. But don't dwell on it now, or you'll give yourself nightmares again.'

251

'You are very kind to think of that,' I said. 'Can I ask one more thing?' I knew I was headed for thin ice now, but I could not help myself. 'I suppose I'm right, saying to them that a fall is even worse than a jump? Even more dangerous, I mean.'

'I would imagine so.'

'And, I suppose, a shove is worst of all.'

There was silence at the other end.

'But can one tell the difference?'

More silence. Alec was making furious gestures at me and I could feel a pulse quicken as it rose in my throat.

'Because they do muck about up there, pretending to push one another and whatnot. It's terrifying to watch. And if I could say I had it from a reputable doctor that a shove and a fall are both worse than a jump and that even a doctor can't tell the difference . . . Well, the thought of one dead and the other in jail for fratricide might have some sway.'

'I think I would rather you did not quote me on this topic,' said Dr Milne, after a huge pause. 'As you say, a reputable doctor has a great deal of sway and has to be very careful.' My mouth dropped open in amazement.

'What?' Alec hissed, jumping to his feet. 'What's he saying?'

'I suppose so,' I said as calmly as I could. 'Well, be assured that if I need to call upon a witness for corroboration, I shall leave you out of it.' I gave my best attempt at a gay little laugh. 'I shan't see buttered scones for days to come, Dr Milne.'

'My condolences,' he intoned, not even trying to match my gaiety.

We rang off.

I tried to relay it word for word to Alec; at least I got the gist of the important bits.

'A reputable doctor has a great deal of sway?' Alec echoed. 'Oh my God, Dandy, he's going to sue you for defamation. You just wait. You're not safe to be let out.'

'I like that,' I said. 'What would you have done? Noth-

252

ing, that's what. And where would we be once you had? Nowhere.'

'Well, where have *you* got us?' he said.

'I've shown Dr Milne up for what he is,' I said. 'I always knew he was. The way he spoke about the girl that very first time – you weren't there, Alec, you don't know. And now it's quite sure. Just because she was a servant (he thought) and had got into trouble he didn't even bother to wonder whether she had jumped or was pushed. Didn't even think to question Lena's version of things. A snob and a fool.'

'A snob and a fool now thoroughly on his guard. I wish you had talked things over with me before launching into it, Dandy. That was a very silly thing to do.'

So, from self-taught philosopher to reckless idiot overnight. There was ages until the dressing bell, but I stamped off anyway, feeling under-appreciated and sick of the lot of them. (I was even cross with Donald and Teddy for the playing on the roof.)

Grant, evidently, was in one of her mellower moods and did not seem put out to be summoned early. She had taken delivery that afternoon of a collar and cuffs in mauve rabbit-fur edged with seed pearls, which she planned to attach to a lilac chiffon evening wrap of mine. I could not remember ever hearing of these monstrous articles, much less rubber-stamping their purchase, and when Grant opined that there was plenty of time to get them on in time for dinner that night I panicked.

'Bit of a waste, isn't it?' I asked, cajolingly. 'Only Mr Gilver and Mr Osborne to see them.'

Grant sighed.

'Yes, I daresay, madam,' she said, laying the collar back in its tissue paper nest. 'When's the next time anyone will be here?' By anyone, I knew, Grant meant any ladies. We make no pretence about that.

'As soon as I can arrange it,' I said feelingly, stepping out of my dress and turning to let her unbutton my underbodice. 'I am sick up to my teeth of men and boys, Grant. I'd join a convent for tuppence.'

'Oh, madam, no,' she said, genuinely shocked. 'Grey serge and no lipstick. And all that praying must give them knees like leather. They must thank heavens habit hems never go high enough to show them.'

Grant's take on the preoccupations of nuns, utterly serious and utterly typical, cheered me up no end.

'Well, all right,' I said. 'Not a convent. Perhaps a harem.' I suspect she is unshockable, but it does not stop me from trying. She smirked at this, though, and I saw that I had failed again.

'What have "men" done anyway, madam?' she asked presently through a mouthful of hairpins. I have offered many times to hold the pins and pass them to her, but I do not pass them quickly enough or hold them out at the right angle and she is best left to manage it herself.

'Nothing out of the ordinary,' I said. 'Just been unwilling to face up to the plainer side of life and made everything more difficult as a result.'

'Oh, that,' said Grant. 'As to that, madam, the kitchen cat brought in a mouse this morning and started to eat it right under the upper servants' breakfast table, and guess who crawled under with a bit of newspaper and got it away from the little beast? Mrs Tilling. Mr Pallister was the colour of milk.'

'Exactly,' I said, lifting my chin while she untied my dressing cape. 'What if the mouse had still been alive, though?'

'Lord, I'd have run a mile!' said Grant.

'Me too,' I said, and even the thought of it made me tuck my feet up off the carpet. 'Men do have their uses,' I concluded.

'No doubt about it, madam,' said Grant. 'You said yourself you'd prefer a harem to a convent.' (When it comes to shock statements, Grant outstrips me without trying.) 'But birth, death and nappies, as my mother always used to say.'

I stared at her.

'Birth, death . . .?'

'And nappies, madam. Things men don't do. Are you all right?'

I didn't answer, but continued to stare.

'Madam?'

'I shan't need you tonight, Grant,' I said. 'And tomorrow is your day off, isn't it? Well then, let's say I'll do without you in the morning too.' I stood and turned slowly, arms out, while she inspected me.

'I hope I haven't said anything to offend you, madam,' said Grant. 'I meant nothing by it.'

'Absolutely not,' I said. 'You've been very helpful.'

I waited until she had cleared the end of the passageway and disappeared through the door to the servants' stairs, then, shoes in hand, I crept along to the guest wing on tiptoe. Before I reached Alec's door he emerged dressed for dinner but, seeing me, he backed into his room again and drew me after him.

'Is your valet –?'

'He's long gone,' said Alec. 'What is it?'

'I'm going to come upstairs straight after dinner,' I said. 'And then tomorrow the story is that . . . let's say . . . Daisy Esslemont rang very early and I've gone off to see her at Croys. I shall think of some reason Hugh won't question. Actually, I'm going to drive to Gatehouse tonight.'

'You're not tackling Dr Milne on your own,' said Alec. 'He's backed into a corner, Dandy. There's no telling what he might do.'

'I'm not tackling Dr Milne,' I said. 'Alone or otherwise. I'm going to track down our witness and I need to leave tonight in case Dr Milne has the same idea.'

'Our witness? What makes you so sure we have one?'

'We do.'

'And what makes you think it won't be as bad an idea for you to tackle him on your own as –'

255

'It's not a him,' I said. 'It's a her.'

'Who?' said Alec.

'I don't know her name or where she lives,' I said. 'But I know she exists. She's the person who laid out Cara's body before the undertakers took it away. And unless I'm very much mistaken, she is also the local midwife. She will know not only that the girl she laid out was not a servant, but also that she was still pregnant when she died, and perhaps – since she's probably the nearest thing there is to a doctor for those who cannot afford Dr Milne – she might also know that Cara's injuries came from being shoved over, not from jumping off any landing. I don't know how they managed to hush her up, Alec – money probably – but I shall unhush her if it's the last thing I do. Now go and entertain Hugh while I prepare a few things and . . .' I hesitated and may even have blushed although the lamplight was too low for him to see me. 'Could you possibly make sure that he has a great deal to drink tonight at dinner and after? I don't think he's likely to come to my room, but it's best to be sure.'

By ten o'clock, dressed in a warm coat in case I ended up sleeping in the motor car, I was huddled in the porch of the side door plucking up the nerve to start walking. The stable block is just around the corner of the billiard room and across the yard and it was a trip I made daily without thinking, being generally too impatient to wait for my little Austin motor to be brought round. Now though, as I set off, the carriage house doors seemed to dwindle into the distance and the yard stretched endlessly in front of me. The stone chippings too crunched explosively under my tread, like horses eating apples, and my neck grew stiff with the effort not to peer around me.

Alec had urged me to take his hired motor but my own, ramshackle as it might be, was at least familiar and was small enough for me to roll it out of the garage with one foot on the running board and one on the ground. This I soon did, then hopped in and pulled the door to without slamming it. I hoped against hope that it would continue to roll down the gentle slope of the yard and the back drive and that I should not have to start the engine until safely away from the house. It was agonizingly slow at first, barely moving. I could hear individual stones on the drive popping under the tyres as I inched towards the first of the gates, then gradually we gathered some speed, hurtling down the bumpy drive and shooting at last out of the gates on to the road and away.

It was light by the time I pulled off on the moor above Gatehouse, but too early for visiting, and I thought anyway that my mission would be the better for waiting until I had rested. Now, sick and gritty-eyed with exhaustion, I did not feel I could rely on myself to navigate the extraordinary interview I hoped was to come. I walked around the motor car a few times until my back and neck began to ease and then got into the passenger side, curled up and closed my eyes.

Awakened by the sound of a cart clopping past on the road beside me, I opened my eyes on to dazzling brightness and felt sure I had slept away the morning, but a glance at my watch told me that it was only just seven o'clock. Melting hot in my thick coat, still screwing up my eyes against the glare, and with my throat so dry that it clicked when I tried to swallow, I started the car and began the descent towards the town. Fearing to drive down the main street and pass Dr Milne on an early call, however, I veered off to the west at the fork in the road and from there picked my way among the criss-crossing lanes towards the sea until I arrived at my destination, stopped the car and let myself in at the gate. The cabbages looked in very good heart, I noticed as I made my way to the front door, hardly any slug holes at all.

I saw through the kitchen window that Mrs Marshall was dispensing porridge to an astonishing number of assorted large sons and small grandchildren and she came to the door with the ladle still in her hands. She cried out in delight at the sight of me and lifted her arms like a runner breaking the winning tape (causing flecks of por-

ridge to leap off the ladle and spatter the floor around her).
I wondered for a moment why my appearance should
cause such immoderate joy, and then I remembered that
the last thing I had promised was to tell her when naughty
Cara was found and brought home again. My face must
have betrayed something of what I felt because hers fell,
and her mouth was turned down at the corners as she
nodded me towards the parlour and returned to the
kitchen.

'Just leave they plates and get on with you,' I heard her
say. 'Jock, Willie, your pieces are ready standing at the
back door. Peggy, tie your ribbon or you'll lose it. Jean, put
the wee one's boots on his right feet before you go. And
don't any of you come through the room, mind. Granny's
busy.' She sidled back into the parlour and sat opposite
me.

'Mrs Marshall, I'm so very sorry,' I began. 'But I don't
have time to tell all just now.'

'From your face, I don't think I want to hear it,' said Mrs
Marshall. 'Just tell me, was she in thon fire, after all?'

'No,' I said. 'She is dead, I'm afraid, but she didn't die in
the fire. I'm sure of it.' I felt a fraud and a heel at the relief
that suffused her face, slackening the drawstring purse of
her mouth and softening the swimmy old eyes in their
baskets of wrinkles.

'So what are you after?' she asked, in a bright voice.

'I need to speak to whoever it is around here who lays
out corpses,' I said. 'I don't mean the undertaker.'

'You mean Nettle Jennie,' said Mrs Marshall.

'Yes,' I said. 'I expect I do.'

'I'll tell you where to find her, madam, and glad. She has
a wee hoose on the Cally estate up by Gatehouse, just on
the edge. But you mind out for yourself when you go
there.' I looked at her enquiringly.

'The thing is, you see, madam, Nettle Jennie is a
witch.'

I had anticipated as much. For all that reading the Bible
and feeling glum were still the only Sunday pastimes in

the respectable homes of Scotland, one only has to mention felling a rowan tree or eating a wild mushroom to realize that St Columba did not make a very thorough job of it. And I have no call to be superior for my legs were trembling as I approached Nettle Jennie's house. It was a tiny building, but with something about it that hinted at a nobler purpose than a worker's cottage sometime in its history. Small wonder, though, that the local witch was welcome to it: it was gloomily situated on the banks of a slow-moving burn surrounded by large trees, and midges were dancing in the air and rising from the ground in front of me as I made my way through the long grass to the door.

Almost too grotesque to be anything but comical was the way the door swung open as I approached it and a disembodied voice said: 'I've been expecting you.' Almost, but not quite, and I was equally balanced between trepidation and amusement as I bent my head under the lintel and entered.

The interior was dark but while the darkness of Mrs Marshall's cottage rooms came from the thick walls and tiny windows, here it arose from walls panelled with black wood and from the fact that, although there was a large arched window of leaded diamond panes set in the end wall, most of the light from it was blocked by a collection of stoppered bottles, one jammed into each diamond, wedged right in if they fitted, held in by putty and string if not. The effect was that of a home-made stained-glass window, and it was this thought which led to the realization that Nettle Jennie's house had once been a chapel. I wondered if this added to or detracted from the lore. It seemed rather macabre to me. The woman herself as well, once my eyes adjusted to the dimness, was revealed to be satisfyingly to type. Thick, grey hair in a plait, the creased dark skin of a gypsy and eyes set so deep in shadowed sockets that their light was the dull gleam of velvet rather than any kind of shine. Set against all of this, however, was her blue work dress and clean white pinny, and her voice

– clear and sweet, and pure Galloway in its vowels. She had been at work on some greenery, piled on newspaper on her table, and she returned to it now, stripping leaves from branches and separating them into piles. Not having been asked to sit, I leaned against a cupboard and watched her.

'I saw you at the inquiry,' she said. 'And I heard you were asking questions.'

'I dearly wish you had come to me then,' I said. 'What a lot of bother it would have saved.'

'That's not my way,' said Nettle Jennie. 'I keep myself to myself and people come to me. They wouldn't come if they thought I'd go running with tales.' I could see the sense in this, but I slumped with disappointment.

'I don't suppose then,' I said, 'that you would be willing to be a witness. To come to the police, I mean.'

'Well, now me and the police, we keep our distance, see? Suppose you tell me what it is you want to know.' She nodded towards a chair at last and I sat, while she carried on with her picking over of the stems and branches. Every so often she would put one of the leaves into her mouth, as I have seen Mrs Tilling do shelling peas in the yard in the sunshine. The leaves might have been spinach for all I knew, but still it made me shiver.

'Well, the little kitchen maid who died at Reiver's Rest,' I began.

'Was no kitchen maid, for a start,' said Nettle Jennie. 'That's the first thing.'

Hallelujah! At last, for the first time in all these months, there was someone else besides Alec and me who was willing to say so.

'I worked that out,' I said. 'She was Mrs Duffy's daughter. But anything you can tell me from having seen her will be invaluable. Next, I think she was murdered, and here is where I very much hope you can back me up, because I have no proof of it at all, beyond my conviction.'

'That's not so easy,' said Nettle Jennie. 'She'd tumbled down, the poor lass, no mistaking that. But whether she fell or was pushed, how would you know? How could you say?'

'You don't think she jumped then?'

'Made away with herself? Is that what they told you?'

'They told me as big a heap of nonsense as they told everyone else. But it was one of the possibilities. She was trying to miscarry the baby, you know, and she jumped too far. Isn't that what they told you?'

Her hands stilled for the first time and rested amongst the leaves.

'What?' I said. She shook her head at me.

'That wee lass couldn't have been trying to get rid of a baby,' she said.

'Why not?'

'There was nothing there to get rid of.'

'Are you sure?' I asked and she bridled.

'I've brought enough into the world to know,' she said. 'Aye, and seen to it that plenty never arrive.'

'But I know she was pregnant,' I said. 'The doctor told me.'

She snorted.

'The doctor! *What* did he tell you?'

'He said it was as easy for him to tell if a girl was – I can't remember the expression he used exactly – but as easy for him as for me to tell a man from a woman. And "tell-tale marks of pregnancy". I know he said that.'

'Aye, she had the tell-tale marks of pregnancy all right,' said Nettle Jennie, and she watched me, laughing at my irritation with her air of mystery. Something was ringing bells, right at the back of my mind. I squinted up at the cloudy green and brown patchwork of her home-made window and remembered sitting in another church, looking at stained glass, listening to the minister. Man that is born of woman, he had said, reminding me of Alec stuttering while he tried to say 'with child'. And suddenly I had it. Suddenly I could remember precisely the words that Dr Milne had used. Those 'tell-tale marks' had said to the doctor – and should have said to me – not that the girl was pregnant when she died but that sometime in her past she had borne a child.

Cara had had a baby. For, of course, there *are* no clear marks of being newly pregnant beyond the obvious change in one's outline. On the other hand I very vividly remembered how cheated I felt after the first time (no one having even hinted at it) to find that I had changed quite markedly and, it appeared, permanently. Even when the baby was safely in the nursery wing with Nanny and there were several shut doors between him and me I could not lie in my bath and pretend it had not happened, not unless the water were very heavily dosed with bubbles and those horrid marks, looking like little pink anchovies draped all over my bosom and stomach, were deeply submerged. This then was what Cara dreaded Alec seeing on their wedding night.

'But why would Dr Milne be so sure she was pregnant again?' I said at last.

'Give a dog a bad name and hang him,' said Nettle Jennie. 'That's all he would have seen. The *doctor.*' This accorded perfectly with what I knew of Dr Milne.

'Could you tell from looking at her how long ago it was?' I asked.

Nettle Jennie shrugged.

'Three, mebbes, four years. Something like that. Now, I'm not being rude, but can I ask you just to step into my garden while I do something here. These are my grandmother's recipes and there's no one knows them but me.'

What an old fraud, I thought, as I hurried out. Grandmother's recipes, indeed. As if I cared what she did with her vegetation. But I was grateful for the chance to think.

All kinds of things began to drop into place. Lena must have known about this baby; she must have been instrumental in bundling Cara away to have it quietly somewhere. And this must be the hold she had over her daughter. Yes! This must have been the power she wielded to make Cara take the diamonds to be sold. I wondered whether her father knew about it. Not, I rather thought. Whether Clemence knew? Not, again. Lena always prided herself so on protecting Clemence from the sordid things in life. This would have been top of the list of things to protect her from. So Lena must have handled it all. Perhaps she had got a little cottage all on its own somewhere, just as she had the next time she had something to do that better had not be seen. With a rush of certainty, I thought of the pictures of Cara, beaming and golden – glowing, as they say – against the setting of some unknown cottage somewhere. A cottage Lena had tried to copy at Kirkandrews years later. I thought of Sha-sha McIntosh telling me about the crêpe-de-Chine dress 'fearfully baggy' from countless ages ago. Four years would be countless ages for one so young, I was sure. But who was Cara smiling at in those beautiful pictures? Not her mother, certainly. Her lover? Had her mother allowed him to visit her? I could not see Lena letting this happen for the sake of love's young dream. But she might, I supposed, if it gave her a hold over the boy as well as the girl, whoever he was.

This much I was sure of. Cara's secret was this baby from years ago. And this was what she had to tell Alec. Now I could see why none of the other options would help her. Postponing the wedding could not get rid of those dark rings and pale stripes. Seducing Alec would only bring discovery sooner. And this was what Lena found out that night at the cottage, what drove her to fury. But wait. That could not be. Had I not just worked out for myself that Lena must have known all along? She could not have managed Cara's confinement *and* have been shocked into madness by its sudden discovery. Here were echoes again of that feeling that Lena was split down the middle. Could she be? Could her rigid respectability, her obsession with keeping the vulgar at bay, have led her to that special kind of forgetting that Austrian doctors tell us of?

Nettle Jennie was at my elbow suddenly, holding out a

263

glass of some pale cloudy liquid. It might have been lemonade, I suppose, but I declined.

'Like I'm saying,' she began, 'I don't meet trouble halfway. I stay out of things, but this time . . . I don't know.' She drifted into silence for a while and then began again. 'That was her own lassie? That was her own wee lassie she did that to? I might could come to the police with you, if you thought it would help put her away.'

'But you said you weren't sure it *was* murder,' I said, puzzled.

'Not that,' she said. 'I mean what she did after.'

'What are you talking about?' I said. 'What did she do to her . . . after?' I was not sure that I wanted to hear this.

'There was some things could not be helped,' said Nettle Jennie. 'Her feet, like, were soft and there was nothing could be done about that, but she ground dirt into them, split the nails and dirtied them. She scrubbed her wee fingernails away to nothing, but she couldn't put calluses where no work had put them. She rough chopped her hair at the ends and greasied it up, bit of dirt, but I could tell it was good healthy hair underneath it all, even combed all up the wrong way into rats' tails.

'She grubbied her neck for her, put dirt in her ears. I cannot be sure, but I think she went out to the closet and got muck to put in her mouth. I never smelled anything in my life like the smell of that wee girl's mouth when I laid her out. But she couldn't do anything about her bonny white teeth. Cover them in night soil, make them smell so bad the doctor wouldn't go near, but it all came off with a swish of water.' Nettle Jennie shook her head and clicked her own strong yellow teeth together.

'I've been to plenty a corp I wished I had gloves for, I can tell you. Years of dirt, ground in. Linens never been off them for months. But this one was all wrong.' She turned to me suddenly plaintive, a look of real pain in her eyes. 'What did she do that for, eh?'

'It fooled the doctor,' I said.

'But how could she do that to her own wee girl? Soil in

264

her mouth? How could she?' I was startled. I should have thought that one in her occupation would be past such sensibility. She drew herself up.

'I'm a woman just like you,' she said, with such remarkable appositeness that I wondered whether she might be a witch after all. 'I do what I have to do, for it must be done by someone. But I couldn't do it for one of my own, not as tender and as gentle as I am. And as for back-combing the hair on the head you've just smashed in, on the neck you've just broken –'

I put out my hands to try to block her words, and she stopped at last, turned abruptly and went back into her house. I followed.

'What you've just told me only confirms it, but I thought so anyway,' I said, standing in the open doorway. 'She is mad.'

'She must be,' said Nettle Jennie. 'If that's what happened.' She looked slyly at me and repeated it. '*If* that's what happened.' Facing the sunlight, her hooded eyes were easier to read and I saw an unpleasant look there now – cunning and taking some pleasure in the cunning. 'Wouldn't you like to know?' she said. I nodded. 'We could find out,' she said in the same slightly wheedling tone. 'We could ask the wee lassie.'

'What do you mean? How could we ask her?' I said, thinking of ouija boards and upturned glasses.

'I'm sure she would tell you. She knows you're trying to help her.'

She looked up at her curious window, pointing at the row upon row of odd bottles. Medicine bottles and scent bottles, beer bottles and oil bottles all corked or stoppered with scraps of rag. I moved towards the window and peered at them.

'They're empty,' I said. 'What do you mean she would tell me?'

'They only look empty,' said Nettle Jennie, right behind me. 'She could tell you with her dying breath.'

I turned, to see her smiling at me. She mimed breathing

265

out, emptying her lungs, then she bent as though to kiss an imaginary face and mimed sucking in hard. Lips pursed shut, she plucked an empty bottle from the shelf at her side, blew into it and waved it at me, one strong brown thumb over the neck, cackling.

Chapter Eighteen

I was miles from her house before I could stop the cackling laughter ripping around my head, halfway home before my blood stopped thundering. Perhaps it was just as well, for without nerves and shivers to help me I should never have had the strength for another long drive. As it was I just about held together, but my little motor car was fizzing hot and had developed one clank and two different grinds under its bonnet when I hauled into the stable yard again, twenty hours after quitting it. It gave one last smoky bang and came to what felt like a permanent stop.

Alec, who had evidently been watching for me, came around from the drive with Bunty in tow, and as she and I fussed over each other, I quickly told him the bare bones of my news: the baby from years ago, the desecration of Cara's body, and a little about Nettle Jennie herself.

'Completely hopeless?' he asked.

'If you'd only been there,' I said. 'With such a witness to lean on, *we'd* be lucky not to be committed, never mind her. But, speaking of lunatics . . . What she said about Lena can't be ignored. We shall just have to go to the police on our own and do our best. Let me wash and change and then we'll talk it through.'

We entered the house through the gun room door, which was nearest, and as we hurried along the passageway Hugh popped his head out of the library.

'Well?' he said. 'How was she?'

I blinked at him and then at Alec. What had Alec been saying?

267

'Yes, how was *Daisy*?' said Alec with a penetrating look at me.

'Oh! Daisy! She was . . . um.' A sudden brainwave. 'She was utterly beside herself. And I think, I really do, that she should go to the police. Don't you think, Alec? Blackmail, after all, is a crime.'

'Of course,' said Alec. Then he added stoutly, 'Absolutely. You should ring her right now and tell her, Dandy.' We began to walk very fast.

'Blackmail?' said Hugh's voice behind us. 'I thought it was moths.'

I asked for Croys and waited, drumming my fingers impatiently and staring at Alec without seeing him, while the operator put me through, the bell rang out and the butler answered. Then I fell to earth with a thud as he told me that Mrs Esslemont was away. I sent him to get Silas.

'What will I say?' I hissed to Alec, with my hand over the mouthpiece. 'Silas doesn't know half of what I've been up to. Will I try to fill him in?'

'Just ask him where Daisy is,' said Alec. 'She may only be out for tea with the vicar. Calm down, Dandy, for God's sake, and try to sound normal.'

'Hello?' came Silas's voice on the line. 'That you, Dan? You're out of luck I'm afraid. Daisy's not here.'

'Where's she off to, darling?' I asked, in my best casual drawl. 'How that baggage does desert you!'

'Oh well,' said Silas, obviously quite taken with the chance of some unforeseen self-pity. 'I can't complain, really. She's on a mercy mission. Gone to see Lena Duffy.'

'What?' I breathed.

'I agree,' Silas went on. 'After all that nonsense in the spring, I wouldn't have said Daisy owes Lena any friendship. But Lena rang up this morning and Daisy has gone to help. Something to do with servant problems. No servants at the cottage or something? I wasn't really listening. And then Daisy said she was off, kiss kiss darling, and see you tonight. You know how she is, lots of noise and no detail, but –'

'Silas, I have to go,' I said. 'Stay by the telephone and I shall ring you as soon as I have news.' I slammed the earpiece into the cradle.

'Daisy has gone to see Lena,' I said, and I could feel the colour drain out of my face too as I watched Alec pale. 'She's walked right into it, Alec, and it's all my fault.'

We stared at one another in a lengthening, darkening silence. I was waiting for Alec to say there was no need to worry, not to give way to hysteria. He might have been waiting for me to say the same, but all I could think of was my letter to Daisy, that stupid, cowardly letter, designed only to save my pride. I had told her nothing that could put her on her guard, had primed her with a line which, repeated in all innocence, had delivered her unsuspecting, perhaps feeling confident, straight into Lena's hands.

I fumbled the earpiece out of the cradle again and rattled the lever to summon the operator.

'Edinburgh police headquarters, please,' I said and then shoved the thing into Alec's hands, knowing I could not rely on myself to form words. I sat down on the arm of the sofa and listened to him trying.

'You have to send someone along there as soon as you can,' he was saying. 'I'll give you the address. What? No, there has been no crime committed, not yet – except, yes, there has but unless you get there in time I – What? My name? Alexander Osborne, but it really doesn't matter. Dorset, but listen. Listen, the woman's name is Eleanor Duffy and the address is 28 Drummond Place in Edinburgh. There is a lady visiting there, a Mrs Esslemont . . . Now look, I am trying to tell you in the plainest possible terms, that Mrs Esslemont – This woman has murdered once already and . . . I am not drunk. Please! Someone must go to the house and get her out, before –'

He crashed the telephone down and shook his head.

'Waste of time,' he said. 'If Daisy comes to any harm

I shall string that idiot up with my own hands. Ring the Duffy house, Dandy.'

I summoned the operator again, and with a tut and a sigh, as though for all the world this was not exactly what she was paid for, she put me through. As it rang out, I tried to compose a speech.

'Where is the telephone?' I said. 'Do you know?'

'In the hallway,' Alec said and nodded, knowing exactly what I was thinking. 'Ask for Daisy,' he went on, 'and then tell her simply to walk out of the front door and not stop.'

And yet, even then, even as late as that, I found myself frowning and felt my face twist into an embarrassed grimace at the thought of Daisy breaking the bounds of convention at my behest, walking away from her hostess's house without her hat or her gloves and not taking her leave. Had Daisy come to the telephone, I wonder still if I should have been able to issue the command, or whether I should have said that of course she might go and say goodbye to Lena, even finish her tea. Luckily, I was not put to the test.

'Mrs Esslemont, madam?' asked the butler, coldly. 'I'm afraid you are mistaken. Mrs Esslemont is not here.' My heart – I think it was my heart although it seemed rather lower in my body than that, lower certainly than the place one presses when one's panic is feigned – whatever it was anyway it gave a lurching bump, but I managed to keep my voice light.

'Might I speak to Mrs Duffy then, please?'

'Madam is at the Perthshire house, madam,' said the butler, if possible even more frostily.

'I – I thought it was shut up,' I said, relief washing over me in waves of warm and chill. Daisy would find no one at home in Edinburgh and come back safe and sound.

'Madam has gone for the day,' said the butler, his voice now sharp with disapproval. 'Gone to meet a friend there.'

I let the earpiece fall and ran for the front door, leaping

down the steps to Alec's motor car, going over on my ankle in the gravel, but managing to right myself. I got the car into gear first try after Alec, eyes wide with alarm, cranked the starter. We could see Donald and Teddy standing on the lawn, mystified, as we sped down the drive.

'They're at Dunelgar,' I said. 'We can be there in half an hour.'

That half-hour was the worst experience of my life, childbirth included. We shot along the high-hedged lanes, careening round bends, spraying gravel, churning earth on the verges. My ankle shrieked every time I stepped down on the pedal, but I could not stop. Over and over I heard Silas's voice in my head: 'kiss kiss darling, see you tonight, you know how she is'. The affectionate exasperation, something he never troubled to hide and which had always made me feel shut out and envious of her, now hammered at me. I glanced at Alec. His knuckles were as white as gnawed drumsticks where he held on to the dashboard, and his face was stricken, a rictus only just held at bay in his clenched jaw, but he at least had no reason to blame himself for what was happening, might be happening, surely could not be happening. I snapped my eyes back to the road and pressed down harder, wincing.

Mercifully we met no jostling sheep plugging any of the little roads, no ambling lethal cordons of cows. Only one small child in a grubby pinafore playing at a puddle outside her front gate caused me to swerve and I felt the claws of a hawthorn hedge screech along the paintwork.

'There can't be . . .' said Alec at last. 'Can there be . . . Is there any innocent reason for Lena to meet Daisy in a closed-up house all alone?'

I shook my head.

'And why on earth would Daisy agree to go?' he demanded, worry turning him querulous. 'What is it that Lena knows about Daisy, Dan?'

'I've no idea,' I said. 'And that should at least have made me cautious about . . . Oh Alec, if only it weren't for my

271

letter. Or if only I had rung Daisy sooner, she would never have gone. At least she would have taken Silas or a servant.' The steering wheel slipped in my hand as a sudden thought crashed in upon me. 'Perhaps she did. Perhaps she took – oh, what's his name? – Menzies, the chauffeur. He's enormous, and he adores Daisy. If Menzies took her perhaps everything will be fine.'

Shock cannot be sustained for long periods of time. I have found this, and not only shock but any extremes of feeling at all. Perhaps, though, it is only me and perhaps this means there is something vital lacking in me, that I cannot keep being worried or miserable without respite for even half an hour. Anyway, I clutched at the possibility that Daisy, far from being alone in a deserted house with Lena, had rolled up with the burly and devoted Menzies at her side; Menzies, who would surely hear a raised voice resounding through empty rooms.

Another fact I have learned about shock and panic, however, is that after a rest one can return to them refreshed, as though one had simply spat on one's hands and taken a better grip. So now the twist and grind of tension simply shifted focus, and instead of yearning just for arrival I could feel myself keening forward in my mind to the sight of Menzies and the Rolls.

'And you're sure, are you,' said Alec, 'about what Lena was holding over Cara? The baby?'

'Nettle Jennie was sure,' I said, 'and I'd trust her before Dr Milne any day. Now hold on.'

We were turning into Dunelgar at last, past the little lodge house with its windows boarded up, through the one gate that lay open, only inches to spare on each side. We roared along the drive, squinting at the cars drawn up by the front door, Lena's Bentley and what? What was behind it?

'It's the Vauxhall,' said Alec. 'She's on her own.'

We skidded to a stop at the far side of the circle, I not trusting myself to steer any closer to the stone parapet and the other cars, my arms now flickering with fright and my fingers slipping numbly over the wheel. Alec sprinted up the steps to the door and I hurried after him, hopping and stumbling now on my swollen ankle. He wrenched the heavy door open – it was not locked – and together we stepped inside.

The shutters all around the hall were closed and light seeped in around their edges and cut slices through the dark. Reeling from the effort of standing still, we waited and listened, beginning to see shapes in the gloom, sheeted humps of furniture. Beyond them, all the doors were shut and there was not a sound.

It was almost seven o'clock and we had no idea when Daisy had set out, how long she had been here. The two cars still outside were a good sign, I thought, and it was some crazy kind of comfort to know that Lena was capable of long careful planning. Perhaps we were not too late. I forced back down the thought that came hard on the heels of that one, that we also knew she capable of action, swift and brutal.

Alec had thrown back the dust sheet on a side table by the door and was rummaging under it. He gave a grunt of satisfaction and straightened, a candlestick in each hand. He held one out to me.

'Gilded bronze,' he whispered. 'They weigh a ton.'

'But there are no candles,' I whispered back. I saw the outline of Alec's hair move slightly against a thin shaft of light as he shook his head.

'Oh,' I said. 'I see.'

'Ssh,' said Alec. 'Come on.'

Holding the candlestick across my breast like a shield, I limped after him. The rug was rolled and tied in sacking along one wall and our footsteps sounded as loud as knocks on the bare floor, even louder as we came out into the stairwell and they caught the echo. I strained to hear another sound, a voice or a breath or even the whisper of cloth as someone moved, but all I could hear was the sound of myself listening, a tinny crackle in my ears which – I could not decide – was either my imagination, or was born of the intensity of my concentration, or even was always there but never heeded until this moment.

Softly we opened door after door, the latches protesting after their long disuse and the dirt in the hinges scraping, but in each room we saw nothing but white shapes and the silent dance of dust. Any of these muffled chairs might have an occupant. Any of these swathed, lumpy tabletops might be concealing Lena, curled and silent, and breathing as shallow as she could with her heart thrilling, or might, I knew, shroud Daisy, more silent still and beyond our help.

We stepped back to the foot of the stairs and paused before beginning to climb. The carpet on the stairs had been left in place or at any rate the felt backing had and we rose up each step without a sound. I felt my lip start to tremble and sensed the candlestick threaten to slip in my sweaty hands. I let out a breath in the smallest whimper I could, terrified that if I held it in any longer, it would end in a sob.

'Have you seen something?' said Alec, so quietly it was as though his voice was inside my head.

'No,' I breathed back. 'It's my foot. I twisted it.'

I suddenly realized that it *was* my foot and, bending, I set the candlestick down and closed my hand around the worst of the pain. It was hard and hot, bulging up around the top of my shoe. I lifted my heel, but resting all my weight on my toe was worse. Alec crouched beside me and felt first my good ankle and then the other, squeezing a little too hard and making me gasp.

'Wait here,' he said. 'I'll go on on my own.' He must have been able to see me shake my head. 'Well, all right, but take my arm.'

Thus we went on, I leaning heavily on Alec's free arm, clasping his wrist tight and biting down on the knuckle of my other hand to stop the tears. Dread, shame and pain wrestled one another inside me, until each seemed to withdraw to a different part of me and settle there, the pain clenching my jaw, the dread of what was to come

274

pounding an ache like a fence-post into my head behind
my eyes, and the shame of it all – Silas's voice – lodged like
sandbags in my guts.

At the top of the stairs a passageway stretched out in
both directions. To our left the meagre light slowly ran out
and the corridor sank into gentle gradual darkness like a
mouth, like a throat, but to our right we could see the
passage turning a corner. We could see the angle of the
wall and the sharp shadow it cast reaching towards us;
somewhere along that way was an unshuttered window.
Without speaking we started to move towards the light,
and as we turned the corner, the brilliancy of it shooting
out around the door at the end seemed too much to be the
mild sunshine we had left outside on the drive. The door
seemed to seethe with the effort of holding it and when
I reached out and turned the handle it was as though the
light itself burst out.

Almost in the centre of the ballroom, small and dark
against the soaring windows and mirrors all around, Daisy
sat primly on a wooden chair looking at her feet. I blinked
and shook my head, and then I saw that her feet were
taped up in what looked like a bandage and bound to one
of the chair legs, together and to the side, crossed at the
ankle just as we had been taught to sit at school, but her
hands were behind her back instead of in her lap and the
upright set of her shoulders came from the rope holding
her hard to the chair-back, without which not only her
head would be drooping.

I started towards her, with a howl of sour despair rising
up inside me, but at my movement her head jerked up, her
eyes rolling above the tape on her mouth, and her whole
body began to surge, the chair creaking and rocking with
each heave against the ropes. Alec got to her before me,
worked her mouth free of the gag and knelt to tussle with
the cord around her wrists as I took her head in my arms
and held it.

'She said no one would ever find me,' Daisy said, working her face free of my grasp. 'She told me no one would

275

ever find me and Silas would never prove anything. But she must be mad. I kept telling her half a dozen people knew I was here and she couldn't hope to get away with it, and that's when she gagged me.'

Alec freed her wrists at last and hunched over her ankles.

'Can you walk?' he said. 'Has she hurt you? Because as soon as these ropes are off you must run. I shall have to carry Dandy, so you must run along beside us.'

'No,' I said. 'I'll start now. I'll be out before you. I'll hop.'

Alec put out a hand and gripped my arm so tightly my fingers tingled.

'Don't go out of my sight,' he said, still working at the bandage with his one free hand. I moved back to stand by Daisy.

'Where is she?' I asked, but before it was out of my mouth I heard footsteps, brisk, light, tapping towards us. A door in the panelling opened slowly outward and I caught a glimpse of a dark stone-lined corridor, a service corridor. Lena nudged the flap of the door wide with her hip, her eyes down, concentrating on the crowded tray of objects she carried.

We stood frozen while she negotiated the door, even Alec's hands stopping their worrying to watch Lena edge into the ballroom and look up from the tray. Slowly, she took in the sight of us. Then she turned with a quickness that startled at least me and hurled the tray back through the gap in the closing door to scatter its contents on the stone floor of the passage.

I never knew what she had planned for Daisy, never saw what was on the tray, but the sounds it made when it fell stayed with me for years no matter how I tried to keep them out of my ears, and more especially my dreams. Metal rang on stone, glass shattered and heavy, dull objects thumped and rolled away. Lena smoothed down her apron – it was not until then that I noticed she wore an enveloping white apron – and walked towards us. She looked

276

quite as tranquil as I had ever seen her. More so perhaps, I thought, as she drew near. Her face had a limpid serenity that I had never seen there before, and it was more grotesque than rolling eyes and drooling mouth would have been. I thought again of Alec and his pie and the headless Sergeant Pinner, imagining that Alec would have had just this smooth look on his face as he ate. It was the look of madness, when all the guy-ropes of the everyday have finally been shrugged off and the mind floats up and is gone.

Lena looked at each of us in turn, smiling gently, then rested her gaze on me and spoke.

'Tell me then, my dear. *Have* you been watching me?'

I nodded, and Lena nodded along with me, still smiling.

'I thought so. I thought so,' she said. 'And so it is all my own doing. I tried to use you, my dear Mrs Gilver. Perhaps if I hadn't invited you to Kirkandrews to witness our tragedy . . .? Tell me, what did I do wrong?'

I gaped at her but then it dawned upon me that this was not meant to open a moral debate but merely to ask where she had betrayed herself to me, and when I tried to think of an answer I found I could not. Where *had* she gone wrong? Where had the suspicion come from, seeping invisibly like gas, until one was enveloped in the miasma, cut off from all the sight, sound and smell of the world but still unable to believe any of it was real?

Smiling, she waited for me to speak and as she did the smile changed, becoming as gaudy and jagged as a lizard's fan.

'You don't even know, do you?' she said, speaking now through clenched teeth, making thick white spots of saliva gather at the corners of her mouth. 'Bumbling cow of a woman that you are. I chose the stupidest person in the room. So stupid. How I should hate to be you – Dandelion Gilver – bumping around in the fog like a sheep, too stupid to see how stupid you are . . .'

'No need to run through the whole farmyard,' said

Alec's voice, steady but strained. 'And you're wrong as it happens. It's not stupidity, it's goodness.'

Lena threw back her head and whooped.

'Goodness? *Goodness*?'

'Goodness,' said Alec, 'which could not help but see evil in front of it. Dandy's goodness meant that she could smell you like a rotting corpse. I don't expect you to understand. Something as vile as you are can't hope to recognize it.'

I wished he would stop. Lena was beginning to seethe, visibly, rocking back and forward on her heels. I had no fear that she would overpower Alec and escape but I wanted desperately to talk to her and get some answers before she crawled into her madness and pulled it over herself for good.

'Why did you do it?' I asked, my voice loud enough to cut through Alec's hectoring. She rounded on me, but I refused to flinch.

I asked her again.

'Why did you do it?'

'Are you too "good" even to imagine, then, Mrs Gilver?'

'Not at all,' I said, surprising myself with the level drawl I managed to get into my voice. 'Only I should like to know if my theories are accurate. Why did you do it? Why did you start it?'

'Because,' she said, stepping very close to me so that the spittle fell on my face as she spoke. Alec rose and moved towards us, but I put up a hand to stop him.

'Because,' she said again, 'they were mine.'

'Of course they were yours,' I whispered, sickened, amazed that I could still be sickened by anything. 'But why would you want to hurt them?'

'You stupid woman,' she said. 'You stupid, blind pig of a woman. Not the girls. The diamonds. Those diamonds were mine. I loved them and they were nothing to him, just as they should have been nothing to you.' She rounded on Alec and, unable to meet his eyes, glared at his chest. 'You and that little tart and all the little tarts you

278

would have bred. It was an outrage to think he could give them to you when they were mine.'

'So you stole them,' I said. 'But –'

'I didn't steal them,' said Lena, suddenly very loud. 'You can't steal what is already yours. I simply took them. He would have left them to that little tart along with everything else and I couldn't stand for that.'

'But then you went too far,' I said. 'You tried to steal them twice and when it seemed as though nothing would ever bring it to light you told Cara to sell them.'

'She couldn't have anyway,' said Daisy. 'They belonged to her father.'

'They belonged to *me*,' said Lena. 'They were mine. They have belonged to the ladies of the Duffy family, generation after generation for three hundred years.'

'Cara was a lady of the Duffy family, you old fool,' said Daisy.

'Oh yes,' screamed Lena. 'Cara, precious Cara, precious Cara Duffy. Little tart.'

'And why pick on us?' Daisy demanded. 'What have I ever done? What has Silas?'

'Filth,' spat Lena. 'Parading around all that money and underneath, nothing but filth.'

'You're mad,' said Daisy. 'You're not even making any sense.'

Lena's eyes rolled.

'So you told her to sell them,' I insisted, laying a hand on Daisy's shoulder trying to quiet her, trying to keep Lena with us. 'And then what?'

'She couldn't be trusted,' said Lena. 'Much better, really. Much neater that way. I had the use of her and then she could go. She was going to get all of it, you know. He just couldn't see past his precious little darling. He didn't know her like I did. What a dirty little slut she was. She had to go.'

There was one question I knew I must ask.

'Could you have done it? Could you have killed your own child in cold blood?'

'Is it too awful for you to imagine?' said Lena. 'With all your *goodness*. Could I? Of course I could. I'm vile and evil, Mrs Gilver, I'm wicked and mad. So my own child doesn't matter any more to me than an ant under my shoe. Weren't you listening?' Her eyes were glittering with amusement now.

'But you didn't get the chance,' I said, and I saw her face flash with something I did not understand, just for a moment.

'Of course I had the chance,' she said. 'What are you talking about? I made the chance, and I took the chance.'

'But something went wrong,' I insisted. Her eyes flashed again.

'What are you talking about?'

'Something changed your plans. What happened? What did she tell you to make you so angry?' Lena's eyes were still huge with fear but her shoulders dropped a little.

'She told me what she had done. What she was. Who could bear to hear what a stinking, filthy tart she was all along?'

'But you knew that,' I said. 'You said you knew what she was.' Lena looked away from me and I saw a cold resolve settle into her face. Then she took a huge breath, threw back her head and shrieked.

Still screeching, she took three enormous steps backwards so that all of us were in the sweep of her gaze. There was something ridiculous about the extravagance of the steps, like a second-rate Shakespearean actor of the old school, or like the game I used to play as a child. Giants' Steps and Babies' Steps, it was called, and that was what Lena's giant steps looked like, as unreal and yet as deliberate as that.

'I killed her,' she screamed. 'Do you hear me? I killed her and if I hang it will still be worth it.' She spoke as though she were Boadicea giving her battle cry, as though she were Joan of Arc declaiming her creed, triumph in her voice and her shoulders thrown back to take the arrows in

her breast, but her eyes were the eyes of an animal thresh-
ing in a snare as the gamekeeper draws near it. I stepped
towards her, staring, peering deep into that animal's
eyes.

'How could you?' I said. 'How could you do that to your
own child?' The fear flared again; I saw it. Something small
inside her had leapt up and just managed to see out of her
eyes for one second before it fell back down. Then she
regarded me with some of the old calmness, and she spoke
softly to me, just to me, too soft for the others to hear.

'You stupid woman,' she said.

I stared at her, feeling something shift, but it was far too
deep to tell what it was, and then she turned on her heels
and ran.

Alec took two steps after her, stopped, wheeled back,
swayed for a second. We could hear Lena's footsteps racing away.

'Go,' I yelled at him.

He skidded over the ballroom floor and was gone. The
ring of his shoes on the bare floor joined the clatter of
Lena's heels and then both became muffled as they
reached the top of the stairs and flew down over the felted
treads. A scream, then a confusion of thumps and knocks,
a shout from Alec, and silence. I knew at once what had
happened.

Carefully, I lowered myself beside Daisy and stretched
out my throbbing foot before bending over the ropes.

'I left my candlestick on the stairs,' I said. Then I looked
down and smiled as the tangle under my fingers began to
loosen. 'Typical. Boys are never any good at untying
knots.'

'Hence penknives,' said Daisy, getting stiffly to her feet
and shaking herself free of the coils. 'Now, put your hands
around my neck, darling, and let me help you up.'

We had just begun to limp across what looked like an
acre of gleaming floor, her two numbed legs about as
useful as my good one, when Alec appeared in the door-

way, his face puckered, one of Lena's shoes dangling from his hand.

'She tripped,' he said, walking slowly towards us. 'I tried to catch her. I almost caught her.' He looked down at the shoe, regarded it for a long time, then set it carefully on the floor and swung me up into his arms.

'I can offer you an arm,' he said to Daisy, but his voice was strained, and even as he spoke he braced his legs – I am no sylph, even had he not been shaking with exhaustion – and so Daisy assured him that she was fine.

At the head of the stairs he turned and began to shuffle down awkwardly sideways, almost pressing me against the banisters.

'No,' I said. 'Let me see her.' So he faced around the way he was going again and down we went towards Lena.

One of her hands was hooked through the banister rail by a snapped wrist and her head lay crushed against her shoulder. Her face was hidden, only the nape of her neck showing. I could see pins sticking out from under her old-fashioned bun, plain metal pins never meant to be seen, and I was surprised by the skin on her neck, soft and plumply crumpled, with some sparse downy hair, too short for the hairpins, which had sprung into curls.

Daisy stopped as she drew level and crouched down to look at her.

'Are you sure?' she said.

'Absolutely,' said Alec. 'We must go and find a telephone and ring the police. I'll put Dandy in the car and come back for you.'

'We can't just leave her here alone,' said Daisy. 'Take Dandy to a doctor, Alec darling, and telephone from there. I shall wait here and keep watch. Yes, yes, I promise not to touch anything. But we can't leave her alone.'

I should have offered to stay. I did not know then that my ankle was broken, and Daisy had had it much worse than me, tied up and thinking she was going to be hurt. I should have insisted that I stay with Lena's body. Why did I not? Simple: I was scared. I still did not feel safe. But safe from what? From the horror of what we thought she had done? That was what I told myself. That was how I explained why I still felt lost and how I made sense of the shifting inside me, slow but relentless, like sand on the ocean floor.

Chapter Nineteen

'And what was the candlestick doing on the stairs?' asked
Inspector MacAlpine, yet again. Even the constable in the
corner, taking laborious notes of my answers, looked up
with an exasperated sigh and flicked back in his pad to
read what I had said last time.

'I put it down because my ankle made it difficult to
climb the stairs without holding on,' I said.

'And you picked it up because . . .?'

'We didn't know who was there or what to expect. For
all we knew there was a gang of thugs around every
corner.'

'And you were there because . . .?'

'We were concerned about Mrs Esslemont. When we
found out she had agreed to meet Mrs Duffy in a deserted
house we thought undue pressure might be brought to
bear. As it was. I told you, when we arrived Mrs Esslemont
was tied to a chair.'

'And you broke your ankle . . .?'

'I cracked a small bone in it getting into the car. I slipped
on the gravel. But I didn't even notice until I was halfway
up the stairs.'

'Didn't notice a broken ankle,' said the inspector blandly
but quite firmly.

'Chipped,' I said, just as firmly. 'A very small bone.' It
was too exasperating the way he kept worrying over the
one thing that was absolutely true while missing the great
gaping holes, but I could hardly point that out.

'And what happened next, Mrs Gilver?'

The constable sighed yet more audibly, loud enough for his superior officer to throw him a glance from the corner of his eye. Hugh, stolid and dumbstruck beside me, followed the glance and blinked at the sight of the uniform as he had every time he had looked at every uniform in the last week. He was there ostensibly to be my supporter and protector but he looked so poleaxed that, if anything, I tried not to speak too bluntly for fear of upsetting him.

'We found Mrs Esslemont in the ballroom and untied her and Mrs Duffy ran away, tripped on the candlestick and fell down the stairs.' The servants' passage, its doorway well concealed in the panelling, had not been found in the police examination of the scene and so the scattered contents of the tray had escaped the need for explanation.

One thing should be made quite plain: Alec and I had not cooked anything up on that first journey in search of a doctor and a telephone. It just so happened that in answering the questions put to us, in separate rooms, by a startled sergeant in Alec's case and a bewildered constable in mine, we did not chance to mention Cara. I was horribly aware even then, of course, that while my interrogator might think he was being so rigorous as to be forced to offer two apologies for every one question, I knew that he was merely nibbling around edges of what would choke him if he were to take a proper bite.

I think it was the fact of Daisy that allowed us, in conscience, just to answer each question as it came and resist pouring out the whole story. We did not see Daisy before her first interview, in her hospital bed in a private room with what she reported to be a very dashing Chief Superintendent (Daisy always does land on her feet), and she might easily have reported word-for-word everything that passed between Lena and me. At that point I should have resigned myself to telling all to Inspector MacAlpine and should have excused myself for not having done so before by pointing out truthfully that I had answered every question asked. That was the other point which helped Alec and me repress any guilt: we managed interview after interview, day after day, not to lie. The Silas, Daisy and the diamonds end of the affair held together so well on its own, you see, that nothing alerted the policemen to something's being hidden and Daisy, although quite without any natural reticence, presumably still had an eye on Silas's flotation and wanted to side-step as much scandal as she could. I expect that is how it was, although we have never spoken of it.

And so, the records show, no crime was committed. At least not by anyone in a position to be brought to book for it. Lena's death was found to have been an accident, as indeed it was. As for her attempt at extortion, even had Silas and Daisy been minded to drag it all out, the general assumption that she had planned it all alone meant that her death put an end to any thoughts of redress. And as Lena herself had pointed out, since one cannot steal what is already one's possession, the theft of the Duffy diamonds turned out not to be a theft at all, but only one of many instances that year of an old family attempting to shed some of its assets in unsettled times.

If somewhere in a police station in Edinburgh an officer scratched his head and wondered whether the name of the poor lady who fell down the stairs in a country house in Perthshire was not the same name that had been shouted down the telephone to him by some madman gibbering about a murder in Drummond Place, then we can be sure that he did no more than scratch his head before he put it out of his mind.

Hugh remained as perplexed as ever about how I had got myself mixed up in it all. Yet more evidence of my silliness, I expect he thought, *if* he thought. Silas had to be told everything, of course, and when my cheque came it bore his signature. Furthermore, Daisy, who answered the telephone when I rang to protest about the shameful enormity of the sum, said that was Silas's doing too and if I felt like talking to a brick wall she would call him to the telephone, but really darling, there was no point, as he was

286

determined to reward me for saving her life and if one looked at it that way, wasn't it rather insultingly stingy.

'You sound cross,' I said, wondering whether I shouldn't repay something after all, if it was causing trouble between them.

'As well I might,' Daisy said. 'Not only have I saved our flotation – through your genius, darling, of course – but I have almost been killed too and one would think Silas owed me some extravagant gift or at least that I should have my every heart's desire for a while. As it turns out, however, it's quite the reverse. I am to present him with yet another son in the spring. Don't laugh, Dandy, it's too bad. Relief and too much champagne, you see. Oh well, I suppose it might be a daughter.' She sobered, with a sigh. 'Speaking of daughters,' she said but stopped, and so when the girl cut in to tell us our time was up there was silence on the line and we felt too foolish to ask for another three minutes.

No sooner had I hung up the earpiece before the telephone rang again and the same aggrieved voice – I should like to box that girl's ears – told me I had another caller. It was Alec.

'I'm in Edinburgh,' he said. He had gone home to Dorset, I think to quiet his mother (understandably rattled by the news of yet another death in the family he had been to join). 'But I'm just about to start for Dunelgar to meet Gregory. Can I pick you up on the way?'

'Have you decided to tell him more?' I asked. 'Have you changed your mind?'

'I've been summoned,' said Alec. 'And I can't make *up* my mind, much less make it up and then change it. I'll see what he has to say, but I need an ally.'

I had to agree, of course, but I felt very little enthusiasm for the visit because I had been trying my best to keep Gregory Duffy out of my thoughts. The daughter who had so clearly been his favourite was dead, his wife was dead, and as for his other daughter, the mystifyingly dispreferred Clemence – and it really did mystify me any time

I considered it – his current treatment of her was a puzzle I could not begin to solve.

I had always been more taken with Cara myself and I expect the same was true of most people who knew them both. There had been something so fresh and sweet about her little monkey face that had to be found charming and Clemence's beautiful mask and cold elegance could not compete. I should have thought, however, that a parent could love them both and love their difference more than any sameness. But Clemence was off to Canada after all. I had learned this from Mary, who had thrown up the area window and called to me as I descended the steps of the Drummond Place house after leaving a card of condolence on the day of Lena's funeral.

'I couldn't think for the life of me what the noise was,' she said, looking more than ever like Mrs Tiggywinkle as she leaned out over the sill above a frothing tub of washing. 'I thought wee boys were whacking the railings.' Sure enough, the best that could be said about the sound of the wooden clog strapped on to my plaster, the steel tip of my cane and my one proper shoe was that it was percussive. Grant was all for keeping me in the house for six weeks, such pain did it give her to see an outfit of hers wrecked by the white lump sticking out from the bottom of my skirt.

'How are things?' I called down to Mary, with a glance up and down the pavement to check that I was unobserved. (Drysdale, agog at the wheel of the motor car, would have to make of it what he would.)

'An earthquake would be peace perfect peace compared to this place,' she said. 'Miss Clemence left from Leith two nights ago, gone to meet the liner at Gibraltar. She didn't even stay for her mother's funeral and if you know why, madam, don't tell me. The less I know about any of this the better. I'm off at the start of the week. Down the other end of the street there, to a lawyer and his wife and three wee ones and another one coming, and I'll be well shut of it.' She looked over her shoulder as if at a sudden noise and then with a wiggle of her eyebrows she thumped the window down and was gone.

So Clemence was already started on her long journey and would miss her mother's funeral. I doubted if even Mr Duffy would go and there was something dreadful, I thought, about a funeral with only the minister and the other officials, even for Lena. I only thought that for a moment, mind you, before I shook myself with disgust at my mawkishness. That kind of flabby sentiment – thinking that there is good in everyone – is responsible for a great deal of harm.

Why then, I wondered, after Alec's telephone call, was I trembling at the thought of telling Mr Duffy the truth?

Had I seen him at any time in the weeks since Lena's death, I should have had a convenient answer. No one with an ounce of compassion could have piled more pain on to the shrunken shoulders of the old man who opened the door to Alec and me later that day. I gasped at the sight of him, and instinctively went forward to take his cold, papery hands in my own. He squeezed them and gave a nod to Alec.

'Osborne,' he said, and I was relieved to hear some of his old self in the curt, barely polite, masculine greeting.

The shutters were open today, but otherwise the hall looked as it had the last time, with the rug still rolled and the furniture still sheeted. He led us to the back of the house, and I was glad not to have to climb the stairs with my cane, and even gladder not to have to pass the exact spot. We went through the baize door to the servants' quarters and I suddenly knew where we were going. I did not follow them up the narrow stairs, but waited in the ground floor passageway resting my foot, listening to them walk along the stone flags above my head and then stop. They stood still for five minutes and more, perhaps talking although I could not hear their voices, and then they moved again, slowly, back to the head of the stairs and down to join me.

'You look cold, my dear,' said Mr Duffy. 'Come out and

289

sit in the orangery and we shall have some whisky. I'm afraid I can't rise to tea.' He smiled, holding out his arm, and led us through another maze of passages then out into the light of a conservatory, empty of anything but a few tough-looking palms. It was dusty and neglected, but comfortable in the warmth of the afternoon sunlight.

'What made you go along that passage, sir?' said Alec, once he had fussed me into a comfortable chair and lifted my legs on to another. Mr Duffy handed me a beautiful old glass one-third full of whisky and sat down with his own, gesturing Alec to go and fetch one from the decanter.

'I was searching the house,' he said, 'looking for the diamonds.' Alec looked around, startled.

'And did you find them?' he asked.

'Oh yes,' said Mr Duffy, taking an appreciative though dainty sip, an old man kind of sip, from his tumbler. 'I knew she wouldn't have sold them. She loved them, you know. Really loved them. The Duffy diamonds. I think they were the only reason she married me.'

I took a gulp from my glass. I abhor whisky, and can usually only choke it down with a great deal of very cold water. In fact, I think it's best to do what the Americans do – ice, lemon and soda – but Hugh will not hear of it. I shuddered as it spread through me, the liquid setting me on fire all the way to my stomach and the fumes rising up and coming out of my nose. I can well believe cars can go for miles on the stuff if the petrol runs out.

From the table beside him, Mr Duffy lifted a small stout chest and passed it to me. It was plain mahogany with silver hasps and a silver crest worn with polishing in the middle of the lid. He waved at me to open it. Inside, bedded snugly in velvet nests, were more cases, lizard skin this time I thought, six lizard skin cases from a huge bulbous one in the middle, to a tiny one like a bread bun, almost too small to support the elaborate hinges. I noticed the scuff marks and the snags in the soft silver of the locks. One by one, I opened the lids.

The stone in the centre of the necklace caught the sunlight and made me blink. People called it pear-shaped; 'a pear-shaped blue-white diamond' was how it was always described in the society pages when it was worn at Court, but I thought it looked like a quail's egg. It *was* blue-white, even against the faded pinkish silk of its case, and the light skipping off it was as cold and as sharp as icicles. Two more of the same stones in the earrings, three in the headdress, then the small ones in rings and bracelets, all looking like little nubs and chips and crystals of ice. They were mesmerizing, quite breath-taking the way they seemed to hum and shimmer with light. But hard on that thought a voice in my head said: two lives lost. Pink cheeks, brown eyes, red blood, all lost while these blue-white stones glittered on and on.

'She loved them so much,' said Mr Duffy. I closed the cases and shut the lid of the chest. 'I should have been warned right then. No one who can feel real love for something as useless as a diamond could possibly be a wife. Or a mother. You only have to look at Clemence to see that a mother with that kind of flaw is a dangerous thing. She passes it on in the blood and then she teaches the child that there is nothing wrong with it and so any check that there might have been is missing.' He swirled his glass around and stared down into it.

'Of course *I* could have been the check, but all I thought about was my beloved girl. And Clemence turned out as cold as her mother before her. Not a bad girl – hard to like, you know, very proper, very concerned about right and wrong – but nothing really bad about her.'

He fell silent again and then roused himself with a brave smile that it hurt to see.

'Nothing can bring her back,' he said. 'I realize that I am quite alone now, but still I want to know what happened. It's clear that Lena was planning to kill poor Mrs Esslemont that day if you had not arrived in time. That in itself does not surprise me, but I don't know why. I want to know why.'

Alec stared at me and then looked away out of the dusty

window and across the gardens, and his message could not have been plainer. I cleared my throat.

'We believe, I'm afraid, that Lena killed her daughter.'

'Cara?' said Mr Duffy.

'Yes,' I said. I should not be afraid to use her name, I told myself. I should not hide behind 'her daughter', 'your wife', 'her sister', but should speak plainly. 'Lena used Cara to expose the theft of the diamonds and then planned to kill her to ensure her silence. I know it seems unbelievable –'

'But it doesn't, my dear,' said Mr Duffy. 'Haven't you been listening? Lena loved them more than almost anything else in the world and she was quite ruthless. So I am not at all surprised. Anyway, I knew, I suppose. At least, I never believed the fire was an accident. Oh, I did not want any more trouble than I could avoid, certainly did not want a murder trial. With my beloved girl gone, what was the point? All I could do was get rid of the pair of them as far as possible as soon as I could.'

'Was Lena's intention to go to Canada with Clemence, then?' I said.

'Yes, I expect so,' said Mr Duffy. 'Not that I cared where she went. I couldn't cast off Clemence into destitution – it wasn't her fault who she was and what she was and, as I say, perhaps I should have tried harder not to let her turn into her mother's child, but by then it was too late.' He shook himself out of the reverie into which he was sinking. 'I suppose Daisy Esslemont knew something, then? But how did she get involved?'

I told him and he listened with no more than a rueful shake of his head.

'Quite ruthless, you see,' he said. 'Of course I knew what had happened when Lena started all the nonsense with the cleaning. The jeweller came to me and told me about the pastes and I said to him just to give the things back to Lena and say nothing. Then I quietly stopped paying the insurance premiums, in case she should get greedy. I am surprised at her going after the Esslemonts in particular, though. Why them?'

'We've never been able to work that out,' I said.

'But I'm not surprised in any general sense,' Mr Duffy went on. 'She was a greedy, ruthless woman. But not really bad, I don't think.'

I wondered how much whisky he had drunk before Alec and I arrived. Even if he did not know the truth yet, how could he say that a woman who had killed her own child in cold blood was not really bad? Perhaps the big gulps of whisky had affected me too, for I was not aware of deciding to speak, but simply found myself speaking.

'She was bad, Gregory. Worse than you yet know. Cara did not die in the fire.' His head jerked up and I saw a quick leap of hope in his eyes.

'No! I'm sorry,' I said, 'she is certainly dead. But Lena killed her in anger, killed her brutally. It almost ruined everything. She was ruthless, you are right to call her so. But there was rage and evil in her too. It's as though she was two quite different people. She laid all her plans and then just smashed through them as though they were nothing.' I was speaking without a trace of kindness now. 'Cara, your beloved girl, is buried in an unmarked grave not a mile from your house in Edinburgh, buried as a servant, given a death certificate full of lies by an idiot of a doctor who cares only about niceties. I'm sorry, Gregory, but Lena was not just greedy and ruthless, she was evil. She must have been, to do such a thing to her child.'

Gregory shook his head at me, smiling, and I thought once more that he must be drunk.

'Lena would never have harmed her child, Dandy my dear. Lena kill her child? Why, her child was the only *living* thing in the world she ever loved.' I stared at him, and felt Alec turn and stare too. Those deep down things were shifting again, bumping gently against each other, making low echoes I had to strain to hear.

'Let me tell you,' said Gregory. 'I must start from a long way back, I'm afraid, but it's the only way to explain.

293

'We went to Ontario straight after our honeymoon and before we had docked I knew what a mistake I'd made. Of course, no one else knew a thing. As far as anyone was aware, we left in '99, a happy young couple, and came back five years later a happy family with two little daughters. No. No. The truth was this. I went on a long trip up-country shortly after we got there and when I came back my wife tried to pass off her condition as happy news, but I was not such a fool as all that. I was only a big enough fool to throw myself immediately into the arms of someone else, and so before the year was out we did indeed have two little girls, one hers and one mine, born four months apart.

'If the lady who was Cara's mother had not died, I might have – I like to think I might have – dared to divorce Lena then. But on my own with a baby girl, all I could think was to make a deal. I should give a name to her brat if she would make a home for mine.

'And so we went on. I wanted to make a family for the girls, but Lena would have none of it. Clemence was hers alone and it was only too plain that all she wanted from me was a share. Her share, she called it. Clemence's share. Such arrogance. I gave up trying to tell her that she had no right to anything, that Clemence had no call on me, and then I grew stubborn. I stopped discussing it, but I determined that neither Lena nor Clemence would ever see a penny of my money nor an inch of my land. I was going to settle everything on Cara. Oh, I know this place and Culreoch must go through the male line, but they are nothing really, white elephants. Cara would have been a very wealthy woman.

'Lena was incensed, of course. And I should not be surprised if the idea of killing Cara started as long ago as then. I think she had forgotten the details of our arrangement. At any rate, she was shocked that I did not intend to settle anything on Clemence and she blamed that for Clemence's inability to attract a husband, but I always thought that had more to do with Clemence herself, poor thing. Lena wasn't supposed to tell her that I was not her father – we agreed that neither of the girls would know – but I think she must have. Certainly she managed to stamp out any chance of affection between us. She spent her entire life bringing Clemence up and it's a dangerous thing for a child – too much devotion, and a constant drip-drip of hints that she'd been wronged – it turned her out so prim, but with no real goodness underneath.

'Towards the end of the war, Lena came to me and said that since Cara was to have everything else, was I really going to split up the diamonds and hand Cara a share of them too? Didn't I see it made more sense for all of them to come to Lena and thence to Clemence in time? I laughed, and she didn't understand why I was laughing. I asked her what on earth made her think that she and Clemence would have any of my diamonds? I can still remember her face. It was as though I had told her the sky was the ground and the ground was the sky. She loved them so much, you see, so much, that the idea that they were not hers was quite unthinkable.'

What he was saying made perfect sense, but what a sorry, silly little mess it was. Surely they could have done better than that. Could not Gregory have broken through the walls Lena put up between him and Clemence? Could he not have seen that his devotion to Cara, while it bathed his own daughter in warmth and light, did Clemence damage? I could well believe that Lena had spent her life pouring poison into Clemence and twisting her little mind into horrid shapes, and although I had never thought it before, I could see he was right about what lay behind the mask – prim, cold piousness – but if all Gregory had ever given her was his name he was as much to blame.

'And you see now, don't you, Dandy my dear, why I say Lena is not actually as bad as all that. There was something wrong with her somewhere deep down, something missing where the rest of us keep our morals, but harm her own child? She would never have done that. That, perhaps, is the only thing she and I shared. We each of us would have gone to the ends of the earth for our girls. We each of us would forgive any wrong.' He shook his head and spoke even more softly. 'The only thing we had in common. We loved our little girls.'

The three of us sat in silence for a while until, the sun having moved behind a tree on the lawn, the room started to feel chilly and my toes sticking out of their plaster cast in their little sock began to nip with cold.

'So Alec,' said Gregory, in a brisker tone, 'it is yours for the taking. All of it. And please don't spend your life in mourning. I should like to think of this place ringing with children's footsteps, even if they are not to be Cara's children after all. The Edinburgh house you will probably sell, I expect. Terribly dull kind of a life for a young woman, and I don't expect that you will feel the same compulsion as I did to keep your wife dull and quiet for fear of what she would do if you let her have her head. Choose wisely, when the time comes.'

'I hope, sir,' said Alec gallantly, squirming a little, 'to be an old man myself before any of this becomes a matter of concern.'

'Well, I'm afraid you will be disappointed then,' said Gregory, in the same brusque voice. 'I have nothing left now and I have no intention of going on. I'm an old man anyway, but however short my time is it's too long to spend missing my girl and thinking of all the things I could have done better. I shan't do it here, of course, or anywhere else that will make a mess and a fuss for you, but you must prepare yourself for it soon.' After a long pause, he spoke again. 'I would like to see her grave, though. I would like that very much.' And then, business-like and chilling: 'Alec, let's you and I meet at the cemetery at ten tomorrow morning and you can take me to see her grave.'

Alec and I stared at each other glumly, each hoping I think that the other had something to say to him that might change his mind. After a few minutes of silence we

296

rose to leave and drove back to Gilverton without speaking.

'You stupid woman,' said Cara, wagging her finger at me as she wheeled past me in the glittering ballroom. 'You stupid woman,' she called over the shoulder of her partner, possibly Alec, before he bore her away. She was wearing some kind of shroud, but a shroud encrusted with diamonds from the neck to the hem and all of the dowagers gathered around the dusty windows of the ballroom amongst the palms whispered greedily and reached out to touch her as she passed. 'You stupid woman,' she shouted from the far end of the room, bellowing to make herself heard above the din that was drilling into my head, making the chandeliers tinkle and causing little falls of dust from the ceiling. The noise grew louder and louder and I noticed now that it was not music after all, but footsteps. It sounded as though dozens of tiny little feet were spattering back and forth on the stone passageway above our heads, thundering about in all the rooms around us, drumming up and down the felt-covered stairs and clattering around and around in the echoing hall below.

I lay still, waiting to see if it made as much sense awake as it had in the dream, and then, realizing that it did, I clapped my hands, threw back the bedclothes and pulled the bell. It was seven o'clock. Three hours before they were to meet at the cemetery, and just enough time, if I was lucky.

Grant appeared, shiny-faced and frowning in her nightclothes, a frown which deepened as I told her to get Drysdale to bring the car round right now and to help me on with some clothes, any clothes, and it did not matter which.

'I'll just run your bath, madam,' she said, to give her an excuse to leave the room and indulge her huff.

'I've no time for a bath,' I said. 'Help me with this damn leg, Grant, please. I'll have two baths when I get back.'

297

Fifteen minutes later, I was in the car at the front door just in time to see Hugh open a shutter in his room and stare blearily out at me.

'Pallister,' I said, leaning out of the window and fixing him with the best haughty stare I could manage – Pallister had of course considered himself obliged to dress and present himself to see me off, for how could he have felt chagrined at the trouble I was putting him to if he had not made sure to be put to it? 'Pallister, since you're here. Please will you try to contact either Mr Duffy or Mr Osborne or ideally both. Tell them I am coming to town. Tell Mr Duffy to wait for me.'

Pallister blinked pompously. He is the only person I have ever known who can do this.

'And where might I find the gentlemen, madam?' he asked.

'I have no idea where Mr Osborne is,' I said. 'Try his mother in Dorset and see if she knows. Wake my husband to get Mrs Osborne's number if you need to.'

With this shocking suggestion, I swept away.

Nothing could have pleased Drysdale more, even at this hour, than to be told to drive to Edinburgh as though his life depended on it, and I had to stop him five minutes into the journey and move into the front seat for fear I should be sick in the back. He got me there, though. I sat with my fingers crossed that we should not meet some zealous policeman on his way into work on an early shift, but he got me there. We drew up at the cemetery at ten minutes past ten. I got myself out without waiting and hobbled on my cane to the far gloomy corner where I could see the two figures, heads bowed, at the foot of the grave.

'Alec! Mr Duffy!' They turned and I saw that not only Gregory Duffy's but Alec's face too was wet with tears which neither of them troubled to wipe away.

'Did Pallister ring you?' I asked, but knew at once from their puzzled expressions that he had not – had not even tried, I would bet – and so if I had only been another half an hour, Gregory Duffy would have walked away and we might never have been able to find him. I determined to award Drysdale a huge tip, and to 'get' Pallister, as my boys say, the first chance I had.

'What is it?' said Alec.

'Did you tell Mr Duffy anything else this morning?' I said. Alec shook his head, still puzzled I think, but also with a growing look of relief. My heart swelled with pride, or with something anyway, to think that even though he did not know what it was I had thought of, knowing I had thought of *something* was enough to relieve him. I leaned my cane against my leg and put out my hands to take Gregory's in mine.

'Mr Duffy, Lena lost her temper, more than that – went mad – because she found out a secret that Cara had been keeping for years. You don't know, do you? Lena's life had gone wrong, you see, because she had the affair and so when she saw someone who had made the same mistake getting away with it and being rewarded with everything Lena thought was hers . . . Or maybe when she thought that her girl, who was good, was to be overlooked in favour of a girl who had been bad . . . I'm not explaining this very well and, you know, none of it matters.

'What does matter is this. I have a piece of wonderful news for you. Some time ago, we are not sure when, Cara had a baby. You have a grandchild, Gregory, Cara's child.'

'Are you sure?' he asked, in a whisper.

'No,' I said. 'I mean, we're sure she had the child, but we don't know that it survived and we have no idea at all where it is, but . . .' I stopped as a new idea suddenly emerged, like a whale from the breakers, in front of me.

'It's worth a try,' said Alec.

'A try?' said Gregory, rounding on him. 'It's worth more than a try. Cara's child? The ends of the earth, Alec, the ends of the earth. You'll understand that one day. Now,' he said, turning back to me, 'where do I start? What do you know?'

'Well,' I said, 'I know who the father is, so you can start

299

there. If the child survived he may well be paying for its upbringing somewhere, or if it's been given away he might at least know who it was . . .'

Gregory Duffy's spurt of energy had faded again and he waved me and my bright suggestions into silence, looking down once more at the grave.

'Why didn't you tell me?' he said softly.

Alec and I made our slow way back to the gate and sat on a bench watching him.

'You know who the father is?' said Alec as soon as we were out of Gregory's hearing. 'When did you find out?'

'It just came to me,' I said. We sat in silence for a moment.

'Well?' said Alec at last. 'Who is it?'

'Oh, come on,' I said, almost laughing. 'It's obvious. Think about it for half a minute and you'll see.' Alec frowned at me and then he opened his eyes wide and groaned.

'Do you think Gregory will find it?' he said.

'Yes,' I said, 'I think he will. If it had been Lena who arranged it all, the information might have died with her. But as it is, I think he will.'

'But why have you changed your mind about it being Lena?' said Alec. 'I can't keep up.'

'Because she can't have known,' I said. 'The baby was the thing she found out about that last night at the cottage, remember.'

'Of course,' said Alec, then he frowned again. 'Only . . . if that's true then what *was* it that Lena knew about Cara? What was it she was holding over her?'

'I don't know,' I admitted. 'But we can't have it both ways. She can't have known all along *and* suddenly found out.' Alec conceded this with a sigh, then he nodded towards Mr Duffy.

'Do you really think it's a good idea?' he said. 'Gregory looking for this baby? I hate to think of more trouble coming to him. I don't think he could bear it.'

'I shouldn't worry about that,' I said. 'The question of

300

whether or not it's a good idea doesn't enter into it. He has no choice. He's seen only too clearly what can go wrong with secrets, how useless it is to keep the surface smooth when things are all wrong underneath. He won't let Cara's baby grow up as Cara did, out of place.'

'But how did you know he wouldn't be angry?' said Alec. 'I can imagine some fathers spitting on their daughters' graves if they suddenly heard what you just told him. I mean, look what Lena did when she found out.'

I nodded slowly.

'But Cara wasn't Lena's child,' I said. 'You heard Gregory: it doesn't matter what your own child does, you would do anything for her, forgive her anything.'

'What's still puzzling me,' said Alec, 'is that for someone who was supposed to have a great hole where her morals should have been, Lena certainly showed enough outrage when she found out about Cara's baby.'

'That was the whole point,' I said. 'She suddenly found out that this girl into whose lap everything was to pour, was just the same as she was and while she had been punished, Cara was to be rewarded.'

'Yes, but Lena wasn't punished, was she?' said Alec. 'She had her houses and her diamonds and her respectability. So long as she kept quiet. It was Clemence who was punished.'

I nodded but said nothing. Alec went on.

'It was poor Clemence who suddenly found out that the "golden girl" had done the very thing that had brought such misfortune on her head. Clemence's head, I mean. Anyway,' he went on, 'even if Gregory had been as angry as Lena was, it might have had the same effect – to break the spell and stop him from feeling he couldn't go on. Is that what you thought?'

'Such depths of cynicism, Alec,' I said. 'Why won't you hear what you're being told? He could forgive Cara anything, would go to the ends of the earth for her no matter what she had done, loved her more than life itself.'

'I suppose so. Like Lena loved her diamonds.'

'She loved her daughter too,' I said, but he did not hear me. He was standing to meet Gregory who had turned at last away from the grave and was walking towards us.

'That's the one thing they had in common,' I said. 'They both loved their little girls.' I saw Lena's face again as it had been in the ballroom – defiant, triumphant, laughing at me, yet still trying to hide the fear in her eyes. What had she to fear by then? What was she still hiding? 'I killed her,' she had said, so dramatically, heroically. But of course she had killed her; that was never in question. 'It was me,' she had said. Of course it was. 'And even if I hang it will still be worth it,' she had said. But worth what? What were the diamonds if she hanged? Nothing. And what else was there?

I watched Gregory walk away from his daughter's grave, and knew that he would gladly have taken her place. I thought of Lena in her grave, and of Clemence halfway to Canada, and I remembered Lena's face as she spoke those last words, just to me.

'You stupid woman,' she had said.

Finally, the last piece fell into place. No, I thought, grasping my cane and preparing to stand. No, Lena, not so stupid after all.

Acknowledgements

I would like to thank Teresa Chris, Krystyna Green, Ken Leeder, Peter McPherson and Imogen Olsen for all the work they have done to turn a story into a book. My friends and family have been cheerleaders in all but the pom-poms and I salute them. Special thanks must go to Cathy Gilligan for friendship, wisdom and inspiration. Finally, I am delighted to have this chance to thank Neil McRoberts for his love and support and his unflinching faith in me.

Acknowledgements

I would like to thank Chris, Teresa, Krystyna Green, Ken Beeton, Peter McPherson and Imogen Olson for all the work they have done to turn a story into a book. My friends and family have been cheerleaders in all but the pom-poms and I salute them. Special thanks must go to Cathy Gilligan for friendship, wisdom and inspiration. Finally, I am delighted to have this chance to thank Neil McRoberts for his love and support and his unflinching faith in me.